ULTIMATE JUSTICE

A Trey Fontaine Mystery

Ryder Islington

Ultimate Justice
A Trey Fontaine Mystery

ISBN: 978-1-905091-78-2
Paperback version
© 2011 by Ryder Islington

Published in the United Kingdom by LL-Publications 2011
www.ll-publications.com
57 Blair Avenue
Hurlford
Scotland
KA1 5AZ

Edited by Leslie Brown
Additional editing by Zetta Brown
Proofreading by Darcy Bowen
Book layout and typesetting by jimandzetta.com
Cover design by Linda Houle © 2011

Printed in the UK and the USA

Ultimate Justice (A Trey Fontaine Mystery) is a work of fiction. The names, characters, and incidents are entirely the work of the author's imagination. Any resemblance to actual persons, living or dead, or events, is entirely coincidental.

All rights reserved. No part of this publication may be copied, transmitted, or recorded by any means whatsoever, including printing, photocopying, file transfer, or any form of data storage, mechanical or electronic, without the express written consent of the publisher. In addition, no part of this publication may be lent, re-sold, hired, or otherwise circulated or distributed, in any form whatsoever, without the express written consent of the publisher.

ACKNOWLEDGEMENTS

Zetta Brown of LL-Publications who took a chance on me. Leslie Brown, a great editor whose dedication and unceasing aide brought this book to its full potential. Mark Mahoney, a deputy in Bossier City who not only took the time to read the script, but also provided technical details on Louisiana law. The Shreveport Nola Stars—K. Sue Morgan, Jennifer Blake, Kathryn Usher, and Sally Hamer—who offered advice and encouragement. Jean Walton, who took a storyteller and helped turn her into a writer. Patricia Rowell, who read, edited and gave unconditional support to this project.

FBI Special Agent Rae Monet of the Violent Crimes Major Offenders Unit, Retired, who provided technical support in all FBI matters. Dr. Cynthia Lea Clark, Psy.D., CHS-IV, MHt, Forensic Psychopathologist, who provided medical advice and technical support.

Dedication

To my husband Irv and our son Roger who supported my desire to write. And to my best friend Glenda Infante, who believed in me from the start, never wavering through all the rejections, revisions and revolting developments. You are the definition of "friend."

Prologue

WILE E. WAYNE
Boudreaux Park
Raven Bayou, Louisiana

Saturday Early Evening, 28 May 2005

WE SET on the swings, watching the man and the little girl. He showed her a picture, probably the old lost dog trick. Then he pulled her in the woods by the park. We knew what he was fixin' to do.

Shadows made her blond hair look dark. We heard the commotion at the ball field where somebody whacked a ball, but not a single grown-up was on the playground.

My belly took a tumble. "Ever body's heard o' this kinda stuff, but nobody ever sees it. Ain't nobody around to see it now but us."

Just 'cause the man smiled and set down on his heels so he didn't look so tall and scary, didn't mean he could be trusted. Drew watches those TV cop shows, so we all seen how there's evil men ever where.

"We have to stop him," Drew said and stood, her long tan legs moving away. She picked up her brown bag laying at the edge of the sand and ran toward the trees. Her blond ponytail flapped around her shoulders. It could have been a racehorse's tail. I always wanted blond hair, 'stead of the dirt colored stuff I ended up with.

Rocky followed us, a little slower. Then, of a sudden, my feet took off on their own and left Rocky, and Drew too. My neck tingled. Sometimes it does that when something bad's coming.

When I hit the thick of the trees, I slowed down. The other two caught up with me and we slunk through the woods, quiet like. Drew passed us our knives. She kept both of 'em stashed in her bag, so nobody knew.

I watched Rocky's face for a second. "Feels good, huh?" I said.

Rocky smiled. A long time passed since he held his old skinning knife. The cops took it forever ago, but he finally got it back. He used another one for a long time and I could tell he didn't 'preciate it so much. Me, I kept mine hid so good the cops never found it.

Rocky pushed his straight dark hair off his face. "Why's the little girl alone? Why'd her mama let her wander off?" he whispered, and hung his head. That's the most Rocky said in a long time. Daddy taught him to keep his mouth shut or else.

I looked up at him. "Maybe her mama didn't care. We know how the mama pretends she loves her kids, but it's all fake. Mamas who love their kids don't let mean men hurt 'em."

We heard him then. My feet pumped faster and faster and my left hand gripped the hunting knife. I slowed down, creeping, listening, Drew and Rocky right behind me. The sound of leaves crackling grabbed my feet and made me stop. My heart sounded like a paddle ball bouncing inside me. I snuck toward a shuffly noise.

Then I saw them—the girl sleeping on the ground while he took off her clothes. Drew's throat made an awful croak.

"You know what to do," I whispered.

Drew moved toward him slow and slinky-like, and unbuttoned the top of her sleeveless shirt and smiled. "Hey, handsome."

He turned and looked over his shoulder. His lips smiled but the rest of his face didn't. He didn't have time to bat an eye before I stepped out in front of Drew. My foot hit his ribs and knocked him over. That kind of kick would make me a super star, if I was playing soccer. "Surprise," I said. I whupped up on him. He rolled onto his back and a grunt whooshed outta his mouth. His evil eyes stared right at me and I saw fear skip through 'em before the mad started to show. He looked bumfuzzled clear through.

The man was big. I'd end up sorry if I didn't do something fast. I landed on him and shoved the knife in deep. He bled like a stuck hog. His arms fell away, and his eyes scrunched up with pain and a look I didn't know. Maybe he was confused, or scared. Ever what it was, it served him right. And ever what plans he had weren't gonna happen.

Blood covered my left hand. "Warm. Velvety."

Drew got on her knees next to the girl, but she didn't move. She was all still and asleep. She looked sorta dead. The girl's skin looked too white and her long hair tangled into a halo around her head. Drew cuddled the girl up into her lap and talked real soft like. She's pretty good with kids. She's sorta like a little kid inside and she kinda knows how it feels to be scared. She ran her fingers over the girl's forehead. We seen good mamas do that when their babies got sick.

I picked up a rag and sniffed it. "Smells of a dentist office." I looked at Drew. "We can't leave things like this. If she wakes up and finds him bleeding and looking kinda dead, she'll feel more scared than ever." Besides, I had a special surprise in the truck for him.

A dog barked.

"Grab a leg," I told Rocky, and we pulled the man deeper into the woods. For three scrawny kids, we did okay. Noises stopped us. We stood still, trying to be super quiet, but we huffed and puffed so hard we scared our own selves. We decided faster was better, even if somebody might hear us.

Sweat ran down my back as we dragged the man over old leaves and tree roots until we found a place to rest a minute. "Go bring the truck down the ole' dirt road off the highway," I told Drew. She's the oldest and she's got another year till she gets her license, but she always takes us places.

Another yap from the dog and I knew it was near where we left the little girl. A sissy scream blasted through the trees. I stopped, breathing hard, listening.

A man's voice.

And a woman's.

She kinda cried.

The dog whined.

More crunching leaves. They found her.

Rocky smiled and I reckoned we thought the same thing. He squatted by the man's head. "Daddy was a hunter. He taught me how to handle animals," he whispered, his first finger layin' against the dull side of the blade, just short of the gut hook.

"He ain't lying. Daddy taught Rocky how to hunt 'em, skin 'em and dress 'em, and he's real good at it. He can even tan the hides," I said.

The man didn't respond. He weren't gonna. He was sleeping, peaceful like. We dragged him up close to the dirt road on the other side of the woods. When Rocky finished with him, people would know the man was bad. Rocky had a way of making wickedness spill right out in plain sight. It was something to see. I looked down at the man's empty eyes. That's when I figured out he already died, and there was one less monster in this world.

Dead.

Me, Wile E. Wayne. I done went and killed another person. But he started it! And he weren't no person. He weren't even good as a animal. "I guess up till now he thought he was pretty slick, smart, and sneaky. Uncatchable. Ever what he thought, it was before he met me, and I ain't named Wile E. for nothing."

Chapter One

Friday Early Morning, 3 June 2005

INTERMITTENT FLASHES of the camera gave Trey ugly glimpses of the scene—cobwebs—a broken shovel—a roll of rusty wire—

The body.

Quick flickers of light enhanced the details as the camera clicked—the petite body in a semi-fetal position on the bare dirt, back to the door. Click—naked and bruised, hair matted with blood.

Click—camouflage-mottled skin, swollen and distorted with gases.

"Shit," he mumbled, forcing a smile, trying not to gag.

His reaction to the dead woman gnawed at him. He'd been on the job with the bureau nine years, long enough to become immune to grisly images of death, so what was it about this scene that affected him so deeply? He'd learned to distance himself from the carnage that came with his profession, or so he thought. He closed his eyes and drew a deep breath as a disturbing thought crossed his mind. Maybe he was losing it. Maybe being shot had done something to his mind. *No. That's not it,* he thought. It was just seeing such a scene in his own hometown.

Back when he was a boy, the population was about nine thousand. Now it was closer to fifteen thousand, with two casinos. He hadn't spent more than a weekend here since going off to Quantico. He took another deep breath, lifted the camera hanging from his neck, and limped a few feet away to get an overview shot of the shed.

Turning away, he wiped rain from his clean-shaven face, swallowed hard, and focused on the small forest across the road, trees fighting for life against the choking kudzu and poison ivy thick as the set of a jungle movie. Rain ran down his forehead from his short-cropped hair.

His Hummer, called "Streak," for the silver-gray paint the color of a lightning bolt, sat at the edge of the dirt road not far from the deputies and crime scene techs who combed the weeds inside the splintered rail fence. They swarmed over the Louisiana mud, fire ants searching for a lost colony. A couple of officers tied off the ends of the overhead tarp and started stringing lights.

Right hand stuffed in the front pocket of his black jeans, Trey stood between a dilapidated tool shed and a shanty some poor Louisiana family had once called home. Paint peeling. Windows broken. The small porch sagging on one end.

He took a breath and turned back to the crime scene. His eyes adjusted from dark clouds and pouring rain to the even darker shadows beneath the canvas canopy. He stared into the maw of darkness, the open door to the outbuilding in question. The canopy gave the detective some relief from the rain and would allow the coroner to remove the body without washing away evidence.

Trey's cell rang.

"Got answers for you." It was the smooth Southern drawl of Tamlyn Washington, intelligence analyst down in the New Orleans field office.

"Shoot."

"May tenth, Ilene Grant reported her sister Kelli Stevens missing. This is the last girl working at Bayou Lights Casino who went missing. And you'll love this. Four days ago, Michael Grant reported his wife Ilene missing as well."

Sisters, he thought. "Is Ilene linked to Bayou Lights?"

A service officer set a box of supplies near the detective. Trey hadn't seen him before, but there was no mistaking the family resemblance. Straight, dark hair. Gray eyes. Large dimples. Patrician nose. He was a damned Boudreaux.

"Nothing suggests that," Tamlyn said.

He refocused, pulled out a notepad and pen. "I'm ready."

Tamlyn described Ilene Grant and as much of the particulars as she'd found.

"Much obliged."

"Is it fun to work a case in a casino? I've heard things about Bayou Lights. Hopkins said it was probably a pain in the butt." Tamlyn giggled.

"Cute. Tell Hopkins...Never mind. I'll tell him myself." Bobby Hopkins had been his partner for a little while and there was nothing he loved more than to razz Trey about getting shot in the butt.

"Hey, Trey...How's Ace doing?" Tamlyn asked.

He bit the inside of his lip. "Just as expected. She's the rising star. Thanks for asking how I'm doing."

"Oh...Hey—"

He pressed the END button. Tamlyn had only been with the Bureau for a year, but she was a good analyst. One day when he was feeling more generous, he'd have to take the time out to warn her about his partner. Bobby Hopkins was a bad influence on young women. Bobby Hopkins was a bad influence on everyone.

The service officer walked away before homicide detective Russ Coleman could introduce them. "A Boudreaux on the force?"

"Yeah." Russ worked the camera. "Near about a deputy. Hope I'm out to pasture by then. The youngest boy. Has a year to go but he's on it. How's Georgia?"

Trey stepped back. "Mom left town for a conference yesterday. She'll be in Baton Rouge until Monday. Then she's going on a cruise with a friend." A sigh of relief managed to escape his lips and Russ chuckled. He offered a faint smile. Russ knew him too well. "Brother-in-law of one of the missing girls filed a missing persons report on his wife." He gave Russ the rest of the details. Unless an I.D. proved the body to be of one of the missing women linked to Bayou Lights, he had no business here. Hell, he had no business here anyway.

Trey wouldn't have gotten the call if any other detective were in charge of the scene. It pays to be an agent in your home state. It's even better if your godfather is a senior detective for the Sheriff's Department.

The camera clicked away in Russ's mocha-colored hands as he took interior shots of the outbuilding. Below the camera, Trey noticed the gray in Russ's goatee. *He's getting old*, Trey thought.

When the flashes stopped, the body became barely visible through the dimness within.

A portable light had been hung and a generator kicked on. Trey flipped the switch. The sight made his heart thump against his ribs. Bile burned the back of his throat and he swallowed hard. He'd seen hundreds of bodies and had smelled worse things than this. Maybe he should have taken a little more time off after the shooting. Maybe being wounded had affected his mind. *No. That's not it. My mind is fine.* He took a breath, lifted the camera hanging from his neck, and limped back a few steps to get another wide angle shot.

He had intended to keep his hand in his pocket like a good observer. It wasn't his damned case, but he was antsy, ready to do something, not just stand around being useless. Besides, doing something would give him an excuse to stay at the scene.

Since the shooting, he'd been given nothing but scut work. And now he was Ace's babysitter. While she went undercover on a potentially huge case, he played boyfriend, a perfect position for collecting info from her and updating her on any new evidence. It wasn't a perfect position for Trey.

The last nine years with the Bureau had taken him across the country, though he worked out of the New Orleans field office. The bad guys had taken to traveling, forcing agents to pursue. But he'd never had to pursue one to Raven Bayou. He only remembered one murder in this town in all of his childhood. This town was an oasis, so different from the big cities. And now his safe oasis was the scene of an ugly murder, a place where young women were disappearing.

Squatting near the door of the shed, he winced as the half-healed wound in his butt sent a shot of pain up his hip. He returned to his standing position, eyes glued to the child-like body of a woman.

Could be either of the sisters. Or not. With her back to him and her skin stippled, he couldn't tell much about her, other than her hair was dark brown and relatively straight, though neither of those things could be relied upon in determining ethnicity anymore. People colored, straightened, or permed their hair on a whim these days.

He slid the button on the digital camera hanging from his neck and snapped a few shots. It would be easier to see the truth when the pictures were printed in black and white. His mind filtered through the thousands of photos and textbook descriptions of decomposition and its many manifestations, calculating how long this body might have lain here.

After a breath, he stepped back and returned his right hand to its proper hiding place. The size of the body was a match for Ilene Grant. That wasn't much. When all the evidence was in, he'd load it into his computer and make some calculations. Then he'd have something concrete to work with. If Russ needed his help, Trey would be ready.

Russ took a few more shots before putting his camera down and beginning a sketch.

"Any crime spree against females I don't know about?" Trey shifted his weight.

"Naw."

"Any similar crimes?"

His godfather gave him a quick look, jaw flexing. "Nothing leading to death. Had a rape and beating of a young woman, Endri Cheramie, a month or so ago. In the hospital two weeks." He looked down at the body. "Guess we'll know more after this autopsy. I suspect this one wasn't raped, and the cases aren't related."

"I know, your famous gut." Trey noted the name *Cheramie* on his pad.

"And over forty years doing this."

Trey averted his gaze and kept his mouth shut. He scanned the site again and saw that Russ was the only detective there. "Where's your partner?"

"On her way. Some people sleep in till five, sometimes even six." Russ didn't bother to look up, but a teasing smile appeared on his lips for a second.

"Her?"

"Taylor."

"Taylor who?" Trey said.

"No, Gemini Taylor."

"Gemini? Like in twenty years ago, Gemini."

"That would be the one." Russ raised his gaze. "You know her?"

"Everyone in Raven Bayou at least knows of her. She was a couple of grades ahead of me in school." He rubbed two fingers up the ridges between his eyebrows. "I can't believe she came back here."

"I think a coyote just ran over your grave, Bub."

Was it just a coincidence that Taylor and Trey were in town at the same time? It had to be. There was no such thing as fate. Not like he meant anything to her. She probably didn't even remember him. But he sure remembered her. The bad girl of Raven High.

"I'll check with them." He motioned toward the techs, heads down like hens after scratch.

Russ nodded and went back to work.

Trey limped, carefully avoiding possible evidence beside which sat bright yellow markers. *Most of this shit's probably just trash someone threw out a car window.* Mud seeped above the soles of his black boots, staining the sides an ugly brown.

He pulled a small mint tin from his pocket, opened it, removed two Lortab, and tossed them past his tongue, dry-swallowing without so much as a flinch. A tingle ran up his spine and tickled his neck, and he took a quick peek behind him only to find his godfather's eyes boring into him. Having an almost familial relationship with a detective was a dagger. And both edges were razor sharp.

Sliding the tin back into his pocket, he walked through the field, his mind sorting through his calendar. How many more weeks before he could return to regular duty?

And while women Trey had never met suffered at the hands of some sociopath, the one who made him crazy was back in town. Gemini Taylor. The girl with the—

"Hey, watch it!" A voice snapped Trey out of his reverie, just as an elbow hit his ribs. He stumbled forward before catching himself, grabbing the tech's arm to keep from falling.

"I...uh." He was an idiot, off in another world. An irretrievable, unwanted world.

A headache began to make itself known and Trey rubbed two fingers up the lines between his eyebrows. It was a struggle to keep his hand from reaching back to soothe the throbbing wound on his left butt-cheek. It had been seven weeks since a bullet pierced the muscles there. The jolt of running into the tech reminded him of how much damage had been done.

"Find anything?" he finally managed.

The officer patted a flat canvas tote hanging from her shoulder, the kind techs use to carry paper bags of evidence. "Not much. Probably nothing that will help. The guys are working on a tire print." She nodded toward a couple of men squatting in the mud.

Trey could see one of them siphoning off the thin chocolate pudding from the porous bayou soil. Water continuously seeped up through the ground, shifting grains of dirt, changing the depth and shape of the print. Fortunately, if they could catch the print, they would be able to tell a lot about the vehicle that left it. If there had been any footprints, they were gone now, washed away by the heavy rain, which had just started to let up.

"Thanks," he said and headed back toward Russ and the body. When he reached the canopy-covered crime scene, he passed on to Russ what little info he'd received. "I'll do a little research and get back to you."

Trey headed to the silver-gray Hummer at the edge of the road. He climbed into the seat and dug his phone out his pocket, but before he could dial, a flash of baby blue in the rearview caught his eye.

A Caddie parked a dozen yards behind him. His fingers tightened on the phone as the driver unfolded herself from the vehicle and pulled out a large war bag. Tall, lean, muscular-but-feminine-Germanic build. She bumped the door shut with her butt. He easily recognized that figure. She was more beautiful than he remembered.

Flawless pale skin. Full lips and straight nose. Cherokee cheekbones. He couldn't see her eyes, at least not with his vision. But in his mind's eye he'd never forgotten their dark hazel green or the thick, mahogany lashes framing them.

He remained perfectly still, his gaze glued to the small image in the mirror. She stepped out of view, but his gaze didn't move. He closed his eyes and pushed his emotions aside. If Trey had learned anything over the years, it was that there was no room in his life for feelings.

He opened his eyes, flung the phone onto the seat, and fished the mint tin from his pocket. After tossing down another Lortab, Trey started the big SUV.

Gritting his teeth, he put the vehicle in gear, concentrating on a three-point turn. There must be somewhere else for him to be, something else for him to be doing besides sitting here reliving the past.

Chapter Two

DETECTIVE GEMINI TAYLOR
Rural Neighborhood Crime Scene
Raven Bayou, LA

Friday Early Morning, 3 June 2005

ROTTING FLESH.

The stench made Gem cringe. It was the odor that fills the air and seeps through the windows just before passing road kill. Except this was worse. It was human flesh, a stink she couldn't forget. One that wouldn't wash away in a summer storm. Even a glob of Vick's under the nose couldn't mask it.

The same stink had assaulted her as she'd parked her Caddie earlier. It came from an area about three-and-a-half miles west of the Boudreaux mansion, the landmark used by everyone in the parish to measure distance.

She was glad to be driving her Caddie. Not many detectives were grateful when their assigned unit was out of service. Gem's was an old sedan with its best days behind it. That car sat *in* the motor pool more than *out*. She appreciated its cooperation—she and the car had a mutual dislike of each other. She preferred driving her own roomy tuna boat to anything from the department, stingy mileage reimbursement and all.

She had arrived a little after eight o'clock. Already the handy-dandy clock/thermometer suction-cupped to the windshield of her vintage Cadillac read seventy-seven degrees. When the storm blew out, the sun would turn Raven Bayou Parish into a kettle of steam. Residents would feel like mudbugs at a crawfish boil.

Dropping her big black war bag on a rotten tree stump, Gem rubbed her shoulder. She squeegeed her hair between her hands, funneling water down the back of her shirt.

Her new partner Russell Coleman ignored her. His wide frame angled between her and the body, blocking her view. His hand moved quickly across a sketchpad. His simple gold wedding band too scarred to pick up light.

She wondered how long he'd wear his ring. How long he'd let the past eat at him before he figured out he'd made the right choice. She only hoped when the jury finally came in they made the right choice too, for his wife's sake.

When Gem went through the academy in Dallas, she never dreamed she'd return to Raven Bayou and work with the detective who'd screwed up Daddy's case. She wondered, fleetingly, if Coleman really cared about finding the truth.

Gem came from a family of lawless gypsies. Her daddy had settled in Raven Bayou only because he'd found a way of getting money for very little work without having to leave town afterward. Mama was the only honest one in the family. Being the opposite of her dad was what Gem was born for. Justice was more important to her than life. She looked at the battered body in front of her and remembered justice hadn't been done twenty years ago.

"Okay, who drives the Hummer?" she asked Coleman's shoulder, almost shouting to be heard over the buzzing flies, humming like a swarm of honeybees and the fat raindrops pelting the canvas-and-plastic canopy erected above the shed.

"FBI." Coleman never looked up.

Gem blinked. *FBI agents in a Hummer?* "What're they doing here?" She heard the defensiveness in her own voice as she turned to see the big silver-gray SUV pulling away. She didn't plan to share with the FBI. She wondered if the criminal might be famous. Or maybe the victim was. "Got an ID already?"

"Naw, but they—" Coleman's head jerked toward the Hummer, "—got some missing women. Our vic might be one of them."

The sound of the generator and the falling rain hitting the low-slung canopy grabbed her attention. Coleman silently concentrated on his work.

Gem turtled her head down into her shoulders and watched the canvas, necessary in this wet climate, vibrate, knowing that at any minute the canopy would collapse and she would suffocate before she could fight her way out of the heavy plastic-lined canvas. The canopy popped up and down in the wind, almost touching her head. She understood the fear was unrealistic, but knowing didn't make the fear go away. She hated low ceilings, or cars with no headroom.

"So, who called it in?"

"The neighbor." Officer Jamison Boudreaux hung a high powered light on the canopy support and pointed west, his baby face contrasting with his rail-thin body. "Said her brats came in from playing yesterday and complained of the stink from here. They came back from feeding the horses this morning and bitched again. She thought someone ought to check it out." He gave her a quick glance, his gray eyes filled with contempt, and turned his back in an action clearly stating she wasn't worth looking at.

"Okay, great," Gem said and watched Boudreaux walk away. His wasn't the first cold shoulder she had received in her short time here. She didn't remember him from when she lived on his daddy's estate and didn't care about him now. Jamison Boudreaux was a spoiled rich kid. His daddy was a big shot, a drunk, and a killer.

She watched Coleman work. He reminded her of the old witch woman of the local legends and ancient stories who knows more than anyone could imagine but still lets her charge make a *faux pas* so she can say, "Now you've learned how *not* to do it, try this." Only problem was, Coleman didn't know it all. He just thought he did.

Coleman said they had a lot in common. He was the only African-American detective and she the only woman, at least the only homicide detective who was a woman. *The other woman detective wouldn't dirty her hands on a homicide,* Gem thought with a grimace. Then again, no one would find Gem on a street corner in fishnets and spiked heels, freezing her butt to bust a john.

She had to agree with her partner though. At least in one way they were alike. A black man got little more respect from the department, or the public, than a white woman.

They also had that night twenty years ago in common, but she didn't want to think about it while looking at yet another dead body. Coleman stopped sketching and squatted near the door.

"What is it?" she asked.

"A bolt." He snapped a photo of the grease-encrusted piece of metal before flicking off a couple of leaves with a gloved hand. Laying a paper ruler next to it, he took a couple more shots. The flash lit up the corpse just inside. Each burst of light from the camera burned the vision into her retina. Permanently. How many other dead bodies were burned there?

Gem looked over her partner's shoulder. She couldn't see his face hidden behind the hood of his raincoat. Her gray three-quarter trench hung loose and so lightweight she hardly knew it was there. Binding clothes made her uneasy. Actually, anything binding got to her. And hoods spooked her, limited her vision.

Sharp cracks rang out from the tarp as it pulled loose at one corner. Wind whipped it in short snaps. The noise of the generator distracted her and the shadows playing on the naked body didn't do her stomach any good either.

She put on her "Taylor face" and became hard, separating herself from the victim. It came naturally. Letting someone else stand in front of her and deal with the slimy underbelly of life. Every cop did it.

Stepping out from under the canopy, she tilted her face up and opened her mouth to take in the rain. *If we could only bottle this nasty rotted flesh odor, and uncork it in a courtroom. Then jurors would get the horror of death. It might be just what they need to get them to take a stand against bastards who kill people like they're swatting flies.*

The deep breaths she drew did nothing to clear her head. Her lungs were so saturated with the putrid stench that when she exhaled, she tasted it. Pain echoed in her brain as a small voice inside whispered: *just get it over with so we can escape the smell of evil filling this place.*

Despite the current circumstances, she loved this kind of case. She could do without the odor, as well as the headache, but if she could help catch a killer, it was all worth it. This assignment told her she'd finally made it.

"Reckon she ran to the shed to hide. Somebody locked her in," Coleman drawled, pointing to a small pecan limb on the ground by the door. "First on the scene found that in the hasp."

Gem looked at the doorframe and metal hasp flecked with tree bark. She turned back to Coleman.

He stared out into empty space, shook his head. "What you think?"

She scanned the area through the pouring rain. One house to the west, one to the east, and a few more dotted the distance. Coleman lied. The victim didn't run to the shed to hide. Where did she run from? "Somebody put her here."

Coleman's eyes crinkled at the corners in a teasing smile. One of her partner's quirks. He would lie, and then wait to see if she'd be swayed by his opinion.

"A crime of passion, maybe a husband or lover," she said. "Somebody with a low I.Q. How smart could he be? He thought no one would find her here. Any footprints? Tire tracks?"

Coleman pointed to the small plastic markers on the ground. "Techs're working on it."

She mulled over the possibilities. A naked body. Sex crime? The killer could have torn her clothes off in a rage. Or maybe he just wanted to embarrass her. Would they find his DNA in the pile of clothes tossed in the shed?

No matter how many murder scenes she saw, one question still sat in the back of her mind even though she already knew the answer. What kind of person could do this to another human being? It took someone who understood what death was and believed this particular death would make the killer's world a better place. Even in the heat of passion, this was true.

"Good morning, Coleman. Detective Taylor," Barlow Parkins, the coroner, had arrived. "What have we here?" His eyes roved over the body.

It was the second time this week someone had addressed her as detective while calling Coleman by his last name. She hoped it was just because she was new.

"I think she was beat to death," Coleman said as he folded his notepad and slipped it into his pocket. He threw his hood back and ran a hand over his fuzzy buzz cut. "I'm fixin' to head back to the station. CSU finished checking for trace and prints outside. No footprints inside." He looked at her. "They'll work the perimeter till Barlow's done." He nodded out toward the field where techs scanned the ground and knelt over evidence.

For someone whose life is a train wreck, Coleman holds everything together pretty well. Maybe when the trial is over, he can get back to living a normal life—whatever that is for a sixty-something-year-old black man in the Deep South, she thought.

"All the outside diagrams out to five yards are done," he said as he pointed to a file sticking up from his bag. "When Barlow's finished here, forensics can come on back. We need statements from neighbors. I'll be back in an hour. I got to take care of something on the Cheramie case."

The name Cheramie made Gem stop and think.

Endri Cheramie was full-on Cajun. Gem could tell by the name. Something about the Cheramie case haunted Coleman. Just mentioning her name made him tense. It refocused his energy, and muddled his thinking. Gem couldn't afford for him to be muddled. He was her way in. She vibed him some calm and went back to work.

Chapter Three

Friday Mid-Morning, 3 June 2005

RUSS LEFT TAYLOR to deal with Barlow and sauntered over to the tan Crown Victoria, his detective unit. The rain had almost stopped and the sun peeked between the clouds for a moment. He slipped his raincoat off and tossed it into the trunk beside his war bag. After throwing out a few requests to the techs, he climbed into the driver's seat and glanced back at the crime scene where his partner was still talking to Barlow by the door to the outhouse. He wondered what they were talking about.

His mind had been so aggravated since his wife Julie died he didn't even know they'd posted the opening for a detective. It was hard enough to keep his mind on the job. He totally blanked on the doings of the department.

Now Taylor was his partner. Well, as long as they worked together, he could keep an eye on her. Russ cranked the A/C and buckled his seatbelt. Did she remember anything about that night all those years ago? He checked his rearview mirror as he pulled away from the scene. After over forty years on the force, he'd seen a lot of incest victims. Gemini Taylor didn't act like one. Either his guess about her dad was wrong, or she had learned to put it behind her.

Thinking on Taylor wasn't the only thing on his mind. Trey sported a hellacious wound. Russ worried it had done more damage to his mind than his butt. Trey's reaction at the news of Taylor being back in town was troubling. He wondered if there was something between Trey and Taylor, or if his godson's reaction was the result of Taylor's past.

Another look in the mirror was useless. With her back to him, Taylor's gray coat blocked his view of the doorway to hell, the likes of which Endri Cheramie had lived through. It was over three weeks since Endri was raped, beaten, and left for dead, and Russ still had no leads. It was one of those aggravating cases where the victim wouldn't cooperate and every lead turned out to be wrong.

And Endri chose now to talk to him. No one, not even Endri, understood how important she was to him. While Russ diagrammed this morning's crime scene, SSO Keisha Bettencourt called him to say Endri had phoned. Maybe the girl finally decided to spit out the truth. So far she claimed to remember nothing, but his gut told him it was a lie.

The department didn't let employees use personal phones for department business, not even cells, so he had to make the call from the station. Whatever it took to get Endri to talk, this was one case that would be solved, and solved by him. He owed her that.

But it was hard to be mindful of Endri's case, or anything else, while the jury was still out on Alton Boudreaux. Just thinking the man's name burned him from throat to belly button.

The Boudreaux name was big in the state. The family was more than rich, and as the fortune passed down through the generations, so did the arrogance. Alton Boudreaux owned more than his share in both departments. Even though he was a bit overweight and had a nasty temper, women fawned over him like he was some handsome movie star. Boudreaux was surrounded by yes men and fooled some people with his air of Southern grace. But inside, Alton Boudreaux was more like a New York mobster or a rich politician. He expected everybody to do as he said. Or else.

Russ swung the Crown Vic around the courthouse square and into a space behind the Civic Building. This had always been the hub of the city with a full square dedicated to county and city business. The old courthouse sat in the center with administrative buildings, parking lots, and a small city park on the four surrounding streets.

He wondered if he should have left Taylor alone in charge of a murder investigation. Before he could dwell on the thought, his cell rang again. He pushed the car door open and peeled his sweaty back from the seat.

"Coleman," he answered as he stepped into a puddle of water.

"Where are you?" It was Bettencourt.

"Coming in the back door. What's up?"

"Lieutenant Loe needs to see you, *viffe*."

Fast? He translated the Cajun in a heartbeat. *Why fast?* Bettencourt's soft tone made him swallow hard.

Russ checked his watch. Nine-fifteen hours. "Where is he?"

"In his office."

Russ quickened his step as he made his way through the maze of halls and rooms to his supervisor's office. Maybe the jury was in. If the LT was asking for him, it must be bad. Russ frowned. *They must've let the bastard get away with murder.*

Lieutenant Loe sat behind an old wooden desk in a small office off the detectives' bullpen, his adjustable chair as high as it could go. At just over five feet tall and only twenty-eight years old, Loe needed all the magic he could build himself up with, even if it meant fooling himself into thinking he was a big man.

Russ took a deep breath and tried to get his calm back. Hoping Endri would be patient, he eased into the padded armchair across the desk from the short, skinny, younger mutt who was his supervisor. The lieutenant sat stiffly over a file, reading and taking notes on a small pad. Russ waited.

"Boudreaux doing okay out there?" The boss said, still not looking up.

Russ's heart jumped when he heard the name. Then it came to him that the man meant Officer Boudreaux. The son.

"He's not fond of taking orders. Has an attitude when it comes to women."

"I'm afraid I have some bad news, Coleman." Loe's gaze locked on the file as he changed the subject.

The bastard got off. Russ wrapped his fingers around the arms of the chair, trying to find a solid grip. *The damned white jury let the son of a bitch get away with murder.* He braced himself as a little burn of acid hit his stomach again.

"This morning there was a carjacking a few miles out of town. The victim is at Mercy Hospital in critical condition."

Sweat tickled Russ's forehead, his hands slicked against the armchair.

"I'm sorry, Coleman. It's your sister Darlene."

His gut cramped up, trying to empty itself. He swallowed hard and sat up straight. Russ had been on this end of the conversation before. Once. Once was enough.

His two sisters were all he had left. Darlene was the baby, seven years his junior. Any thoughts of Boudreaux or even Endri flitted from his mind like scared pigeons. "Her grandkids?"

"Her husband dropped them at school so she could go to a business appointment. She was on her way there when it happened."

"Patsy been called?"

"She's already at the hospital. And she called the husband. Arrangements are being made to get him and the children together and deliver them to—"

Russ nodded. "I need to go." The heels of his hands pressed into the arms of the chair as he sprang to his feet.

"I'll have someone drive you."

"I'll drive myself." He did an about-face.

"I think it would be best if you let someone—"

Russ was already trotting down the hall. He heard his boss yell something, but it was like a mosquito buzz as he headed out the door and jumped behind the wheel of his suburban.

Chapter Four

WILE E. WAYNE
Rural Neighborhood Crime Scene
Raven Bayou, LA

Friday Mid-Morning, 3 June 2005

I STOOD BACK watching Gemini work. She was doin' okay today. I was glad 'cause there's them days when she don't. Sometimes she has that dumb, clown-face kinda smile. It must work though, 'cause I never saw her throw up at a crime scene.

She looked plum tuckered out to me. I wondered if something was bothering her, or if she was just working too hard. Sometimes Gemini does that and she don't take kindly to people reminding her of it.

I decided not to stay all day 'cause there was nothing for me to do but stand around with my hands in my pockets. Besides, I hated to see the lady like that. Hated the smell too.

It reminded me of the dead raccoon Daddy found in the woods once and put on Rocky's head so he'd look like Davey Crockett. Said it'd teach Rocky to be quiet. To be a real tracker and hunter.
Rocky didn't like it, but he kept his mouth shut. Up till then, the worst Daddy ever did was rub him with the entrails of a dead skunk. Daddy said it was to hide the human smell, but he didn't put none on hisself. I was sure glad he couldn't catch me.

Chapter Five

GEMINI TAYLOR
Rural Neighborhood Crime Scene
Raven Bayou, LA

Friday Mid-Morning, 3 June 2005

GEM FOCUSED on the coroner squatting near the shed door, his latex-gloved hands examining the bloated body. Barlow reminded her of Higgins on that old Tom Selleck TV show that ran on *Nick-at-Nite*. Face clean-shaven, except for a pencil mustache, short hair combed straight back, a bow tie enclosed in his button-down collar, and suspenders tight against his back.

She would forever link him with his smells. Every strand of his thin hair stayed firmly in place with mousse. A dollar to a knothole said his brand was Nexus. His face shone with the aftershave he dabbed on after his morning soft-as-a-baby's-butt shave. His shirt, stiff with starch, reminded her of her mother doing laundry. She wished she could smell those things right now. The thought made her wonder if Barlow deliberately went through his grooming ritual to help mask the smell of death he dealt with every day.

When he visited the bullpen, the multiple scents were somehow comforting. She'd spent little time with him before today, but Barlow was so open and easy to talk to, easy to get to know. He held the position of deputy coroner long ago when she was sent away. She remembered sadness in his eyes when he picked up her daddy's body. No one was aware that she'd seen it.

"How long before we have anything?" she asked, feeling the pressure of being the only homicide detective at the scene. What if she missed something? Or did something stupid? What if she lost track of time? She had no idea how long she was supposed to stay there. She looked at the oversized man's watch on her wrist. Daddy's watch. It ticked off the seconds slowly, trying to make her believe she had all the time in the world. She owned more watches than she knew what to do with, so many she didn't even know where they came from.

"Give me a minute. If you have all the pictures from this angle, I'll turn her over." Barlow looked at her expectantly.

"Coleman got 'em," she told him. "Go ahead." She took a camera out, ready to get some shots from different viewpoints. Barlow rolled the victim over and Gem swallowed hard. For the second time that day she smiled to discourage her gag reflex.

This woman didn't die of a beating, as they had assumed. She didn't run into the shed to hide.

Maggots crawled, not only from ears, eyes, nose and mouth, but from three gaping holes in her upper abdomen. And underneath her, only a small amount of blood stained the ground.

Gem snapped short stories at the crime scene. Later they would be patched together with the autopsy report and other info to create a mural of truth, if truth could be found. Sometimes, to catch a killer someone had to search deeper than the evidence and use more than the conventional tools of the trade.

"The killer brought her here after she died." Barlow confirmed her thoughts. "She suffered a severe beating, probably with fists, before being stabbed. This is all conjecture, of course."

Gem was relieved to hear the woman had died before being locked into the dark, spider-filled standing coffin of an outbuilding. Her heart ached for the victim and Gem wondered how long the woman endured pain and humiliation before this final assault.

After almost fourteen years working for the Dallas PD, this wasn't her first dead body. She'd seen every form of human butchery and every kind of human sewage. Most people would consider this nasty, dirty work. Gem did too, but when this ugly part was over, the hunt would begin.

Her head buzzed at the prospect of an enemy to hunt. She lay awake at night trying to outsmart the bad guys. She made lists, took notes, obsessed over details. This body begged her for justice, and Gem would work furiously to provide it.

She'd been excited this morning when Coleman called and told her they had a dead one. The hyper-focused adrenaline rush of her first real murder case was similar to her first day of school as a kid or her first job interview as a teenager.

But now, watching Barlow work, the excitement was gone, washed away by shame, a deep sadness for the dead woman and a new resolve to put the victim at the head of the line and stop worrying about her own selfish goals.

She finished with the pictures. Barlow printed the victim while Gem talked to the techs about what had been found. Not much. The rain had stopped. Gem paced the area for the next hour as possible scenarios flickered through her mind like old home movies. A husband threatens to kill his wife and no one is around to stop him. A woman fails to provide love and someone decides the punishment for her failure. A man gets violent when he drinks and finds his wife's body lying nearby when he sobers.

She took a breath and pulled her mind back to what needed to be done next. She'd think about motive later, after she'd finished the next item on her list: possible witnesses.

INTERVIEWING the local residents ended up being a fruitless ninety minute exercise. Gem walked to the few surrounding houses and talked to whoever was home. No one admitted to seeing anything or anyone. She sensed that they were all afraid, but none gave any indication of guilt over this particular death.

She headed back toward the crime scene to see the silver-gray Hummer creeping down the dirt road. It came to a stop.

Her hackles rose. This was her case. The FBI was not needed and definitely not wanted. She threw her bag in the back seat of the Caddie, tossed her raincoat on top, and strode straight toward the Hummer until the driver stepped out. He was dressed in black jeans and tee, with a lightweight gray jacket, his hair just long enough for her to see the curls popping out.

Trey Fontaine.

There was no mistaking him. At the age of twelve he was a handsome boy. Now he was definitely a man.

He walked toward her, which put him in control. That would never do. She wiped her face clean of emotion and headed out again.

They stopped two feet apart, eye to eye. Despite her desire to deck him, or at least give him a few choice words to chew on, she wouldn't do or say anything to bring shame to Aunt Ginny. Gem mentally checked herself and put on her Taylor face. Shoulders straight, chin high, maintaining eye contact. "Is there something I can do for you?"

"Just wanted to take another look around." Fontaine stood squarely in front of her.

"You have no jurisdiction here, so, really, there's nothing you need to see." Suddenly, Gem was painfully aware that she'd had a large cup of coffee and could use a breath mint.

"Russ called me," Fontaine said. "We have an open case involving missing women."

"Well, this one isn't missing."

"You know who she is?"

"I know she was murdered. Were your missing women murdered?"

"How long have you been back?"

"So, you do remember me?" She gave him a cold smile that never reached her eyes. "Well, let's solve our problem first. We have a murder victim, and until she is connected to your case, she's mine."

Fontaine shifted his weight to his right hip and slipped a hand in his pocket. Instead of steeling himself against her, he eased into a casual posture and offered a smile. He had backed down. Not at all cop-like.

He must be trying to get me to relax, catch me off guard. Maybe he thinks I'm not serious. Anger made her a little light headed, and right now she was steaming. She crossed her arms in front of her and took a deep breath. "Look, I don't need FBI here giving me problems. So, are we clear?"

Fontaine smiled and Gem thought she would explode.

"Yes, Ma'am."

"Good. Now, if you'll excuse me, I have work to do." She turned and left him standing in the road, feeling his gaze on her as she went to her car and pretended to be busy.

The engine of the big SUV turned over and she heard the sounds of the tires on the road. She put the top down on her convertible and sat. He would never know what that moment twenty years ago meant to her. It was the first good thing she'd ever done. *Get over yourself. Just keep your mind on the case.*

She tried to relax on the drive back to the station, the whooshing air proving cool and fresh on her skin, and blowing away thoughts of Fontaine. In their place came visions of her last visit with her mama.

In the back of her mind, Mama's voice echoed in harmony with other voices, the entire chorus trying to convince Gem to return to Dallas and ask for her old job back. Yes, starting a new job was a little scary, and putting her career on the line in a hick town full of sexism was not her smartest move. But damn it, she deserved to be a detective. And to be one here, where she might be able to right an old wrong, was worth the fear. Worth what she would have to put up with from most of the men in the department. No, she could *not* walk away after getting this close. Those taunting voices insisting she turn tail and run was just the scaredy-cat in her.

She blasted the radio. Her hands became vices on the steering wheel. She'd be damned if she would run.

The smell in the air improved significantly as she got closer to town. The white leather interior of her car reflected the sun and was moist from the thick air. More than anything, Gem wanted a shower to wash the stink of death from her.

Chapter Six

TREY FONTAINE
Georgia Fontaine's Residence
Raven Bayou, LA

Friday Mid-Morning, 3 June 2005

TREY SAT at his mother's antique desk, staring at the laptop. Black and white pictures of the crime scene flashed on the screen, timed with the click of his mouse, but his mind was not on the crime scene. Instead, it was on a dirt road from twenty years ago similar to the one from an hour ago. Taylor had certainly learned to be territorial.

Behind his ear lay a receiver so small it was held with a tiny round Band-Aid. Through it he heard Ace as she flirted with casino customers. Under her voice rang the bells and whistles of one-armed bandits, the hum of hundreds of gamblers.

Around Trey's neck hung a leather thong with a silver medallion, a jumble of Cherokee symbols engraved on its surface. The speaker attached to the back of the medallion lay against his throat, picking up his voice and carrying it to the receiver behind Ace's ear.

Though he was playing boyfriend to Ace's undercover cocktail waitress, he knew hardly anything about her. His linguistic training told him she was from Virginia, and his ethnicities training said she carried both Cherokee and Jewish blood. But that said nothing about the person inside. What he did know was that women were disappearing, and Ace was on the job.

Now it was time to put his "handler" hat back on and make contact with the undercover Ace. "I didn't know flirting with the customers was a requirement of the job."

Ace didn't comment, so he waited, his eyes drawn to the computer screen as it flashed gruesome images.

Ace yawned. "Oh, I'm tired."

"Was that for me?"

"Um hmm."

"Everything okay?"

"Um hmm."

"You need anything?"

"I need a nap."

"Smile, Sugar. You got a couple hours to go yet," a male voice said close enough to Ace for Trey to hear. He picked up enough in those few words to know the speaker wasn't native to Louisiana.

"Tap a couple of times when you're clear and I'll update you," Trey told her.

Minutes ticked by with no response from Ace. By the time he heard the taps on her choker, his mind had wandered back to the crime scene, with Taylor on the periphery. He told Ace of the body this morning, and that Ilene Grant was the sister of the last girl missing from the Bayou Lights Riverboat Casino.

His phone rang. "Hold on, Ace." He answered his cell. "Fontaine."

The strain in Russ's voice made Trey wince. "I'm on my way." Trey stood, a sharp pain shooting down his leg. "Ace, my aunt had an accident. She's at the hospital. You're good?"

"Go."

Trey hustled to the driveway with a limp, pulling out the mint tin as he went. His heart raced. He jumped into the Hummer, the pain shooting up toward his spine as he resisted flooring the accelerator. His body shook and his throat tightened. Aunt Darlene—he'd called her that since he was old enough to talk. He'd known Russ and his sisters his whole life and couldn't imagine Aunt Darlene as a victim.

He maneuvered Streak through the traffic, his thoughts wandering to the many times she'd taken him wherever he needed to go, him with his light skin and she with her dark, and dared anyone to say a word.

Shit. First Russ's wife Julie. Now Aunt Darlene. Could she have fallen victim to the same person responsible for the missing women?

And then there was the Cheramie case. Russ said she'd been in her vehicle when she was attacked, same as Aunt Darlene. Were these two crimes racially motivated? An African-American woman driving a nice mini-van, running her own business threatened some. And Cheramie was black too.

Maybe Darlene was just a convenient target.

Or maybe was it personal.

Chapter Seven

RUSS COLEMAN
Raven Bayou Community Hospital
Raven Bayou, LA

Friday Late Morning, 3 June 2005

THE CLOUDS rolled back, turning a bleak day into brightness. It didn't seem right that the sun should come out when he was so overwhelmed. *It can't be a coincidence. Not Endri and Darlene.*

The man at the information desk directed him to the Intensive Care Unit. Russ didn't need directions. He'd been there before.

His sister Patsy sat in a green chair in a green hallway, surrounded by green silence. Their eyes met and she patted the chair beside hers, working up a smile he knew was fake. He didn't want to smile either.

As he passed a doorway marked WAITING ROOM FOR ICU, the drone of a television and the sounds of a mother trying to soothe a cranky infant reached him. Sitting in the chair, he took a deep breath, preparing for the worst.

Patsy took his hand. "She's in recovery."

"You've seen her?" He swallowed hard and fought back the dampness in his eyes, ready to blame it on the cottonwoods and pollen.

Patsy shook her head. "When I got here, she was in the operating room, but as soon as she wakes up, they'll let one of us in for ten minutes ever hour. Frank will pick up the young'uns. When they get here, I'll take them home with me so he can stay."

He nodded, knowing Darlene's husband would want to spend every minute he could with her. Just as Russ had spent every second he could with Julie, in this same hospital, in this same unit, with this same terror hanging over his head. The thought put him into a panic again.

She might be as bad off as Julie was. She might be in a coma. She might never recover. *No! Darlene has to be all right. She can't die. I can't lose her too.*

He wrapped his arm around Patsy's shoulder, more for his comfort than for hers. A chill touched him. Hospitals were always cold, but suddenly his bones were ice.

They waited forever before a gurney came rolling up the hall, two white clad employees guiding it gently as they avoided looking at Patsy and Russ. A nurse opened the door, and then pulled it closed behind the rolling bed that held his sister. Thirty minutes later the door opened and the same nurse made eye contact with Patsy.

Russ pulled out his badge. "Raven Bayou Parish Sheriff's Department. Need to see Darlene Vance," he said in his best official voice.

"She's resting now. You'll have to talk to the doctor before questioning her," she said with quiet authority.

He cleared his throat. "I'm her brother." He slipped his badge back onto his belt hoping he hadn't blown it.

She looked him up and down and peered past him to Patsy who must've confirmed his statement. "Ten minutes, and then you have to go."

"Thank you." He followed her to the bed where his sister lay. Movable curtains, same as an emergency room, separated other patients from her.

He wanted to touch her, but Darlene looked too frail. Instead he stood perfectly still and watched her breathe. The steady movement of her chest rising and falling mesmerized him, and he lost track of time. His mind traveled back to eighteen months ago when Julie laid there, her chest rising and falling with the sound of the respirator that kept her alive. Boudreaux had been arrested a week after the hit-and-run. A month passed before doctors convinced Russ of the futility of continued life support, and he let them pull the plug.

It took threats of a civil rights lawsuit to make the D.A. add the charge of vehicular manslaughter to Boudreaux's case. What was it to the fine citizens of Raven Bayou if one more black woman was murdered? Sure she was the wife of a detective, but after all, he was just there to fill a quota. No one really cared.

Of course, the defense attorney fought all the way, insisting that Russ had made the final decision and was therefore responsible for his wife's death.

Whatever else happened in this world, Alton Boudreaux would pay—had to pay—for what he'd put Julie and Russ through. The muscles in his jaw tightened as he gritted his teeth. *Boudreaux better pray to God the jury finds him guilty. If that drunken bastard gets off...*

Too much. It was just too much. Julie. Endri. And now Darlene. He swallowed hard and took a deep breath. One thing at a time. As soon as Darlene was okay, he'd find the bastard who did this, probably the same man who put Endri in the hospital.

He bent close to his sister. Her face was unrecognizable, but the small scar on her forearm said it was little Darlene who lay there. He'd been babysitting the day she wrecked her bike and cut her arm. Even at fourteen he stayed calm and levelheaded, applying pressure to the cut. He carried her next door and Mrs. Dubois drove them to the hospital. His father gave him a look for letting the baby get hurt, but Mother praised him for his quick thinking.

He had let no one see his terror. Now only a small, pale scar reminded him of how he'd prayed for her not to die that day. It had just been a simple cut, but he'd never been so scared. Darlene needed more than his prayers now, and he needed more than praise to make it all better.

The nurse returned to usher him out. He wanted to protest. He hadn't had a chance to talk to Darlene. She didn't even know he was there, just as Julie hadn't been aware of him those weeks she lay unconscious.

But the nurse reached up and put a hand on his back, led him out to the green corridor where Patsy still sat, and closed the door behind him.

Chapter Eight

TREY FONTAINE
Raven Bayou Community Hospital
Raven Bayou, LA

Friday Late Morning, 3 June 2005

TREY WHIPPED into the hospital parking lot, leaving the Hummer illegally parked. He rushed through the emergency room door and straight to the elevator. After Julie, he knew the way to ICU by heart.

He found Russ and Aunt Patsy sitting in the hall. "How is she?" he asked as soon as Aunt Patsy looked his way. Russ didn't respond, didn't even seem to know Trey was there.

"She's stable. Had a little trouble, but the doctor says she's doing a lot better now." Aunt Patsy's eyes held fear, but her back was straight, her head up.

"She's critical," Russ added.

"Russ spent a few minutes with her. Frank and the young'uns will be here soon. Why don't you boys go on back to doing what y'all do?"

Russ returned from wherever he'd been. His gaze went to Aunt Patsy, and then to Trey, his expression never changing. Trey thought Russ looked totally lost and really needed to hear him speak with that calm stability that always brought strength and comfort.

"Can I see her?" Trey asked.

Aunt Patsy explained the rules, though it wasn't necessary. He'd been here before. "Go on, now. I'll be right here till Frank comes, and I'll keep in touch with the nurse's station. Y'all can't do any good here. Go find the animal that did this." She patted Russ on the back, and then pulled Trey into a hug before shooing him off.

"Aunt Darlene knows a lot of people. Did she ever mention Ilene Grant or Kelli Stevens?" Trey asked.

"Not to me," Aunt Patsy said. "Why?"

Russ stared at him, a warning.

Trey collected his thoughts. "I don't know what I'm thinking. They had an appointment with Mom a few days ago and I just thought since Mom and Darlene are both real estate agents..." he lied. "It's just been a long day, Aunt Patsy." Trey gave the woman a hug and the two men walked down the hall to the elevator. Russ remained silent, his face expressionless.

"Does Aunt Darlene know the Cheramie girl?"

"No. Endri lives in the Cajun track. I don't think they ever met." Russ clamped his mouth shut, jaw muscles flexing.

"Four women attacked in two months. There's got to be a connection."

"Four?" Russ said.

"Ilene Grant, her sister, Cheramie, and Darlene." Trey ran his fingers up between his eye brows. "But we don't know anything yet about Ilene's little sister. She could be part of your case, or she may have run away. I imagine living with Michael Grant can't be fun for a teenage girl."

"Who'd steal a mini-van?" Russ said.

Trey ignored the question, and then finally said, "How did Darlene look?"

"Not good."

In Russ's voice was the constancy of a life lived in one spot, an immovable object untainted by time or distance. The knowledge comforted Trey. He had the urge to touch Russ, to do something. He didn't. Instead he trained his eyes on the elevator doors until they opened. They walked slowly through the emergency waiting room and out the automatic doors.

Russ stopped, and remained silent for so long Trey wondered what his next move should be. Back to business. That was always safe.

"Any info on the doer? I figure he's young. Criminals get better with experience. Either he hasn't learned not to leave witnesses and evidence, or he's a flier, high on meth or rock."

"Yeah," Russ said, his eyes off in the middle distance.

"Maybe he stole the mini-van to sell for dope money, but mini-vans aren't that hot. And it's not the typical MO of a rapist. They need to have control. Better to get a woman in his car, rather than steal hers. Too dangerous."

"I know. Seems personal to me too." Russ frowned.

"Did you get an I.D. on the body this morning?"

"Pretty sure she's Michael Grant's wife. His payroll stub was in the clothes in the shed."

"Damn," he said and Russ nodded. "I wonder if the four women are connected."

"I don't think the crimes are connected. Cheramie was raped. Ilene Grant killed. Her sister is missing, although she could just have got mad at someone and lit out," Russ said.

Trey didn't say the explanation didn't feel right. He shrugged.

Russ looked at his watch. "I reckon Taylor will be at the station by now. I better get back."

"Sure you're up to it?" Trey asked.

"I'm not sure of a thing. But Wilkes is working Darlene's case and my bet is he's in the pit." Russ finally looked at him.

Trey nodded. "Think I'll tag along."

"Meet me at the station." Russ turned and headed toward the emergency entrance parking lot.

Trey trotted to the Hummer, his mind reeling as he drove the short distance to the Civic Building. The Cheramie girl. Aunt Darlene. Ilene Grant dead, her sister missing. Some might think this quiet town had been visited by some kind of lunatic. But Trey didn't believe in all that psychobabble bullshit. He knew this kind of killer was just another human being. Probably a man who used excuses to do whatever he wanted. Psychologists called them damaged. To him they were selfish manipulators wanting immediate gratification.

He called Tamlyn for an update on Ilene, her sister, and her husband. "And I need a favor. I need a background on Gemini Taylor."

"Who's she?" Tamlyn asked.

"Now she's a detective at the Sheriff's office. The question is, who was she? Just do a preliminary for me, Tamlyn. Please."

"Okay, Trey, but I hope you know what you're doing. Local cops get cranky enough about their cases. Now you're actually checking out one of *them*."

"What they don't know won't hurt me. No need to put it in writing. Just a quick run through."

"If you say so."

"Much obliged." Trey tucked the phone away, his mind immediately returning to Aunt Darlene and the body found this morning. Ilene Grant was a white woman. The more he thought about it, the more he recognized the differences in the women. Two white, two black; two young, two middle aged. There were cultural differences, class differences. It didn't make sense that the four were connected. But Endri Cheramie and Aunt Darlene...maybe.

The sun shone brightly in a vivid blue sky dotted with ugly clouds the color of dirty steel. A light wind marched them across the sky, cloaked-soldier style. Today, they had been the enemy, washing away evidence.

He pulled into the rear parking area, and even with his mind in turmoil over this morning's events, his eyes scanned the lot for the Caddie. He breathed easier when he confirmed it wasn't there.

Chapter Nine

GEMINI TAYLOR
Sheriff's Dept.
Raven Bayou, LA

Friday Noon, 3 June 2005

GEM PARKED in the employee lot. She left the top down and hurried into the building, her hair absorbing the heat of the sun's rays. Humidity seeped into her skin like a steam bath. A silver-gray Hummer sat in the lot. Trey Fontaine was here.

The courthouse sat across the street, the parking lot on the corner reserved for jury members. It was full. Everyone knew there was only one jury trial in session: Boudreaux.

In the station, the women's locker room buzzed with third-watch arrivals hurrying to get ready for briefing. Olive green pants and tan shirts filled the room. The sounds of final gun checks echoed. Clips locking into place, slides snapping back, safeties clicking on and off, metal snugging into leather or nylon.

The combination to her lock made her fingers dance. Five left, twelve right, fifteen left, and the lock fell open. No time for a shower. A clean white camisole shirt and light blue jacket, and she was ready to continue the day.

The detective's pit was Gem's favorite place at the station. Open, roomy, and far enough from the office and intake to avoid chatter and other distractions like the smell of a drunk covered in piss and puke. Or a victim's family crying.

Russ Coleman sat with the phone to his ear, his body radiating tension. In a chair at the end of his desk sat Trey Fontaine. His broad shoulders filled a black T-shirt under that thin silvery jacket.

When Trey was twelve or thirteen, he was as big as most sixteen year olds. He grew into a big man. Though only about six feet tall, he was broad-shouldered and well-muscled. He'd be about thirty-two or thirty-three now. She'd have to remember to ask when his birthday was. His light brown eyes were even more penetrating than when he was a boy and rimmed with thick, dark lashes.

She dropped the ten-print card on Bettencourt's desk, and grabbed a couple of paper towels from the table where the coffeepot held something akin to the mud on her shoes. On the way to her squeaky chair, she passed an empty desk where today's newspaper lay open to the B section. When she got close, she read the headline:

BOUDREAUX JURY STILL OUT
WHILE MANSION BURGLARIZED—
250K IN JEWELS STOLEN.

She was a little woozy and faded for a second. *Lack of food. That must be it.* When she got her wits back, she found herself sitting in her chair opposite Coleman with Fontaine staring at her intently.

Her mind froze, locked on his presence. A noise kept trying to get through to her. Finally, she figured out it was the voice of a fifteen-year-old girl seeing a new man in town she admired. Gem hated it when civilians came to the station. She knew that being on the job required dealing with the public, but the station was *her* house, and she didn't appreciate strangers in it.

Coleman hung up and was talking to her, but she couldn't figure out his words. She wiped her shoes off, schooling her face, peering toward him. He scribbled on a notepad, eyes downcast.

"No comment?" Coleman asked.

She had no idea what he was talking about.

"I told you this morning about the FBI. Now you're not interested?" He waved his hand in front of her face.

Gem figured out he must've introduced Trey while her mind ran rampant. She hadn't heard him and wondered if he'd just told her why the FBI was here, what they wanted. No way would she ask.

Fontaine stayed silent, one ankle propped on the opposite knee. A bear paw of a hand lay curled casually around the leather boot as he sat watching her, a cougar near a rabbit hole.

"Let's try again. This is Trey Fontaine. He's with the FBI and the dead woman might be part of a case he's working."

It was a real struggle for Gem to keep herself focused on Coleman. "What's going on? I thought I'd see you back out at the site."

Their desks were set up against each other, giant old turtles trying to decide if they wanted to mate. The idea had been to make more room for foot traffic. The result put their faces just a few feet apart. Still, Coleman avoided looking at her. Something bothered him, something personal. This wasn't about the Cheramie case, or about the scene they'd processed this morning.

"Is there something you need to tell me?" She was pretty sure the jury wasn't back yet. It was the only thing she could think of that would make Coleman so keyed up. If they came back with not guilty...

Coleman stood and tossed his keys to Gem. "Let's go. I'll tell you on the way."

Fontaine came out of the chair and rolled it back to a nearby desk. His right hand eased into his pocket. She noticed his eyes turned a little hard with the movement.

"To where?" She followed Coleman toward the hall. Fontaine trailed behind.

"Carlin Construction. Michael Grant works there and his wife Ilene went missing four days ago."

"And you think she's our vic?" She hurried along beside him.

"I know she is."

"How?"

"The paystub in her pocket. Stole a print of her right thumb. That confirmed it." He offered a notebook. Inside Gem found copies of DMV photos of Ilene Grant, and Michael Grant, her husband. The only vehicle registered in either name was a tan '99 Ford Taurus.

"Ran the print through NCIC. Ilene Stevens had a driver's license in California till ten years ago. Two years before she came here, she changed the name on her license to Ilene Grant. Her Louisiana license has a Verbois address. Husband reported her missing four days ago, said she'd left the day before. This case is already colder than a well digger's ass. We'll be lucky to get anything from the lab by Monday."

It was standard procedure to run the print locally, and in this case that would have been enough since Ilene Grant was a schoolteacher. But running a local known victim through the National Crime Information Center to get an I.D. wouldn't have crossed Gem's mind. She thought of the woman only as a victim, not as someone with a possible criminal past, which would normally trigger her to run an NCIC check.

She made a mental note of this little trick and wondered what else Coleman would share with her in the next few months. Could she get him to help her re-open Daddy's case? Word had it she had only a short while to pick the man's brain before he left the job for boring pastures, but Gem didn't believe Coleman would retire as soon as she was trained. Russ Coleman would work until the day he died. And if she could just say the right thing, maybe the time would be used to find Daddy's killer.

As they went out the door, she filled him in on what Barlow said and what they'd found at the scene. "So, we're gonna interview the husband's boss?" she asked Coleman, and then swung her gaze to Fontaine as he opened the rear door of the Crown Vic and squeezed himself in. "And what do you think you're doing?" she asked.

Trey didn't respond.

Gem opened the driver's door, slid under the wheel and looked at Russ. "You gonna tell me what's going on?"

"Not exactly," Coleman said.

"Not exactly?" she repeated and again turned on the FBI agent, "Fontaine!"

"Hey, I couldn't get out now even if I wanted to," he replied.

"Fine, but why did you get in in the first place? Are you still after this case?"

Coleman said something Gem couldn't quite hear, and then, "Let's gnaw on this later. I have other stuff to worry about. My baby sister Darlene was carjacked this morning. Somebody dragged her out of her mini-van and beat the shit out of her. I think she maybe was raped, but she's not talking to anybody. We've been at the hospital with her."

Gem felt knee-high to a piss ant for her earlier tone. Coleman's mouth formed a hard straight line, the muscles of his jaw pumping as he gritted his teeth.

She sighed and tried to concentrate on her driving. The two-lane highway was deserted but for them. The Crown Vic rolled down the road well over the speed limit. She dodged potholes and the bones of the occasional road kill. Every once in a while she'd check her rearview, only to meet Fontaine's gaze. The voice inside giggled. But on the outside she was fuming at Coleman for letting an agent come with them, especially since he wouldn't tell her why.

Coleman was silent. Gem wondered how he was holding up under the doubled stress of what happened to his sister and the trial.

She understood his feelings about the trial. The jury was out. Most officers believed Boudreaux deserved a long prison term, if not the death penalty, but their beliefs weren't based on respect for Coleman. Or friendship. Gem heard the things they said behind his back, probably close to the same sort of nonsense they spread about her when she wasn't in the room. But everyone knew Boudreaux. He was a manipulator, good at getting others to do his dirty work. Boudreaux would buy his way out of this.

She glanced again at the man whose life would be most affected by a not-guilty verdict. He stared out the side window, no doubt overwhelmed with worry and memories and anger.

Maybe a not-guilty verdict was just what Gem needed. There would be no justice in Boudreaux going free. She wondered if it would it make Coleman more open to the possibility that justice wasn't served all those years ago.

Chapter Ten

TREY FONTAINE
En Route to Pellin, LA

Friday Noon, 3 June 2005

TREY WAS IN a tight spot, literally as well as figuratively. The rear seat was designed to keep prisoners controlled, with a hard, narrow bench, no window controls or operating door handles, not even enough legroom for his feet to sit flat. His knees pressed against the back of Russ's seat, cutting off circulation to his toes. It was turning into one of those days when he was unable to focus.

In front of him sat his godfather and the woman who single-handedly set the gold standard for women in his life. It was hard to believe that one moment in time could create such an indelible image in his mind. One moment, and Gemini Taylor became the ideal.

Neither of them spoke. He knew the reason for Russ's silence. What made Taylor so quiet was the mystery. Her eyes occasionally flashed at him in the rearview, and he saw a slight crinkle at the corners of her eyes as he caught her furtive glances at him.

Surprisingly, an old pain stabbed him in the chest. His memories of her were tied to the devastating year when he lost his dad. He wondered if he could get the mint tin from his pocket. Certainly not without pressing his knees harder into Russ's back and his butt farther into the seat. He turned his gaze to the window. They were nearing Pellin. Soon he would have to get out of the car and pretend everything was under control.

Chapter Eleven

JAMISON BOUDREAUX
Sheriff's Dept.
Raven Bayou, LA

Friday Noon, 3 June 2005

WHEN JAMISON returned to the station, he heard rumors of a carjacking involving Russ Coleman's sister. The detective had gone to the hospital— good news for Jamison. He detested that nigger. He also needed a few uninterrupted minutes of privacy to do some investigating himself.

The front office was down to a skeleton crew with almost everyone at lunch, their time staggered so someone left every fifteen minutes. He approached through the rear hall into the personnel section, found the file he wanted, and then went to an empty cubicle in the traffic bullpen. The tab was neatly typed: TAYLOR, GEMINI.

Jamison opened the file and read over the application:

> *Received GED at age 18.*
> *Commendation for involvement in warrant execution resulting in several arrests of child pornographers; Meritorious Commendation for saving a life...*

The bitch was a fucking hero.

Jamison hadn't been born yet when Taylor's dad was killed in the house on the backside of the Boudreaux land, less than a quarter mile from Boudreaux Stables.

Even if he had been around back then, his grandmother never allowed Jamison to play near the row of houses reserved for employees or the children who lived there.

Jamison closed the file and peeked around the cubicle divider. The front office was empty. He returned the file.

The rumble in his belly said it was time to eat. Heading out the rear door to one of the units needing service at the garage, a blast of moist heat slapped him. The cruiser shook as he turned the engine over. He rolled down the windows and drove to Sonic, sat and ate as he pondered the dead body from this morning. Jamison had only caught a glimpse of the naked figure lying inside the dark outbuilding, but there was something terribly familiar about it.

Tossing his bag of trash under the menu sign, he drove the unit to the garage, and then called to have someone pick him up. It was only half a mile from the station, but it was hotter than hell and he didn't intend to spend his time walking. He would be glad when this year was over. Next year he'd be a correctional officer, and a year after that, he would qualify to carry a weapon. Being the one giving orders would be sweet. Enforcing them would be sweeter.

Five minutes after he called, Bettencourt arrived to pick him up. "I have twenty things on my desk today. Can you run a set of prints?" she asked.

"Sure. Whose?" He liked it was better when she asked instead of ordered. He didn't mind doing the grunt work. What bothered him was taking orders from another service officer, not to mention a damn woman, and a nigger at that.

"The body found this morning. Just need a confirmation of I.D. for the file."

At the station, he scanned the print and entered info. He gazed around the holding area for prisoners. "Arrestees" they were called. "Prisoner" was a better term, though "scuzball" was his favorite.

One cell held an old guy with a scraggly white beard and grungy red suspenders, so drunk he couldn't keep his chin off his chest. He needed lessons from the old man. Jamison smirked. Alton Boudreaux could out-drink anyone in the parish.

The computer beeped and Jamison returned his attention to the screen. His heart began to race and his throat constricted in a feeling he remembered from when he was a boy and something made him cry. A few keystrokes brought an image on the screen and confirmed his fear.

"Fuck!" The word came out in a violent whisper. The body in the outbuilding wasn't just another victim. *This must be why that damned nigger and his bitch were so quiet around the station. They enjoy their little secrets.*

He turned his back on the glass partition and leaned against the wall. No matter how hard he fought, he couldn't hold back the tears. Ilene Grant was the only one who'd guessed his secret. The only one who didn't think he was stupid. She taught him to read. In all his life he'd never met anyone so gentle and patient. And he loved her.

Chapter Twelve

TREY FONTAINE
Construction Site
Pellin, LA

Friday Early Afternoon, 3 June 2005

TREY CONSIDERED Michael Grant's possible involvement in his wife's death. Tamlyn had called with the backgrounds on the Grants. The man was a heavy equipment operator and cement truck driver who met Ilene in California and brought her to southwest Louisiana. He was also a gambler who spent most of his off time at Bayou Lights where the sister Kelli Stevens worked.

Back at the station, Trey had reviewed the missing persons report taken from Ilene Grant regarding her sister and perused notes from the first interview by an officer from the Verbois station. The notes indicated that Ilene had been upset over the disappearance of her sister and had gone for a walk.

There might have been motive for Grant to kill his wife, and possibly even his sister-in-law. Maybe Michael Grant's price for Kelli moving in with them was a piece of ass. Maybe Ilene had found out. Maybe Kelli saw something Grant did at the casino, something he didn't want his wife to know.

Taylor pulled the car over at the edge of the road in front of a construction site. Trey counted about ten houses being built, five of which framers attacked with hammers and nails. The other five were empty, their cement foundation still dark with moisture.

He waited impatiently, knowing the inside door levers didn't work. Someone had to let him out. Taylor snapped out of the unit, leaving Trey to fend for himself. Russ rescued him and the three of them approached the worksite, Taylor in the lead. Trey watched her take command of the situation, exuding confidence. Without even having seen her work, he knew she was a good cop. She cloaked herself with different personas as she talked to different people to make others feel at ease or under pressure as the need arose.

He straightened himself and focused on the foreman, comforted by the nine-mil against his ribs and the snub-nose at his back, though he wished it wasn't necessary to wear a jacket in this heat. Suddenly he hoped this wouldn't become a competition between them. Their first battle, when Trey was in second grade, had ended with a bloody nose. And it wasn't hers.

Chapter Thirteen

GEMINI TAYLOR
Construction Site
Pellin, LA

Friday Early Afternoon, 3 June 2005

PELLIN WAS nineteen miles from the Boudreaux mansion. By the time they reached the worksite and found the foreman, the temperature had gone up two degrees. Clouds were nowhere to be seen. It was a perfect picture.

But pictures couldn't convey the thickness of the air that made her clothes damp like they weren't quite ready to come out of the drier. At least the air smelled of cut wood and cement. That she could live with.

"Mike left early today." The foreman's tone was short and to the point. Having better things to do with his time than talk to the likes of Gem, he looked at his watch, and then directed his gaze back to the site where his men had slowed their pace.

"Is that something he does often?" she asked.

"He leaves when his part of the job is done. He finished about two-and-a-half hours ago. Normally, he'd go to another site, but there's nothing close, so I sent him home." He looked at Coleman like he was garbage, and then ignored him. She figured Mr. Foreman didn't care much for her either. Or more likely, didn't care to be questioned by a woman. His eyes went to the agent at her elbow several times though Fontaine hadn't asked a single question.

"What kind of worker is he?" she asked.

"Arrives on time. Does his job." He shrugged, his gaze landing on her just long enough to state his opinion, daring her to dig deeper before returning his attention to Fontaine.

"What time does he usually clock in?" she said.

"Six." He pulled a worn bandana from his pocket and wiped sweat from his face and neck. Gem held back a smile at the dainty paisley print in his dirty paw. His answers gave not a hair more than necessary.

The only person whose gaze he met was Fontaine's, and it was with a sour look on his face. Apparently, he didn't like law enforcement at all, though he did at least show a little respect for Fontaine by looking at him.

"Do you know where he lives?" she asked.

"Verbois. Has a trailer out there on Crowder Road."

"Thanks." Gem bet a dollar to a mud pie this guy had been to the Grant home more than once. The average employer didn't know the name of the streets his employees lived on. She checked her watch. Two-ten.

"Guess we have a drive ahead of us," her partner said as they headed back to the unit.

They rode in silence while fury emanated from Coleman like a tidal wave of Louisiana hot sauce. Though his anger and frustration were not directed at her, she could see it getting stronger and looking for a target.

Gem understood why Coleman's frustration would boil over into anger after such a day as this. He was up before daylight, called out to a dead body in the pouring rain. Endri Cheramie, the victim on a case that had come to a standstill, wanted to talk to him privately. And his sister had nearly been killed, which took precedence over Cheramie's plea for contact. Darlene's case echoed Cheramie's. Sheer frustration would have forced Gem to take a pound of flesh out of someone. Anyone.

He had allowed her to conduct the interview of the foreman, but she suspected he would take charge when they found Michael Grant. That anger would shoot out soon, and Gem hoped to be in the bleachers when he took aim.

IT WAS a long trip to Verbois, a small map-dot forty-five minutes from the other side of the Boudreaux estate in east Raven Bayou Parish.

After Gem gave Coleman some time to think, she asked, "So did you learn anything on the Cheramie case?"

His shoulders tensed. He was ready for a fight, and his gaze shifted up and to the left, a sign that he was trying to come up with the right words. Or the right lies.

"She's having nightmares, not doing so good. She wanted to talk to me without her mom knowing. I explained about my sister, that I can't come right now and gave her my cell number. She'll call me this evening." He might as well have said what he was thinking: *To hell with the department and its rules.* His eyes told Gem not to comment.

Fontaine leaned forward, his head almost between Coleman and hers. "Tell me about her case."

Coleman gave him a quick rundown of Endri's case.

"Has she talked to anyone? Given any pertinent info?"

"No more than to say she went to the club with a friend who gave Endri her car keys and left with a boy. Endri planned on driving her friend's car home. She stopped at a light when a young man hopped out of a small gray pickup and into her passenger seat."

"Forced her to drive out of town and park. Raped her, beat her, and then dropped her on this side of Breaden Street Bridge, less than a block from downtown. Found the car at Strawberry Pond."

"Similar to Aunt Darlene. Any witnesses?" Fontaine asked.

Gem's ears perked up. *Aunt Darlene? Could these two really be related?*

"The question of the day. Her friend confirmed the first part of the story. The club was full, but no one saw a thing."

"Could she and Aunt Darlene be linked to the disappearances?"

She thought about what Coleman had tried to tell her earlier in the office while she was in la-la land. If Trey was asking now, it couldn't have been about *this* conversation. She sighed heavily.

"I doubt it," was all Coleman said before he turned his head away, ending the conversation. They all returned to silence.

The discussion about the young teen reminded Gem of her own childhood. Her mama spent her whole life working to support her daughter—and Daddy. She was gone before Gem got up most mornings and worked until after dark. Gem woke many summer mornings alone in an empty house, the door standing open. Though Daddy had a job at the Boudreaux stables, he was too lazy to work. Mostly, he drank. And he was an ugly drunk. He tolerated no disobedience from his only child.

By the time Gem was five she knew the facts of life much too well. For many years she wished she'd she been born a boy. She was pretty sure Daddy wouldn't have hated a boy enough to punish him as he did her.

Besides, Gem thought if she'd been a boy, she'd have been stronger, more capable of fending him off. He wouldn't have gotten away with stuffing a boy in a steamer trunk for hours at a time. At least that's what she'd thought back then. A boy would've had the courage to fight back, or tell. Gem tried to tell once, but Mama shushed her and told her they'd talk in the morning. They never talked in the morning. Mama was always gone.

Gem peeked over at her partner and wondered if he had any idea of what she'd been through as a child. He'd been upset ever since they'd been thrown together. But considering what he'd suffered in the last year and a half, no one could blame him. For the most part, Coleman was as cool and collected as Gem remembered him. Even with everything going on around him and in his world.

She hoped he didn't still see her as a victim. She wanted him to see the capable Gem, the Gem who had a job to do and got it done. She needed him to need her or at least appreciate her. How could she tell him she knew he'd made a terrible mistake twenty years ago? More importantly, how could she get him to reopen the case?

The Crown Vic rolled to a stop and she stepped out onto the gravel drive. The trailer sat back off the dirt road on a small rise. Trees formed outlines of what were probably individual lots. A Monarch butterfly drifted lazily past her face.

Fresh cut grass, kudzu, and a slight whiff of petroleum filled the air but she barely noticed. Her full attention was on that tin box called a home. Even something as big as a singlewide trailer was too small for her comfort. The metal door stood open, only a screen separated her from the dark cave within.

Memories flashed through her head like hot electric currents making her senses react as they had when she'd been locked in a closet or made to crumple her body up into a small heap in the bottom of a trunk with the lid closed down.

She took several deep breaths to regain her composure and prepare herself for the inevitable. Ready or not, her job was to go in there and inform the man they'd found his wife's body. The only thing that bothered Gem was the "in there" part.

She let Coleman lead the way and stayed at the bottom of the steps while he knocked. The wood-framed screen door rattled and shook, bringing a sudden silence to the birds in the nearby trees. It didn't take long for them to start chattering again, probably discussing the arrival of three strangers into their otherwise peaceful world.

Fontaine stood inches behind her. It was irritating as all get out, mostly because she knew he was doing the chivalry thing, letting the lady go first. Aunt Ginny's voice rang out in her head. "Show your appreciation when a gentleman is kind," she would say.

Hope welled in her that Michael Grant had already left and someone else would tell them to go away. But Grant's tan Taurus sat not ten feet from where she stood. A glint of sun reflected off the front bumper, but a noise pulled her attention back to the screen door before she could check it out.

Grant wasn't anywhere near the picture on his DMV. And the accompanying description—one-hundred-fifty pounds, black hair—was even further from of the truth. He had put on at least thirty-five pounds since the license was issued. His hairline headed for the back of his neck, and what was left of his hair was more salt than pepper. He was a snaggle-toothed bubba if Gem had ever seen one. Around his eyes, he reminded her of Daddy. Or maybe it was just because Daddy and Grant were both evil. It didn't take long to place him in that category.

After introductions, Grant allowed them in. Coleman went straight to the kitchen table, just a few feet from the door, and asked if he might sit. One of Coleman's tests.

Gem was surprised at Grant's sociable attitude. Not many bubbas would allow a black man to sit at his own supper table.

Glad to be in the background for now, she stepped inside and Grant pulled the screen door closed. It was stifling. The swamp cooler was off and only a small ceiling fan stirred the oppressively hot air. Grant offered her the only remaining kitchen chair as if her fragile self might crack if her dainty size ten feet had to hold her up. What a gentleman.

"Mr. Grant, I think you're the one who needs to sit," she said softly, relieved for an excuse to stand. She stayed near the door, her gaze sweeping through the trailer, and then out to the yard.

She'd lost track of Fontaine and was surprised to find he had passed her and stood at the edge of the carpet, akin to a puppy trained not to set foot in the kitchen. His eyes bore intently into Michael Grant.

The trailer smelled of cheap aftershave, burnt toast, and copper. The metallic odor of blood was hard to get rid of. Dirty dishes overflowed the sink. Gem wondered if the murder weapon lay among them.

Fear seeped from Michael Grant through his thin, white, sweat-soaked T-shirt. His breathing changed to the variety that brings on dizziness and fainting. Doctors called it hyperventilation. Gem called it terror. Grant's right hand nervously found the watch on his left wrist, turning and adjusting it. Tick, tick, tick.

Chapter Fourteen

Friday Early Afternoon, 3 June 2005

TREY NOTED Gemini's unusual behavior. Her skin blanched to the hue of skim milk as she entered the trailer, and there was a slight tremor in her hands. Though she looked terrified, her back remained straight. She focused on the two men sitting at the kitchen table.

He turned to the man who sat across from Russ and didn't think anyone could look more nervous than Michael Grant. "Mr. Grant, do you gamble?"

Grant's gaze slowly focused on Trey, confusion furrowing his brow. "Who are you?" he demanded.

Trey pulled his badge from his pocket and introduced himself. "Now, answer my question."

Grant paled. His breathing changed and his hands shook. "On occasion."

"At Bayou Lights?"

"Wh...What's that got to do with Ilene?"

"Answer the question, please."

"Yeah. Ever once in a while. Hell, yeah. Ever body in the parish has! So what? It ain't illegal." Bullets of sweat broke out on Grant.

"How long was your sister-in-law in town before she disappeared?"

"My sis...Kelli? I don't know. A few weeks. What's going on here? I thought this was about Ilene." A little color crept back to his face.

Trey watched the man's expression change as fear replaced confusion, and then anger, and then back to fear. It all took place within a couple of heartbeats, telling Trey the man's concern was more for himself than for Ilene or Kelli.

"Did Ilene gamble?" Trey asked.

"Hell no! No wife of mine's gonna go in those places. Not that it's your business."

"Mr. Grant, your sister-in-law and your wife both went missing within a two week period. We're trying to find out what happened to them. Can you think of anyone who might be responsible for their disappearance?" Trey shifted his body a little, trying to relieve the pressure of the gun lying against his back.

Grant took a deep breath and blew it out. "No. I told all this to the cop who took the report. Now, you got some news, or what?"

"Do you know the owners of Bayou Lights? Or any of the employees?"

A little fear flickered again in Grant's eyes. "Not personal. You think somebody from the casino killed Kelli and Ilene?"

"One more question, and then we'll get back to your wife. Why did Kelli Stevens come to Louisiana?"

"Look, Mr. FBI Man, I already been through this shit. She got an offer for a job, I guess."

"You guess? You don't know? Who offered her a job?"

"Ilene said Kelli met someone in Los Angeles who said there was a woman in Vegas looking for girls to work in a casino. Kelli went there and worked for a few months. Then they offered her a bonus if she'd move here and work at Bayou Lights."

"And why did she move in with you?"

"I thought you said, 'one more question?'"

"Do I need to repeat myself?"

"Ilene wanted her to."

"No other motive?"

"Motive? Now see here, I don't know where the girl ran off to, but I ain't got no motive against her. Now, what about my wife?"

Russ cleared his throat and took control. "Mr. Grant, you told the officer who took the report that your wife went for a walk Monday evening and never returned. Why didn't you call that night?"

Grant's face reddened and he squared his shoulders. If anything would make him blow, it would be an interrogation from a black detective. But Trey would get back to him. The burning question right now was how did he know his wife was dead?

Chapter Fifteen

GEMINI TAYLOR
Michael Grant's House
Verbois, LA

Friday Early Afternoon, 3 June 2005

GEM WONDERED why Fontaine pushed the casino questions, but her thoughts were interrupted by Coleman's next statement.

"Sir, I'm afraid we have some bad news. We found your wife's body this morning," he said coolly.

"I...I thought she left me," Grant said quietly. He stared through Russ. His face grew paler with each passing second.

His fake concern sent her radar into full throttle. She understood a woman leaving him, but wasn't convinced he was heartbroken about it. More likely, he was mad that she dared to leave.

"When did you last see her?" Coleman lowered his eyes to his notepad.

Grant laced his fingers together into bloodless knots. He was deciding if he should lie. "Monday. I came home from work and she was pissed off. She went stompin' out the house and walked down the road. I thought I'd give her some time to cool down, but when she didn't come back by sunset, I went hunting her. The next morning I called the police."

Gem pressed her lips together. No doubt he'd gone hunting for her. Hunting's what bubbas do. Her bet was he'd found her.

"Does she have family? Parents? Siblings, other than Kelli?" Coleman carefully moved his gaze from Grant. A smart move, Gem realized. Someone with her partner's strengths could make an innocent man nervous. A guilty one might clam up with fear. *This must have been what he used to get a confession out of an innocent person while Daddy's killer went free.* Her muscles tensed at the thought.

"Both her parents are dead, but she has another sister in Dallas."

Coleman scratched the details on his notepad as Grant gave them. "Did you contact her?"

"No, I...I didn't wanna piss Ilene off more. I figured she'd come home, and then be mad at me again if I'd told her sister about this leaving stunt." His soft tone was edged with anger.

Gem sneaked a look at Fontaine. He stood, right hand in his pocket, weight shifted to his right hip. Could he smell the hint of copper?

The louver windows were closed up tight, with heavy gold drapes all but pulled together. Just an inch of sunlight slashed across the room, piercing her eyes and continuing right through to her brain. Her temple pounded threateningly, but the pain quickly faded.

"Do you mind if we look around?" Coleman asked calmly, though tension surrounded him with a black aura.

Grant's chin dimpled as he pressed his lips together. His eyes blazed with fear and surprise. "What for? I'm a private person. Don't like people going through my stuff."

Gem rubbed her arm over the holster lying against her ribs, hoping she wouldn't have to use it. She'd never shot anyone, though she'd drawn down on perps more than once.

If he got permission, Coleman would make it cursory. Her gaze came back around to Grant, who hadn't shed a tear, though his face paled and beads of sweat the size of peas formed at his brow. His hands were too busy reporting his nervousness to wipe away the evidence on his forehead.

Gem thought it would serve him well to die in the same fashion as his wife, to go through what he put her through. *Too bad I'm one of the good guys.*

Chapter Sixteen

TREY FONTAINE
Michael Grant's House
Verbois, LA

Friday Early Afternoon, 3 June 2005

THE MAN hadn't asked anything about what happened to his wife, a fact that would raise any cop's suspicion.

Russ asked a few more questions while Trey looked around the living room at the brown carpet, scarred coffee table, and red velvet couch. All of the furniture could have been thrift shop specials.

"Sometimes we can get a hint of where someone planned to go by what they left behind," Russ tried again. "It will only take a minute."

Grant hesitated before replying. "Just don't be handling stuff," he said and stood to keep an eye on Russ as he walked through the narrow trailer.

Trey saw nothing worth noting in the front room. Taylor's gaze swept the kitchen.

"Thank you, Mr. Grant." Russ said when he returned. "When can you come down to Raven Bayou? We'll need someone to identify the body."

"But you said it was her. I hafta work."

"You work Saturdays?"

Trey fought to keep a straight face as Russ easily manipulated the man. He didn't need Grant to I.D. the body. Fingerprints and dental records would provide the proof they needed. The I.D. was an excuse to ensure Grant came to the station voluntarily, without considering an attorney.

"I'm sure your boss'll understand. After all, you just lost your wife. It's standard procedure in these cases to have a family member identify the body. If your boss has any questions, he can call me." Russ took a card from his pocket and laid it on the table.

"Well, I don't work tomorrow. I can come in the morning, I guess. You gonna be there?" Grant leaned back and squeezed his arms over his chest. Took the bait just like a rabbit. Or a rat.

"Yeah, I'll be there. That'll be fine." Russ's voice flowed like honey.

Grant nodded, eyes downcast, hands fumbling in his jean pockets.

They could have taken him in for questioning, but Trey knew as well as Russ that it was better to know the answers before asking the questions.

Taylor pushed out the door, breathing deeply as she hustled down the stairs. Russ followed with Trey right behind him. Before heading for the unit, Taylor walked over to Grant's Taurus. She bent and looked at the front bumper, and then the tire, before returning to the cruiser.

As soon as they were all in the unit Taylor asked, "Did you smell blood in there?"

Russ shook his head, not even bothering to look at her, while Trey's gaze bored into the back of her head. He hadn't smelled anything except sweat and garbage.

"What was so interesting about the car?" Trey asked.

"New damage to the front left bumper. Also, a chunk of rubber out of the tire."

THE RIDE BACK to Raven Bayou began in silence. Russ was probably thinking the same thing Trey was; Michael Grant showed no emotion except nervousness. Not the shaking of the soul at the loss of a loved one but shaking of the hands, like a man struggling to control a dangerous secret.

Trey knew the difference. He rubbed his hand over the pocket holding the mint tin. It was after seventeen-thirty by the time they rolled into the rear parking lot. The Civic Building closed more than a half-hour ago leaving the station as the only entrance. Taylor heaved her door open as she dragged the shifter into park. Trey never saw anyone so anxious to get out of a car.

They followed the maze of hallways to the coroner's office. Barlow confirmed the preliminary findings he'd given Taylor about the beating, but had nothing more. "Avlee took scrapings from under the nails and casted the wounds. She also has the bloody clothing."

"Thanks, Barlow," Russ said.

They arrived at the CSU lab just as Avlee Waters the lab tech was leaving. "Hey, the Bobbsey Twins," Avlee said with a smile, her white teeth gleaming against her dark Seminole skin.

"Got anything for us?" Taylor asked.

"Not yet. Two other cases in front of yours."

"But ours is a homicide. We're looking at the husband and we need all the help we can get," Russ put in.

"The carjacking case gets my attention next. How's she doing?" A kindness shone in Avlee's dark eyes as she looked at Russ.

"I called the hospital an hour ago. She's stable but critical," Russ said.

"She's in my thoughts. In the meantime, the burglary of the Boudreaux mansion has the mayor in a panic. A.C. Boudreaux is one of his biggest supporters. I'll get to your case as soon as I can." Before either of them could reply, Avlee trotted down the hall.

Chapter Seventeen

GEMINI TAYLOR
Sheriff's Dept.
Raven Bayou, LA

Friday Evening, 3 June 2005

AVLEE'S DARK SEMINOLE eyes held a secret. Besides being good at reading people, Gem had gone to school with Avlee. They weren't close. Gem had never been allowed to get really close with anyone as a kid, but Avlee was open to anyone around her.

She was the mystic type, always wanting others to "find themselves" and "figure things out." But that wasn't why she was being close-mouthed today. Her smile at Trey raised Gem's hackles. Avlee knew more than she was telling, but Gem couldn't say a thing in front of Coleman.

Gem observed her partner, his head hanging down, shaking side to side in disgust. She'd only worked with him for a few days but could see his wick getting shorter, and when he blew, the explosion would be ugly. Russ Coleman was a dedicated detective, a methodical worker and a man who rarely allowed emotions out to play. At least on duty. Yet, several times in the last few hours, Gem watched tension grip his face and wrinkle it into a scowl. If she were one to pray, she'd pray for the man who hurt Darlene. He'd need all the help he could get if he ever faced Coleman. This was the part of him Gem wanted to get hold of. This was the Coleman she wanted to work with, the part she needed.

As they walked back toward the pit, thoughts of the Boudreaux trial returned. Her watch said six-oh-five. Court closed almost two hours ago. Surely they would have heard.

Reports needed to be written, but it was late. "So I take it we're working tomorrow. Where do we start?"

"With Michael Grant," Coleman said as he picked up his bag.

"Coleman, Taylor?" Lieutenant Loe's voice filtered through the room. Gem bit her lip to keep from smiling at his soft, feminine voice. It had been obvious since day one that Loe's short man complex went into overdrive with her height.

She watched Coleman and Trey nod to each other, whatever that meant, and then she and Coleman headed to the boss's office. He motioned them to sit. A file lay on the desk in front of him.

"Sorry about your sister, Coleman. How's she doing?" The lieutenant shifted his gaze from Coleman several times before managing to gain control and look him in the eye.

Lieutenant Loe's breathing increased. He shifted tensely in his chair, emotions written clearly on his face. It wasn't easy for such a young man to bear so much responsibility. Clearly, Coleman intimidated him, probably because of the older man's experience. Or maybe he was afraid Coleman could read him as she did: unsure and a little weak. Or maybe Loe's nervousness was rooted in the color of Russ's skin.

"Thanks. She's stable. She'll come out of this. I want the case." It was a useless gesture on Coleman's part.

The lieutenant cleared his throat. "You know better. Wilkes is on the case. He's a good man."

"At least let me help him with leg work," Coleman said.

"You leave it alone."

The muscles in Coleman's jaws bunched up as he gritted his teeth.

"You and your sister are two of a kind. Stubborn. Did she tell you anything?" Loe asked with almost no intonation.

Coleman shook his head. "No one can get anything out of her. She's refused a rape kit and says she can't remember what the man looked like."

Both sat quietly, waiting. Loe held a pen in his hand, his thumb making it click-click-click.

Gem's throat constricted and she swallowed hard. "Sir, I could go talk to her." The "sir" almost stuck in her throat. It wasn't her thing to volunteer any more than it was to call a man like Loe "sir," but Coleman would appreciate any help she could give and it was the least she could do.

"There's a rape crisis counselor there, but Darlene refuses to speak to her," the lieutenant continued. "What makes you think she'd talk to you?"

"Maybe she won't, but it's worth a try. She won't talk to a man and there's no one else to send." *Unless you count the vice detective who doesn't know a victim from a cucumber.*

"I promised your partner I'd put my best people on this." His eyes swept from Gem to Coleman and back. "Wilkes is a good man. He'll find the bastard who did this."

"Finding him won't help much if your only witness won't cooperate," Gem said a little more sharply than intended.

This would have been the perfect time to back off, but she'd never been one with perfect timing. She could see Coleman's interest in what she said. Shifting to the edge of the chair, she leaned forward. The lieutenant didn't have a problem looking *her* in the eye. She hoped this wouldn't be one of those times when she'd opened her mouth and inserted her foot. Aunt Ginny said that was Gem's specialty.

"Taylor can be pretty stubborn too, Lieutenant," Coleman said. "I'd feel better if you let her try."

Gem couldn't decide if she wanted to kiss Coleman or smack him.

The lieutenant's gaze fixed on Gem, his eyes cold. "Hold your reports and go," he ordered in a tone as if it were his idea.

Gem nodded. Loe said something else to Coleman, but she didn't pay attention. Her mind was already trying to wrap itself around what she'd just gotten into. She'd just volunteered to talk to a woman who had been beaten, maybe even raped. It was the worst part of the job. Even worse than telling a victim's family about the death of someone. At least with death, the terror ended.

She stood and pushed her chair out of the way, ready to attack what she hoped would be the last major event of the day.

"Report any thing you learn to Wilkes. Immediately. And see me Monday morning with your findings," Loe said, his face emotionless. "Early."

Definitely an appointment with the firing squad, she thought.

When they came out of Loe's office, Trey still sat at the end of Coleman's desk. Gem headed straight for the locker room, took a quick shower, and hurried to her car. The bottle of lemon shampoo had served its purpose. She no longer smelled of death.

Chapter Eighteen

TREY FONTAINE
Sheriff's Dept.
Raven Bayou, LA

Friday Evening, 3 June 2005

"WHERE'S YOUR CAR?" Trey called to Taylor as Russ headed for the Suburban.

Taylor nodded toward the back of the lot.

"I'll walk you," he offered. "Been a helluva day."

They were silent until they reached the Caddie and Taylor tossed her bag onto the back seat. He thought about asking her out, but decided against it. This was not time to get involved.

A low whistle escaped his lips. "A '59 Eldorado convertible." His hands caressed the chrome window trim, gaze sweeping over the classic automobile. This was the kind of high school sweetheart a man remembered forever. He'd been so focused on Taylor this morning he'd barely paid any mind to her chariot. Now he couldn't take his eyes off it.

"And I thought you were being chivalrous," she teased as she rattled her keys.

He swung the driver's door open and smiled at her. "So, do you have plans this weekend?" *What the hell am I doing?*

"Plans? Uh, just some research. Maybe a day out."

Trey still held the door. He had the urge to make her slide over so he could drive this baby but closed the door gently instead.

"How about I pick you up for breakfast in the morning?"

Gemini eased the key in the ignition and looked up. "Are you a gambling man?"

"Huh?"

"I'm betting you can't find a place where I'd enjoy eating breakfast."

"It's a bet. Pick you up at eight?"

"Nine? I'm not really a morning person."

"Nine, your place."

"You know where I live?"

"No. But I have resources."

Trey watched as Taylor drove out of the lot. When she was out of sight, he pulled the mint tin from his pocket and popped two Lortabs in his mouth. *It's not a date. It's just breakfast. I'm just trying to get to know Russ's partner. That's all.*

Yeah. Right.

Chapter Nineteen

GEMINI TAYLOR
Raven Bayou Community Hospital
Raven Bayou, LA

Friday Sunset, 3 June 2005

THE SUN slipped behind the trees and a warm breeze rustled the leaves and stirred the smells of Raven Bayou. Gem had promised to be ready for Fontaine tomorrow morning. He didn't say where they would go and that was fine by her. Maybe Fontaine would be more likely to help her with Daddy's case than Coleman, or perhaps Fontaine could convince Coleman to reopen the case. Gem was ready to use whatever means necessary. The sooner the better.

Her hands squeezed the steering wheel so tightly they hurt as she drove to the hospital. Disappointing Coleman was not an option. Nor was failure. She hadn't been close to many men in her life, and most were users in one way or another. But Gem sensed gentleness in Coleman. He'd survived a haunted past and understood the pain of others. If she managed to get answers from his sister, Coleman would owe her.

Whatever had to be done to get Darlene Vance to talk, Gem would do it.

The information desk directed her to the ICU where the nurse told her to have a seat in the waiting room while she paged the doctor. When the nurse shut the door, Gem turned toward the waiting room but stopped at the sight of a pretty African-American woman sitting in a chair across from the closed doors.

"Couldn't help but overhear your conversation," the woman said and introduced herself as Patsy Watson, Darlene's sister. Gem listened attentively as Patsy told all she knew. Her voice was filled with concern for both Darlene and Coleman. It made Gem wonder what it would be like to have a sibling to share with, someone to care about. Someone who cared about her.

A picture of two little girls playing behind a rose bush flashed in her head, and her heart pounded with their joy. Then, just as quickly, the daydream flickered into black, like the end of an eight-millimeter tape.

"They been trying to push me outta here all afternoon. Don't take to blacks in the hallways," Patsy said.

"You seem to be holding your own."

"They ought to know by now. I been in this hall with half my family one time or the other."

The nurse called Gem into ICU and led her to the doctor. "Mrs. Vance suffered severe trauma about the head, a break to the mandible, a severe lacera—"

"Could I get the English version, please?" Gem interrupted, thinking how impressed he was with himself. It was hard to pay attention to his droning with the hospital smells attacking her. No matter how much disinfectant they used, the stench of urine lingered. Along with the heavy, copper smell of blood.

"Her left jawbone was broken, and she has a deep cut above one eye. Massive bruising. We're keeping her in ICU for the night due to swelling of her throat. Bruises on her neck indicate someone choked her. She's stable but needs plenty of rest."

"Thanks."

Still, Gem wasn't ready for what waited on the other side of the curtain. Darlene Vance was in no condition to answer questions from her or anyone else.

Darlene's eyes were swollen nearly shut, black and purple skin bulged out into multicolored golf balls, cuts on her brow from the beating now sewn with black railroad tracks of stitches. The left side of her face was bandaged.

With her jaw wired shut, and a massive dose of fear leaking from the slits where eyes should be, Gem couldn't bring herself to ask personal questions. But she believed she understood Darlene without either of them saying a word.

Darlene Vance was strong, able to withstand whatever the world threw at her without breaking. If she was withholding information, it was to protect someone other than herself. She had lived through torture and terror, and was still fighting. To Gem, that was proof of her strength.

Gem had never been allowed to associate with African-Americans as a child, except for Reena who was half white and whose mama worked for Alton Boudreaux. Daddy hated it. He hated anyone different from him, which turned out to be most people. But her family lived on Boudreaux land and Reena was one of Boudreaux's pets, so Daddy tolerated the friendship between the two girls. Gem'd been gone from Raven Bayou for half a lifetime so she didn't remember ever meeting Darlene Vance.

And now here Gem stood, feeling a strong sense of kinship for this woman who had been so bitterly mistreated. It would be easy for them to connect. Gem could empathize. *Here goes*, she thought. It was time to stop thinking and do something.

"I'm Detective Taylor. Call me Gemini. I'm out of Raven Parish Sheriff's Office, where your brother works." There was no need to tell her she was Coleman's partner. It might make the woman overly cautious.

"Are you feeling any better?" *What a stupid question. But what do you say to someone in this condition?* she thought.

Darlene didn't attempt to answer, just reached a hand weakly toward Gem who took it, not sure what the woman wanted.

Darlene's fingers were icicles, long and thin and bloodless, but her grip was stronger than expected. Gem stood there for a long time, allowing Darlene to hold her hand the way she would hold on to a sister.

"Just relax, Mrs. Vance. We'll find him and put him away."

More tears rolled down the woman's cheeks. With one hand, she motioned for pen and paper. Gem found a tablet on the bedside table with notes already scribbled and crossed out. A pen lay beside it. She handed them to Darlene and waited, and then read the note.

Said he'd kill my family if I told.

"You're safe, Mrs. Vance, and so is your family. If you help us catch him and put him away, he won't get out for years."

Scared. She wrote. *He knows where Russ works, knows about Patsy, my husband, grandkids.*

"Mrs. Vance—Darlene, I'll make you a deal. You give us what we need, and we'll provide complete protection until he's put away. Permanently."

He's crazy.

Gem freed her hand long enough to retrieve a chair while trying to ignore the closed-in feeling of having the curtains drawn.

"Let us do what we have to, before he hurts someone else." She waited and hoped, but Darlene Vance really mirrored her brother in one way. Stubbornness. For a long time Gem sat there, holding Darlene's hand. So long, in fact, Gem began to nod off.

HER HEAD suddenly snapped up and she blinked her eyes into focus. She'd actually fallen asleep. "It's late. I should go." But Darlene's grip tightened and her face filled with fear again.

Still holding Gem's hand tightly, Darlene bounced their joined hands on the mattress. She wanted Gem to stay, not just in CCU, but here, at her bedside.

Please don't go. Rest here, she scrawled crookedly, the pad supported by her thigh so she didn't have to release Gem's hand. Darlene put the pad on her tummy and patted the bed, motioning for Gem to come closer. She couldn't tell the scared woman no. Darlene squeezed Gem's hand and pulled Gem gently toward her.

Hesitantly, Gem leaned forward and laid her head on the edge of the mattress. Darlene sighed. Gem closed her eyes, a flash of something shiny reminding her about Grant's car bumper. She thought only to rest a minute or two, but the drone of the complex machinery monitoring Darlene's every breath and heartbeat lulled her away.

Chapter Twenty

WILE E.
Raven Bayou Community Hospital
Raven Bayou, LA

Friday Night, 3 June 2005

I PEEKED at Miss Darlene. She looked like a broken angel in the light coming from the bulb over her bed. A bandage covered her head and her face was bruised and swole. A needle burrowed in her hand, an ugly, blood-sucking bug, taped down so it couldn't get in deeper.

Must of been one evil man to do that to a lady. It reminded me of the men who was the reason we left town the first time, and I wondered if one of 'em did this. 'Course, they hurt kids more than ladies.

Gemini sat, bent over, asleep, with her head on the bed by Miss Darlene's good hand. I pushed my hair back from my eyes. The only thing that makes me madder than for a man to be mean to a lady is for him to be mean to a kid.

The more I watched the two ladies, the more mad I was. I heard Miss Darlene not tell what the man looked like. She was so scared. I wondered what I could do to help her feel safe. I reckon if I knowed who did this, he'd best be gone, 'cause I can be mean as the devil when I get mad.

Chapter Twenty-One

GEMINI TAYLOR
Raven Bayou Community Hospital
Raven Bayou, LA

Friday Night 3, June 2005

BEHIND HER CLOSED EYES and even breathing, Gem's mind returned to a sunny evening when she was a little girl, playing with her only friend. What was left of the spring sun shone deep gold through the trees in the distance. Reena and little Gem ran, laughing and playing tag, their bare feet flecked with black soil. Reena's legs were longer than Gem's because Reena was older, but Gem urged her feet to go faster until she finally touched Reena's caramel skin.

"You're it!" Gem yelled and ran around the fat trunk of an old magnolia whose branches shot out from just above her head and hung to the ground, heavy laden with rubbery leaves and giant white blossoms. Reena bent and chased Gem around the tree so close behind that the older girl's warmth enveloped her.

The sweet scent of her starched sunsuit mixed with the smell of magnolias. The thin cotton hugged her body and the straps were tied so loosely that they fell off her shoulders.

"Well, what are my two favorite girls doing out here? It'll be dark soon."

Gem stopped so quickly that Reena bumped into her before managing to come to a standstill. The smell of cherry pipe tobacco made Gem shiver as Mr. Alton closed in, stopping where the tree branches barred his advance. He wore a light blue suit, and fancy black shoes. Mr. Alton always wore a suit. He was taller than Daddy, and wider too.

"So, which one of you wants to help me down at the stable? We have a new foal that needs checked on." His smooth, tan face wore a smile, and his dark hair shined with the fragrant oil he always used.

Both girls backed around the tree until its trunk hid their bodies from him.

"Come on now. Don't make me choose," he cajoled and took a pull from the fancy carved pipe.

Gem's heart pounded so hard she bet Reena could hear it. She didn't want to go with Mr. Alton. He did things she didn't like. But she didn't want Reena to go either 'cause he might do it to her. Just as Gem was about to step away from the tree and reach for his hand, Reena ran from behind and hurried to his side.

"There's a good girl. Let's go see Mona Lisa's foal." He took her hand and they walked away.

Gem came out from behind the tree and followed at a safe distance until they reached the top of the knoll behind the barns. Then she stopped and watched as Reena walked quietly beside the big man, his quiet voice barely audible.

Reena and Mr. Alton were so far away that Gem couldn't hear him talking anymore. Reena turned and gave Gem one last look, her soft gray eyes showing a mixture of fear and dread. Reena was the willing sacrifice.

Gem had seen Reena go to the stable with Mr. Alton before. Reena knew what was going to happen, and she went anyway. Hot tears stung Gem's eyes and ran down her cheeks.

She turned to run toward the house but ran face first right into Daddy's dingy, stinky undershirt. Daddy knocked her down with a backhand for it. He was skinny, but strong.

"What you think you're doing, spying on Mr. Alton?" he barked as his pock-marked face turned into a scowl.

Gem stood and dusted off the back of her sunsuit.

"Get yourself to your room and stay there till I call you. Better than that—get to your closet. No supper for you tonight, little Miss Nancy Drew."

Gem turned to obey but not quickly enough. His boot landed in the small of her back and she found herself sprawled on the ground. Her hands and knees were skinned, but she bounced up onto her feet and hightailed it across the yard, not stopping until she reached her room, fear welling in her chest as she neared the closet door. Reluctantly, she opened it and looked inside.

She had to tee-tee really bad, but if Daddy came in and caught her in the bathroom...she looked around the room. Someone watched her, someone hiding in the shadows. Gem hurried into the closet and closed the door behind her. But the feeling someone was watching didn't go away.

SOMETHING CRAWLED UP her spine, making the hairs on her neck stand. She raised her head from the mattress, still feeling the uncanny tickle of someone spying on her, but a look around made a liar of her instinct.

The curtain was closed three-quarters of the way and only Darlene and Gem were there. Even the nurses' station was empty. The other patients slept. Gem combed her fingers through her hair and yawned.

Her back was stiff from the hard plastic chair. She stretched as Darlene watched with a look of concern. The weight of Darlene's stare must have been what woke Gem up. When she apologized for having fallen asleep, Darlene wrote two words on the notepad.

Do it. She closed her eyes.

Gem understood the request. It took more than an hour for a nurse trained in evidence gathering to arrive and prepare. Gem held Darlene's hand during the exam. Fear and pain poured from Darlene as the nurse slid the cold plastic speculum into her and told her to relax.

Gem fought back tears. "I'm proud of you, Darlene. You're doing the right thing. Don't worry. We'll find the bastard who did this. You just may be saving someone else from going through all this."

When the nurse finished, Gem plastered a half-hearted smile on her face and squeezed Darlene's hand.

"Don't worry. We'll take good care of you and your family. I promise."

Chapter Twenty-Two

RUSS COLEMAN
Sheriff's Dept.
Raven Bayou, LA

Friday Night, 3 June 2005

RUSS HUNG UP the phone and palmed his face. Avlee wouldn't get to the Grant case till morning. She could only do so much. Putting a burglary at Boudreaux's mansion in front of any case made him want to hit something.

He wondered if deputies guarded the jury. How many could be paid off by Boudreaux? Russ sipped his cold coffee and made a face at the bitterness, his stomach burning.

Tomorrow he'd review Endri's file. It had been twenty-five days since Endri's attack. Even if they figured out who attacked her, the typical victim wasn't willing to get on the witness stand and live through it all again. Didn't want her life to become a public story. Didn't want her sex life talked about in front of her mother or to be called a whore by some attorney.

But Endri wasn't typical. Endri was special. Russ considered himself good at reading people, and he read Endri as strong and stubborn and not likely to let anyone to get away with hurting her.

With Darlene going through the same thing, it was twice as important to find the useless ass responsible. *There must be a link*, he told himself. Maybe he'd missed something.

A call to the hospital confirmed Darlene would be moved to a semi-private room in a couple of days. He talked to the nurse who told him his other sister went home and a female detective was just leaving.

He threw his war bag in the back of the big, forest green Suburban, whipped over into a brightly lit gas station, and laid out almost thirty dollars by the time the pump clicked off. He went inside for a large cup of black coffee before heading home.

When he got back to the SUV, he saw it. A single sheet of plain white paper, folded once, lying on the driver's seat. Russ stretched across the seat and put his coffee in the cup-holder on the console. He unfolded the paper.

DROP THE CHERAMIE CASE OR
NEXT TIME SOMEBODY DIES

Instinctively his hand went to his weapon as he swept left, and then right. The station was busy, but no one stood out. His gaze flew from one person to the next, from one vehicle to another. He slid the gun back into its holster, swallowed hard and looked back at the note. The attack on Darlene had been his fault. Whoever almost killed Endri was willing to go to great pains to make sure Russ stopped the investigation. His heart pounded harder and lightning shot through his jaw as his teeth ground against each other.

Next time somebody dies.

HE PARKED in the two-car garage beside the smoke-gray T-bird coupe that hadn't moved in months. If he kept anything of hers, it would be the car. Russ had teased Julie more than once about her loving the car more than she loved him. Her only response was always a silent, cat-that-ate-the-canary look.

And then there was the house. It was time to sell the big monstrosity and find something more suitable for a widower, something simple. Julie once told him that if anything ever happened to her, she wanted him to go on with life. She called him a man with a spirit to be shared with the world. Right now, he didn't feel too spiritual.

Just as he stood out of his car, his cell rang.

"*Bon soir*? Detective Coleman?" Endri's voice sounded faint and frightened.

"I'm here, Endri. What is it you wanted to talk about?" After a long silence, he asked, "Are you still there?"

"*Oui*." She sobbed before continuing, "You will drop the c...case. No more *fouiller*, no."

"What do you mean, 'no more digging!' The bastard tried to kill you! Endri what's wrong?"

"Let it pass by. *Mais la*. No more. Me and Maman, we be fine."

"No! Wait! Endri—"

Click.

The whole day had gone this way. Did the girl know something about the sender of the note? He stared at the phone, but it held no answers.

NEXT TIME SOMEBODY DIES.

"Damn." Adrenaline kicked in, making his skin tingle and his hair stand on end. He jumped back into the Suburban and drove like a madman until he reached Raven Bayou Road and had to slow down so as not to miss the narrow turn off into the small Cajun community.

Old men and women sat in twos and threes on the porches. Children played in yards. Cajun music floated through the neighborhood. He was in front of the Cheramie home in minutes.

Sweat covered his face as he stepped out of his SUV. The front door to the house was closed, and pounding on it produced nothing. She could've called from anywhere. Or she could be lying dead on the floor on the other side of the door.

He walked around the house to the fence. A small lock secured the gate. No one came to his shout. Thin lace curtains remained closed. With the lights out inside, he saw nothing, and without something concrete, he had no reason to break down the door.

He climbed back into the SUV, his nerves sending mixed messages of fight and flight. He pulled out the cell and called the hospital to check on Darlene.

Wherever Endri had called from, danger sat with her. There was no doubt in his mind that these two cases were linked. And he was the link.

Lost in thought, Russ eased through the area where his illegitimate daughter had grown up. The woman who adopted Endri promised she'd never tell the girl about her past. Endri didn't need to know she'd been abandoned. Russ made sure she had a good life here and made sure there was a college fund for her. She'd never wanted for anything important. And her adoptive mother loved her wholeheartedly.

MORE HUNGRY THAN TIRED, Russ swung by the Rusty Badge for a burger and beer. The place was full of deputies, firemen, and other city and parish employees. Russ found a soda-fountain table with two tall barstools under it. With a heavy sigh, he pulled out one and sat. The waitress arrived and Russ was pleasantly surprised to find there was a new woman in town.

"Evening. What can I get you?" she asked. Her nametag said CORA. Her face said, "Leave me alone."

Russ gazed at her for a minute, taking in her pretty, heart-shaped face and skin the color of light coffee. "A burger, medium rare with everything, fries, and a Miller Lite draft."

Her light gray eyes looked familiar. Her dark hair was pulled back in a bun. Her face looked young. Maybe late thirties.

"Got it." She walked away without so much as a smile. Tight black jeans revealed a shapely behind and small waist. He enjoyed the view until the crowd closed around her. He looked for friendly faces. Not many in this crowd. Few of them would even speak to a black man, even one who might have to back one of them up someday. He hadn't gone out with friends since Julie's death.

Cora returned with his beer, interrupting his remembrances. "Burger's almost ready." She stepped close to set the frosted glass down. He smelled cigarette smoke and some clean fragrance, her soap or shampoo.

"You're new in town?" He took a long draw on the beer. It was icy cold and good going down.

"You could say that. I lived here when I was a kid, but we left town before I started high school. I'll get that burger for you."

She turned away. He figured she must be just as alone as he and understood how such a pretty woman could walk around with a cheerless attitude.

Coming back with his food, she set the basket down and grabbed his glass. "I'll top that off for you," and before he could object, she returned with a full frosted glass.

He wanted to speak before she turned to go, but his energy had bottomed out and his mind didn't offer up the proper words. She slipped the check under the edge of the cardboard coaster and disappeared again.

He ate his meal alone—in the midst of the crowded bar and grill. After leaving enough on the table for the meal and a decent tip, he dragged his butt out to the Suburban and headed home.

Pulling the SUV into the garage, he closed his eyes for a second. On the video screen beneath his lids he saw Cora's gray eyes and full mouth. With a deep breath he locked the Suburban and went inside. The solarium called to him. He made himself comfortable on the wicker loveseat and just listened to the quiet.

In the corner stood a rubber mat, rolled like a carpet. It was what he used when he prayed, a thing he hadn't done since Julie went to the hospital. She always said he was disciplined and she could set her watch by his morning coffee and paper, or his evening prayer. He unrolled the mat and sat, folding his legs in front of him.

Twenty minutes later he knew what he must do. Tonight he would start sorting things. Tomorrow he would call the realtor. And next week, he'd look for a small house in the country where he could set the clock by his morning coffee and paper.

Chapter Twenty-Three

CORA LYON
Boudreaux Estate
Raven Bayou, LA

Friday Night, 3 June 2005

CORA LYON took a deep drag off her cigarette as she wheeled her midnight blue Firebird close to the barn. The summer sounds of crickets and bullfrogs stopped for an instant before continuing their serenade. She leaned against the fender and enjoyed the light breeze until the cigarette was nothing but a filter.

Before going inside, Cora looked up the hill toward the big house. The Boudreaux mansion. Everyone in the parish knew the mansion, and the family. Even Cora, who'd been back in town for only a short time, knew how powerful they were.

She smiled as she sauntered into the barn. This was her first time back in the parish in more than twenty-three years. She'd known the Boudreaux name forever, though she was born in Kentucky and spent most of her life there.

The stud nickered. Cora grabbed a scoop of grain and dumped it into the hanging trough. A glance between the wooden slats told her the bandage on its injured leg was still intact. Without thought, she lit another cigarette. Alton Boudreaux would birth a foal himself if he ever caught her smoking in the barn. The horse raised his nose from the trough and nodded, a little worried neigh rumbling from his muzzle, but the smoke didn't stop him from chewing.

Boudreaux Stables was famous in Kentucky, but that wasn't why she knew the name. It was one she'd heard from her mama ever since she could remember. And now Cora was here, at the very place she was conceived.

Corina LeBeau had been given her mother's maiden name, a name familiar to the local town folk. Using Lyon as a last name meant no one in town had any clue who she was.

Before she was done, everyone would know the truth. Either they would love her or hate her. Didn't matter much either way.

Chapter Twenty-Four

RUSS COLEMAN
Sheriff's Dept.
Raven Bayou, LA

Saturday Morning, 4 June 2005

SATURDAY MORNING the newspaper said the jury had not reached a verdict on the Boudreaux case. They would convene again Monday morning. Russ had been at the station for two hours, his mind divided between the Grant case, the call from Endri, and the need to wrangle info out of Wilkes on Darlene's case.

The phone made him jump.

"Hey, you left a message to call you?" It was Avlee.

"Figured you'd be in today. You alone in the lab?"

"Of course. I think you and I are the only dedicated workaholics left in the department. Besides, come on...a murder case!"

"I'll be there in a minute." He hung up, pulled a thin file from his war bag and grabbed his coffee. It took a couple of minutes to get there.

Avlee sipped on her own mug, eyeing him from over the rim.

"I need a little help with something," Russ said. "But I'm not ready to share. Think you could do me a favor?"

Avlee shrugged. "This has to do with your sister's case?"

He rubbed a palm over his short hair and sighed.

"Let's see what you got." She slipped on rubber gloves.

He laid the file on the counter in front of her.

She opened it. "Interesting," was all she said. With smooth-tipped tweezers, she picked up the note and put it under the microscope, moving it slowly beneath the narrow view of the lens as she checked first one side, and then the other. "You touched it without gloves?"

"It was in the seat of my SUV. Didn't know it was evidence till I read it. Unless you find something on it, I'd rather not mention it to anybody right now."

"I can live with that. When I'm done, I'll call you."

Russ went back to the pit and called Wilkes. His voice was gravelly as he answered the phone.

"Hey, it's Coleman. I need to talk to you."

"I'm about five out."

"I'll meet you in the parking lot."

Wilkes was a good judge of time. Within five minutes he'd parked. "What's up?" He slid out of his pickup, unfolding his long legs. His short, curly salt-and-pepper hair stuck out around the edge of his billed RBSD cap.

"I think Darlene needs protection."

"Why?" Wilkes started walking toward the building, tugging at the tie around his neck.

Damn. He didn't want Wilkes to ask questions. "I think she was attacked because of me. I've been working that aggravated rape case, and now Darlene was attacked the same way. Trust me on this."

The detective stopped and turned to face Russ, his voice lowered conspiratorially, "You're gonna have to give up more than 'trust me,' Coleman. What's going on?" His blue eyes peered, unblinking, at his friend.

Russ dropped his gaze for a second, but he couldn't think of any way to keep it a secret. "I got a phone call from Endri Cheramie, the girl who was attacked." He waited for a nod of confirmation. "Said she wanted me to drop the case. Sounded really scared. I think maybe someone was forcing her to call me."

"And what's that got to do with your sister?"

Wilkes would find out sooner or later, so Russ told him about the note.

"Son of a bitch!" Wilkes lowered his voice, looked over his shoulder at the door. "Where is it?"

"With Avlee, but I asked her to keep it quiet for now. If this gets back to the LT, he'll pull me from that case too. Damn. He'd probably put *me* in protective custody." Those last words came out between gritted teeth.

"Look. The only way to get guys guarding your sister on the clock is to go to Loe. But there's no policy against visiting friends off duty. I know a few guys who owe me. Between the two of us, we should be able to keep someone there until she's discharged. If she gets released before we have someone in custody, who's to say we can't decide to have a long-ass welcome home party at her place?"

"That'll be trouble for you."

"No trouble. The guys owe me big and they'll do what I ask. How many can you get?"

"Trey, me, maybe Taylor," Russ said.

"Well, you've got me, and I can gather at least three. We can do it."

"Thanks, Wilkes." Russ sighed with relief, and started walking again. "It's good to have a friend on the job."

Wilkes followed. "Hey, us old farts have to stick together. Have you talked to your partner since last night?"

Russ shook his head.

"Darlene talked. Said a skinny young man with blond hair opened the passenger door when she rolled up to a stop sign. She tried to fight him, but he forced her to drive to some isolated area." Wilkes looked cautiously at Russ. "He raped and beat her, and then shoved her out of the mini-van and drove off. When we find the mini-van—and we will—we'll compare the odometer to whatever info the husband has and see how far the doer went. That's all Taylor told me. Did Darlene tell you anything?"

"No." Russ spoke slowly, trying to keep the emotion out of his voice. "She was asleep when I went in. Think I'll go visit her for a while."

Wilkes had been his friend for decades and in all that time, Russ had never seen him wear the expression Wilkes probably thought of as compassion but to Russ looked like pity.

"Don't worry, we'll catch the asshole." Wilkes patted Russ on the shoulder. "C'mon, let's get it done."

RUSS SAT with his sister in the semi-private room she'd been moved to. His cell rang. It was Wilkes.

"Caught a case you might be interested in." Wilkes spoke softly. "A man's body was found on the back side of Boudreaux Park by two hikers thirty minutes ago."

Russ leaned forward and rubbed his hand over his face. "I have to make sure Darlene is covered before I can leave. There's no one to cover until nine. Do you really need me?"

"I think you'll want to be in on this one."

"Has he been I.D.'d?" Russ asked, wondering what Wilkes could be getting at.

"Not yet, but he was stabbed in the chest. Abdomen split open from heart to pubic bone."

Chapter Twenty-Five

TREY FONTAINE
Gemini Taylor's house
Raven Bayou, LA

Saturday Morning, 4 June 2005

TREY PARKED in front of Taylor's house at oh-nine-hudnred. The house had been a barn in its former life, but now it was a small, two-story home. He knocked on the door, and Taylor whipped it open almost immediately.

She was dressed and smiling. Maybe she was glad to see him, even at this time in the morning. He appraised her clothing: white sleeveless tunic, brown chinos, sandals. "You look great."

She grabbed her bag and followed him to Streak. "I love this thing."

"Yeah, it's my baby."

"It has four-wheel drive, so you can go anywhere. Right?"

He nodded. "It's designed to take off road." After handing her up into Streak, he climbed into the driver's seat and left the drive by way of the shallow drainage ditch for her benefit. He received a beaming grin for his effort. She settled herself like a teenager on a carnival ride, singing along with the music from the radio, her brown leather bag lay in her lap.

As he turned onto Old Latree road, she became quiet. The two-lane blacktop was smooth, thanks to Alton Boudreaux, whose property lined one side. The other side was wild with trees and vines, so dense it looked impenetrable. Trey noticed Taylor's hands wrapped tightly around the seatbelt, knuckles white as she stared out over the hood. He said nothing.

Suddenly, her mood changed and she appeared to relax. She crossed her legs and sat up elegantly before she hooked a stray strand of hair behind her ear and turned to him again. "Is breakfast still a secret? I'm famished."

"It won't take us long to get there, Taylor."

"Ginni."

"Huh?"

"I prefer Ginni. It's my nickname."

"You don't look like a Ginni. Where'd that name come from?"

"Aunt Virginia."

"Okay. Ginni it is." That would take some getting used to, but he guessed people did have a right to use whatever nickname they chose. It was strange how her articulation changed when she said it, reflecting how she'd spent the last twenty years in Texas.

She ran her hands over the leather interior, uncrossed her legs and propped a sandaled foot on the dash. "This is really a radical ride." Again she appeared relaxed and happy. And young. She looked antsy, unable to make up her mind as to her mood.

"'Radical?' It's been a while since I heard that word."

"Stick around. There's lots more where that came from. So, where're we going?"

"Down the road. Boudreaux Park."

Silence engulfed the other side of the Hummer.

"Don't worry. I brought everything we'll need to enjoy it. I intend to win the bet." A quick glance in Taylor's direction told him she wasn't impressed. Maybe it was one of those female hormone things. Or maybe he was just trying to read something into every move she made. "We don't have to go there. I know a little restaurant a few miles away that serves a big country breakfast. Sue's Kitchen. Serves gravy, biscuits, eggs, grits."

"No grits." Humor returned to her eyes. "You *brought* breakfast?" Her articulation changed just enough to get his attention.

"Yes." He was pleased at her surprise. He'd done something right.

"Is it better than Sue's?" She dropped her foot to the floorboard, leaned forward with both hands braced on the edge of her seat, and gazed at his face intently.

"I don't know about better, but I guarantee there's not a single grit in it."

She laughed and it was like they'd been together since childhood.

Streak eased along Old Latree Road, past the Boudreaux Estate and the stables. The big white barn reflected the sun into his eyes. He turned west on Old Cypress Road and stole a glance at Taylor. She was quiet, her face blank.

"Are you okay?" he asked as she sat silently, her eyes glued to the road ahead.

She didn't speak, but nodded. He was unconvinced. Her face looked white, the skin translucent. A sheen of perspiration met her hairline.

The road curved around the back side of Boudreaux land. Three houses sat back off the road, each with outbuildings behind them. This was where Gemini Taylor had changed his life.

He turned quickly to catch a glimpse of something shiny. Before he could get a look, the brightness disappeared, leaving nothing to see except the last old house and barn. The glint came from the direction of a partially opened barn door where the sun shone through, but he was too far down the road to see what it was.

Besides, what he wanted to see was the gorgeous woman sitting beside him. The same beautiful girl he'd seen on this same road years ago, who had called a halt to the relentless teasing by his buddies and consoled him over the loss of his father.

He brought his gaze around to Taylor and saw fear in her eyes. "What's wrong, Gem...Ginni?" he asked, hoping he hadn't made a mistake in coming this way, past the house she grew up in.

She blinked. Her gaze focused on him. Seconds ticked by. Then her lips curled up again. "Nothing. It's just...been a long time. And you don't have to call me that. I know you're not used to it."

He smiled, relieved. Getting used to a new nickname was difficult enough without it coming on a first real date. Especially this first date. *This is not a date!* "Good. You'll always be Gemini Taylor to me."

He wondered if she was homesick, missing her father as much as Trey still missed his. Or if she was afraid of the memories. "We could stop there on the way back, if you want."

She turned her gaze to her side window and rubbed both temples with her fingers.

"Headache?" he asked.

She brought her attention back to him and nodded. "When I was little, I got my brain fractured." She turned away again, looking out into some place he couldn't see.

Whatever she's feeling, she doesn't want to share. He wondered if she'd forgotten their kiss.

"I'm glad we're almost there. I haven't been to the park in ages. Are the swings still there? I'm hungry." Her voice was light and airy. He expected a giggle any time now.

"Yes, they are. We can eat. Then I'll push you on the swing," he offered. Again her eyes lit up for him.

He parked in the gravel lot and jumped down from the seat. "I'll be right there." He hurried around to help Taylor down, but she was faster than he and had already leapt from the seat to the ground, avoiding the running board.

Trey went to the back door and took out a picnic basket and blanket, pressed the key chain alarm, and led Taylor, shouldering her oversized bag, toward the play area. A few people gathered on the bleachers around the ball field at the other end of the park. A game was scheduled for today.

"How about here?" he asked as he stopped a few yards shy of the monkey bars. Taylor nodded and he set the basket down and spread the blanket. He couldn't help but notice her gaze resting on the swings. "Hey, I thought you were starved."

"Just five minutes?" she pleaded.

Trey followed her as she hurried to the swings and chose the middle one. She sat, wrapped both hands around the chains and backed up as far as she could before raising her feet.

He positioned himself behind her and pushed, remembering the hundreds of times he had come here to sit on the swings and think.

Taylor continued to pump until she swung almost as high as the bar holding the chains. He stopped pushing, but she didn't stop pumping, using her whole body to keep the momentum going until she was breathless.

Leaning against the steel upright, Trey watched and listened as Taylor laughed with joy.

"You really needed a day off!" he said as she dragged her feet until the swing stopped.

"I haven't done that for a while."

He offered a hand and she took it as they walked back to the blanket. Her skin was soft, her grip gentle. Trey liked how she stood shoulder-to-shoulder with him, and her stride equaled his. He usually had to slow his pace so as not to drag his date. Taylor walked easily at his side.

She sat Indian style and made herself comfortable.

Trey eased down to his knees. Holding back a grimace, he rolled onto his right hip, and propped himself on his right hand. Opening the basket with one hand, he laid out breakfast. Taylor pulled lids off plastic bowls. "Fresh fruit and whipped cream. Boiled eggs and sharp cheese. Walnut brownies and chocolate chip cookies," he said as she explored.

Taylor clapped her hands.

He pulled out a thermos. "Hot black coffee. And there's French Vanilla creamer and sugar. Did I forget anything?"

"All my favorites! How did you know?"

"A little birdie told me."

"I just bet," she said as he handed her a plastic plate and she loaded it. "So, why did you ask me to breakfast?" She created a sweet concoction of the coffee and sipped.

"Since you've been gone for so long, and yesterday was such a bad day, I thought you could use a break."

"Darn. I thought maybe you actually wanted to spend some time with me." She threw him a flirty smile.

"Do you remember that time on the road?" It was hard to look into her eyes as he said it, but he forced himself.

"You mean when I kissed you?" Her tone was nonchalant.

"You did more than kiss me."

Taylor laughed out loud. "I heard the talk between you and your buddies that day. Your face was so red. I didn't know if you were mad or embarrassed. It pissed me off. I wanted to give them something to think about." She nibbled on fruit, but her gaze didn't leave his face.

"Well, thanks. You certainly gave *me* something to think about." He smiled.

"I'm sorry about your dad. I never told you this, but I hurt for you back then. Those boys...they didn't see your pain."

He swallowed hard. "I can't imagine why you remembered that, but thanks."

She stared intently into his eyes. "The town was so small back then. I didn't remember any other person being killed in Raven Bayou in my whole life. And then a cop was killed." When she'd finished, she reached for his hand and held it firmly, her thumb rubbing over his knuckles.

Trey took a deep breath and looked into her eyes. "How about we talk about something else?"

She turned her gaze to the swings, and then swept around the park. "Okay. If you could have anything in the world, what would it be?"

Trey thought a minute. "A brother."

"Really? Why?"

"I had lots of friends growing up, but none that I've known and stayed close to throughout my life. I'm a little jealous of people who grow up with lots of siblings. After Dad died..."

Taylor allowed the pause for a beat before speaking.

"Go on."

Trey still didn't trust his voice. His eyes dropped to where they were connected, their hands warm with contact. The memories of his dad, of his dad's death, flooded his mind. He wasn't ready to go there. Loosening his hand from hers, he stretched out on his right side, resting on his elbow. "I thought we were going to talk about you?"

"Okay. We can talk about me. When I heard the FBI was poking around in my case, I thought you were planning to steal it." Taylor rubbed her temples.

"I get that a lot," he said. "Headache?"

She nodded.

"Turn around," he said, beginning to push himself up. But before she could move, something grabbed his attention.

"What's that all about?" he asked as two units sped along a dirt road toward the trees. A noise behind him caught his attention and he turned to see Russ coming out of his Crown Vic. Not a good sign.

Trey stood. Taylor followed. Russ rushed in their direction, his face grim.

"Sorry to intrude on your day, but a body turned up." His gaze went straight to the trees. "Saw the Hummer sitting here. If you guys are interested."

Both men turned their attention to Taylor whose face had gone pale.

"I'm sorry, could you repeat that?" she asked with a stronger voice than Trey had heard all morning.

"A body."

She focused on Trey for an instant, and then did a full circle, looking around the park. "Where?" Her shoulders straightened. One deep breath and her voice had changed again, becoming a little deeper, and much more professional.

Russ pointed. "About a quarter mile through the trees, right off the old dirt road.

Taylor returned to the blanket, pulled the straps of the leather bag onto her shoulder and trotted toward the woods. It would be much shorter in distance to just cut across the grass and through the woods, but it would mean leaving the unit behind.

She disappeared into the woods, body erect, and all business. Something crawled up Trey's spine, making the small hairs on the back of his neck stand on end. He ignored the tug on his brain and followed Russ to the unit. No sense adding Streak to the half dozen units that must be down the dirt road.

Dozens of questions popped into Trey's head as the Crown Vic bounced down the narrow road. He wondered how long the body had been there and what kind of person would leave a body in the woods so close to a frequented park. And the big question was whether this victim was related to the recent murders.

"Endri called me last night. Said I need to stop working her case. She was scared as all get out. On the way home, I stopped to get gas and somebody slipped a note on my seat saying if I didn't back off the Cheramie case, next time someone would die."

"Why the hell didn't you call me?" Trey said.

"No need. I drove over to Endri's. The house was dark. No cars out front. Nothing you could've done, except get a good mad up."

"Damn. Any ideas where it came from?"

Russ shook his head. "All I know is the bastard who attacked Darlene is scared. He thinks I know something."

"What?"

"Bub, if I had a clue, I'd know who to beat the shit out of."

The Crown Vic came to a stop behind a patrol unit and he saw the CSU van as well as an unmarked. He and Russ opened their doors simultaneously onto the flurry of activity.

The one-lane dirt road wended through the woods, ending out on Gypsom Highway. Weeds and saplings fought for sun, and the grass stood at least ten inches tall.

The smell of rotting flesh filled his nostrils, narrowing down a time line for him. This was not a fresh kill, nor was it weeks dead.

Trey stuffed his right hand in his pocket and followed Russ to the body where Taylor squatted, her gloved hands patting down the victim who lay on his side.

"Wilkes took the wallet," one of the deputies said. "We ran the ID. Fred Terrand. Thirty-two. Address in Ruston."

Trey watched Taylor work, her hands sure. She might have been working a crossword puzzle for all the emotion she showed. Her face was not a foot from the maggot-infested wound on the victim's chest.

It occurred to him that this was her way of coping with her past. Gemini Taylor didn't remind him of a young girl now. The smiles and youthful behavior had been replaced by a tough exterior. From the expression on her face, the interior could be just as hard.

"Looks like he's been dead at least four or five days," Russ said in a hushed tone, "not much more than that. Hard to tell in this weather, and him being exposed to animals and whatnot." His gaze focused on the victim's face. "His name sounds familiar."

"It should," came a voice from behind them. Wilkes stopped beside Russ. "Terrand. He's a convicted pedophile. Registered sex offender."

The body had been exposed to weather and animals. There wouldn't be much trace left. They would do a cursory check before transporting and follow-up later.

Russ and Taylor stood by, unable to take their eyes from the body as Trey watched. "You look like you've seen a ghost," he said to Russ.

Russ turned. "No. But it's the second body I've seen with those exact wounds." His thought came out in a whisper.

"There's been another murder lately, like this one?" Trey asked.

"No. " Russ glanced at Taylor.

Trey thought for a moment. *Taylor's dad was killed like this?*

"Meet you at the station," Russ said, and then made for his unit.

Trey knew it wouldn't be long before Wilkes sent them packing anyway. Russ and Taylor were assigned to the Grant case, and Grant was scheduled to come in. Wilkes would take this one.

After a few minutes, Trey and Taylor left the scene, walking back through the woods to the blanket that lay on the grass. Silently, they packed up the food and rode back to the station.

MICHAEL GRANT had arrived at the station twenty minutes before they did. When they walked into the lobby, they found him pacing back and forth, worrying his watch. He wore a frown and directed an angry stare at Russ who suppressed a yawn as he led the way through the halls and pushed through the double doors going to the lab area of the coroner's office. Taylor stayed in the hall with their grieving widower. Grant stuck a hand in his pocket and jiggled the change there. *Another one of his nervous tics,* Trey noted.

"Ready for the viewing?" Russ asked Barlow.

The coroner nodded and wheeled the gurney alongside a curtained wall.

Russ stuck his head out the door and nodded to Taylor. Grant fiddled with his watch, his gaze moving around the room.

"This way, Mr. Grant." She motioned and Trey watched as they walked, Grant trailing behind, suddenly not so anxious to see what awaited at the end of the hall. "In here," Taylor said. The door to a small, well-lit room with a glass wall squeaked open. "Are you ready?" she asked. Grant nodded. "All right, Coleman."

Barlow opened the curtain and Ilene Grant lay in full view, covered to the neck, her face gray with blue splotches from the beating she'd taken, the green tinge of bruising ugly in the glare of fluorescent lights.

Trey saw Grant's head jerk up spastically, confirming the identity of the body as well as his disbelief. Seeing his wife's corpse four day's dead through fright-filled eyes looked a lot different than whatever Grant had seen the day of his wife's death, even if he'd been enraged and decided to teach her a lesson. Barlow closed the curtain.

Trey and Russ met Taylor and Grant in the main lobby. "Are you feeling okay?" Russ asked.

Grant nodded, his face blanched.

"Let's just take a little break." Russ led the way, Taylor and Trey brought up the rear behind a sweaty Grant, whose life had just taken a major turn for the worse.

The interview rooms were just off the hallway, a few yards from the pit, and just big enough for a small table and four chairs. Each room had a window facing the hall. Trey settled himself in the observation room next door.

Russ stepped aside and pointed Grant to a chair against the far wall, and then took a seat with his back to the window, leaving a chair for Taylor near the entry. She left the door open and sat.

"Now Mr. Grant," Russ started, "I want to go over this again, but first, I need to read you your rights."

Grant leaned forward, shaking his finger at Russ. "Look here, I don't know what you're thinkin', but I ain't done nothing, so I don't need no rights read to me."

"It's just standard procedure. Nothing to worry about."

Grant nodded his head, though he looked uncertain. Russ read from the card, and then gave Grant a declaration to sign, swearing he understood each of his rights.

Taylor scratched notes as Russ grilled the man politely. Trey thought of his dad as he watched Russ calmly and expertly do his job. Questions poured forth without hesitation, standard questions about when he left work, when he arrived home, what his wife's exact words were before she walked out. What time she left. Had she ever done this before. And what time he went looking for her. Who her friends were and where he thought she went.

Russ was relentless. Grant all but hyperventilated as he alternately worried the watch on his wrist and laced his fingers into a tangled white mass.

"You want something to drink, Mr. Grant?" Russ finally asked.

Grant's head bobbed up and down along with his Adam's apple.

"A soda?"

Again, only a nod. Apparently he wasn't sure he should speak.

"Excuse me a just a minute, Mr. Grant." Russ stood and looked at his watch. Trey did the same. Eleven-oh-five hundred hours. Taylor stepped out of the way and waited for Russ. Trey met them in the hall.

"He's guilty as hell," Russ said to Taylor. "If he didn't do this, he had it done, but my money's on him. I intend to keep him here as long as possible. See if you can get in touch with his sister-in-law in Dallas. Find out her opinion of him. You know what I need. Then get back here and be 'bad cop.' "

She nodded and hurried down the hall while Russ retrieved a soda. Trey kept an eye on the suspect until Russ returned. They took their respective places and again Russ went over the questions, trying to get the man to slip up, change his story, or commit some error that would give Russ probable cause.

Trey pulled the mint tin out, popped a pill in his mouth and leaned a shoulder against the wall as he watched a master work.

Chapter Twenty-Six

RUSS COLEMAN
Sheriff's Dept.
Raven Bayou, LA

Saturday Morning, 4 June 2005

RUSS SAT with his wrist on the table, pen between two fingers, bouncing the tip and the end alternately against the notepad. This rat was guilty. He could smell it.

When Taylor told him about the wounds on Ilene's body, he'd known it was someone close. Only two kinds of murderers stabbed in the heart, the professional, or somebody who wanted to punish what they saw as a black-hearted animal. "When Mrs. Grant got mad and left the house, what kind of shoes was she wearing?" Russ asked.

"Don't know. Don't give a shit about her shoes," Grant said in what looked like a Jack Nicholson impression, all the way down to the little head waggle and the tight-lipped smile at the end.

"What kind of clothes did she wear? Shorts, or long pants? Maybe a dress?"

"I don't pay no attention to Ilene's clothes!" His voice boomed.

"You don't have any idea what she was wearing?"

"You married?" Now speaking softly, knowingly.

Russ nodded, trying to play "good cop." He could see Grant's confidence growing, could hear it in the man's voice as he answered questions with a range of emotions from hostility to arrogance.

"How long?" Finally, Grant's gaze came straight at Russ, daring him to answer.

"What difference does it make?"

"Me and Ilene been married twelve years. I ain't noticed what she wears in a long time." A flash of indifference on his face proved him true to his word. He relaxed now, folded his arms across his chest in a pose of confidence.

Russ pretended to look at his notes. *Where the hell is Taylor?* "I'm confused about something. When we came out to your house to tell you about your wife's death, you said you thought she'd left you. Did she pack a bag?"

"I told you she just got mad and walked out. Didn't take nothing."

"Not even her purse."

"No!" Grant shifted in his chair, took a deep breath and pressed his lips into a thin line.

"So she had no money, no I.D., no credit cards. How did you think she could get away?"

"I wasn't thinking 'bout that. All I knew was she was pissed off as a bull with no dick on breeding day."

"What made you think she'd left you?"

"She didn't come back!" The man's eyes threw blazing arrows, and Russ could see he was ripe for blowing. He couldn't wait for Taylor. He'd have to do it himself.

"Mr. Grant, did you ever hit your wife?"

The man's eyes shifted from side to side. "No. We argued before, but what couple don't? You're acting like you think I done that to her. I know you ain't got no evidence or else you'd have me in jail, so now look here, Coleman, if you're finished with your questions, I'll just head on outta here."

"You can call me detective." Russ stood, motioning for Grant to follow. Grant obeyed. Russ grabbed his arm and propelled him down the hall, feeling the resistance and fear in Grant's body.

Small holding cells were located near the back door next to a counter where officers processed detainees for transport. Past the counter, a windowed computer room was used by personnel who watched detainees while answering phones or prepping reports. Russ led the man to a chair near the counter. "Don't move."

"Keep an eye on him," Russ told the tall, blond service officer. She nodded and returned to her report, eyes bouncing up to Grant and back down to the desk.

Pacing not only proved to be a stress reducer but was also helpful with problem solving, so Russ headed down to the morgue, his mind working out the logistics of Grant as the murderer.

Chapter Twenty-Seven

TREY FONTAINE
Sheriff's Dept.
Raven Bayou, LA

Saturday Morning, 4 June 2005

TREY LEFT THE OBSERVATION ROOM.

Leaning against the wall, he tried to clear his mind. After a few minutes, Russ came down the hall. "How hard would it be to find Arnold Taylor's murder book?" Trey asked.

"There's a copy in my desk. Why:"

"I'd like to see the similarities to Terrand."

"Come on" Russ said.

They expected to find Taylor in the pit, but didn't. Russ pulled the book from the bottom drawer of his desk.

"Don't let her see you with it," he whispered.

"Why do you have a copy?" Trey asked.

"It was my first official murder case. Imagine. Only black detective makes good." Russ shrugged. That said it all.

A few minutes later, Trey sat in one of the interview rooms, the blinds pulled and door closed, concentrating on the old Arnold Taylor murder book. The pictures were gruesome, the original report detailed. The coroner's report was very enlightening. Arnold Taylor was forty-eight years old at the time of his death, five-foot-seven, and 160 pounds. Two knives had been used to kill him, one a seven-inch hunting knife, the other a skinning knife. Maine Taylor identified both as belonging to her husband.

There were also rips to the anus and colon, evidence that someone had rammed a large object into the orifice repeatedly. According to the complete report, the unidentified object was never found. An eerie prickle ran down Trey's spine. These kinds of injuries were so personal. Only someone who hated him would commit such a violent act.

Trey stared at the picture of Taylor's dad lying in a pool of blood. The body found this morning had been gutted by animals, but there was no doubt the wounds were similar to these. Russ was right. The autopsy on Terrand would prove interesting. Trey wondered who had enough details of the Arnold Taylor murder to be able to copy it so closely.

Chapter Twenty-Eight

RUSS COLEMAN
Sheriff's Dept.
Raven Bayou, LA

Saturday Morning, 4 June 2005

"HOW'S IT GOING, BARLOW?" Russ hoped he could avoid a long explanation of the Ilene Grant autopsy and findings. Barlow tended to ramble. Anytime the man started a sentence with "That reminds me of the time..." Russ excused himself.

"I've finished with the exterior. Time of death was sometime between Monday night and Tuesday early morning. The wounds were likely made with a butcher knife. We found brown fibers on her leg. Avlee took them. I'm working this one myself. Care to watch?" He pulled the sheet from the woman's nude body lying on the cold stainless steel table, the Y-incision clean, skin and muscle folded back to expose the entire abdominal cavity.

She'd been washed, her bruises now very visible, her pale skin dull in the florescent light.

Russ tried to look away but his eyes didn't cooperate. He couldn't stop staring at the small, lifeless body of Ilene Grant. The woman had been tortured, probably over several hours. Some of the bruises were massive black continents surrounded by oceans of green. Damage from the wounds in her chest was so obvious, even Russ could identify them.

"Is there something in particular you wanted to know?" Barlow asked as he grasped a scalpel in his hand.

Russ brought his gaze to Barlow's face. "I'm looking at Michael Grant, the husband, for this one. Anything you can tell me would be helpful."

Barlow nodded agreement. "This victim was beaten about the face so badly she was unrecognizable. Bruises and broken bones indicate he kicked and stomped her before stabbing her here, here, and here," he pointed. "Death was the result of the stab to the heart. She was not sexually assaulted, but was found naked. He wanted to humiliate her, Coleman. My opinion is that this was personal.

"The killer was right-handed, taller than the victim but not by a lot, strong, most likely male. He probably transported her in a vehicle with a brown interior, or wrapped in a brown rug. I told Avlee to send her findings to you immediately." The doctor's gaze met Russ's head on, and he offered a smile before reaching into the victim and lifting out her liver.

"Thanks, Barlow." Russ took his normal long strides through the halls as he turned over the information in his head.

He came around the corner into holding, his footsteps echoing against the cement floor. With a ten foot ceiling and open cells, the area was cavernous and the most functional part of the building. He found Grant sitting on the stool, chafing his watch around his wrist.

"Let's go have a talk."

"I thought you were through with me."

Russ wondered if the man had found some confidence in the fact that he was still free. "You're not going anywhere right now." He walked side-by-side with Grant back to the interview room. The man sat while Russ closed the door.

"Looks like you have some explaining to do. The coroner found brown fibers on your wife's clothes and body. What do you know about that?"

"Nothin'."

"You think strings and lint would remain on her for hours while she was out walking around?" Russ asked. He was betting Grant didn't know enough about forensics to answer the question. Silence proved it to be true. "What color is the interior of your car?"

"Brown." The man swallowed hard.

Russ made a note. "Leather or cloth?"

"Cloth."

"And the carpet in the trunk?"

"Brown, I guess." This came out with a deep sigh. Grant laced his fingers together and dropped his hands below the edge of the table, his gaze following the movement as if they were disconnected from his body.

Russ paused, silent, his gaze boring into Grant like a drill. When he spoke, it was soft. "You know what I think?" He held his voice to a low rumble. "I think you beat the hell out of your wife. I think you tore her clothes off. And when she lay on the floor helpless—" He stood, palms on table, hovering above Grant, "—you took a knife from your kitchen, stabbed her in the chest, put her in the trunk of your car and drove her to the other end of the parish where you tossed her clothes into an abandoned garden shed, stuffed her body in it and left her to rot."

Grant's eyelids opened wide, his jaw dropped, and his body rocked slightly in his chair. But nothing came from his mouth.

"You have nothing to say about that, Mr. Grant?"

"I think you're just too lazy to go out and look for the real killer so you're gonna try blaming me, and me just losing my wife! Why ain't you out looking for who done this?"

Russ narrowed his eyes, gritted his teeth, and stared coldly at the man. Silence fell like a wool blanket over the room. The men were face-to-face, only a small table separated them.

"If you aren't the killer, then I'm sure you'll want to cooperate completely to help us find the one responsible."

Grant nodded, eyes like slits of suspicion.

"Then why don't we go out to your place and get some samples of the carpets in your house and car? We can compare them to the evidence, and if you're innocent, it will prove it."

The man pondered the words for a minute, his forehead wrinkled, and his teeth grating over his bottom lip.

Russ held on to a thin strand of hope.

"What if the killer done it in the house? What if he used my car? No, I don't think it's right, using stuff from my own house. If I have to, I'll get me a lawyer."

"Well then, I guess I'll have to get me a warrant." He mocked and stood, pushing his chair in. "Let's go."

"Where're we going now?"

"You're going back to holding. I'm going to see the judge." Sometimes those words scared the bejeebers out of criminals. Not this time. Just to make his point, Russ pulled a pair of handcuffs from his belt and snapped them around the man's wrists. Then he walked him back to the stool by the computer room's glass wall. Russ motioned for him to sit and nodded to the officer. The same blond scowled at Grant.

Russ would explode if he didn't get something out of Grant. They didn't have enough to get forensics into the trailer. Not yet. But he'd use everything he knew to keep Grant from walking out the door. If Grant was the killer, he'd skip before the weather changed. And in Louisiana, that was pretty quick.

Time to call Avlee. At least she could get scrapings from Michael Grant's nails. Not that it would do any good. Ilene Grant had been dead for about four days. Even a pig like her husband would have washed his hands a few times by now.

Chapter Twenty-Nine

GEMINI TAYLOR
Sheriff's Dept.
Raven Bayou, LA

Saturday Late Morning, 4 June 2005

HELEN BRAMMER turned out to be a sweet, smart woman who had worried about her sister for years. She sensed unhappiness in Ilene during phone calls and when reading Ilene's letters.

After a twenty-minute talk, Gem went to the ladies room, and then returned to her desk to find Coleman waiting for her. Coleman's voice echoed as Gem walked into the pit. "Where've you been?" he asked, his frustration clearly visible.

"Ten-one," she replied sharply. "I spoke to Helen Brammer. Not fond of her brother-in-law. Thinks he's too crude and dumb for her sister. She took the news hard. Said she didn't doubt," Gem posted the quotes with her fingers, "'that bastard' was responsible. Helen asked her sister if Grant ever hit her and Ilene said no.

"But she'll testify Grant was emotionally abusive, calling names and saying mean things to Ilene, saying other women were prettier and smarter. Ilene and her hubby argued a lot and Grant never learned how to fight fair."

Coleman sat silently. Gem sensed his eyes following her as she parked herself at her desk and yawned. Irritation rolled off him, making her skin prickle. She was sensitive to angry men.

"I turned into not-so-good-cop while you were busy."

"Next time I get to be bad cop."

"What makes you think there'll be a next time?" He said it with such a straight face that, until she caught the slight smile, Gem thought maybe he was serious.

She stood, stretched, and headed toward holding, Coleman on her heels. Michael Grant sat in the brightly lit room, sweat covering his face despite the air conditioning. The smell of sweat, urine, open sores, and filth on most detainees became unbearable in a closed room unless the A/C was cranked.

Gem turned on her "good cop" persona, took her cuff key out, and removed the bracelets from his wrists. "Mr. Grant. I'm sorry it took us so long to get things in order. If you'll come with me, we can finish up and let you get going." She motioned for him to follow her and the man gave Coleman a look saying that at least the little lady knew how to treat him.

Gem held back a grin and handed her partner the cuffs. Coleman strode behind Grant as she led the way to the pit.

"You just have a seat here in my chair, Mr. Grant and I'll make sure we've got all we need. Don't go anywhere. I wouldn't want you mistaken for a suspect and locked up. We'll be right back."

She figured Grant believed he had them fooled into thinking he was innocent. As long as he was confident that he wasn't a suspect, he wouldn't run. Maybe he'd even make a mistake.

Avlee arrived and bent over their suspect's hands, gathering potential evidence.

Coleman collected everything they might need for the afternoon. "I'll meet you outside," he said and headed for the men's locker room, leaving her to deal with Grant. When Avlee finished, Gem walked the man out the front door of the building.

"What's that mess over my hands all about?" he scowled.

"Just proving you had nothing to do with your wife's death." Gem lowered her voice, "That way my partner has no reason to keep bothering you. I finally convinced him that you don't look like the killing type."

He smiled smugly, his shoulders straightening a little.

When they reached the sidewalk Gem stopped and gave him her best smile. Men usually fell for it. "Thank you again, Mr. Grant. I'm sorry for your loss. If we learn anything, you'll be the first to know." She offered a hand.

The man ignored it and faced her squarely, his eyes narrowed. He whispered, "You ain't gonna find nothing. It ain't healthy sometimes, finding out things that ain't your business."

Hatred rolled off him with his sweat and slapped her face while his threatening tone washed over her and chilled her to the bone. Pain hit her temples so hard she squeezed her eyes shut and held her head with both hands. When it dawned on her that she was showing weakness in front of an aggressive man, she forced her eyes open, but Michael Grant was gone.

Chapter Thirty

TREY FONTAINE
Crime Scene Behind
Boudreaux Park
Raven Bayou, LA

Saturday Noon, 4 June 2005

WILKES, AVLEE, ONE CSU TECH AND TWO DEPUTIES. Trey kept his distance as the team collected evidence in an eerie silence. Even the birds knew something serious had happened.

When Wilkes dropped his recorder from his lips, Trey moved closer. "How's it going?"

"Looks like he was dumped here. Techs found some drag marks under the leaves, but the drag trail is completely washed away after about twenty feet." He pointed in the direction of the marks and Trey saw how the body must have been moved from the direction of the playground. This made sense if he was a child molester. *He was probably in the park and someone followed him into the woods.*

"You know anything about the Arnold Taylor case?"

Wilkes shook his head, his face emotionless, except for the bulge of muscle on his jaw as he gritted his teeth. "Coleman worked that one, but from what I heard, it was pretty much open and shut. I'd been a detective for a year when he caught that case. I was out of town with family. First vacation I took after getting married."

Trey nodded. It was good to see the man cared about Russ. He chose his next words carefully. "Did you see the body, or the file?"

"Maybe if you have questions, you ought to ask Coleman."

"I have. He showed me the file. I'm just trying to make some sense out of the fact that your body here has the same wounds as Arnold Taylor. So, did you see the body, or the file?" he repeated.

"No. Heard about it. Same wounds, huh?" Wilkes looked down at the recorder in his hands.

"Russ got a confession on that case, but this looks a lot like the pictures of Arnold Taylor. You think they could be connected?"

Wilkes finally looked into Trey's eyes. "It's been twenty years with no similar crimes. Far as I'm concerned, this is an isolated case. If I come up dry with leads, I'll talk to Coleman, but I don't intend to open that can of worms. No need causing unnecessary problems."

"You might talk to Barlow after this autopsy." Trey motioned toward the body. "And just compare the similarities."

Wilkes nodded and turned back toward the body. He spoke quietly into his recorder, and then turned back to Trey. "If anyone but you made that suggestion, I'd be all over 'em."

"Russ is a good cop. I'm not saying he did anything wrong. All I'm saying is it's odd. Two murders with similar wounds in the same town. Maybe a copycat. Maybe someone who knows about the first case. Maybe no connection."

"I'll let you know what I find."

"You can reach me on my cell," Trey said. *And I'll contact Tamlyn and have someone check NCIC for murder victims with similar wounds. If it turns out that several cases are similar, it could be a copycat. Or it could be partner of Arnold Taylor's killer.*

Wilkes took the card Trey had written his number on and went back to work while Trey backed off, his mind accumulating facts.

When Trey reached Tamlyn, she had the info on the Grants as well as on Gemini Taylor. He pulled one of Russ's business cards from his wallet and read the fax number to Tamlyn. "Hold on to the Taylor info until I call again."

"You got it," Tamlyn responded and hung up.

Chapter Thirty-One

GEMINI TAYLOR
Sheriff's Dept.
Raven Bayou, LA

Saturday Noon, 4 June 2005

GEM STOOD on the sidewalk out front. She had no idea how long she'd been there, but the sun was blinding her as Coleman pulled up in the Crown Vic. Jumping into the passenger seat, she buckled up and they headed down the main street of town to grab lunch before going to Verbois to interview any neighbors they might have missed the first time.

She closed her eyes and rubbed her temples. Someone inside her head was trying to force his way out using a pick-hammer and the pain hadn't let up one bit since Michael Grant threatened her.

Her bag sat on the back seat. She couldn't reach it, not even the outside pocket holding her migraine pills. She waited impatiently while Coleman drove to the restaurant of his choice. They passed Bubba's Bar-B-Q, The Fishin' Hole, Craw Daddy's, a Waffle House and two buffet chains.

Gem smiled when Coleman wheeled the big car into the lot of a Southern Maid. It wasn't what Gem had in mind, but who was she to argue? She unzipped the small outer pocket of her bag and grabbed the prescription bottle before locking up.

They came out with half a dozen donuts and two large cups of coffee, his plain black, hers French vanilla. He flipped her the keys and she slid in under the wheel. Coleman stared at the donut with a guilty look on his face like someone stood over his shoulder waiting to admonish him at the first bite.

"One won't hurt. Moderation is the key." Gem's teeth sunk into a luscious mouthful.

Coleman looked at the box with four more donuts in it.

"Yeah, moderation." He took a bite while she pulled out of the lot.

"How is Darlene this morning?" she asked.

"She seems better. How did you get her to talk?"

Actually, she didn't have a clue, so she lied. "It's a secret between us girls."

They rode in silence the rest of the way and arrived in Verbois a little after 1 p.m. Humidity hung thick in the air, causing their clothes to cling within two minutes of leaving the comfort of the unit.

The trailers on Crowder Road were a half-acre apart, most sitting back off the road, with mimosa trees and brush between the lots. A few were fenced and contained large dogs whose fur bristled upon their arrival.

"You want to split up and get it over with?" she asked.

"No. Sometimes a woman can get further than a man in these situations. You lead. I'll pitch in if I have any bright ideas."

What he really meant to say was a white woman would get further than a black man.

The closest trailer to the Grant home was locked up and no one answered the knock on the door. They had better luck at the second one on the same side of the road as the murder scene. A woman answered the door and introduced herself as Molly Akin. Probably in her late thirties, she was short, and a little overweight, but her sunny smile made her pretty, and likeable.

"Call me Molly."

"We're here about Ilene Grant," Gem said.

Miss Molly's expression went from smiling to concern. Her brow knitted together tightly and her lips turned into a thin straight line. "If you two'll have a seat on the porch, I'll get us some iced tea. Sweet or unsweet?"

"Sweet Ma'am," Gem said, followed by Coleman's "Unsweet, thank you," and they sat on the unfinished wooden chairs under a ceiling fan that did a surprisingly good job at cooling them.

"Here we go." Miss Molly served large glasses filled to the rim, her dark curly hair hanging into her face as she leaned forward. "Now what is this about Ilene? I haven't seen her for several days. So, is there really something wrong? She usually walks this road every morning with her little Cheaters."

"Cheaters?"

"A Yorkie. She walks him morning and night. I've been worried sick over her."

"Miss Molly, I hate to be the bearer of bad news, but Ilene is dead. Her body was found yesterday morning." Gem didn't think this was news to the woman. She knew.

Tears shone in Miss Molly's eyes. "So it's true. I'd hoped it was just one of Mike's stories. He tells some doozies. What happened?"

"She was murdered."

"What is this world coming to?" Molly Akin mumbled. Gem knew the feeling too. That was probably why Miss Molly lived out here in the boonies, off the beaten path of the psychos and maniacs. Except for, possibly, Michael Grant. "Is Cheaters alright?"

Gem looked at Coleman before answering. "We don't know Ma'am. We didn't know about the dog until you told us. How did you learn about Ilene's death?"

"Wes, my husband, saw Mike last night at the Dew Drop Inn. They drank a couple of beers. Mike said Ilene had walked off and never came back. Said the police found her body. Didn't say much more. Then Wes came home."

"When was the last time you saw Ilene, Ma'am?" Gem asked.

"Well, let's see. It must have been Monday morning. Sometime around six. She usually walks...walked Cheaters after Mike left for work. It's hard to believe she's gone. Who would do such a thing?" She leaned forward.

"We don't know yet, Ms. Akin—"

"Missus."

"Yes, Ma'am. Have you noticed any difference in Mr. Grant? Has anything changed?"

Molly Akin gave Gem a fearful look but there was no surprise on her face at the suggestion that Michael Grant was responsible for his wife's death. Miss Molly shook her head.

"Have you ever heard fighting coming from their house?"

Miss Molly's gaze quickly fell. "Sometimes Mike yells at Ilene. It's been going on ever since they moved in. But, I just can't imagine him killing her. He's..." She squeezed her lips together in an effort to stop the gossip from leaking out.

Gem tried to control her breathing as she asked, "He's what?" She had a feeling this woman was going to be very helpful.

"Just so..." Miss Molly looked around hesitantly. "Cowardly," she whispered.

Gem's eyebrows tweaked up.

The woman read the inquisitive look and responded. "He yells and screams, but I've never seen him confront anyone except Ilene. She told me more than once that Mike accused her of cheating on him. That's why she quit teaching. He was jealous of male teachers. Even complained about the way she dressed in front of the boys in her class. Accused her of showing off in front of them. But, as far as I know, he never said a word to any of the men."

"Did Mr. Grant tell your husband when Ilene walked away?"

"Not that I know of, but he'll be home soon. You could talk to him. Where was she found?" Her pale blue eyes bore intently into Gem's.

"We're really not free to give details, but it was at the other end of the Parish."

"That doesn't make any sense." Miss Molly cast her gaze to the wooden floorboards of the porch. "How did she get way down there? Her sister lives in Dallas. She has no friends outside this town. And she doesn't drive."

"She has a driver's license," Gem said.

"But she was in an accident a few years back and it scared her so terribly that she hasn't driven since. Ever."

"Does she entertain during the day?"

"Entertain?" Miss Molly asked innocently, her brows furrowed.

"Does anyone visit her at home?"

"Not anyone I've seen, except an occasional neighbor for a cup of coffee. And that Jacks guy. I told her to watch out for that boy."

"What boy?" Gem and Coleman said in unison.

Chapter Thirty-Two

TREY FONTAINE
Sheriff's Dept.
Raven Bayou, LA

Saturday Afternoon, 4 June 2005

TREY TOOK the pages from the fax machine next to Bettencourt. "Thanks. I'm expecting a few more pages. If you don't mind, I'll just sit here and wait for them."

"You'll have to. I'm off in a few minutes."

Trey waited until Bettencourt left before calling Tamlyn and giving her the okay to fax the Taylor info. After receiving everything, he went out to his Hummer to read. There wasn't much on Taylor. Just her driver's license from Texas and the full set of prints they took at both departments. Trey didn't know what he'd expected to find. The fact she'd been hired meant there was nothing in her background of any importance, at least not as far as crimes. Somehow the lack of info comforted him.

It was time to check in with Ace. He turned on the communication set and listened.

"Is all well?"

"Um hmm."

"I'm heading over there to see if anyone can tell me why Michael Grant's so nervous over his gambling."

"Um hmm."

THE BAYOU LIGHTS CASINO sat on the Tangipahoa River, just north of Highway 190. Trey parked Streak in the lot of the casino, across the street from Boudreaux's River Queen. Both casinos were held by corporations, but Boudreaux was the majority shareholder of the River Queen and he owned nearly twenty-five percent of Bayou Lights. The parking lot was full. Noise echoed through his receiver so loudly he had to switch it off as he approached the brass framed glass doors.

He popped a Lortab and walked onto the casino floor where hundreds of slots rang and played carnival music. A thick haze of smoke filled the air and half a dozen servers weaved through the crowd, taking orders.

He moved slowly past the rows of slots, past the roulette wheel, and toward the blackjack tables. The thought of talking to a dealer or two slipped his mind when he saw Alton Boudreaux sitting at a poker table. A beautiful woman in a sparkling gown stood behind him while he puffed on a cigar and studied his hand. She looked bored.

Trey could see the similarity between the senior Boudreaux, and his sons Jamison and Monty. Especially Monty. Thinking of the older son brought a bout of guilt, followed by hatred. First, hatred of Boudreaux for raising his sons to be what they were. Second, hatred of Monty for his part in Trey's father's death. And finally self-hatred for his own part in the same crime.

Trey walked into the dark lounge a few yards from the poker table and ordered a draft. He watched Boudreaux toy with the gamers. The man folded his hand, tossing the cards toward the dealer. Trey couldn't hear what Boudreaux said, but he saw the barracuda smile.

Boudreaux played a few more hands, and then excused himself from the game. He offered his arm to the woman, who looked relieved. Trey followed, stopping here and there feigning interest in a game.

After a few steps, the woman pecked Boudreaux on the lips and walked off toward the elevators. One of the slot machines caused a frenzy and Boudreaux hurried in that direction. Trey followed at a discrete distance.

"Well, look there, Miss Rose. You hit a jackpot." Boudreaux put an arm around the older woman who smiled and patted his cheek.

"It's 'bout time. I been nursing this baby all day," she said.

"Congratulations," Boudreaux told her and started to walk away.

"Alton, I swear this damn thing is broken," an old man in turquoise pants said before Boudreaux made his escape.

"Now, Roscoe, you know better. Why, these slots payoff better than any in the state and you know it."

"If that be true, then this one's broke 'cause it's been eating my money all day."

"I'll tell you what. You go tell Felix that Alton said you get a free dinner tonight." Boudreaux shook the man's hand, practically pulling him off the black padded stool. "Maybe after a good meal, you'll have better luck."

The old man walked away, muttering to himself.

A bald man in an expensive suit approached Boudreaux and whispered in his ear. Seconds later Trey saw Boudreaux walking toward him.

He offered Trey a hand. "Good afternoon. My name is Alton. Welcome to Bayou Lights."

"Thanks," Trey said as he shook the man's hand, wondering what the hell was going on. "I'm Trey. Is this your place?"

Boudreaux nodded. "Of a sort. I have an interest in it." His chin raised a notch as he admired the room. "Will you be staying?"

"No. Just stopped by for a beer and maybe a hand or two of blackjack. How's the food at the buffet?"

"Excellent. Tell Felix at the register to put it on my tab."

"That's very kind," Trey said, knowing the casino lost no money by offering free food here and there. "I have a friend who comes in sometimes. Name of Michael Grant. I thought he might be here tonight."

Boudreaux paused as he removed a handkerchief from his pocket and wiped his lips. "I don't believe I know anyone by that name. Sorry."

"Thanks anyway. Nice meeting you," Trey said and left Boudreaux standing alone. Walking toward the blackjack tables, Trey wondered if everyone was welcomed personally by Boudreaux. The man obviously didn't know who Trey was. If he did, Trey was sure he wouldn't be kind. After all, the Fontaine name was linked with Monty Boudreaux's death.

He sat at the blackjack table and played a few hands, losing all the cash he had on him, which fortunately, wasn't much. As he walked toward the front door, Trey saw one of the security guys watching him. Trey's presence had made someone nervous. Now all he had to do was figure out who, and why.

Chapter Thirty-Three

GEMINI TAYLOR
Akin Residence
Verbois, LA

Saturday Late Afternoon, 4 June 2005

"ILENE NEVER told me his whole name, but she calls him Jacks. He's been sniffing around her like a hound." Miss Molly took a sip of tea.

"Who is he? Where does he live?" Gem scooted to the edge of the chair, ready for the hunt to begin in earnest.

"I don't know, but he's way too young to be chasing after a woman Ilene's age, especially since she's married. Ilene kept saying he's just a harmless boy."

"How old is he and what does he look like?"

"He must be nineteen or twenty, shorter than you, I think." She nodded toward Gem. "Neat-cut dark hair. Bone skinny. Dresses like a fashion model."

Coleman sat forward, a pointer on the scent. Gem was tempted to scratch him behind the ear and tell him he was a good boy. Instead she resumed her questioning. "When did you last see him?"

"It's been a while. Maybe a week or ten days." Miss Molly wiped the condensation from her icy glass and took a sip of tea.

"So he came to her house?"

"Yes. Just drove right up like he owned the place."

"What did he drive?"

"A gray pickup. A little one."

"Could you be a little more specific?" Coleman threw in before Gem had the chance.

"Wish I could. But I avoided the place when he was there, so I never got a good look at the truck, or at him."

"Why was that? Were you afraid of him?"

"No. I just didn't want to get into Ilene's problems."

Gem turned and looked at the Grant home a good forty yards away. "How often did he come around? How long did he stay?"

"For a while, a couple of years ago, he was here two or three times a week. Then, somewhere along the way, he started coming less. I'd say that lately it's been more like once every couple of weeks. Didn't stay long. Ilene started standing out in the yard to talk to him."

"But he used to go inside? A couple of years ago?" Gem asked.

"Yeah. I think he was still in school back then."

"Seen anyone else, any strangers around lately?"

"Are you thinking she had a man friend?" Miss Molly shook her head. "She never did anything or said anything to make me think she ever stepped out on Michael."

"I'm just wondering if someone from out of town might have come here, killed her, and took her body away." Gem hoped this would trigger a different conversation from the woman.

"I ain't seen no strangers around here in years." Miss Molly gathered the collar of her shirt around her neck nervously, as if vampire bats might fly by any second.

A pickup churned dust in the yard. Wes Akin, Miss Molly's husband, was home. After introductions, Wes Akin answered a few questions, adding nothing new.

"Thank you for your cooperation, Mr. and Mrs. Akin." Gem stood and Coleman followed. "One more thing, Ma'am. Have you seen Cheaters since Monday?" She looked into the woman's eyes.

"No. And Ilene would never go anywhere without him. She loved that dog."

THE REST OF THE AFTERNOON proved unproductive. No one saw or heard anything. They decided to check out the Dew Drop Inn, Mike Grant's favorite haunt, before returning to the Grant home, just in case the dark-haired kid was a dead end. Dust flew as Gem pulled into the dirt parking lot and parked in the shade. She popped the door open, swinging her feet into a deep pile of rubbery, dry magnolia leaves. "I'll nose around out back." Sometimes she just needed to be alone for a few minutes to think.

Coleman slid out of the car and went inside.

They met back in the car in less than five minutes.

"Bartender says Grant comes in almost every night for two or three hours," Coleman said. "Drinks beer, shoots pool, tells jokes, and then leaves. He confirmed that Grant and Mr. Akin were here last night, sitting together. And he remembers Grant being here every night for the last two weeks. That gives Mr. Akin's story credibility. But the owner can't swear to what time Grant arrived or what time he left this past Monday."

"I think we should go see if our favorite suspect is home. I want to see Grant's face when I ask him about Cheaters. I don't think we should mention Jacks until we've checked him out," she said.

"Yeah. We don't need another death to investigate." Coleman buckled up as Gem wheeled the big car around and headed back to the Grant place. Luck finally prevailed. The tan Taurus sat in its space in the drive and only the screen door was closed.

Coleman knocked. They heard Grant bark, "Just a minute."

Gem moved up onto the step beside her partner. Grant arrived at the door, his chest bare, a towel in his hands with which he casually wiped his armpits. His beer belly hung over his belt. Second trimester was Gem's guess.

"Mr. Grant," she said in her most humble voice, "sorry to bother you. We have a couple more questions."

He didn't invite them in this time. "Like what?"

Before Gem could answer he disappeared and she heard Coleman's weapon slide from its holster. Almost instantly Grant returned, slipping his arms into a shirt.

"What happened to Cheaters?" she asked and heard the gun ease back home.

Color drained from Grant's face and he hesitated before answering, "I ain't seen him since Ilene left."

"Did she leave him here with you?"

"Hell no! I don't baby-sit no dog. She carried his ass."

"Why didn't you mention him while we were at the station this morning?" Coleman asked gruffly.

"Damn dog ain't important. Ain't like someone'd kill her just to get that mutt."

"Are you going out?" Gem forced a smile.

"Always do. Goin' down and have a few beers. We all gotta grieve in our own way. You done with me?"

"Yes. Thank you. Sorry to have bothered you. Have a good evening." Gem led the way to the car and drove slowly, her eyes constantly searching the rearview mirror. Coleman lowered his sun visor and used the vanity mirror to do the same, but when they reached the main road, Grant still had not appeared.

IT WAS CLOSE to six o'clock when Gem plopped down at her desk at the station and sighed.

Coleman started working on the supplemental report while she booted up her laptop and worked on the initial report.

"I'm outta here," she said a half hour later. But she didn't go home. In the parking lot, she took off the white button-up shirt, leaving her in a cream undershirt. She slipped a hair band on, pulled a box out of the trunk and tossed it onto the back seat. Top down on her Caddie, she headed north again, toward Verbois. The sky was a beautiful turquoise. The evening air was delicious as it blew through her hair. It would still be light when she reached her destination.

A little voice in her head whispered for her to be careful, to keep her distance until they were ready. Gem couldn't search the place without a warrant, but she could keep an eye on the man.

Chapter Thirty-Four

RUSS COLEMAN
Sheriff's Dept.
Raven Bayou, LA

Saturday Evening, 4 June 2005

RUSS WATCHED TAYLOR hoist the heavy bag and walk out of the pit. Before calling CSU, he pulled the small magnetic phone book from his wallet and buzzed Julie's best friend Naomi Pruit who worked at the phone company.

He asked if, come Monday, she could pull the Grant phone records and send them to him. She agreed without hesitation, her voice cracking with fresh grief at the mention of his dead wife. She'd known Julie ever since grade school.

The note he left on Bettencourt's desk read: *Check phone numbers through reverse index. Need names and addresses. Page me if you find anyone named Jacks.*

Two stops and he could go home. Collecting boxes from a local store took only a few minutes. With the back of the SUV full of packing material, Russ drove down the old highway and exited two minutes later on Gypsum Road and wound his way through the short streets to Willow. As he pulled up to the curb in front of the Cheramie house, he noticed Mrs. Cheramie's Mercury Marquis in the drive.

He slipped his jacket on before sauntering up the walk to the front door. The door squeaked open seconds after he rang the bell. It was Mrs. Cheramie. Claudine Cheramie was not yet forty years old. She was staunchly built and wore a flowered house dress. Her skin was the color of cocoa and flawless.

"Good evening, Ma'am. Is Endri in?"

"Sure, 'tective. Come on in. Some news on the case?" she said through full lips and crooked teeth.

"No, Ma'am. I was hoping Endri might've thought of something more. If I could just talk with her..."

Mrs. Cheramie nodded and led him to the living room. He sat while she hurried down the hall. He couldn't make out what they said, but the sharpness of voices made it clear to him that mother and daughter disagreed.

Mrs. Cheramie returned alone, fingering the crucifix she wore on a gold chain around her neck. "I sorry, 'tective. Endri not been herself. She axed if you kin leave a number so she kin call you when she up to it."

"Has she talked to you at all about what happened?"

"Not a lick. Endri ain't talked me up much 'bout anyting in da last few days. I sorry. Wisht I could be more hep. You unnerstan."

Russ nodded. He handed the woman a business card, thanked her for her time, and then walked away, looking back over his shoulder to the windows toward the other end of the house.

Light shone through one window where pink curtains moved. There had to be a way to get to the girl. Russ flung his jacket onto the passenger seat and headed home.

Chapter Thirty-Five

TREY FONTAINE
Near Grant Residence
Verbois, LA

Saturday Near Midnight, 4 June 2005

TREY ARRIVED in Verbois just before midnight. He drove down Main Street to one of the many roads leading up the hill toward the residential lots and mobile homes where the Grant residence was located. One block up the hill he pulled Streak over until the big SUV was almost in the ditch. He got out, eased his door closed, and then walked toward the familiar outline of the Caddie sitting under a huge cottonwood on a cross-street a half-block up the road. The air was warm, and stars blanketed the sky.

"Great—" Trey whispered.

"Crap!"

"—minds..." he finished.

"You scared the hell out of me!" Taylor growled.

Trey slipped over the passenger door of the convertible and into the thick leather seat.

"Can't believe you didn't see me coming."

"What're you doing here?" Taylor crossed her arms against her chest.

"Well, you're in a great mood. I got bored. Got to thinking about Grant. I just came up to take a look."

"Okay, you had your look," Taylor snapped.

"What the hell...? A few hours ago you were all smiles. Who tripped your trigger? Michael Grant's sister-in-law is one of my missing girls." Trey was getting a little tired of her petty, competitive attitude.

She wiped a stray hair from her lips and sighed. "I just hate this waiting. I want to get this guy, and get back to..."

"To what?"

Taylor hesitated before answering. "Look, we all know Michael Grant killed his wife, okay? I just want to get this case over with." She kept her eyes trained on the mobile home at the top of the hill where Grant parked his car.

Trey noticed a box in the back seat, half-full of file folders, and a notebook leaning against them. "What's all that?" he asked.

"Research."

He grabbed the notebook and opened it.

"Hey," Taylor reached for it. "That's none of your business."

But she was too late. He'd already seen enough to know what it was.

"You're working your dad's case." He didn't like where this was going.

"I've been looking into it for a long time. Just...trying to figure it out."

"Figure it out. It's not that hard. The killer is in prison."

"Yeah, right, 'cause Detective Russell Coleman could never be wrong."

"Look, Taylor, anyone in your position would probably have doubts. But I read about this case. There was a confession. Finger prints. Blood. That kind of evidence doesn't lie."

"Says Coleman."

"Says me. Says anyone with a brain." Trey rubbed two fingers up the furrow between his brows. "It must have been hard what you went through. But dragging Russ's name through the mud...I don't see how that'll make you feel better."

"You don't have a clue who I am. You don't know anything."

"You might be surprised at what I know," Trey said.

"Do you know that every spare minute I've had since I was eighteen has been spent trying to solve this case? You have no idea how hard it is for a female rookie cop in Dallas, or anywhere else in the South to get answers. I've driven hundreds of miles on my days off just to talk to a cop who worked a case like Daddy's." She talked fast, and though the volume of her voice was still under control, her body shook so hard Trey could see it, even in the darkness.

"Russ did everything by the book. You've only worked with him for a little while, but believe me, he's a good detective."

"Yeah, well, even good detectives make mistakes."

Trey's fist hit the dashboard. "Bullshit! I thought you liked Russ."

"There's a murderer out there," she said between gritted teeth. "Twenty years this guy has been free to kill. It's time."

"If you're right, we would've found the bodies."

"You want bodies? How about a teenage boy in Texas cut from stem to sternum? How about a middle-aged man in Oklahoma with the same wounds?"

"You're telling me a serial killer is responsible for your dad's death? And that same person has been running around in different states, free for twenty years, killing people, and no one has even suspected it's the same guy? That makes no sense. I'll grant you that Terrand's wounds are similar to your dad's, but it doesn't mean there's a serial killer or the same person killed both your dad and Terrand. It could be a copycat."

"Over the past twenty years things have changed. When Daddy died, no one knew anything about DNA. There wasn't a computer in every department. The victims didn't have much in common. Nobody bothered to even check for a pattern."

"How did you find them? How did you even know to look?"

Taylor was silent, her gaze falling to her hands. "I knew Coleman had the wrong person. I searched. I read newspapers. I watched the news. I followed up on every article on every broadcast involving a death with a knife."

"I'm not buying it. Serial killers who stab their victims with knives are generally sexually motivated."

"Generally. Not always. But as it turns out, with every case where I could get at the evidence, there was proof of anal penetration."

"How many?"

"A total of twelve bodies."

"How many with sexually related injuries?"

"Five. That I can prove. A lot of departments didn't want to share."

"And yet you think they're all victims of the same man? You have no proof."

"Look, Fontaine, I want your help. I want the case re-opened."

Trey didn't even bother to open the door. In his anger, he pushed himself up and slid over the top of the passenger door, and then turned toward Taylor. "You bump up against Russ, you bump up against me. I can't stop you, but I can sure as hell protect Russ."

He walked back to Streak but his last words were empty. He couldn't think of one damned thing he could do to protect Russ.

TREY PULLED UP into the garage and pressed the remote to close the door. Opening the back door of Streak, he grabbed some clothes from the drawer under the rear seat.

Exhaustion set in as he secured the house and fell into bed. But sleep didn't come. Determined to force his mind into a beta state, he pushed thoughts of Russ and Darlene away and took a deep breath. When he closed his eyes, flashes of memory made him smile.

The three boys walked down Old Cypress Road on a Saturday afternoon, eating peanuts and sharing a co-cola. Tim started his usual teasing. "You saving that thing for marriage?"

"Naw. He's just scared of girls," Jason said.

"Knock it off," Trey said. Both boys laughed at him.

"C'mon, Trey. You know you're scared," Jason repeated.

"Either that, or you don't like girls," Tim said and tossed a peanut at Trey's head.

"I said, knock it off." Trey was getting tired of the same old teasing.

They had made it past the Taylor house and lengthened their strides, let down by the absence of Gemini Taylor. But then there was that voice.

"Hey, Trey."

They all stopped in their tracks as she approached, wearing a thin T-shirt and cut-off jeans. She was without doubt the most beautiful girl in the world. Trey swallowed hard when she stopped in front of him, her breasts just inches from his bare chest.

"Where've you been? You promised to come back last night but you didn't...you know...to finish what we'd started?" She stuck out a moist bottom lip and ran a finger down his cheek.

Trey heard gasps and sighs behind him, but he ignored them, his awareness glued to those dazzling eyes and pink lips. Gemini grasped his hand and pulled him from the others.

When they were far enough away so they couldn't be heard, she pressed her body against his and wrapped her arms around him. Her lips were close to his ear, her breath causing ripples of pleasure as it grazed his skin.

He fell instantly in love with her. Admittedly, he'd loved her before. But that was from a distance. Puppy love. This was the real thing. His body shivered, every inch of him eager.

"Let those mouthy jack-off bastards think what they want. You're not like them." She kissed his ear, and then brought her lips around to his and slipped her sweet tongue inside.

His hands automatically pulled her tighter to him as she gave him his first real kiss. Her breasts pressed against him and his body throbbed with a need he'd never known before. Suddenly, she stepped back, took his hand, and pulled him toward the oleanders. Trey thought something must be terribly wrong. Maybe she intended to drag him all the way to the house and tell her daddy something. But he followed dumbly anyway. After all, this was Gemini, and she was every boy's dream.

She stepped between two of the tall plants and turned to face him. From the road he was sure it looked like he was taking a leak and he hoped no cars drove by. After another torturously long kiss, she pushed him back a step. Trey stood frozen, his whole body aching. His breathing came fast and hard as she smiled. He couldn't take his eyes off her.

"Sorry to hear about your daddy. Was he a good man?"

He swallowed hard, the sting of tears in his throat. It was all he could do to nod, his mind and body reacting to the raw grief. And the guilt of not acting when he had a chance. If only he'd told someone what he knew, his dad would still have been alive.

Gemini gave both of his hands a squeeze. "Okay, I'll see you then," she said loudly enough for the boys on the road to hear. Giggling, she waved and walked away.

"Hey, man!" George said and slapped his shoulder. "Wow! How'd you do it?"

"Yeah, tell! What was she talkin' about?"

The three boys who surrounded him suddenly showed him a new respect. It was a day he would never forget, nor ever figure out.

Two days later, Arnold Taylor was found dead and Gemini was sent off to her aunt. As it turned out, that was a good thing. Had she stayed, he might never have made it into the FBI, let alone through the academy. He'd been crazy about her back then and would've done anything she asked.

Trey opened his eyes to the guest room of his mother's house. Now that he was older, he could see where his priorities belonged. There would be time for emotional attachment fifteen years down the road, after he made a name for himself and set his career in stone. Then he would have time for a real relationship.

The moonlight shone through the window. He stared at the wall where his mother had hung a framed copy of a newspaper article about his first big bust, and pictures of him. And one of his dad. Trey'd only slept in this room a few times. He would swear it was smaller than before.

Georgia Fontaine was the perfect example of womanhood. Always in a dress. Clean. Always made up. The death of her husband had changed her. Trey could not remember a single loving act from his mother since his dad's death. But there was no doubt about her love for his dad. Even after Tremaine Fontaine died, she still loved him.

Best not to feel than to feel what they'd gone through when his dad was shot and killed in the line of duty. Trey tried to direct his mind to a subject less distressing. Turning onto his back, he threw an arm over his eyes to block out the moonlight. The A/C blew cold against his skin as he lay on the full bed.

Sleep wouldn't return with his mind churning through the past as well as the present. He had to distance himself. His body lay in a cold sweat, tense from head to toe, his heart hammering in his chest, admitting that Gemini Taylor was still the most beautiful girl in the world. And he was still just a little in love with her.

Chapter Thirty-Six

GEMINI TAYLOR
En Route to Raven Bayou
Community Hospital
Raven Bayou, LA

Sunday After Midnight, 5 June 2005

GEM HAD ENOUGH to think about without Trey Fontaine increasingly on her mind.

Fontaine was an FBI agent. He had access to information from all over the U.S. If she could get him to, he could gather info on murders similar to Daddy's and find more in a matter of minutes than she had managed in all those years of searching.

And though she'd been able to ignore the interminable conversations between Coleman and Fontaine throughout the last two days and concentrate on her job, she wasn't able to block out the deep hum of Fontaine's voice in the background any more than the voice in her head frequently talking excitedly about how cute he was.

Those few minutes in the road when Trey was thirteen, or close to it, and she was fifteen, had never faded from her memory. *I must've been crazy. If Daddy had seen what I did, I'd have been in for a beating at the very least.*

She'd always hated being teased, and when she saw those boys mocking him, suddenly, she hated them too.

Of course, there had been no arrangement or date the night before. She just made that up to get them thinking she and Fontaine'd done it, or at least started to. She left it to Fontaine to invent the rest.

If it had been any other boy, she wouldn't have risked the punishment she knew would come with discovery. But Trey Fontaine was mature for his age, very cute, and easy to manipulate. His dad had been killed just two weeks before. Those boys were probably being normal teenage boys having a normal conversation, trying to keep Trey thinking on girls instead of his grief. But teens could be mean and thoughtless sometimes, and Trey's face still wore the pain.

It wasn't an unwelcome chore to be close to him. Though her history had proven she was no judge of character when it came to the men, she knew she was right about Trey.

She felt like she'd done him a favor all those years ago, but now, seeing him face-to-face as an adult, her cheeks warmed every time he looked at her, which was often. She tried not to return the interest, but that was difficult too.

She parked in the hospital lot and forced her mind away from Fontaine, away from the past. There was plenty in the present to concentrate on.

Miss Darlene was asleep when she arrived, but the nurses let her stand by the woman's bed for a few minutes. Sadness and anger filled Gem. Miss Darlene looked so fragile. She was a stranger to Gem but that didn't matter. She was a woman. In Gem's life, she'd seen way too many women hurt.

She left a note for Miss Darlene and talked to the nurse before stepping out into the hall. A deputy sat in the green chair thumbing through a newspaper. Wearing civvies, he looked like just another visitor.

Gem handed him her card. "My cell number's on the back. If you need someone to give you a break, call me. I'll be back for the four-to-eight shift."

Finally, Gem could go home.

GEM SHOULD HAVE just stayed at the hospital for all the sleep she got.

This would be a perfect time to work on the landscaping. Or wash the car. Or review all the info she'd gathered on Daddy's case and plan what to do next, but she was too exhausted to even think about any of that stuff.

Instead, she stepped into a cool shower, letting the water rinse away the day's ugliness and washed her hair. After changing into loose cotton Capri's and T-shirt, she grabbed a diet co-cola and raided the fridge. A few minutes later she made herself comfortable in her favorite overstuffed chair.

She planned to go see Mama today. Now that she lived closer, she'd promised herself she'd visit her at least every other week.

Gem could see the woods through the twelve-foot windows on the southeast side of the house. In the daylight, the sky was so blue it hurt to look at. Beyond the small woods, the water treatment plant lit up the sky every night.

All she had to do was turn her head the other way to see the box. The notes, pictures, witness statements and newspaper clippings. Everything she'd gathered that had to do with Daddy's murder.

She looked at the view of the trees instead.

A pile of mail had stacked up over the last few days. She didn't know how that happened. Sometimes things occurred so quickly she couldn't remember all the events of the day, especially ones as simple as collecting the mail.

Sorting through it, she found a letter from her mother and stared at the return address, the same return address on every letter she'd written since Daddy died:

MARTHA TAYLOR 8512312
LOUISIANA CORRECTIONAL INSTITUTE FOR WOMEN

P.O. BOX 29, ST. GABRIEL, LA 70776

Gem was thirty-four now. When she did the math, she was shocked to realize it was nearly twenty years to the day since Mama was arrested for killing Daddy.

Slipping a finger under the flap of the envelope, she tore it open across the top. The letter was long, as usual, and filled with the day-to-day activities and thoughts of a woman who knew she would never step foot outside the razor-wired fence of a Louisiana state penitentiary.

Chapter Thirty-Seven

WILE E.
Old Cypress Road
Raven Bayou, LA

Sunday 2:30 a.m., 5 June 2005

WE SCRAMBLED OUT of the car and headed for the old barn where the rickety pickup was stashed. Drew climbed in the driver's door and tossed her bag in my lap.

The full moon was all the light we needed. We rolled the windows down on the truck, and me and Rocky relaxed while Drew drove. Nighttime in Louisiana is always the best, especially when it's not raining.

We'd be home by dawn and nobody'd ever know. I was thinking maybe after we was done we could visit the old man. If we watched him a while, maybe we could figure out if we was gonna kill him or not. And then after him, we had to figure out if Fontaine was worth killing, or if he was just all mouth.

The air was cool blowing against my face as we headed north. Rocky set by the window and me in the middle. Anybody seeing the three of us together might think we was a odd looking bunch. Drew has sorta longish, blond, curly hair and blue eyes and her skin is tanned like on the TV commercials. Rocky has dark hair that hangs on his collar and curls some and his eyes are almost black. And me, my hair is straight and my eyes are green, kinda like a cat's. But really, none of it matters. What matters is, we take care of each other. We take care of ever body.

Doing this stuff makes me feel like a super hero. Right from the start, I didn't like the look of the man, but maybe we could talk to him and make him understand. If he wouldn't listen, somebody had to stand up to him. Men beating on women just ain't right, and we intended to let him know what he did was wrong.

When we finally got to Crowder Road, Drew killed the lights and eased past the man's trailer. The blue and white paint was old and dull in the moonlight. Drew drove on while we checked the neighborhood. A dog barked a few times as the truck rolled by. Besides that, it was dead quiet.

Drew pulled up into an empty field a ways past the last trailer on the road. I reached under the seat and found the present I brought and eased out the door. Rocky moved quiet like behind me as we headed to have a serious talk, and maybe some fun.

In ten minutes we was at the back of the trailer. We all slipped gloves on before Drew knocked at the back door.

"Who's that?"

"Open up, Michael. I need to talk to you," Drew called quietly. The door opened, light shining from the small bedside lamp.

"Who...what are you doing here?" Grant stood in his skivvies and a dingy undershirt. His hair looked like a robin's nest, all swirly and sticking out ever which way, and he smelled like beer.

"Just wanted to talk to a real man," Drew said in that voice men like. Rocky and me kinda hung back in the dark until Grant swung the door open wide and smiled. Drew stepped up, and we followed. Michael Grant's eyes looked at us kinda weird, like maybe we was from outer space.

I stepped to the front. "Like she said, Michael, we need to talk to you."

Chapter Thirty-Eight

RUSS COLEMAN
Sheriff's Dept.
Raven Bayou, LA

Sunday Night, 5 June 2005

WHEN HIS CELL RANG, Russ and his brother-in-law Frank Vance were in the hall outside Darlene's hospital room.

"A deputy spotted Vance's—Darlene's—vehicle forty-five miles from where she was found," Wilkes told him.

The mini-van was in Strawberry, a town just large enough to have a blinking yellow traffic light at the main intersection. "You going down there?"

"No. Chance and Bobbi Jo are on their way. I told the deputy to keep watch. I'll have the techs transport it."

Russ knew what that meant. Bobbi Jo Sanders and Chance Cooper were two of the best trace techs in the state. There would be no mistakes, nothing missed. No private tow company messing with evidence. And no lack of enthusiasm or resentment from techs who didn't care much for Russ.

"Thanks, Wilkes." Russ pressed a thumb and forefinger into the burning crescents under his eyes.

"I'll keep in touch." The line went dead before Russ could answer.

Wilkes was one of the few stand-up guys in a department filled with good ol' boys. The only man on the job, other than Tremaine Fontaine, who'd become a genuine friend to Russ and treated him as an equal.

Another hour or two and Russ would be finished. So much for senior detectives having the weekend off.

A FEW HOURS LATER when he dialed CSU, expecting to talk to a machine, Chance answered and said they had info for him. They were waiting in the lab.

"You guys are here awful late," Russ said.

"Yeah, well...Wilkes has been good to us, and besides, your sister didn't deserve this," Bobbi Jo said.

Russ was floored. Neither of these techs had ever been right out rude to him, but he just assumed they were like the rest of his fellow workers, or at least most of them. "Thank you, Bobbi Jo."

"Anyhow, you didn't hear this from me," she said quietly. "Prints inside the mini-van put a Scott Alexander at the wheel." She handed Russ a file. It held an NCIC printout of the suspect, a white male, twenty-two, with long blond hair.

His rap sheet listed, among other things, burglary and several counts of possession. The mug shot showed glassy eyes and scabby skin. Could this be Jacks?

"Wow," Russ said.

"We found fibers consistent with Levi's and a blond hair on the driver's seat. Debris on the floor mat, also mud on the tires and undercarriage. All we need is something to match it to."

Bobbi Jo tugged the file out of Russ's fist, her expression playful. "This goes to Wilkes."

"Thanks." Russ tried to swallow the sarcasm. He didn't want to keep the file, but a few more minutes to look at it wouldn't hurt. "Avlee already gone home?"

Two heads nodded. Answers about the scrapings from under Grant's nails would have to wait.

"Wilkes said he'd put out an APB on Scott Alexander and talk to the watch sergeant," Bobby Jo said.

"He's here?"

"No. I called him."

"Thanks, both of you."

As he headed home, Russ considered how he could use the new information. Alexander was a druggie. He probably didn't have the desire or the brains to plan an attack on Darlene. The note Russ had received wasn't written by a teenage druggie. It came from someone who was smart and probably had access to money or drugs. Scott Alexander was gonna pay, but Russ also intended to find out who sent him. That was the bastard Russ wanted.

AT OH-FOUR-FIFTY-NINE the pager pulled Russ from a dead sleep. It was a number he knew, followed by an 8-1-1, not quite an emergency, but damned important. He dialed.

"We got Alexander in holding," Wilkes's deep voice said.

"On my way." He hung up and called Trey. "They got Darlene's attacker."

"I'm there."

It was the kind of shower Russ'd taken during the academy, two minutes, in and out. Ten minutes later he was on the road. He flipped on his headlights and dialed Taylor's cell. The morning paper sat on the seat beside him. His hand shook as he lifted the phone to his ear. "Is your replacement there?"

"No, but he called. Should be here any minute."

"We got Alexander." His gut tightened. Coffee on top of a nervous stomach. Not a good combo.

"I'll be there as soon as I can. Keep your cool."

Trey pulled into the lot right behind Russ and they walked through processing together.

His stride was always bigger when solid information waited at the end of the trip. A service officer sat at a computer in the glass room, watching detainees while working her log. Five minutes later Taylor joined them.

"Where's Alexander?" Russ asked.

The officer pointed. The three of them swung their gazes around to the scab-faced doper cuffed to a bar along the wall, his chin almost touching his chest as he sat there snoozing, dirty hair pulled back in a rubber band at the base of his neck.

"Wilkes is on his way," the officer said.

Russ barely heard the woman speak over the pounding of his heart. Anger boiled over. Three long steps later and he towered over the scumbag who had attacked his sister.

A few hours ago, when Bobby Jo told him about Alexander, he was angry, but in control. Now...well, now he was mad. Out-of-his-mind mad.

He tangled his fingers in the man's filthy shirt and lifted him until the wall-chain stopped him, his other arm already cocked back for a punch.

"This won't help matters, Coleman! Turn him loose!" Taylor yelled.

The scrawny body hung limp as the perp flinched. Then, without a word, he giggled.

Before Russ could manage to throw his fist into the dazed face, Trey's arms wrapped around Russ in a bear hug. The bag of bones fell back on the aluminum seat, his head bouncing off the wall.

Trey whispered, "You do this and he walks."

Russ stopped struggling.

Taylor filled the gap between her partner and the skinny blond, eyes throwing daggers at Russ. Before he had a chance to comment, Wilkes voice caught his attention.

"Well, Coleman. You're here kind of early. You'd think someone called you or something."

Russ knew Wilkes had to put on an act for the benefit of the others in the room. If the lieutenant found out Wilkes had called Russ and told him about nabbing Alexander, there'd be trouble.

"Taylor and I have a murder case to work. Thought we'd get an early start." Russ took a few steps toward the hall.

"Mind if we watch?" Taylor asked Wilkes with a jerk of her head toward Alexander.

The detective pursed his lips, narrowed his eyes, and then he nodded. Five minutes in an interview room proved Wilkes was wasting his time. Alexander was so gone he could barely talk, though he sneered really big at the mention of the mini-van.

"What were you doing following Darlene Vance?" Wilkes asked.

Alexander giggled. "I was playing Jacks." He mimicked playing the ancient game, throwing up a ball and picking up jacks from the table.

"Take him to holding," Wilkes told the deputy. "Ask the sergeant if someone can take him to the emergency room for a urine sample and blood test, and then bring him back. After Avlee gets a stab at him, he can be transported to the jail."

Taylor called Avlee's voicemail and left a message while Russ did the same with the DA. There was no more they could do until the rest of the city woke up.

Chapter Thirty-Nine

TREY FONTAINE
Sheriff's Dept.
Raven Bayou, LA

Monday Morning, 6 June 2005

TREY AND RUSS stopped at The Coffee House and picked up three breakfasts.

"I'm starved," Trey said as he found the one with eggs, sausage, biscuits and gravy. He ate while Russ drove. "So, the one with hotcakes and eggs is Taylor's?"

"Yeah. She loves sweets. Any time of day." Russ smiled.

"No kidding."

They'd just pulled out of the restaurant parking lot when Bettencourt came across on the radio. "Two-Raven-fifty-six."

"Fifty-six, go," Russ said.

"CSU's looking for you. Results in the Grant case."

"On our way." Russ called Taylor and told her to meet him there. Trey packed away what was left of his breakfast, hoping CSU actually had something they didn't already know.

Avlee sat on a high stool near a counter full of beakers, bottles, and carboys across from an island counter top with a MultiPROBE II Forensic Workstation. Against the walls stood a TriScan document scanner with full spectrum light analysis, a Spectrum Spotlight 300FTIR imaging system for analyzing drugs, and a half-dozen other gadgets. The last large drug bust in the parish had provided all this new equipment. Thanks to asset forfeiture laws, a half million dollars in assets had been seized and auctioned with monies collected going to the county sheriff's office.

Trey had taken classes on the process of crime scene investigation and had seen these modern miracles and how they worked. He was glad it was anyone except him, sitting in the lab. He could never be a lab rat.

Give him the typical FEEBBIE drug testing kit—a plastic tackle box with a few chemicals, a ceramic mixing bowl, and a simple instruction sheet—and he was happy. Anyone who could read could determine within two minutes if a plastic bag contained coke or powdered sugar.

"The scrapings from the vic's fingernails ended up being her own skin," Avlee began. "Barlow found a mark from what was probably a chigger on her leg. She must have scratched it. The brown fibers we found on her and her clothing were from short-nap carpet, most likely from a vehicle interior or trunk. I haven't had time to match it further, but by tomorrow I'll be able to tell you make and model."

She wheeled her stool over to the computer and pulled up some pictures. "The casting of the wounds proved more valuable. The knife was a single-edged ten-inch blade, very thin, and there were traces of raw chicken meat at the entry point of one of the wounds. She was stabbed with a common kitchen knife, one that had been used to cut up chicken not long before she was killed."

"Anything else?" Russ asked while Trey stood back, thinking it was time for another "mint."

"Yes," she said and rolled back to the computer. "The cast of the tire track at the crime scene was also useful. The rain destroyed a lot of the pattern, but we can be sure it didn't come from a truck or SUV. It's a passenger vehicle tire, 75R-14 Weatherall. And it's well worn. The tread is so thin you could see air through it." Avlee grinned at her own wit.

"And?" Russ asked, and Trey could see him lean forward a fraction of in inch, sensing she had more.

She pointed at the photo of the tire cast, her finger following a deep notch. "See this impression? Look closely at its shape."

All of them moved closer and looked. The area Avlee pointed at was a hexagon in the cast, about a half-inch wide and a quarter-inch deep.

"The tire has an indentation made by a something with a hexagon head," Russ said what Trey was thinking.

"Yes—" Avlee started to explain but Russ had already gone, Trey right behind him, and Taylor almost trotting to keep up.

"There was a mark on Grant's tire," Taylor said.

"I saw it. I'll call the DA. See if you can have a couple of deputies out of Verbois Station get out there, pronto. Grab some radios and get the car."

While Taylor and Russ were in high gear with their phone calls and equipment gathering, Trey hurried to the vending machine in the break room and grabbed a soda. On his way to the parking lot he downed a couple of Lortabs

By the time Russ got off the phone and into the parking lot, Taylor had the Crown Vic ready, A/C blasting. Russ threw his war bag into the trunk and jumped into the passenger seat.

Trey wrangled his way into the back. The plastic interior was warm to the touch. With a forecast of no rain and record heat, steam was already building. He was thankful it was summer and would be light for another ten hours. CSU would need the time for processing the residence. Michael Grant would be thoroughly pissed at their intrusion. No one appreciated a search warrant giving complete access to their home. This was gonna be fun.

"Marks is working on the warrant. It should be ready by the time we arrive," Russ said.

Taylor nodded. "And CSU?"

"We'll impound the car, and then interrogate Grant. His knowing that we have the tire cast might swing him, but either way, we'll get a warrant for the house as soon as we prove the tire matches the cast."

"I guess this rules out Jacks. At least as far as Ilene Grant is concerned," Taylor said.

Trey nodded, but Russ had a strange look on his face.

"What you thinking?" Trey asked him.

"Something's just not right about Jacks. That name rings in my ears like I'm supposed to remember something about it."

Trey didn't say a word. It was Russ's great gut instinct again. Trey was just glad to finally be doing something.

THEY ARRIVED to the sight of several cruisers, light bars announcing a mass presence. Humid heat smacked them when they stepped out of the unit. As they walked into the yard, Trey noticed a pile of dirt by a small hole in the ground and beside it, a shovel. His attention was still glued there when someone spoke.

"Morning, Coleman." It was a deputy Trey didn't know.

"What the hell's going on?" Russ asked.

"He's dead," the young deputy said.

"He?" Russ asked.

"Michael Grant."

Russ looked at Trey, and then Taylor, whose gaze was locked on the trailer, her mouth hanging open.

What the hell! Trey closed his eyes and rubbed the lines between his brows. *Kelli Stevens disappears, then her sister Ilene Grant is killed by her husband. And now her husband it dead? Something's not right.* Tension gathered making his jaws clench and his neck kink up.

"When did it happen?" Taylor asked.

"Don't know. Detective's inside," the deputy nodded.

"This is Agent Fontaine. He's with us," Russ said and the deputy waved them under the crime scene tape.

"What's that?" Trey nodded toward the hole in the ground.

"A dog."

Trey started to slip his hands in his pocket out of habit, but the pain in his butt-cheek forced him to cross his arms in front of his chest instead.

He looked around. Had Russ's unit radio been set to scan the channels, they might've known in advance what was happening here, but the radio in the Crown Vic had been full of static caused by the humid weather so no one had bothered to set it to scan.

Another body. Maybe the missing Jacks character *was* having an affair with Ilene. Maybe he took revenge on Michael for killing his wife. How many did that make? Ilene Grant, the sex offender, and now Michael Grant. Several girls missing and two women carjacked and raped. Three weeks ago the biggest crime in the parish had been teenagers' joy riding and the occasional drunk driver.

Trey rolled scenarios around in his head, trying to discern whether all of it was related. Did the sex offender kidnap the girls and rape the two women? No. Records indicated the molester was into young girls, five or six years old. Evidence said Alexander attacked Darlene. Could he also be responsible for the others? One of the girls who'd disappeared was the sister of Ilene Grant, and now she and her husband were both dead.

As Trey tried to line up all the players in his head, he watched Taylor and Russ go about their jobs. Taylor looked deathly pale and shaky. She dropped her bag on the first step of the porch and followed Russ to the hole in the ground.

Trey hung back enough to take in the whole scene. Two uniformed deputies stood within the crime scene tape while a third was outside the fence. A plain unit spoke of the presence of a detective, but Trey didn't see one. He stuck his hand in his pocket and fingered the mint tin. It was almost empty.

From his location near the parked Taurus belonging to Michael Grant, he saw several mobile homes up the dirt road. If anyone was home, they were out of sight, tucked behind their curtains with their A/C's on high. Someone would have to interview all the nearby residents again.

Russ and Taylor stood at the bottom of the steps.

"Shall we?" Russ asked and his eyes focused on the door of the mobile home.

Taylor picked up her bag, but allowed Russ to go first. Trey wondered if she was avoiding the trailer itself, or what waited inside.

Chapter Forty

GEMINI TAYLOR
Grant Residence
Verbois, LA

Monday Morning, 6 June 2005

GEM WAS IN NO HURRY to enter the tin box, but if the body of their prime suspect was inside, she had to. She refused to let her fear control her and stop her from doing her job.

Though her mind was set, her body didn't cooperate. Her feet stopped moving. The heat of the morning was not enough. Her body jumped into overdrive and sweat poured down her sides. *Why, of all places, did the damn man have to pick a sardine can to die in?* She took a deep breath, slipped her sunglasses off, hitched her bag up, and put one foot in front of the other.

Coleman walked in. Gem dropped her bag on the top step and followed, her heart beating a little too hard for comfort.

The fact that Trey the giant was behind her didn't help. His bulk took up a lot of space. With the bright sun shining and all the lights on, the trailer still looked dark and confining.

An investigator stood in the kitchen, a narrow closet door yawning open in front of him.

"Hey, Marcotte," Coleman said and shook the man's hand. "This is my partner, Taylor, and this is Agent Trey Fontaine."

Marcotte nodded to them as he tugged his waistband a little higher on his beer belly.

Coleman stepped up and looked into the closet. "Damn." He moved aside so Gem could take a peek.

Michael Grant had been stuffed into the closet, back against one side, knees against the other, his head falling forward. A puddle of blood, urine, and feces filled the closet floor.

Gem stepped closer and saw the source of the blood. Grant's bare chest was a mass of reddish brown. The handle of a knife stuck out just to the left of his sternum. It was too dark in the closet to see the cuts, but she knew what they'd find when the body was laid out. Three stab wounds to the chest, identical to his wife's.

"I'll get my bag and start the sketches," she said. "Forensics?"

"On their way," Marcotte replied.

She stepped out into the afternoon sun. "Who found him?" She yelled out to the deputies scattered around the yard.

"Me," a tall, broad-chested deputy drawled, a toothpick rolling from one side of his full lips to the other.

"What time?"

"Oh-seven-twenty hours." A very tall deputy with black shiny hair curling around his baseball cap walked up the stairs and stopped one step from the top. His nametag read Deputy Long. *Very fitting*, she thought. He reminded her of an actor from the old movies. Clint Something, who played in a movie about a friendly bear.

Gem hated military time. But those eyes were a deeper blue than the sky, so she forgave him. She looked at her watch. Nine-fifteen. "How many others went inside?"

"Just Marcotte."

"Thanks." Not very talkative, but damn cute. She grabbed her bag and headed back inside. The swamp cooler on the roof was off, which suited her, since turning it on would encourage people to close the trailer door. She dropped her bag on the carpet, slipped on latex gloves, and grabbed her posse box.

"You see the paper this morning?" Marcotte asked.

"Haven't had a chance," Coleman said.

"B section of the *Times* has a story on Ilene Grant."

"Great."

Their voices were thick with sarcasm. The article probably had specifics the department would rather have kept quiet. Easier to filter through the loonies who confessed to every crime in the parish.

"I'll take the outside," Coleman said and Gem heard footsteps, felt them too as the floor shook.

Sweat trickled down her back, soaking the bra band that worked to squeeze from her chest the little air she could get. Ignoring the closed-in feeling, she went about her work, carefully marking the location of everything, measuring the relative distance of objects, one from another. The closet door, drop-leaf table, the kitchen counter. Her mind raced with questions and she almost forgot the smallness of the room. Almost.

She studied the body in the dark closet. The beer belly she'd noticed yesterday that made Michael Grant appear to be a man soft and out of shape, distracted from his otherwise compact and muscular body. From this angle, the light accentuated his short, heavy stumps for legs and ham-sized biceps.

After making a few notes, Gem grabbed her flashlight for a closer look. His face was a bloody mass of tissue, nothing she hadn't seen before. But bile rose in her throat at the sight of that pregnant looking abdomen, open from pubic bone to sternum, skin peeled back from the wound akin to a butchered bear.

Her knees buckled and she sat down hard. She'd seen this before. Flashes of memories flicked through her brain: the metal legs of the kitchen chair, the lime green-and-gold linoleum floor, the ocean of blood creeping away from Daddy's body.

She couldn't do this again. Her throat went dry and she had no control over her breathing, which had turned into short gasps. She scooted away from the closet and leaned against the lower cabinet under the sink. The floor shook again, and continued to shake along with the heavy footsteps coming in her direction. A dark shadow fell over her.

"What's wrong, Taylor?" she heard Marcotte say.

Her vision faded.

Chapter Forty-One

RUSS COLEMAN
Grant Residence
Verbois, LA

Monday Morning, 6 June 2005

RUSS AND TREY were on the hunt for footprints around the outside of the Grant property when Marcotte called Russ from the front porch. The urgency in the detective's voice made them jog to the front door.

Marcotte looked inside the trailer, and then back at Russ. "Your partner got a little shaky, but she looks okay now."

They hurried into the trailer and found Taylor halfway in the closet, her flashlight pointed at Grant's chest. Her shirt clung to her back, wrinkled with sweat. It was déjà vu.

Russ'd been freshly promoted to detective twenty years ago when he took the call at the Taylor house and found her sitting in a small closet, her young eyes hollow. He knew Taylor hated small places.

"What's wrong, Taylor?" he asked.

"Nothing wrong with me, but Mr. Grant don't look so good."

"Take a break. I can finish."

"No," she almost barked. "I'll be done in a minute."

Russ turned to Marcotte and Trey. "She's fine."

Both men exited the stinky trailer, leaving Russ with his partner.

"Barlow can take over. He here yet?" Her voice sounded like a speakerphone from inside the closet.

Before he got a chance to answer, Taylor backed out and turned to face him, a flashlight in her gloved right hand, blood covering the bare skin of her left.

"What are you doing?" Russ asked, not believing what he saw.

She looked at her left hand and her lips curled just enough to make Russ wonder if she was all right. "There's blood ever where," she said.

Russ stepped around her and looked into the closet. Either she had stuck her hand into the open abdomen or into the puddle on the closet floor. He bent and took a closer look at the floor. Nothing to show she had touched it. Blood, urine, and feces looked like a nasty Jell-O.

He turned back to his partner, who rinsed her hand in the sink and dried it on a kitchen towel. "You stuck your hand into his guts? What the hell were you thinking?"

He didn't know if he was angry or scared. Both emotions fought to come out first. He ran a hand over his hair. Twice. What if she'd destroyed evidence? With all of her training, how could she make such a mistake?

"Already had my glove off. Thought I saw something around the blade," she almost whispered.

Russ rubbed his head again and sighed. "Shit. Make sure you put that in your report. If you contaminated the body, if you left any of your DNA on it and the lab finds it, they'll think you were involved."

Russ stepped back a couple of feet and watched Taylor work. By the time she finished sketching and taking pictures, CSU arrived, Barlow right behind them. Taylor stepped aside as four more bodies crowded the room.

The coroner stuck his head in the closet, and then backed out and began unfolding a white paper tarp. After a couple of minutes he returned to the body and came out with a thermometer. "Looks like he's been dead six to eight hours," Barlow said. He stuck his whole upper body in the closet. "When was he found?"

"This morning a little after seven," Taylor said. "So he died sometime near three this morning."

"Any similarities between his wounds and his wife's?" Russ asked.

"Well, Mrs. Grant wasn't gutted, but both have chest wounds, and they look similar. Can't really give you much until I get him on the table." Barlow's face was drawn, lips pursed, when he mumbled, "This does look familiar."

It looked familiar to Russ too.

"Are you finished with your photos?" Barlow asked Taylor as he spread a body bag on the paper.

Taylor nodded and Barlow pulled the body out of the closet, Chance grabbing the legs of the body and helping lay Michael Grant out. While Barlow made notes about lividity, bruising, and other marks on the body, Chance bagged the hands and started his tedious job of looking for trace evidence with a magnifying glass and tweezers.

Russ stood frozen, his gaze glued to the form of Michael Grant. A minute passed before he looked at Taylor. "Barlow has everything under control in here. Can you help me finish outside?"

"Sure. Just let me get the last pictures. Five minutes and I'll be there." She grabbed her camera and snapped pictures of the empty closet and the corpse on the body bag.

Russ walked out the door.

Chapter Forty-Two

WILE E.
Grant Residence
Verbois, LA

Monday Afternoon, 6 June 2005

COPS WERE EVER WHERE, so there was no way for Rocky and Drew to get a close up look. But me, I'm kinda small and quiet and sneaky, so I got a good look at what was going on. I heard talk that the no-count Michael Grant maybe killed his wife and her little sister. He won't be killing nobody else.

Drew cried when she saw the puppy. She loves animals. Then she tried her best to get close to that FBI agent guy. Tray was his name, like a folding table for eating in front of the TV. Stupid name if you ask me. Rocky don't much care for him, either.

Anyhow, it was too hot and sticky, and there was too many cops for us, so we just left.

Chapter Forty-Three

TREY FONTAINE
Grant Residence
Verbois, LA

Monday Afternoon, 6 June 2005

"WHAT'S GOING ON?" he whispered to Russ.

"It's not possible. I feel like I traveled back in time. This can't be happening. I can't imagine how Taylor feels."

"Why?"

"It's just so much like…"

"Like Daddy." Taylor stood on the stairs, her war bag hanging from her shoulder. Trey found no emotion on her pretty face.

"Where do you want me?" she asked.

Russ looked dumbfounded. "I've already done the sketches. How about more photos?"

"Sure."

Trey watched her take shots of Grant's vehicle in relation to the trailer and the road—shots of the hole where the dog had been found in relation to the fence, driveway, and trailer—shots of the front and back steps. He stood back and observed her thoroughness, her intense attention to detail and thought, *She'd make a great agent.*

It was like she could see the sequence of events that had occurred outside the murder scene. She followed the trail of small plastic markers, snapping shots of footprints, tire marks, tools.

It took them two more hours to complete their investigation. With sketches and evidence packed away and specific requests to CSU regarding the knives, the dog, and possible fingerprints, they loaded their bags in the trunk of the Crown Vic.

It took another hour to canvas the area for possible witnesses. The only person they found at home was Mrs. Akin, who said she'd been asleep until after eight-thirty and hadn't looked out the window until a few minutes before they arrived to talk to her.

"I need to drive. I think better when I drive," Russ said and opened the driver's door.

"Good. I could use a break," Taylor said.

Climbing into the back seat, once again Trey had a perfect profile view of Taylor as he sat behind Russ. She looked tired and a little pale. And beautiful.

They reached the city before anyone spoke.

"I'm so hungry my belly thinks my throat's been cut," Taylor said.

"Me too," Russ agreed. "You want to stop for something before we hit the station?"

"I could use a burger and a milkshake." She looked eager.

"Me too," Trey agreed, hoping he could reach his mint tin while they were eating, and thinking a burger was an odd choice for her. He couldn't remember seeing her eat meat.

Russ wheeled the unit into Sonic. Taylor ordered a double cheeseburger and a vanilla shake. Trey and Russ ordered the same and Trey was astonished to see Taylor finish the giant burger. It was understandable that she would've been famished—she never got the breakfast he and Russ bought—but still...

"Where did you put it all?" Trey asked her as she slurped the bottom of her cup.

She answered with a pat of her stomach and smiled. "Now I'm ready for a nap."

Apparently, she wasn't kidding. She leaned her head against the headrest and closed her eyes. Her lashes lay thick upon her cheek and he had an almost irresistible urge to reach up and brush back the wisp of chestnut hair lying against her jaw almost touching her lips.

Russ parked behind the Civic Building and Taylor opened her eyes. She looked no more rested than when she'd closed them, though somehow she looked older than she had just a few minutes ago. They pulled their war bags from the trunk and Russ locked up.

"Go on home, Taylor. We can do the reports in the morning." Russ took his bag and headed for his Suburban.

Trey was exhausted too, but he still had to check in on Ace before passing out. It occurred to him that he spent half his days playing second fiddle to Ace, and the other half trailing behind Taylor. Two beautiful women kept him worn out, physically and mentally, and neither of them really wanted him around.

Sometimes life just wasn't fair.

Chapter Forty-Four

RUSS COLEMAN
Sheriff's Dept.
Raven Bayou, LA

Tuesday Morning, 7 June 2005

"HOPE TODAY is better than yesterday," Russ said as he sat down at his desk in the pit. He, Trey, and Taylor were just settling down when Wilkes came over.

"How's your sister?"

"She's coming home today."

"Heard Grant is dead. How was yesterday?" Wilkes hiked his leg up and sat on the desk.

"It was a long one. How 'bout yours?"

"Mostly drudge. But today...," he lowered his voice. "I'm headed over to interview Scott Alexander."

"Mind if I tag along?" Russ asked. Trey and Taylor leaned forward for the answer.

Wilkes gazed over his shoulder before whispering. "I've been told to keep you out of the case."

"Okay. See you later?"

"Sure," he said at normal volume. "You guys take it easy." Then he lowered it again. "I'm scheduled to interview him in thirty minutes. Room Twelve, parish lock-up."

As Wilkes walked out, Russ's brain went into roller-coaster mode, high one minute and low the next. His first thought was to run full speed across the street, but he couldn't leave right after Wilkes. He would protect Wilkes at all costs. The man had really shown his friendship in the last few days.

"Why don't you two go get us some fresh coffee?" he asked Trey and Taylor.

Taylor's look said she thought he'd lost his mind. "Too hot for coffee."

"You'd best be careful, Russ," Trey said cautiously.

"Well, if you don't want coffee, I'll go get my own." Russ stood and pushed in his chair. Taylor stood. "Where do you think you're going?" he said. "You didn't want coffee. Stay here and work on your report."

Chapter Forty-Five

TREY FONTAINE
County Jail
Raven Bayou, LA

Tuesday Morning, 7 June 2005

RAVEN BAYOU PARISH JAIL was located in the basement of the County Courthouse. The observation room was small and dark. Russ went in first, followed by Trey, and then Taylor who closed the door. They stood near the mirror looking into Interview Room Twelve.

In the next room Scott Alexander sat facing the mirror and the detective. The suspect was not as wide as the chair he sat upon. His arms were dry and several scabs were half scratched off with small smears of blood on the surrounding skin, but his eyes and bearing said he wasn't high any more. His hands shook, and his gaze went everywhere except toward the detective's face.

"You're looking a little rough, Scott," said Wilkes. "Parish jail's a hard way to detox."

Alexander interlocked his fingers and gently bounced the sides of his hands on the table, his lips pressed into a thin slash across his face.

"You want to tell me why?" Wilkes asked.

The arrestee finally looked at the man across the table from him. "Why what?" he said with a scratchy voice.

"Why you ditched the mini-van."

"My lawyer says I don't have to tell you shit."

"Well, your public defender is correct. However, without your cooperation, we can't make a deal. And without a deal, you're looking at some hard time. Angola makes parish lock-up look like a vacation in the Bahamas."

"Don't need a public defender, dude. I got Oliver McCutchen, attorney at law."

Trey looked at Russ for an explanation. None came. Only the flinching of jaw muscles.

"One of the most sought after criminal attorneys in the South," Russ finally whispered.

Wilkes ran his fingers over the pen he held, fondling it lovingly.

Trey grinned. "Let me guess. Wilkes just quit smoking." He was rewarded with a nod from Russ.

"And how did you manage to secure the services of a man whose hourly fee is five-hundred dollars and requires cash up front?" Wilkes asked.

"Like I said, I don't have to tell you shit."

Wilkes fondled the pen for another minute before making his exit.

"That's the end of that," Trey said.

If McCutchen only worked for clients with big money, who had big money and was willing to spend it on the likes of Scott Alexander?

Wilkes came in. "Hearing's scheduled for today at thirteen-hundred."

Russ shook the man's hand. "Thanks," was all he said. After Wilkes walked away, Russ turned to Trey and Taylor. "I'm gonna go visit Darlene for lunch. I'll see you guys later." He headed across the street and down the sidewalk toward the parking lot behind the civic building.

Trey looked at Taylor. "Well, I guess we're on our own."

Chapter Forty-Six

RUSSELL COLEMAN
En Route to Strawberry
Raven Bayou Parish, LA

Tuesday Afternoon, 7 June 2005

"Michael Grant died Sunday morning between oh-three-hundred and oh-six-hundred hours. He was found at oh-seven-twenty hours, Monday," Barlow said. "A hunting knife was used for the three stab wounds and a skinning knife for the long cut. We call that a zipper. See, a skinning knife has what's called a gut hook, used to unzip the gut," Barlow said as Russ and Trey looked at Michael Grant, stretched out on the autopsy table.

"What about the butcher knife found in his chest?" Russ asked.

"It was placed there, and I do mean *placed* there, after Grant was dead. The killer put the kitchen knife into one of the stab wounds, the one that hit the heart," Barlow answered. "Avlee is testing the blood and checking for prints on the kitchen knife. It's my understanding that the other two knives were never found."

"Anything else?" Russ asked.

"He was sodomized with something so big it would have killed him even if he didn't have any other wounds. Just like Arnold Taylor. He also had the same kind of knife and wounds as Arnold Taylor. Nothing else significant. If anything comes up, I'll give you a call." Barlow's tone was even as he met Russ's gaze, but Russ read what the coroner didn't say. That Russ could have been wrong. Or details had been leaked and now there was a copycat. He didn't like either of those thoughts.

Russ looked at Trey. "How about you go find Taylor and y'all meet me at the unit. We're going to take a ride."

"So, are you going to tell me what's going on?" Trey asked him as he started the car. Taylor sat in the passenger seat in a fresh blouse and jacket.

Russ looked in the rearview and met Trey's gaze, and then refocused on the road before repeating what Barlow said about Michael Grant's death for Taylor's benefit. "And then there's the watch."

"What watch?" Taylor asked sharply, sounding a little put off like he had information he wasn't sharing.

"Grant wore a watch. Remember how he fiddled with it during the interview at his house? But there was no watch at the scene. Where did it go?" He gripped the steering wheel tighter, pretending it was Scott Alexander's neck.

"It's not in evidence?" Taylor asked.

He shook his head.

"So, where are we going?" Trey asked again.

"I couldn't figure out who Jacks was, and then I overheard something. The captain is going to a conference in Florida—"

"What does that have to do with anything?" Trey asked.

"He's flying into JAX...J—A—X."

"Wilkes asked Alexander what he was doing following Darlene and he said, 'I was playing Jacks.' He was pretending to be Jacks," Taylor said.

"J.A.X. is someone's initials," Trey said.

Russ glanced in the mirror again and saw the interest on Trey's face. He was finally starting to understand. Russ smiled. "And I think I know whose."

Eyes on the road, Russ reached for a stack of papers on the seat beside him and handed them to Trey. "But more importantly, Alexander knows for sure, and he was released on bail a half-hour ago. And if he knows, then Nick Strickland knows," Russ said as he drove out of town.

"Who's Nick Strickland?" Taylor asked.

"He's Alexander's good buddy. They run together. And they went to school with the youngest Boudreaux. They tend to get in trouble together."

Trey skimmed the first page. "Jamison Alton Xavier Boudreaux, making his initials JAX," Trey read. "A letter of recommendation required for the hiring process, written by Mrs. Ilene Grant. What made you think of him?"

"The description Mrs. Akins gave fits him to a T, and those three boys are thick as thieves. It took a while to set in, but when Loe said 'Jax,' I remembered Boudreaux's grandpa was named Alton Xavier. If we're lucky, Alexander'll be with Strickland, but even if he's not, I'm gonna have a little talk with Nicky Boy."

FIFTEEN MINUTES LATER they rolled slowly to a stop. The trees encroached upon the road and created a tunnel of limbs above it. Just in front of the unit stood an old rusted mailbox with the name STRICKLAND painted on the side in red, and past it, a driveway.

Trey and Taylor followed Russ as he waded into the weeds between the trees. They stopped when the house came into view. Two young men sat on the porch, beer cans in hand. Sitting in the front yard were three vehicles: an old, dark green pickup, a Ford Fiesta, and a small, gray Nissan pickup. Bells and whistles went off in Russ's head. *Finally, a concrete piece of evidence. A little gray truck, just like the one mentioned by both Endri, and Darlene.*

"It didn't take Alexander long to get here," Russ whispered.

"That's Nick Strickland?" Taylor asked.

"Fits his description," Russ answered. "Nineteen years old, five-foot-five, 135 pounds, dirty blond hair."

Strickland's hair touched his shoulders in oily strands. His Western shirt was torn, his jeans hanging from hipbones.

The trio was quiet, trying to hear the conversation taking place on the porch, but it was too far away. The boys passed a bowl between them, the smell of primo weed wafting through the trees.

"You have a plan?" Trey asked.

"Yeah," Russ said, "but you're not gonna like it."

Chapter Forty-Seven

TREY FONTAINE
Strickland Residence
Strawberry, LA

Tuesday Afternoon, 7 June 2005

RUSS BACKED OUT of the weeds and walked down the dirt drive to the house, Trey and Taylor right behind him.

"Afternoon, boys," Russ said. He put a foot on the bottom step of the porch and stopped. "I think it's time we had a little talk."

Russ was right. Trey didn't like it. The strong, no-nonsense tone in his godfather's voice was rarely heard, and it wasn't something Trey ever cared to hear. When Russ got quiet, he got dangerous.

Alexander had bed-head hair, and his ribs showed through the dingy, too-small T-shirt he wore. He held the pipe in his hand and, at the sound of Russ's voice, hid it behind him. Too late. His mouth hung open, obviously speechless.

Strickland looked at Alexander, unsure what to do.

Strickland's eyes were huge with fear, and his pupils dilated from the pot. Trey guessed Strickland was the weakest link.

Russ did a complete turn, slowly looking in all directions before addressing the boys again. He looked at Strickland. "Your daddy around?"

Strickland looked at Russ, mouth agape. He shook his head.

"That's good. That's real good, 'cause I need to talk to you two in private." Russ casually unbuttoned his jacket and swept it behind his arms before slipping his hands into his pockets.

Though Trey was a step behind his godfather, there was no doubt in his mind that Russ's badge and weapon were visible to both boys. Taylor didn't move a muscle or say a word.

"Give me a minute," Trey said to Russ and started walking around the east side of the house. He moved quietly, looking in windows, eyeballing the outbuildings for signs of life. Everything was still. As he came around the back corner, he saw movement and made ready to draw his weapon when he recognized Taylor coming from the other side of the house.

She shook her head. All clear. They returned to the front of the house, flanking Russ. "Looks like no one's here."

"That's good. That's really good," Russ said. "Now, first, one of you is going to tell me who Jax is. Which one will it be?"

The boys looked at each other again.

"Okay, I'll choose. Tell me, Scott. Who is Jax?"

"I don't know what you're talking about," Alexander said.

Trey moved up beside the stairs, so he could see Russ's face and Russ could see him. "Who owns the gray pickup?" Trey nodded toward the vehicle.

"It's mine," Strickland said, his gaze shifting between Trey and Russ, not sure which one would hurt him first.

"You ever loan it to Jax?" Russ asked Alexander.

"You got questions for me, you can ask my attorney."

Russ ascended the stairs and stopped within a few feet of the boys. "If we were here, asking you questions, then that'd be the right thing to say. But since we're not here, that answer ain't gonna help you one bit."

"So, you're playing Bad Cop?" Alexander said to Russ. Then he looked at Trey. "That means you're playing Good Cop?"

"In case you haven't figured it out, I'm not playing at all," Russ took another step.

Strickland cringed and his shoulders scrunched up around his ears. "Yeah, Jax uses my truck now and then."

"Okay, now we're getting to it. Who is Jax?"

"Shut up, Nick," Alexander warned.

"That ain't very good advice, Son," Russ said, now hovering over Strickland.

Taylor made her way up the steps and stood beside Russ. Strickland looked up at her nervously.

Alexander stood. "We know our rights. Y'all can't just come on private property and make us talk."

"Oh, but, we didn't. We're on our way out to Verbois. We haven't seen you guys at all." Taylor stared into Strickland's eyes. "Don't even know where you live."

"Don't make me ask again," Russ said quietly.

"Okay, look. I don't know what y'all want, but we ain't done nothing," Strickland said.

Russ took one step and reached for Strickland's shirt, but the boy fell backwards over his chair to get out of reach. "It's Jimmy! Jamison Boudreaux!"

"Jamison Alton Xavier Boudreaux?" Trey asked.

Strickland nodded as he scrambled up onto his feet and back up against the wall.

"Damn it, Nick, shut the fuck up!" Alexander hollered. Trey hoped Nick was more afraid of Russ than Alexander. The boy was like a skittish colt, gangly and wild looking.

Russ slipped his hands back into his pockets and smiled. "Since you're in such a confessing mood, how 'bout you tell who hurt Miss Darlene Vance?" Taylor asked Strickland. Her volume was low and soft, but she spat the words out through her teeth with a menacing tone.

Alexander watched Strickland with contempt. "Keep your mouth shut!"

"How about Endri Cheramie?" Trey asked, looking at Alexander.

"Fuck you," Alexander replied.

But Nick Strickland was already broken, his huge eyes filled with tears. "I ain't done nothing. Sometimes Jax borrows my truck, but I don't know nothing about what he does."

"Bullshit," Trey said. "Two years ago a deputy stopped a yellow Corvette for reckless driving. Brought in three boys, all drunk. Found a ladies diamond dinner ring in the pocket of the driver, Jamison Boudreaux. All three of you were released to Alton Boudreaux. No file number, so someone talked the deputy on the scene into making this a contact instead of a report. You have a sheet for B&E, and auto theft. And Darlene Vance's van was found here, in Strawberry."

Taylor grabbed Strickland by the front of the shirt, pulled him away from the wall, and then bounced him back against it. "Ain't it kinda strange that Miss Darlene's van was right here in this little town where you live?"

"I don't know nothing! I swear!" Strickland said.

"If I don't get answers, y'all are gonna have a terrible accident," Russ said. "Who raped Endri Cheramie?"

Strickland's eyes bulged as Taylor twisted her grip on his shirt, choking him with its tightness. "Jax! It was Jax! Only, he swears Endri liked it! He said she wanted it! Ain't no way she'll tell! Nobody tells on Jax!"

Alexander turned and headed toward the end of the porch but Trey was faster, vaulting the porch banister and grabbing the back of the boy's shirt. Alexander began to fight, but quickly figured out he was outweighed by at least sixty pounds and nowhere near as strong. Trey returned him to the chair, sat him down hard, and stood over him. The adrenaline had kicked in and he barely noticed the burning of his butt until the action was over. He wished he could wash down a couple of pain pills with some vodka but schooled his face so no one knew there was anything wrong. Sweat ran down his body but not only from the heat.

Trey watched Russ move in on Alexander, put his right hand around the boy's throat, and lift him up on his feet. "Now you listen. Listen carefully. Darlene Vance is my sister."

Alexander dug his nails into Russ's hand, trying to loosen the grip. He struggled to breathe, his eyeballs bulged from their sockets, and his face turned red. He tried to push Russ away but his efforts were useless.

Trey had never seen Russ so angry. He fought the urge to step in. Every few seconds he scanned the area, making sure they were still alone.

With his left hand, Russ threw a single punch to the boy's breadbasket, and then turned him loose. Alexander bent over, arms across his abdomen, choking. He went down on his knees and bent till his head was almost on the wood planks of the porch.

"Before I'm done, all three of you'll wish you were dead," Russ said.

Strickland was only a couple feet away and said, "Man, if Jax finds out we talked, we'll *be* dead."

"Finds out what?" Trey said, glaring at both of them. "We were never here."

Chapter Forty-Eight

GEMINI TAYLOR
Taylor Residence
Raven Bayou, LA

Wednesday Evening, 8 June 2005

THE SKY GLOWED with fiery colors, deep oranges and flaming reds peeked through the trees. They mimicked Gem's emotions. A million things to do before Trey picked her up. A million things to think about.

Gem hadn't been out to a club in years, and though this would be on the job, she looked forward to being with Trey in a social setting. A voice echoed in her head. *Imagine spending the whole night with Trey....Stop that!*

She shook her head to push more complete, more intimate ideas of her and Trey aside.

If they were successful tonight, they might catch a real sadistic bastard. Jax Boudreaux raped and beat Endri Cheramie, but proving it was going to be hard.

Someone viciously murdered Michael Grant. Was skinny little Jamison Boudreaux strong enough to commit such a vicious murder? Was his affection for Ilene strong enough to send him that far?

They didn't even know if Jax would be there. This could all be for nothing. Yet Gem sensed he would be, and that before this night was over, she would face him. And she hoped it was a good thing.

Her head started to pound a little, and a vivid picture of a brain tumor flashed behind her eyes. Maybe if the headaches didn't ease, she'd see a doctor.

She tossed her gun in the evening clutch along with a white hankie and a breath spray. Next she dropped everything else they might need for the night into the medium-sized leather bag she carried everywhere she went.

By the time she was ready, stars sparkled in the indigo sky. The night air was soft and humid. She opened the front door. Too antsy to stay inside waiting, she grabbed the bag, locked the door, and walked down the drive.

From anywhere on her land the view was open and distant. But standing in the dark, Gem's mind played tricks on her. The darkness created walls she couldn't see, pressing in on her like a crowd in a small elevator. Smells overwhelmed her. Coppertone suntan oil. The pungent odor of sweaty clothing. The sickening stench of rancid road kill.

A shudder ran down her spine. She took a few steps. A light from a house down the road came into view. With that marker as her wall, she breathed easier. When Trey rolled up in his oversized Hummer, she would be ready for whatever the night would bring.

Chapter Forty-Nine

TREY FONTAINE
En route to Taylor Residence
Raven Bayou, LA

Wednesday Night, 8 June 2005

TONIGHT HAD TO WORK or they'd lose any chance of catching Jax Boudreaux. Assuming he was guilty. Assuming he was at the club. Assuming Taylor found a way to bait him.

Trey's mind churned with facts and feelings. Not enough of one, but too much of the other. One side of Trey yearned for the kind of relationship his parents had when he was young. But the other side, the logical side, knew that kind of relationship is rare. And Trey had no time to pursue it. Not now.

Nearing a Y in the road, he hooked a right and followed the seldom-used road at the edge of the woods to Taylor's street.

His mind whirled with what Taylor could say or do to set Jax off. Anything that pushed his "inferiority" button would do. Especially in front of his friends. Surely, Jax would be at the Star-Lite tonight. Where else would a rich young man be on a night off?

It was simple enough for minors to get in the club. This was not Washington or Los Angeles. Trey'd spent many a night at the Star-Lite long before turning twenty-one.

Taylor came into sight, standing on the side of the road. He hopped out of the SUV, his feet heavy as he strode toward her.

He'd heard of people seeing "a vision," or calling a lover that, but until now it had just been words. Taylor stood before him in a clingy black dress, her hair pulled up to reveal a slender neck and nicely rounded...everything.

"I know it's not supposed to be a date, but I don't usually pick up women on the side of the road."

She smiled. "I got bored and decided to take a little walk."

Trey offered his arm like a gentleman. Taylor smiled, bent to pick up a brown bag, and walked with him to the passenger side of the Hummer. He managed to beat her to the door, open it, and then pressed a button on the inside of the door. An electric running board slid out.

She pulled a small, black, beaded bag out of the larger leather one and turned to him. "Could you throw that in the back for me?"

Trey took the bag, surprised at its weight as he opened the rear door, and put the bag on the seat. By the time he returned his attention to

Taylor, she had one foot on the running board and was looking for a handhold, her black dress hugging creamy upper thighs. It was going to be a long night.

Putting his hands on her waist, he lifted her onto the running board and enjoyed the view while she squirmed into the seat. He looked down at her shoes. Black heels with some kind of string tied up around her ankles. Dust lent a shadowy look to them.

"Here. Let me clean those off," he said and used his bare hands to wipe the light powder of dust from the black suede. It was all he could do to keep his fingers from scaling those long legs.

When she'd settled herself, he closed her door and climbed into the driver's side.

Taylor rubbed her temples.

"Headache?"

She nodded. "They seem to be bad lately. I took something just before you arrived. I should be fine in a little while." She wiped her hands down the dress. Trey didn't know if she was attempting to dry sweaty palms or stretch the dress down her thighs.

"Think we can do any good tonight?"

Taylor didn't answer, didn't even look his way.

Popping the console open, he pulled out the recorder and handed it to her. He didn't have a warrant to use it, but the worst that could happen was that it would be thrown out as evidence, and Trey had learned that covering your butt was reason enough to record an incident. He could always toss the recorder if it wasn't useful. As long as there was no expectation of privacy, a wire was good on duty or not, though the Bureau considered its agents on duty all the time. How the Sheriff's department would look at it was questionable. Russ and Taylor could deal with that if and when it came up.

Taylor sat, looking at it like something from outer space. "Don't look at me," he said. "I have no idea where you're going to put it."

He tried not to watch as she reached down the front of her dress and made room for the three-inch long plastic case; he sent a quick prayer that one day he'd be reincarnated as a bra.

It took less than five minutes to reach the club. As they pulled into the valet parking area, his mindset changed. This was what it was all about. The job. It was what his dad had loved. It was what Trey loved. He gave Taylor a quick glance. "Ready?"

She nodded, but didn't look ready. Her face paled and her breathing became fast and shallow. Trey detected a tremor in her hand as she smoothed her hair.

"You'll be fine," he said. "Here we go."

Chapter Fifty

GEMINI TAYLOR
Star-Lite Club
Raven Bayou, LA

Wednesday Night, 8 June 2005

"A MILLER LITE DRAFT," Trey said and turned to Gem.

"A Screwdriver."

The crowd was rowdy despite the early hour.

Trey leaned close. "See any familiar faces?"

Gem shrugged to avoid shouting an answer and took a sip of her drink. It was stronger than she liked. They needed to look like they were off duty, which they kinda were because the boss hadn't authorized this little mission. But ordering non-alcoholic drinks would make the barmaid suspicious. They'd just have to sip slowly and carefully.

Trey put his mug to his lips and barely took a sip. Gem, on the other hand, thought maybe one drink added to the pill she took for her head might make the pain go away. Just one wouldn't make her drunk, and if she didn't get this headache under control, she'd get sick and most certainly draw attention.

She didn't sip daintily, but took a long pull on her straw. It burned a little when it hit her stomach. Within minutes the hot burn turned into warmth, flooding her body and easing the pounding in her head.

Trey studied the crowd and she kept an eye on the door. They hadn't been there thirty minutes when Coleman came in and sat at the bar. She couldn't remember ever having seen him dress casual. In a suit, Russ looked bulkier, but the casual clothes showed he was actually pretty lean, just a small spare tire around his middle. His clothes were a little outdated. He looked the part of a man going through a divorce. Or widowed.

Trey ordered another round. A terrible pain hit her between the eyes. She closed them, hoping this wasn't going to turn into a migraine from hell.

Chapter Fifty-One

RUSS COLEMAN
Star-Lite Club
Raven Bayou, LA

Wednesday Night, 8 June 2005

RUSS HAD NEVER been inside the Star-Lite Club, except for an alcohol poisoning case eight years ago. The truth was, very few blacks ever went there unless they were invited and accompanied by a white. A black man Russ's age, wearing a suit to a club...No, that wouldn't work. He had hunted through the closet and came up with black slacks and an ivory-colored shirt. It was the last shirt he remembered Julie buying for him. A lightweight fabric. Cool to the touch. He ran his hand over it, remembering. To top everything off, he wore the gold neck chain holding an ivory-looking flat stone with a tiger carved on it. A gift from Julie on their fifth wedding anniversary.

The past couldn't be changed. With a hard swallow, he'd finished dressing and attached the holster under his waistband to hold a small pistol against his belly.

He threw his small go bag in the back seat and backed the T-bird out of the garage. He pushed in a CD, the smoky voice of Anita O'Day with a sax behind her, and headed for the Star-Lite Club.

There were two lots, one for self-parking and the other for valet. He drove into the self-parking lot and pulled in beside an Explorer.

The music coming from inside shook the windows of the T-bird. The noise of the crowd standing around outside wasn't much better. Most of the partiers were young and white. He scooted around the edge of the crowd and made his way through the mob near the door.

The room was dark, with small lights hanging from the ceiling like stars, and smoke thick enough to give everyone in the place lung cancer and leave plenty for the next crowd. A whiff of pot drifted through now and again.

The dance floor was full, just like the tables. He found a stool at the bar and ordered a beer on tap. The bartender was a slender brunette wearing a pleated-front shirt and bow tie. Even in the neon and star lights he recognized her. "CORA," the nametag said. It was the same one she'd worn at the Rusty Badge.

"Did you quit the grill?" he asked.

She shook her head. "It's just a couple days a week."

Cora took his money and slid a cold mug to him with a half smile. Russ swiveled around to get a full picture of the club. In one corner, a group of young couples sat together, among them one black couple. They appeared to be having fun. It took a while before he spotted Trey and Taylor.

They looked to be an average couple, except Taylor looked as young as the first time he ever saw her. He watched them for a few minutes. Taylor looked all excited, tugging Trey onto the dance floor, Trey wearing an amused grin.

Russ checked his watch. Twenty-one-ten hours. An off-duty deputy was at the hospital. There wasn't much time for getting close to people. As far as he could see, his being here wouldn't help at all. None of these young white people would give him any information or trust him enough to share anything. Maybe Trey and Taylor would have some luck.

Turning back to the bar and the mirrored wall, he came face-to-face with Cora. Her familiar face made him much more comfortable.

"Looking for someone?" Her eyes were on him as she scooped up money from the customer beside him.

He soaked in her gray eyes, her heart-shaped face, her full lips. It took him a minute to remember he hadn't answered her question. "Just needed to get out and relax." He sipped his beer.

"Let me know when you're ready for more." She offered a small smile, and he thought she was a little friendlier than at the Rusty Badge. She rushed around like a chicken with its head cut off, serving one customer after another and he wondered if she really even recognized him, or looked at him.

Russ leaned over his beer and tried to keep his mind on finding Jax Boudreaux. But when he looked up at Cora, a flash in her eyes curled his lips into a smile before he sipped again.

"I work with a young man named Jax Boudreaux. Thought I'd see him here tonight."

Cora's smile disappeared, replaced with a furrowed brow and narrowed eyes. She walked away. Ten minutes passed before a bartender returned to get Russ another beer. A man with no nametag. And no smile.

When he finished the second beer, Russ stood and moseyed toward the men's room. The smell of pot was stronger and the group hanging out at the bathroom door had a bad case of the giggles. Russ didn't think any of them looked clear-headed enough to understand a joke that funny.

After elbowing his way through the young men, he used the toilet, and then skirted the edge of the club. He leaned a shoulder against the wall and watched the crowd for another thirty minutes, finally deciding this was a stupid idea. Russ figured there might be four people in the club who would even speak to him, and two of them were Trey and Taylor.

The thing he did learn was that Taylor could really dance and even Trey showed a little rhythm. And that the bartender didn't talk about Jax. Neither one had anything to do with Endri's attack. Or Darlene's.

He'd stood all he could of the loud music and smoke. Heading back to the door, he finally made eye contact with Trey and shook his head before leaving.

Outside, the crowd still collected, some standing around the door, but mostly sitting on the hoods or trunks of vehicles, drinking and smoking and making out. Walking slowly toward the parking lot, he spied a woman down the block.

A streetwalker. They saw everything. Especially this one.

Russ passed the lot and leaned a shoulder against a brick wall, slipping his hands in his pockets, eyeing the street casually. She took the bait and a few minutes later moved to a couple yards of him, pretending he didn't exist while showing off her goods. She always was good at this game.

The red leather mini skirt showed off long legs and a red halter-top pressed her big breasts together. Her skin looked smooth and soft. She was darker than Julie, but very pretty for a hooker, especially one her age. Bonbon had started working this same six-block area the year Russ became a detective.

"Sure is hot tonight," he said.

Bonbon looked around at him before responding, "Sure is, Honey. What you doing out here 'stead of enjoying the A/C and booty in that fine e-stab-lish-ment?" She broke down the word into its parts. He winced. Bonbon always talked a little too loud.

"Too noisy and crowded in there for me. And with all those people, the air ain't all that cool either. I'm Russ. What's your name?" He turned toward her, his back against the wall. They'd played this game before. Once too often.

"They call me Bonbon, Honey, 'cause I'm a cho-co-late de-lite." She smiled. "You on the job tonight?"

Russ grinned at Bonbon and shook his head. "Just killing some time. Do I look that much like a cop?" The stucco of the building bit into his back, but he didn't move.

"Damn straight. But you look like a friendly one." Bonbon glanced up and down the sidewalk. The crowd still hung all around the club, spilled into the parking lot and street, but no one paid them any mind.

"You waiting for something special to happen?" Bonbon looked him up and down, one hand resting on her jacked out hip.

"I have friends inside, but I don't really want to spend the evening with them." His hand jangled the keys in his right pants pocket.

"What'd you have in mind?" She tilted her head down, looking through her upper lashes, a cat smile on her face.

"We need to talk," he said quietly.

"With all these people watching? You serious?"

"It's important."

"Okay, but make it look good, Honey."

"Let's go," he said and gripped her upper arm. He lead her roughly to his car, opened the back door, snatched cuffs from his bag, tossed her bag on the trunk, and cuffed her hands behind her. "I wanted to let you know how Endri is doing and to ask for your help," he almost whispered.

He saw her tense up like a deer in headlights. She was so still, he couldn't tell if she was breathing. Finally he knew she wasn't going to ask any questions. He pushed her against the car. "Stay there," he said loud enough for anyone interested in his activity.

"Endri's fine," he said as he made a show of searching her. "I saw her yesterday. But she's not telling about what happened. He's young and dark-haired and might have been in a small, gray pickup."

"That's the damn description of half the people on this street, Honey. And there's lots a gray pickups around."

"It was Jax Boudreaux. The bastard nearly killed her. Who knows where he'll go or who he'll do next. I need some help on this."

"You need to let this be before somebody dies. You know how things work. Cain't go pushing around the wrong folks." And then louder, "What's your gig tonight? You want to spend some time with me, you don't gotta take me in."

"Like I'd spend money on you." His back was to the crowd. He smiled, knowing Kiana understood the game.

Russ lowered his voice again. "I promised I'd look after her, Kiana. Some bastard almost killed her."

"Ain't no Kiana here. And Endri ain't my concern. Let it be." She hung her head.

"So you're never going to tell me why you gave her away? You knew I'd make sure you had the money to raise her." Russ said as he picked up her bag and emptied it on the trunk.

He heard her sniffle before saying, "Been enough pain gone around. No need for more. Let it be, Russell."

He refilled her bag, including the pot pipe and a small bag of weed. He could see her tearing up. With his body hidden behind the car, he pulled two twenties out of his wallet and slipped them into her hand as he removed the cuffs.

"Nice doing business with you, Honey," she said sarcastically as she walked away, her hips dancing under the tight skirt.

He heard her cussing like a sailor as she got closer to the crowd, but mostly they all ignored her.

Russ thought of going back inside to tell Trey and Taylor to give it up, but just as he opened his car door, Cora walked around the corner. She crossed the parking lot to an old rusty Firebird, a cigarette hanging between her lips.

When she tried to start it, the car just moaned. Her fist came down on the steering wheel, giving it a good beating. Russ didn't think that would convince it to cooperate.

"Anything I—"

She jumped, her eyes turning into deep steel saucers. "Shit!"

"Sorry. Didn't mean to scare you. Just wondering if I can help?" Russ took a step back and slid his hands in his pockets, showing her he had no ideas about attacking.

Throwing open the door, she stomped to the front of the car and jerked the hood up. Russ followed slowly, giving her space.

Cigarette still hanging out of her mouth, Cora kept an eye on him while trying to jimmy the cables to the battery. She then made a wide path around him, climbed back in, and tried again. It didn't even moan this time. "Bastard's screwed up. Won't be going anywhere tonight." She stepped out, slammed the door, and hung her head back over the engine.

"Can I take you somewhere?"

She came out from under the hood, back straight, looking like a scared puffer fish.

Russ pulled out his ID. "I'm a cop." He hoped to make her comfortable accepting a ride.

"You think I don't know that?" With a headshake, she leaned against the car. "So, what now? You want to search the car? Pat me down?"

"Whoa—I'm not on duty. Just saw a lady in distress and thought I'd come to the rescue."

A hearty laugh worked its way up her throat, and she took another deep draw on the cigarette before flicking it onto the ground and rubbing a black boot into it.

"It's been a long night." It sounded like an apology. Slamming down the hood, she reached through the driver's door window and grabbed her purse. Finding another cigarette, she lit it and looked up at him expectantly.

"You're not going to lock it up?"

"Piece a shit's not worth stealing."

Russ shrugged and placed a hand on Cora's back, guiding her to his car. A look of surprise crossed her face, and another when he opened the passenger door and waited for her to get in.

"Mind if I smoke?" She motioned to the inside of the car. Russ shrugged and closed the door behind her.

"Where to?" he asked as he buckled up.

"Boudreaux Stables on Old Latree Road." Cora inhaled another lungful of smoke.

"Seatbelt, please."

Cora's body molded to the bucket seat. She reached around and grabbed the buckle, pulled it across her body, and snapped it in place. Then she took the cigarette out of her mouth and exhaled enough smoke to kill them both.

"You live at Boudreaux's place?" He pulled out onto the main street.

"I work mornings in exchange for a room in the barn." She blew smoke out her nose and crossed her legs, bouncing the top foot in time to some beat Russ couldn't hear.

He tried to keep his cool while driving toward enemy territory. "You work with horses and tend bar?" The traffic signal turned red as he eased into the turn lane.

"I turn stalls, feed, water and groom the horses, repair tack. With this being summer, the only horse in the barn is one with an injury, so it don't take long. Then I work a few hours as a waitress at the Rusty Badge before my shift at the club."

"Really? And in your spare time?"

She ignored him, lit another cigarette from the butt, and then tossed it out the window. "If I have spare time—I think. Thinking is useless. Idle hands are the devil's tool."

They were silent until Russ turned onto Old Latree Road.

"About another mile, on the right." Cora blew smoke out the window.

Russ knew exactly where Boudreaux lived and where the stables were. He slowed and turned onto the dirt drive and followed the white wooden fence, keeping his wheels on the worn tire trails spread by a wide swath of grass. His heart beat faster than normal, like he expected something to happen.

"There." Cora pointed to the barn.

He parked and went around to let her out, closing the door behind her. Again she looked surprised at his manners. He leaned against the car.

"Thanks for the ride. You can come in, if you want." She headed for the door.

"No, I...shouldn't bother you."

She turned to face him, cigarette hanging from her lips. They were pretty lips. Cora smiled, and then walked in, leaving the door open.

He balked like a wild pony. Found his wedding ring with the fingers of his right hand. Twisted it. No, he wouldn't go in. No point in it.

Instead he went to the driver's side of the car. Fingers on the handle, he looked over the top of the car to the barn door. Leaving it open like that wasn't safe. He went to close it. But he didn't. Pulling his cell from his pocket, he dialed Wilke's number.

"I might run a little late. You got someone to cover from midnight till oh-three-hundred?"

"I can get someone, but that'll leave you to cover until tomorrow night. Do you have enough people for that?"

"Yeah. Thanks, Wilkes."

Inside, bare light bulbs hung from the ceiling down the center of the long barn. It smelled cleaner than he remembered barns smelling. A horse nickered. Checking out the inside, he saw an office to his right and another room to his left. Both doors stood open, but no light came from the office.

He walked to the room where the light came from and stopped. There wasn't much to see, other than Cora. The room was bare. So was she. The woman lay on the bed naked, facing the door, stretching to crush out a cigarette in the ashtray. The look on her face said she knew he would stay. She was right.

Chapter Fifty-Two

TREY FONTAINE
Star-Lite Club
Raven Bayou, LA

Wednesday 11:59 Hours, 8 June 2005

TREY TRIED to keep his gaze moving, to pay attention to the little groups of people who hung together, but every now and then he had to take another look at the striking woman at his table.

Her headache must have faded because she appeared to be enjoying the drink and music. Russ had arrived, stayed for almost an hour, and then signaled his intention to leave. Still no sign of Jax. Taylor had forced him to dance. He was glad to be back at the table.

He turned his attention to a small group of young men who laughed together in the corner. "Excuse me," he told Taylor. "I need to hit the john. I'll be right back." He moved through the crowd slowly and made his way to the other side of the dance floor. In the corner near the hall he hit pay dirt. One of the young men stood behind another, pointing toward the crowd.

"Go for it, Jax. Show 'em how it's done." The speaker was Scott Alexander. The instigator laughed and tossed back a drink as Trey moved through them and past the Armani-wearing Jax to the door of the men's room down the hall. Nick Strickland took one look at Trey and averted his gaze. He didn't say a word.

Trey looked into Jax's eyes and traveled back in time to twenty years ago. He was the image of his older brother Monty. The resemblance hadn't been so obvious when Jax was in uniform and wearing a hat that shaded his face. Trey had never really looked at Jax Boudreaux. Until now. He stepped into a stall long enough to dry swallow a Lortab before making his way back through the crowd. At the table, Jax hovered over Taylor.

"Excuse me," Trey said, and the dark-haired Jax turned toward him. He had to crane his neck to look Trey in the eye.

"Is there a problem?" Trey asked Taylor, his eyes still on the intruder.

"No problem. This little boy was just leaving." Taylor's stare was cold and dark.

Jax threw one last dagger with his eyes before straightening shoulders and walking away. Standing with his groupies, he turned to face the table again. His buddies howled with laughter. A scowl crossed his face as he glared at Trey, and then Taylor.

Trey regained his seat, grinning gleefully at the group when suddenly Taylor's hand landed on his thigh. She was all but sitting in his lap, her cold anger gone, and in its place, intense heat.

"Let's dance." She laced her fingers into his. She stood and tugged gently. It didn't take much to convince him.

On the dance floor, she moved like liquid to the fast music. Trey made eye contact with Jax for a second before bringing his attention back to Taylor.

In her heels she was a tad taller than he, and when she stepped in close enough for their bodies to touch, Trey forgot about Jax, Russ, their mission to find bad guys, his career. He even forgot about the wound on his butt.

Taylor turned away from him, and then backed up until her gyrating body did more than touch him. Her hands reached behind her, wrapped around his hips to pull him closer.

Time stopped as he worked at gaining enough control to put his hands on her waist and turn her around. He willed his body into submission and leaned in close. "Did you get anything?"

The look on her face said she didn't have a clue what he meant. He took her hand and pulled her off the dance floor and back to their table. The beer he'd been sipping called to him. He picked up the glass and took a gulp.

"Come on, let's dance," Taylor said in a whine.

"We need to talk," Trey said seriously, but his face broke into another grin as he looked into her eyes. "You're too distracting."

She leaned into him, her eyes somewhere far away.

"Taylor," he almost shouted. She brought her gaze around to him, and then moved a few inches away.

"Did you get anything?" he repeated.

Her gaze swept the room. She could have been looking for a lost dog. Then her face hardened. She leaned close again, this time avoiding the body contact. "I think I pissed him off."

She took another big swig of her drink, finishing it, and shook the ice cubes. He obligingly took the empty glass and headed for the bar. The server brushed against him with a smile and Trey ordered Taylor's drink. "I'll bring it to you, Honey."

He returned to the table and sat, sending a cautious gaze around the room again.

Jax and his two boys had faded toward the back of the crowd. The drink arrived. Trey tossed a generous tip on the table but ignored the buxom server, his mind once more on the job.

"We wanna dance," Taylor said and stuck the straw between her lips.

Trey leaned close. "No, we don't. Alexander is here with Jax and Strickland." Trey tried to watch the crowd but finally gave up when Taylor drew his earlobe into her warm mouth. A shiver went down his spine. He knew there was no point in continuing the charade.

Keep your head in the game, he told himself. *This is no time to get caught up in a relationship. No time for romance, love, marriage.* But what she was doing to his body had nothing to do with a relationship.

"Taylor, knock it off." He pulled his attention back to the three young men in the crowd. She didn't seem to take him seriously.

What brought his thoughts down the relationship path he couldn't begin to guess. Was it their earlier kiss? It was obvious Taylor wanted him. He was just making more out of this than it really was. He could handle any situation. Except for one small issue. This was Gemini Taylor, the most beautiful girl in the world. This was the person who'd changed his life on Old Cypress Road. The one who made his friends look at him in a new light. Girls suddenly paid more attention to him. He became different. He thought differently. He walked differently. And now here she was, on him like a cat in heat. He had to think back. *When did that kiss happen? Was I thirteen? No. Daddy died six weeks before my birthday. I was still twelve when Gemini Taylor became the one my universe revolved around.*

He wasn't sure what had gotten into her and couldn't decide whether he liked it or not. *Oh, I like it alright. Too much. And not here. And not now.*

It was time to give up for the night, get the hell out of there and deal with Jax later. But when Trey took her hand, he saw her gaze sweep slowly over the crowd as her lips constantly drew liquid through the straw. Something was up. She wasn't drunk. This was a ruse.

"I don't see them," she said. "Let's dance." She tugged at his hand but he didn't budge. Instead he tried to think. Taylor had already put Jax down in front of his friends. Then it dawned on him that she wanted to be on the dance floor so she could keep an eye on Jax and his buddies. Maybe taunt him.

Trey twined his fingers through hers and pulled her out on the floor. Though she appeared to be into the music, her dancing was much more subdued than before.

He noticed her gaze turn toward the back wall where the hallway led to the rest rooms and back exit. After several glances in that direction, she said, "I need to go," nodding toward the hall marked with signs for restrooms and phones. "Be right back." She swept her lips against his, and then headed toward the ladies room.

Trey sat back down, his pants too tight in the crotch for comfort. He sipped the last of his drink and looked around the crowd. Beautiful women filled the room, but none as gorgeous as Taylor.

Pain throbbed in his groin and he shifted, bumping his butt against the back of the chair. One pain was replaced with another and he held his breath to avoid yelling in agony.

He couldn't hear himself think over the loud music. Looking toward the hallway, he couldn't see past the crowd on the dance floor. Restless, he walked back toward the bathrooms.

"Ready for a refill, darling?" the server asked.

He shook his head. What was taking Taylor so long to return? He stood, hoping to see over the dancers. All he managed was an occasional glimpse of the other side, a few blond heads, and the signs pointing toward the restrooms.

A few minutes ticked by before he decided to head in that direction and wait for Taylor at the near end of the hall. But before he made it halfway through the crowd, he saw a swarm of people running away from the restrooms in panic. As he got closer he heard their screams.

Trey pressed through the river of bodies emptying into the ocean of people already gathered at that end of the room. When he finally made it through to the hall, he found it empty. Taylor was nowhere in sight.

Rushing to the ladies' room, he threw the door open. His heart jumped into his throat. Leaning against the stall post, stood Taylor. Her hands clutched a Glock. A few feet away on the floor lay the still body of Jax Boudreaux.

Chapter Fifty-Three

GEMINI TAYLOR
Star-Lite Club
Raven Bayou, LA

Thursday 12:02 a.m., 9 June 2005

COMPLETELY ALONE, Gem maintained her position. Gun trained on Jax Boudreaux, though she knew he was dead. Her elbows ached from their almost hyper-extended angle, locked in position, her hands grasping the Glock so tightly they hurt.

Tears ran down her cheeks, hot against the cold of her face from the A/C.

Boudreaux's fancy blue Armani shirt had a new design, a purple blossom the size of a magnolia bloom and growing, the center pulled into the pulpy hole. Blood pooled in the hole, vibrating with the slowing heartbeat. It reminded her of the scene in *Jurassic Park* when the camera focused on a puddle of water rippling with each step of the giant dinosaur. She struggled to keep the pistol trained on him though the shaking made it difficult. The barrel of the gun bounced up and down unsteadily.

She sensed more than heard someone come in. She knew then that she'd heard nothing since the blast of the pistol. All the noise of the club had disappeared.

"Taylor." It was Trey, his voice soft.

She didn't take her eyes from the man on the floor. The vibration of the puddle of blood had stopped. The pooled blood slowly leaked from the hole, leaving chunks of flesh visible.

"Taylor. It's all right. You can put the weapon down." His voice wavered.

She didn't agree. Her gun remained trained on Boudreaux.

"Taylor. It's over. Give me the gun."

She tore her gaze from the body on the floor for a quick glance at Trey, and then whipped her head back around and refocused. The man hadn't moved. "He's not going to lock me up!"

"No, Taylor. He's not. He's dead. No one is going to lock you up anywhere. You're safe now. Give me the weapon."

It sounded like he was getting closer, but she was afraid to look. Afraid the man lying in front of her would get back up and try again to force her into the tiny metal cubicle.

"It's alright, Taylor. I'm coming over there. Just take it easy."

She heard him take a step. Then another. Her body shook, knees weak. She leaned harder into the metal post of the bathroom stall.

Then Trey was beside her, his warm breath on her ear. His body threw off heat and she wanted nothing more than to curl up in his arms, against his solid chest, and be safe.

His hand trembled against her shoulder, and then her whole body started. She thought for a minute he was afraid too. Maybe he didn't really know if Jax was dead. Maybe he was lying to her.

"No one's going to hurt you, Taylor," he said softly in her ear. The fingers of his left hand slid slowly down her arm. Her heart thumped harder. Her hands tightened on the gun. His fingers stopped at her wrist. His breath touched her cheek as he whispered, "You're okay, Sweetie. You can relax now. He's dead. No one's gonna hurt you."

His other hand moved slowly around her back and pulled her away from the metal support, her left shoulder pressing hard against his chest. His heart pounded against her and she smelled the fear on him.

She leaned into him and his left hand pressed gently down on the barrel of the gun. She didn't have the strength to resist. Her grip eased and the gun slipped away from her.

She took one final look at the body on the floor. It still hadn't moved. Trey wrapped both arms around her and turned her face into his neck. She sobbed and shook uncontrollably.

She heard voices. Someone said to call 9-1-1, but it wouldn't help. She'd watched Boudreaux's soul leak from his eyes.

Why are they shouting?

Trey led her out of the bathroom and down the hall. Deputies. Leather squeaking. Other noises. The crowd faded into the background until the club was empty except for uniforms and a few employees.

Trey tried to get her to sit, but she didn't want to leave the safety of his arms. She sensed another person nearby, and then heard his voice.

"What happened?" It was Lieutenant Loe's voice.

"She went to the bathroom. He followed her in and attacked her. She shot him." Trey answered as if he'd been there. Again, she was aware of the trembling of his body and his hands.

"Where's her weapon?"

That was the last thing she heard. Her knees gave way. Her mind went blank.

SHE AWOKE on the floor, leaning against the wall, still in Trey's arms.

His hand stroked her hair, and he held her close. "You fainted. Everything's gonna be okay. I promise. Just relax."

"I killed him? He's dead?"

"Don't worry. You'll be cleared." He turned his cold lips to her forehead and kissed it. "I gave your weapon to Loe."

I killed a man. Actually killed him. I took a life. Her stomach churned. She put a hand to her mouth. "I'm gonna be sick," she whispered through her fingers.

"Get me a wet towel and a trash can," Trey commanded a young deputy, and the man rushed to do his bidding.

He pressed the icy wet rag on her throat and set the small trashcan near her, pushed stray strands of hair back and wiped her face and neck. "Just relax, Sweetie."

The white rag turned an ugly color, a dirty, red clay kind of color. She looked down, and even in the dimness of the room she could see spots of blood all over her.

She was dirty and sticky. And sick. Covered in blood. She shook uncontrollably and struggled to breathe. "Get it off! Get it off!"

"You're okay, Sweetie. Here, let me..." Trey wiped at the blood, trying to calm her, but she wanted to scream, to run. She wanted to jump in a river and stay there for hours. She couldn't stop the violent shaking, the rising panic.

"Take a breath," Trey said. "You're gonna be fine." He finished wiping her neck and face, tossed the rag aside, and held her.

She didn't know how long they sat there, but it was long enough for Barlow to arrive. The CSU team. Internal Affairs. The Captain. Brass was everywhere. She wondered when Coleman would arrive. How could she ever again think about Coleman's mistake? It surely was not worse than what she just did.

Even through the crowd she could smell the body. The urine and feces, and the other odor that always follows death. Her logical mind said it didn't come that fast, but her nose insisted it smelled the odor of rotting flesh.

She tried to figure out what had happened, how she'd ended up here. She remembered coming to the club with Trey to help Russ. Then something happened. She'd been distracted. More than once. One instant she was on the dance floor, the next she was sitting on the toilet, dress hiked up around her waist, panties bunched around her knees, Jax Boudreaux standing over her.

She couldn't remember what he'd said to her, but she clearly remembered what she said to him. "Why don't you go back to your little buddies? You wouldn't know what to do with me."

She had stood, straightened her dress, the bastard still standing where the stall door belonged. *Then what happened? Damn it! Think!*

Head pounding, she shivered with cold.

Trey asked a deputy for a blanket. "You'll be fine. You're just in shock," he said as he wrapped it around her.

The noise around them echoed in her head. She squeezed her eyes shut tight, trying to block out the light, the past hour, the horrible thing she'd done. He was just a boy. Had his whole life ahead of him. And she killed him.

The blanket helped. She sat back against the wall, tears streaming. *If he'd just not tried to trap me. I could've handled his hands on me, could even have handled his nasty remarks. But when he wouldn't let me out...*

"I'll need a statement, Taylor."

It was the lieutenant.

She opened her eyes and looked up at him. His gold shield shone against the black leather holder tucked in his belt.

"I'm ready." She started to move.

"No, you're not." Trey held her firmly in place. She let him. She wasn't ready. For anything. She watched as Trey's gaze focused on the lieutenant. "Forty-eight hours. Department policy. You have to give it to her. She's in shock. She needs to go to the hospital."

"No!" She almost puked. *No gurney. No straps. No ambulance.*

He stroked hair back from her face. "How about I drive you?"

She shook her head. "I'm alright. Just a little shaky."

Trey was vertical in one swift move, his hands pulling her up beside him. He walked her to a chair, sat her down, and wrapped the blanket around her shoulders.

Loe called Avlee over. "Get what you need before she goes."

Avlee grabbed her go bag and started working on Gem. She swabbed Gem's hands and dress for gunshot residue, took some blood samples from the blotches on her skin and dress, and scraped under her nails. She took pictures of Gem, a close-up of her shoes, and swabbed for blood on the soles.

Gem watched the cotton swabs being sealed in glass tubes. Avlee took one more swab and wiped Gem's lips. Caked, dried blood stuck to the cotton. As Avlee sealed the swab into a tube, Gem melted into nothingness.

Chapter Fifty-Four

TREY FONTAINE
Star-Lite Club
Raven Bayou, LA

Thursday 01:00, 9 June 2005

TREY HAD WIPED most of the blood spatter from her face, the backs of her hands, as well as her throat and chest. No doubt her dress was spattered with blood too, though it didn't show on the black fabric.

He caught her as she melted out of the chair. Hooking an arm around her back and under her knees, he lifted her. Loe shuffled out of the way and stood back, watching.

"Any luck reaching Russ?" Trey asked.

Loe shook his head. "Paged him. No response yet. We need a blood draw and urine test immediately. One of the IA guys can take her to the hospital."

Typical. Trey grimaced. *He's worried about the department and IA, afraid of the headlines: Drunk Cop Shoots Alton Boudreaux's Son.* "Mind if I drive her? He can follow me." Trey tried to make it sound like a request, but he had no intention of allowing them to put her in a unit.

The lieutenant considered for a moment before turning to speak to Wilkes. "Who's going to the hospital with her?"

"I'm sending Reese."

The lieutenant talked to Wilkes, and then returned his attention to Trey. "Take her to the emergency room. Internal Affairs will take her formal Saturday morning." The lieutenant stood and made his way over to the deputies huddled together.

Pulling his chair close to Taylor, Trey put his hands gently on her face and studied her expression intently. Her eyes were glazed over, her mind probably far away.

"A knife. He had a knife," she whispered.

He carried her out. The valet who'd parked the Hummer took off at a trot and was back in less than a minute, leaving the SUV in the middle of the street. He opened the passenger door and Trey lifted Taylor in.

She was coming around as he buckled her seatbelt. He slid behind the wheel.

The hospital was only a mile away. Officer Angelia Reese walked them in, her go bag hanging from her shoulder. Fortunately it was a slow night and they were taken in immediately. Taylor was awake, but pale and weak like she was dying. A nurse drew her blood, handed her a cup and pointed at the restroom.

"I need to wash up," she said quietly.

Trey looked at the nurse, and then at Officer Reese.

"I'll need to take pictures," the officer said.

"I'll get something for you to wear," Trey said and headed for the SUV.

He returned to find the bathroom door closed. Reese and Taylor had to be inside. Trey knocked and Reese cracked it open enough for him to hand in some clothes.

Taylor came out in a baggy T-shirt, sweats, and heels. Her skin was translucent, her eyes looking off into the distance. Her body shook visibly. Reese came out behind her with an evidence bag in her hand.

As Trey started to pick her up, Taylor began to protest, but there was no fight left in her.

Reese was still talking to the nurse when Trey carried Taylor back to the Hummer. She managed to open the door, but he helped her into the seat and fastened her seatbelt.

Climbing into the driver's side, he took a quick glance her way. Her color had returned, along with a languid smile.

"Glad to see you back. I'll get you home." He started to put the shifter into drive but movement out of the corner of his eye stopped him. She had unfastened her seatbelt and slithered over the console until she lay across him, breasts pressed into his chest, head on his shoulder, and one arm around his neck.

"I don't wanna go home," she whispered.

Thankfully the streets were bare as he drove away from the main part of town, trying to concentrate on driving enough to keep the Hummer on the road and not run over anyone.

He'd seen this before. Experienced it too. Often, after a brush with death, people just want to feel alive. It was a natural response, a desire to prove one was still breathing, still able to feel joy and pleasure.

Memories of lying on a filthy carpet while blood poured from his flesh reminded him how close to death he came. One bullet. A little higher or from a different angle. It only took a second. He could see himself there, the recorder digging into his side where it had been taped. *The recorder!*

"Taylor, did you turn on the tape?"

She ignored him, her lips on his neck.

"Did Reese take the recorder?" he said, his voice not as steady as he would've liked. "Give me the recorder,"

She shifted her weight, pulled at the T-shirt, and stuck her hand in the loose pocket of the sweats.

Handing him the recorder, she reached to her waist and pulled the shirt up over her head. A lacy black bra with no straps barely covered her breasts. As she scooted lower into his lap, he took a deep breath and tossed the recorder onto her seat. Dealing with Taylor and trying to drive, he struggled to maintain control of the SUV. And of himself. He pulled over. With the SUV in park, he gripped both of Taylor's wrists. She looked up with a seductive smile.

"Not this way. Not now."

"Oh, come on, party pooper." She stuck out her lower lip in a pout.

He managed to lift her back across the console and retrieve the shirt. "Put it on and buckle up," he said with all the sternness he could muster.

It took a minute to realize he was holding his breath, fighting to maintain control as she giggled seductively, but just as quickly as it had appeared, the teasing smile vanished and tears welled.

"It's okay, Sweetie. Everything is going to be okay."

She didn't move, didn't make a sound.

"Taylor," he whispered. Her body went rigid. She turned her face away from him.

The recorder. He reached over to the edge of her seat, found the recorder and pressed the rewind button. Nothing. He pressed the play button and the spools started to turn. Again nothing. She'd never turned it on. "Shit."

He spoke softly, cautiously, and placed his hand on her shoulder. "I know it's been a rough night. Things will look better in the morning." She didn't look at him, but neither did she shrug him away. He sighed, dropped his hand and said, "We'd better go. Russ is expecting me."

She turned to face him. "Does he know? Does he know what I did?"

"Maybe. The lieutenant paged him."

This time the tears streamed down her face like rivers. She turned toward the door. Her body shook so hard he could see it from where he sat. "I need to tell him. It's important. He needs to know about the knife."

"Okay, let's go find him."

He wanted to hear that part of the story too. She hadn't explained to him about the knife, but there was something about the way she said the word. Knife. She said it almost lovingly, as if the knife were tied to *her*, not Jax Boudreaux.

Chapter Fifty-Five

GEMINI TAYLOR
En Route to Coleman Residence
Raven Bayou, LA

Thursday 2 a.m., 9 June 2005

THE HUMMER'S A/C stirred the smell of blood. Trey said nothing as he pulled away from the club.

Her gaze went to the fancy dash of the giant toy the FBI agent called Streak. She thought about Trey, the Special Agent. Did he really believe her? Or did he have motives for taking up for her that had nothing to do with her being innocent? She pulled her mind from that thought, yet the only other place for it to go was to Jax.

She fingered the sweats. Goosebumps cropped up on her arms and legs, and she shivered in the now-cold air blowing from vents all around her.

Trying not to be obvious, she glanced at Trey. He turned to smile at her, a gentle half-smile to be sure, but still, it looked sincere.

"Feeling any better?" he asked in a mellow voice.

That wasn't what he really wanted to ask. She could guess his real question: How did it feel to kill someone? Her body shuddered with revulsion.

"Yes," she lied. The truth just wouldn't come out. She was a criminal, a murderer. She couldn't confess that to an FBI agent. Especially not to this one.

She watched his lips part, his tongue wet them. A little jolt of pleasure shot through her and she heard the giggle of a very young woman. Her imagination was getting a little too independent, her mind flip-flopping with emotion.

"Can you tell me what happened?"

Her heart hammered and she stared straight ahead, afraid to look at him. Afraid of what she might see. Her throat constricted. She couldn't will her voice to work.

Her fingers sought the small black bag that should have been lying in her lap and panic filled her when she didn't find it. Then she spotted it lying between her and the console. She'd slipped it from around her neck on her way to the hospital. It was in the Hummer when she was in the bathroom with Deputy Reese.

She pulled it onto her lap and gripped it with an iron fist, her lifeline. Something familiar for her to cling to during a crisis.

The clock on the dash said two-twenty-two. They drove into Coleman's neighborhood. Porch lights cast yellow shadows across dark yards. She was in the Twilight Zone, in a town empty of all life after an alien attack. Only the weird music was missing.

Trey parked in the driveway and led her into Coleman's house. It may as well have been his own. "Coffee?" he asked as she sat at the kitchen table.

She shook her head, still afraid to use her voice.

Trey opened a cupboard and in a blink, returned to stand over her. "Take these." He placed the opened bottle on the table and handed her a glass of water. A generic over the counter sleep aid. Something to take away pain and help her sleep. *Am I in pain? Yes*, she thought. She took the pills obediently and sat there in the quiet, gripping the cold glass like an anchor.

"Where's Coleman?"

Trey shrugged. "Sooner or later he'll be here. How about you get some rest?" Before she could respond, he took the glass from her hands, laced his fingers in hers, and led her to the living room. She sat on the couch and looked down at her feet. Those stupid black heels. She'd put them on again, after dressing in Trey's sweats. He squatted and removed her shoes, his hands warm on her feet. He rubbed them the way one does when trying to warm a cold child.

Then he sat at the other end of the couch and patted his leg, an invitation to lay her head there. She leaned over and laid her cheek on his thigh. He pulled the throw from the back of the couch. It fell across her body.

The only sound was a slight whirl from the A/C. The only light came through the archway to the kitchen. She closed her eyes as Trey's hand gently brushed her hair back from her face.

"I didn't mean to kill him."

"I know," he whispered. "I know."

Her body gave in to the exhaustion and she slept.

The clank of the steel doors closing behind her echoed in her dream. She walked down a long, narrow hall, institutional gray. A cold place. Where was she? She turned to look behind her at the reinforced door, the deputies with no holsters on their belts. The smell of confinement—a mix of sweat, urine, and cleaning products that couldn't mask the staleness of recirculated air. Then she knew.

Prison is no place for a claustrophobic detective. Gem had two strikes against her from the start. Her lungs automatically began to struggle for oxygen, her heart racing as though she were running for her life. *Just keep it together. This is not the place to lose it.*

She passed through all the levels of odor, from the smell of bleach in the ground floor lobby, to the iron and rust scent of the hallway and stairs and into the acrid stench of sweat and urine in the second floor waiting room.

Her name was called. After taking a deep breath, she started up the heavy metal stairs to the third floor, the sound of her black heels reverberating in the deep stairwell.

About halfway up, the steps grew metal hands that grasped her ankles. She screamed. In her attempt to get free, she lost her balance and shrieked again. Her world began to spin, but instead of falling down the stairs, her body was supported by what must have been a half dozen people.

They floated her to the top of the stairs where the guard wanded a blue-light over her hand and read the date stamp she'd received at the sign-in desk.

The sight of the bright, purple-looking bulb made her realize her entire surroundings were like an old movie, black and white. Even the guard herself was gray.

Gem stood still, enjoying the air from the oscillating fan sitting atop the guard's table. Then she opened the door to the room where a long counter divided by glass ran from one end to the other. The door slammed behind her. She was trapped inside, the stale air barely circulating. She willed herself to concentrate on why she was here, to remember she was on the visitor side of the glass, at least for now.

Five stools lined the counter, each bolted to the floor, a partition on either side, phone hanging on the right. This room reeked and for good reason. Two vents high on the wall put out air not much cooler than the temperature outside, a nice humid ninety-two degrees. Gem chose a stool and nervously sat. Not having seen Mama in more than a year, she was anxious to tell her the good news.

Through the glass, she watched. A guard opened the door, a solid metal thing with a six-square-inch window through which prisoners and visitors could be watched. The guard allowed Mama to walk through. The door closed with a bang, vibrating Gem's teeth, though the solid walls stood firm. Sweat beaded along her hairline and tickled her neck. Her head pounded like it might explode at any second.

Mama walked slowly toward the stool opposite, wearing the sleeveless black and white striped jumpsuit, a reminder of the archaic legal practices of the Louisiana State Prison System.

With a smile carefully pasted on her face, Mama sat and picked up the phone receiver. "Did Virginia come with you?"

"No, I'm alone this time."

Mama looked so thin and pale. Her hair had gone gray over the last few years, and all of her teeth had been pulled. Her state-provided dentures reminded Gem of George Washington's dental work. "I can come every week now, Mama."

"You don't have to do that, baby girl." The pasty skin of Mama's hand stretched tightly over her knuckles as she gripped the phone.

Gem heard the guilt in her statement. Mama believed she had cost

Gem enough in her life. "It's okay, Mama. I have good news. Remember when I visited and told you I'd put in an application at the Raven Bayou Sheriff's? Well, I got the job! I'm a detective!" Sweat rolled down Gem's sides to the waistband of her pants.

Mama's brows drew together in a scowl. "I told you not to be doing that. You shouldn't be in that town at all, not living there or working there. Why didn't you stay in Lufkin with Virginia? Or in Dallas? You were doing so good."

Other voices echoed her sentiments. Gem looked around the room. Empty. The skin on her neck tingled like someone had breathed on it.

"Mama, now I can really do something good. Finally I can help you. There's been another murder, Mama. Just like Daddy's." Gem's body sat up straighter of its own accord as a contrary little voice told her to leave it alone. "I won't be able to stay long. You remember Russell Coleman, the detective who investigated Daddy's death? He's my new partner."

Tears welled in Mama's eyes. Gem tried not to look, tried to avert her gaze to the high window behind Mama where bright sky stood out against the dull wall.

Mama cried every time. Gem knew her mama didn't mean to make her feel guilty. *It's just part of my nature to accept responsibility for things that happen around me,* she reasoned. Gem was there in the house at the very time Daddy was killed. *I should've been a witness, should've been able to say, "Mama didn't do it."*

"So, according to your letters, you've been reading a lot." Gem tried to remember to smile and pretend she was happy to be here.

"Never had time to read before...I've learned to enjoy it."

"What do you like to read?"

"Psychology. Sociology. Dream interpretation."

"Dream interpretation?" Gem's heart thumped hard against her breastbone. Mama used to ask her about her dreams. The nightmares that woke the household with her screams. Gem could never remember the details. Only the fear. She watched Mama shift her gaze, afraid of what Gem might see in her eyes.

Mama said nothing.

"When are we going to talk?" Gem leaned toward the glass and noticed a reflection of something behind her. She turned and saw a giant playpen. Three young people played in it.

They all watched her as they sat on the padded floor and leaned against the netted side. The girl and one of the boys smiled at her, but the other, the boy with the wavy dark hair stared out of sad eyes. Gem ignored them and turned back to Mama.

"We talk all the time, Gemini. We're talking now."

"You know what I mean. We haven't had a real conversation in years. Not about the important things. We never really had that talk. Mama, I know you're innocent. If you'd just tell me the truth, maybe we could get you out of here. Why did you confess to a murder you didn't commit?"

Something warm and wet reached Gem's feet and she looked down to find a pool of blood rising above the soles of her black heels. She didn't remember putting those heels on.

She turned and there on the floor laid Jax Boudreaux, his face black and white-gray, his eyes smiling. Gem noticed his glittery watch, but it was on her wrist instead of his.

Her breath caught in her throat. She shut her eyes and tried to scream. Nothing came out.

"Gemini!" her mother yelled into the phone, and Gem opened her eyes. The blood was gone. So was the body. Even the reflection in the glass had disappeared. She turned and looked over her shoulder. The playpen and its occupants had disappeared too, but she could feel their presence.

"You're my daughter, Gemini. My only daughter. I don't want you doing this." Mama's voice lowered, "I'm fine here. This is where I belong. Please, Honey, leave it be." Her eyes shone with tears, but Gem wasn't about to back down. They were talking about Mama's freedom. Gem intended to see this through whether her mama wanted her to or not.

"Mama...Now that I'm a detective, I finally have the resources to work your case. Just tell me what you know, what you saw!"

"My case is closed." Tears poured over her lower lashes, over her high cheekbones. They dripped off her chin. Fear shimmered in her eyes.

It was then that Gem's resolve cemented in her mind. Whatever, or whoever, scared her mama this bad, Gem would find out. And when she learned the truth...

Gem's hands hurt as they strangled the phone receiver. "Mama, you have to tell me. I promise I won't let anyone hurt you."

Mama could be stubborn, but Gem sensed her mama wanted to tell. To finally unburden herself of the truth she'd held in check for so long. There had always been a connection between them. Gem knew what Mama was thinking, and Mama knew Gem's mind. They were two birds who had formed their own flock and moved through the air in tandem, their turns and dips perfectly executed side by side, without communicating.

"Tell me," Gem whispered, gripping the receiver with both hands, the fancy watch so loose on her wrist it clanked against the countertop.

Mama's body shook, wracked with sobs. She squeezed her eyes shut, a river of tears gushing out.

"Tell me," Gem said a little louder into the phone, a little closer to the glass.

"Gemi—" she choked.

Mama hadn't called her Gemi since she'd started kindergarten.

"You know...as much of the truth as I do...maybe more," she said in halting breaths. Tears covered her face and mucus ran from her nose to her lips. With one hand she wiped her face, and then rubbed the hand along the leg of her jumpsuit. Her scowl returned. She stood. The phone disappeared from her hand. Next went the glass, and then the counter.

Gem grew dizzy as the room changed. When her head cleared, she found herself standing inches from her mother. The wall behind Mama had disappeared too. They were on the ground floor with no wall between the room and the green grass of a beautiful field. They were a few steps from freedom.

Mama swallowed hard and looked Gem in the eye. "We aren't going to talk about this anymore."

"We have to! Don't you under—"

"Here's something for you to understand." Mama's voice lowered but became hard. "If you keep asking about that night, I'm gonna not see you again. The only power I have left is the right to refuse visitors. I'll not have you digging into this, Gemini. You drop it and go on about your life, or don't bother coming back."

What could she say to make Mama see how much Gem needed this? How much she needed it herself? Gem could finally learn what happened that night. And the one person who could help her most would not.

"Mama, whether you help me or not, I'm going to do this. If I can prove someone else killed Daddy, you'll be free. If you'd just—"

"I love you, Gemini...Good-bye." Mama returned the receiver to its hook. She walked silently to the door, never looking back. As the door closed behind her, the walls began to waver.

Gem looked behind her and the wall where the playpen had been was only inches from her. She closed her eyes. Then her gun was in her hand and Jax stood in front of her. A wall pressed against her back. Jax took a step forward, the wall behind him following.

"Back off!" Gem shouted just before she saw the glint of the knife. Then the gun went off.

She blinked and, by some magical power, she was no longer in the prison but lying on a couch with a firm thigh beneath her cheek. The throw lay over her. Under the cover Gem checked both wrists.

But there was no watch.

Chapter Fifty-Six

RUSS COLEMAN
En route to Coleman Residence
Raven Bayou, LA

Thursday, 9 June 2005

RUSS QUIETLY closed the door of the T-bird and started the engine. He watched the main house, hoping no lights would come on, hoping no one would come running with a shotgun.

Creeping slowly down the driveway to the main road, he looked in the rearview a hundred times, hoping to catch one final look-see of Cora before going home.

A quick glance at his ring finger brought a stab of guilt. His gold band was still there, the last reminder of a wonderful marriage. A wonderful life. He was glad to be in the car, a solid piece of metal hiding him from heaven. Had Julie seen through the barn roof? She'd always been able to see inside his heart. Where was his heart an hour ago?

There was no excuse for his actions. He followed Cora into the barn like a dog in heat knowing for sure what he'd find, what he would do.

A shiver ran down his spine. He couldn't help himself. Cora was so full of passion. So giving. So broken. She never spoke a word about her past, but Russ was aware of her pain.

Julie, please forgive me. Father, please forgive me. Cora, please forgive me.

He drove on automatic pilot, not aware that his was the only car on the road. Suddenly he was home. The Hummer sat in the drive behind the Suburban.

When he stepped inside, he saw them. Trey sitting on the couch with Taylor's head on his lap. The serious glint in Trey's eyes said there'd been trouble. Taylor sat up and pulled the throw around her shoulders while Trey turned on the table lamp.

The hair on Russ's neck stood on end. "Darlene? Is it Darlene?" He held his breath.

Trey shook his head and Russ let the breath go.

"I killed him," Taylor said.

"Who?"

"Jax. And Coleman...he had a skinning knife."

Chapter Fifty-Seven

GEMINI TAYLOR
Coleman Residence
Raven Bayou, LA

Thursday, 9 June 2005

"WHAT HAPPENED IN THERE?" Russ asked.

"I was using the toilet when he opened the door on me—"

"You didn't lock it?"

"Never." Even Gem could hear the fear in her voice.

Both men nodded in understanding.

"We said a few words. He grabbed my breasts...I slapped him away..." She tried to remember exactly what had happened, but the vision wasn't clear. Closing her eyes, she concentrated on Jax standing in the doorway. "He grabbed my breasts. I slapped his hands away. I said, 'You're not dealing with a small, defenseless girl now. Back off before I have to hurt you.' He sneered at me, like it was a joke, like *I* was a joke, and leaned against the stall wall..."

GEM SAT in the bathroom stall, Jax Boudreaux blocking her way out.

"You think because you're tall, you're too much woman for me? Or is it the gold shield? Tell you what, why don't we go for a ride? My 'Vette's out back."

"Get the hell outta my way, you little prick." She stood to pull up her panties and straightened her dress. Her heart raced. The walls were closer together than before. She shook, the old fear creeping up.

"We know about Ilene Grant. And also about Cheramie," she said.

Jax Boudreaux's lips curled into an emotionless grin. "I don't know what the hell you're talking about."

"'Move!" she shouted and shoved him, but he was planted hard in her way and, despite his slender build, was stronger than she'd expected.

His shoulders squared and his breathing got faster. "Look, bitch! I don't know who you've been talking to, but if you fuck with me, it'll be the last thing you ever do."

Gem could see the walls close in around them. He was close...too close. She backed away and into the corner of the stall. The walls were getting tighter and tighter...The muffled sound of the music thumping in the lounge beyond only reinforced her sense of being enclosed, but she refused to let him see her scared.

"Get the fuck out of my way!"

Jax leaned in, a big grin on his face. "What's wrong, Taylor? You don't like doing it in public places?"

She shoved him with all her might. He stumbled backward. His feet tangled around themselves so he landed on the floor. She tried to step past him but he caught her ankle and pulled. She went down hard, almost hitting her head on the sink. Instead, it bounced on the floor, making her dizzy.

He climbed on top of her. She heard him say something...a whisper...

The mixture of sweat and urine and aftershave filled her nostrils and panic vibrated in her chest. She fought him off, opened her purse and pulled out the pistol. Getting to her feet, she put her back against the post of the stall and aimed. He lay between her and the door.

"Coleman has a copy of the letter from your file. We know everything."

Not even lying on the ground and looking into the barrel of her Glock could wipe the smug contempt from his face. "You think I'm afraid of you? What? You and that nigger bastard gonna get me in trouble?" He stood, took a step. His hand eased into his pocket, his fancy watch glittering from his wrist.

"Stop!"

Jax smiled and slowly took a knife from his pocket. With one finger he opened the blade, and she saw the gut hook on the end.

"Back off, Boudreaux. Don't make me hurt you." She was completely cornered, the stall post at her back.

"So, there's a letter in my file. She was my teacher. So what? I can make the letter disappear. Hell, I could make *you* disappear."

He was less than three feet away, still blocking her exit, when he stopped. The sneer returned to his face. "Mess with me, bitch, and I'll have you put under the jail. I'll lock you up for so long you'll forget what daylight looks like."

Gem's heart hammered in her ears. "Just back off!"

And then he lunged...

Chapter Fifty-Eight

RUSS COLEMAN
Coleman Residence
Raven Bayou, LA

Thursday, 9 June 2005

RUSS WATCHED TAYLOR close her eyes and stay that way for a few minutes.

"Lieutenant Loe paged you but said you didn't respond. I called your cell. Got the message that it was out of service," Trey said.

Russ looked down at his waistband where his pager belonged. Not there. Then he remembered. When he dressed to go to the club, he left it on the dresser, thought it looked too cop-like with his casual clothes. And when he hung up the cell after talking to Wilkes, he'd turned it off.

Taylor's face was pale. Her brows were drawn together over her puffy eyes. She huddled close to Trey, looking for warmth. Or protection. She was scared. With good reason. Alton Boudreaux's son was dead and she was the shooter.

IA would be all over her soon. Boudreaux would push to have her fired and on trial for murder. As soon as he heard the news, he'd be on the phone with the mayor demanding her arrest.

"Listen to me, Taylor," Russ said.

She looked up at him, and he saw fear and shame fighting in her eyes. "We'll get through this. You didn't do nothing wrong."

"But—"

"No buts. You're a cop, a good one. Your file speaks for itself."

"What if they think you sent me there to kill Jax?"

Russ slid out to the edge of the chair and leaned forward like a catcher at home plate. "Don't worry about me. I can take care of myself. Just tell the truth. You'll be fine. Trey and me, we're here for you. Go home. Get some rest.

Tomorrow you'll need to think this through, but not right now." Russ looked at his watch. "I have to get to Darlene's. You've got my cell number. I won't turn it off again. If anybody from the department calls you or comes to see you, call me. You got that?"

Taylor nodded, the tears almost gone now. He went to the fridge and grabbed a bottle of water, and then returned to the chair.

When he tilted the bottle to his lips, his gaze fell on his wedding ring. Setting his water on the coffee table, he slid the ring up his finger, turned it round and round on the tip, and then gently laid it beside the bottle.

"I have to change before I go." Russ looked at Trey. "Take her home.

Call me if you hear anything."

He went to the bedroom to change. He heard Trey excuse himself and follow. Russ sat on the edge of the bed and slipped off his shoes.

"What's up?"

"Nothing's up. Just have to get to Darlene's."

Russ pulled his belt from the pant-loops, laid it on the dresser, and then dropped his pants and sat. He looked up at Trey as he folded the pants over the back of the small chair near the bed and slipped off his socks.

Trey stayed still, leaning against the doorjamb. "Didn't Julie tell you to get on with your life? Russ...Julie's gone. I know, she was wonderful, and you were madly in love with her, but she's gone. It's been a long time. Did you expect to never have feelings again?"

Trey didn't move, didn't say another word. Russ could take no more. "How did you know?"

"You never take your ring off, not even to wash your hands. Something's up. You've been gone for hours without calling in. Phone's turned off. Your face was grim when you came in, even though you knew nothing of what had happened at the club. And you took off your ring."

Russ rubbed a palm over his head. "There's a new lady in town. I've been out to her place, if you could call it that."

The A/C clicked on and a sudden stream of air brushed his neck, bringing back inappropriate memories. With one quick motion he pulled the shirt over his head and tossed it in the nearby hamper.

"She made me feel alive again for the first time since..." It came out as a faint whisper.

"Good. When do I get to meet her?"

Russ looked at Trey like he'd lost his mind. "Let's not make any wedding plans, Bub."

Trey smiled. "I'll take Gemini home."

Russ nodded and headed for the shower. He heard Trey call out a good-bye.

Fifteen minutes later, Russ walked back into the living room, picked up the Suburban keys from the table near the front door and stopped with his hand on the knob. The gentle clink of his wedding band against the metal was missing. He raised his hand and looked at the pale circle and heavy indentations on the third finger of his left hand.

After a deep breath he returned to the coffee table, picked up his wedding band, and closed his palm around it.

Chapter Fifty-Nine

GEMINI TAYLOR
En Route to Taylor Residence
Raven Bayou, LA

Thursday, 9 June 2005

THE THERMOMETER on the dash of the Hummer read seventy-five degrees, but Gem was still cold.

"Did they find the knife?" she asked.

"I'm sure they did. Don't worry. You're a good cop, Gemini. You'll be cleared. Here we are." He set the brake and turned off the engine.

Something nagged at her brain. There was something about the knife that she needed to know. But for the life of her, she couldn't turn it into a picture she understood.

Dizzy, she climbed out of the SUV. Her stomach rumbled with hunger. Her mouth tasted like chalk. Trey wrapped an arm around her shoulder and pulled her close.

"My bag." She pointed to the back door. He looked torn between getting the bag he'd locked away for her and letting her stand there alone while he retrieved it. She pulled the key off the snap inside her evening bag, realizing the lieutenant had taken her gun. But her small purse wasn't empty. She felt Daddy's watch there.

The purse was heavy and it crossed her mind that she'd somehow ended up with someone else's bag, but all she cared about right now was getting inside. She couldn't force the key into the doorknob for her shaking. Trey took it from her and a second later she was inside. The A/C blew cold against her.

It was pitch black, but she didn't move to turn on the light. She didn't want to see whatever was on Trey's face. She turned to him in the dark, gave him a quick hug. "Thank you. I'm going to bed now."

"I'll stay." His hands were on her, caressing her back gently, reassuringly.

"No. Really, I'm okay. Please. I just need to be alone."

"Are you sure you're ready for that?"

She didn't answer right away but figured her hesitation would only make him more determined to stay, to protect her.

"I'm sure."

He didn't move.

"Trey, thank you for taking such good care of me. But I'm a big girl. I need some rest. I'll be okay."

"Promise you'll call me if you hear anything. And if you can't sleep, call me and I'll come back."

"Okay. I'll call Russ and you every time the phone rings."

"Call me when you wake up?"

She nodded and brushed her lips across his cheek. He retreated to the Hummer.

She climbed the stairs in the dark, slipped off her shoes and crawled into bed, dragging the thin spread up to her shoulders. She drifted off immediately, and the dream from earlier returned.

Mama in prison. Jax dead on the floor. A playpen full of older children watching her. The walls closing in...

Her face was wet with tears when she woke. The bedspread lay wrinkled and wadded under her where she'd tossed and turned in her sleep.

It was more memory than dream. At least the conversation with Mama was. It had taken place less than two weeks ago. Right after Gem arrived in town to accept the job.

No doubt her fear of confinement triggered the vision of the stairs grabbing her. But she didn't have a clue where the three children came from.

Gem stripped off the T-shirt and sweats and tossed them in the laundry basket. She climbed into a hot shower. Mama had told her from the beginning not to come back to Raven Bayou and never to go digging into the past.

This woman gave birth to me. She worked hard every day to provide for me. She's been locked away for twenty years. For the rest of her life.

It didn't feel right.

THE SUN shining through the window nearly blinded her. Gem stood under the running water and tried to wash her mind. Then she noticed something strange. She didn't have a headache. No pain at all, except for the sore spot on her hip where...

Oh, God. I killed Jax.

The tears started again, burning hot against her cheeks. Sobs racked her body. She let the hot water run over her until it ran out, and then stood in the cold until she shivered.

She couldn't get the picture of Jax out of her mind. The vicious way he lunged at her. The emptiness of his eyes as he stared off into nothingness.

Her stomach convulsed. She ran for the toilet, hit her knees and retched. She was empty, but it didn't stop the waves of nausea. The dry heaves. When it finally stopped, she was too weak to move. The shower was still running, but she had no strength to get up and turn it off. Instead she sat wet and naked on the cool tile floor, arm across the toilet bowl, forehead on her hand, shivering.

Before she went to the academy, she'd been asked a dozen times if she thought she could handle having to kill someone. In classes, teachers ran scenarios where they considered how it would feel to take a life under certain circumstances.

Not like this.

Those words sounded familiar. She'd heard them not long ago, but she couldn't remember where. The phone rang.

She thought about getting it, but didn't. After the fourth ring, the machine picked up.

"Gemini? Are you there?" It was Trey's voice.

She pushed herself up and turned the shower off, wrapped a towel around herself, and went to the bedroom to pick up the receiver. "I'm here."

"We need to talk."

"About what?"

"Not on the phone." His tone startled her. She invited him over and hung up. The clock said nine-oh-eight. She dried off and dressed, brushed her teeth, and ran a brush through her hair. By the time she popped the top on a diet co-cola, the doorbell rang.

Trey's emotions were clear. His lips were pressed together in a straight line, his jaw set. He walked in slowly, hands in his pockets, eyes narrowed.

Her living room was not furnished for company. The large, old table with chairs around it was covered with files, photos and boxes. She led him to the counter dividing the kitchen from the great room, where two swivel bar stools sat. He still hadn't spoken.

"Talk," she said and sipped from her can.

"I need you to tell me again exactly what happened." He leaned forward, elbows on knees, his face only inches from hers.

His intense stare told her he knew something. Something terribly important. And he was trying to help her.

She swallowed hard and thought before speaking, choosing her words carefully, watching his face. Occasionally, as she gave him the facts, he nodded understanding. She talked him through the entire incident, and then waited.

His lips compressed into a thin, hard line. His chin dimpled from the pressure. He leaned back, rubbed a hand over the back of his neck, his eyes still glued to her. Then he made the movement that told a lot about him—he rubbed the lines between his brows with two fingers. Whatever was right behind that spot held something in and he didn't want to let it out.

He exhaled and slumped a little. "They didn't find a knife."

Her skin prickled. Hair rose on her arms. Her heart skipped a beat and thudded in her chest, vibrating up into her throat. "That's impossible! He had a knife. A skinning knife!" The blood drained from her face and the back of her throat burned with threatening tears. "I swear, he had a knife," she said mostly to herself.

"There's more."

She looked up at him. How could there be more?

"It's Boudreaux."

For a minute she thought he meant Jax. But no, it was Alton. Alton Boudreaux.

Her nausea rose again. Trey went to the sink and wet a paper towel, returning it to her so she could wipe her face.

A vision of two little girls running around the trunk of an old tree filled her head. Reena. Was she real or just a girl in a dream? Just someone Gem made up so she'd have one friend? Why had she thought of Reena?

"What about him?" she asked, very afraid she knew the answer.

"The mayor has demanded a full investigation, not just of Jax Boudreaux's death but also of you, your entire past. And Russ."

"That's ridiculous! Russ has nothing to do with it."

"You know the mayor's in Boudreaux's pocket and Boudreaux hates Russ. If Russ hadn't pushed so hard, Boudreaux would never have been charged. There would've been no trial. This is his chance to turn the tables and make it look like Russ had you kill Jax to get even somehow. For Julie. Before this is over, it's going to get really ugly."

"Where's Russ?" *When did he become Russ to me?*

"At the station, far as I know. Probably working the Grant case. The lieutenant is expecting you to go in for a statement Saturday morning."

She stood, intent on going right that second to see Russ. He needed to know how sorry she was. Correction: *she* needed him to know.

But before she'd taken a step, Trey caught her arm and held her hostage. His fingers encircled her wrist tight. In a panic, she jerked her arm free and got into a defensive posture. Trey reacted instinctively too, moving so fast the bar stool bounced against the floor.

"Didn't mean to startle you," he said, "but before you go in, you need to think. Who's your union rep?"

"I don't need anyone with me. You think I did something wrong? I'm telling you, he had a fucking knife!"

"I believe you. I just don't know how you're going to explain it's missing." He set the stool back up on its legs and sat with his left butt cheek hanging off the seat. "With the mayor pressuring the chief, there's no telling what will happen. You could end up being charged, considering it's your word against the physical evidence, or the lack of it."

He was right. All they'd have to do was charge her. Her career would be over. Boudreaux had the clout to push the mayor and the DA into anything.

"Avlee is the rep. I'm sure she's in," Gem almost whispered.

"Call her first. Arrange to meet her privately. I have something I have to do today, but can we get together tomorrow? I might need some input from you."

"What kind of input?"

"I'll know more in the morning. Make your call."

Chapter Sixty

GEMINI TAYLOR
Taylor Residence
Raven Bayou, LA

Thursday, 9 June 2005

GEM CALLED TREY to let him know what happened with Avlee. He'd told her he might need her input, but she had to go to Dallas and get a complete copy of her jacket. Gem had to make it her priority.

"How about I take you?" Trey said.

"I thought you had something to do today. It's 250 miles."

"I'll do what I have to do tomorrow. I make good time in Streak. I can pick you up in thirty minutes."

"I'll be ready." As soon as she hung up, the phone rang. It was someone from the front office with appointments for her to see the shrink and submit to a polygraph on Friday, both for the administrative investigation.

She wasn't looking forward to going back to Dallas PD, but there was too much in her personnel file to have it faxed. There was no telling who might be put in charge of making and mailing a copy for her. It might take days. Or weeks. And it might not be complete. This was too important to depend on someone else. Especially since at least one person in personnel hated her.

She was waiting by the door when Trey arrived. Jumping in the Hummer, she found two cups of coffee in the console between them.

"French Vanilla Café." He handed her a steaming cup from the FastStop. She'd been out of bed almost an hour and a half without her morning fix and sipped the sweet coffee gratefully. On the floor in front of the console sat a small box with a cord running to the dash.

Trey opened it and said, "Banana nut? Or Chocolate?"

"Chocolate."

He handed her a warm muffin, and then pulled out onto the road.

"Cold diet co-cola in the chest." He gestured toward the back where an ice chest sat within reach. Trey'd thought of everything. And had collected it all in less than half an hour. A man after her own heart.

"So Avlee thinks having your jacket from Dallas might help her?"

Gem nodded and sipped. They were already on Highway 63, headed northwest. "I have letters of commendation, merit raises. Avlee'll make an appointment with the union attorney for tomorrow." *So we can figure out how to defend a murderer.* "You said you might need my input about something?"

"There's a new woman in town. Cora Lyon. She has no sheet."

That name had a familiar ring to it. "So?"

"She arrived three weeks before Ilene Grant was killed. It's something to check out."

"But according to Avlee and Barlow, Michael killed Ilene."

"Yes, but who killed Michael? Jax Boudreaux was a suspect, but we didn't find any physical evidence."

"Damn! The knife," Gem said. "Jax had a skinning knife in the bathroom. And someone used a skinning knife on Michael Grant."

"We have to find that damned knife," Trey said, mostly to himself.

They were silent. Gem didn't want to think any more right now about the knife. It made her crazy. "You think Cora Lyon is the only new person in town? Hundreds of people, maybe thousands, come here to gamble every week. As far as that goes, I've been in town less than a month." Gem noticed his cruising speed was above seventy-five on the narrow two-lane road. She tugged on her seatbelt, just checking.

"Cora Lyon came from Kentucky, but her family wasn't from there." Trey glanced Gem's way. "She was born Corina LeBeau. In Raven Bayou."

Corina. Reena. *The little girl in my dreams. They must have been memories*. Reena is real.

"Did she live on the Boudreaux estate?" Gem asked, knowing the answer.

"Yes. Her grandmother was a housemaid to the Boudreauxs. Corina's mother was only thirteen when she gave birth."

"Who is her daddy?" Gem's heart skipped a beat with the question.

"Birth certificate says 'father unknown.' "

"You think she came back here to find out who he was? And then what? Blackmail him? Kill him? You know Michael Grant was from California. It's not likely he was here back then, so he's not her dad."

Trey nodded. They sat in silence. Reena. Gem remembered her so clearly, her long grasshopper legs and dark curly hair with golden highlights from the sun. Reena was her friend. Did Trey know already? Was that why he wanted her input? Reena was maybe five years older than Gem. She'd be almost forty now.

Gem leaned her head back and closed her eyes. The vision of Reena and her playing came right back. They played hide and seek in the barn where Daddy kept his old truck, and among the oleanders along Old Cypress Road.

The silence stretched well into an hour. Pictures of the past flashed in her mind. But it was the last picture that broke the silence, the one of Reena walking slowly away, her hand held by Alton Boudreaux.

Gem's eyes flew open, and she gasped.

"What?" Trey's foot eased off the gas peddle.

"I guess I fell asleep. Had a dream." Gem took a sip of the not-so-warm coffee and studied her surroundings. They'd already reached Interstate 20 and were heading west. They'd be in Dallas soon. Trey must've been averaging ninety miles an hour.

"So, any ideas about Corina?" he asked.

Gem thought before answering. "Where's her mother?"

"She died a few weeks before Corina came back to town."

"Maybe she has family here. Maybe she returned because it feels like home. Maybe her mother took her away and she didn't really want to go so she returned after her mother died." Even Gem didn't believe a word of that.

If Reena was anything like Gem, she'd have wanted more than anything to get away from Raven Bayou when she was little. Only something vital would draw her back.

THE PERSONNEL OFFICE was empty. A sign on the inner office door said J. Manelli. The door was closed.

Gem sighed in relief. With any luck, Janelle Franco was gone, out to lunch, moved on to another department, or another planet.

Trey and Gem sat in the uncomfortable chairs for ten minutes before a young woman showed up behind the counter. It wasn't anyone Gem knew.

"Hi. I'm Kim. How can I help you?"

"I worked here as a deputy from 1991 till a few weeks ago. I need a complete copy of my personnel file for the Raven Bayou Sheriff's Department." Gem showed her ID.

"I'm a temp, so I need to get permission." Kim knocked on the inner door.

"Enter," said a woman's voice.

She did, and a heartbeat later opened the door for J. Manelli.

"Shit," Gem said under her breath.

Janelle looked as arrogant as ever. Her brows wrinkled above her pale eyes, and she crossed her arms in front of her, like she was protecting herself from an evil visitor. "Gemini Taylor, what are you doing here?"

"I need a copy of my jacket."

"So Kim tells me." Janelle Manelli's eyes went from Gem to Trey. "Is this your latest...?"

Trey didn't respond. Neither did Gem.

"I believe I have a right to get a full copy of my jacket. Shall I copy it myself?" Gem said.

"I don't think so." Janelle turned to Kim and lowered her voice, but not quite enough. "Copy her file. Make sure you receive payment before handing it over."

"How long do you think?" Gem asked.

"Give me an hour." Kim smiled and walked away.

Trey and Gem headed back out to the Hummer. Gem took a deep

breath, her eyes cast to the ground. It took a couple of minutes before she spoke. "I can't believe somebody actually married her. Two years after I started here, I went on a couple of dates with Tony Franco. He was a deputy. His sister, Janelle, told him there was something wrong with me. When Tony mentioned it to me, we argued. It ended our relationship."

"What made her say such a thing?" Trey asked.

"Who knows? I don't have a clue what she's talking about. She doesn't know me. She claims she's 'feels like there's something off about me.' "

"Don't tell me she's talking about her instinct?" Trey scoffed. "The look in her eyes when she saw you was weird. She must be some kind of nut case. That's the kind that usually gets promoted."

"We never even talked except when I was first hired and had to have all my pre-hire crap done. You know, physical, polygraph, psych. She scheduled them all."

Trey looked at his watch. "Lunch?"

"I'm starved." She climbed back into the Hummer.

"I can solve that problem." Trey retrieved the ice chest from the back, and then climbed behind the wheel.

Gem set the chest between her feet and explored. Inside she found half a dozen plastic containers with turkey, cheeses, grapes, strawberries, cut up veggies and ranch dip. She recognized the Styrofoam from FastStop.

The man was definitely a keeper. He knew how to spoil a woman. They ate and took a short walk before returning to the office. Gem paid for the copies and walked out with her jacket. When they were inside the SUV, she looked through the file before they left. It looked complete.

After a gas and bathroom break they headed south on Highway 69.

"Are you in a hurry to get back home?" he asked.

Gem checked her watch. Had she driven herself, she wouldn't have made it to Dallas yet. She shook her head, looking out over the wide-open land.

"Good." He pulled onto a narrow road heading east.

"Where're we going?"

"The Frontier River."

A few miles down the road, Trey turned south onto the dirt and drove another mile before parking beside a blooming mimosa backed by a small stand of trees.

"Let's go for a walk." He hopped out.

The temperature was pushing ninety-five and Gem began to sweat before they'd walked a hundred yards. Trey held her hand. There was no trail. The ground was strewn with rocks, so she watched every step to avoid twisting her ankle.

The sound of the river drew her attention. "Wow!"

In front of her was a small waterfall, the river rushing over several boulders ten or twelve feet high. It was an oasis in the middle of nowhere.

Trey pulled her to a large flat-topped rock, leaned against it and turned her to face the river, her back relaxed against him. Despite the heat a hundred yards away, this place was cool, with a light breeze blowing a lighter mist of water against them.

He wrapped his arms around her and rested his chin on her shoulder, their cheeks touching. They stayed like that, frozen like an old snapshot and watched the river, listening to the crash of water throw itself over the rocks and down to the riverbed.

"How did you find this place?" she whispered.

"I had a buddy in college. He came from Tyler and his dad used to bring him here as a kid. It used to be bigger and the fishing was good. We came here for a weekend. In a few years it will probably be gone."

"It's beautiful."

His chin touched her shoulder as he nodded.

"You camped out?" she asked.

"You say it like you're shocked."

"The way your Hummer is stocked, I just can't imagine you camping out in the wilderness."

He loosed his arms and suddenly her feet were dangling as he picked her up. "Really? Can't imagine it, huh? Can you imagine how cold that water is?" He started walking toward the river.

"Don't you dare!" She wrapped her arms around his neck and locked her fingers together.

"So, you *can* imagine it." He kept walking.

"Trey, I swear, if you throw me in there, I'll kill you!"

"Oh, but what a way to go."

"Trey! Stop! Put me down."

He stopped at the edge of the water. "Here?" he asked. The spray of mist coming from the waterfall dampened her skin. "Take it back."

"I take it back. I take it back! You're the great outdoorsman!"

He turned away from the river and allowed her legs to dangle, but didn't let her feet touch the ground. His arms wrapped around her ribs, pressing her breasts into him as she looked into his eyes. "Just to let you know, the water isn't really cold," he said.

Gem's breathing was labored and not because he was crushing her lungs. When his gaze went to her mouth, she knew he was going to kiss her.

His lips were smooth as glass, soft and full, and when his tongue met hers it sent electrical currents shooting in all directions.

He eased his hold on her, and she slid down his chest until her feet were planted firmly on the ground. His embrace remained tight, like he was afraid to let go.

"My mother should be back in a few days. I was thinking of having a barbeque at her place a week from this Sunday. Will you come?"

That last question put a smile on her face. "You want me to meet your mother?" Her temperature suddenly cooled. "I'll be in jail by then."

He put a finger under her chin and tilted her head up. Their eyes met. "I'll break you out if I have to."

"In that case, yes. I'd love to meet your mother."

His arms relaxed their hold and his face turned somber. She wrapped her arms around his neck and leaned against him, lips close to his ear. "Do me a favor," she said in what she hoped was her most sexy voice.

"What?"

"Put your hands in your pockets."

He gave her a questioning look, but slowly did as she asked, anticipation on his face. She took a half step back, brought her palms up to his chest...and pushed with all her might.

Trey landed butt first in the flowing water, a sharp inhalation declaring his shock. "Shit!"

She tried to outrun him, but it was hopeless. She laughed uncontrollably as he picked her up and carried her back to the river. She screamed and pleaded to no avail. He walked to the middle of the current, which was no more than thigh high, and then turned and headed for the waterfall.

The water hit her and she struggled to free herself, but Trey kept a firm hold on her as the cascade hit her. She thought she would drown.

When he finally stepped back and allowed her to breathe, he was grinning. His eyes sparkled. She couldn't resist. Her arms were already around his neck. She forced his head down to her.

His lips were cool, but inside his mouth she found heat. He dropped her legs and curled his body into her.

Gem shivered inside and out.

He took her hand and led her out of the water. The warmth of the sun felt good as they walked toward the Hummer. From the look of their clothes, the water had not been anywhere near clean.

"Now you've done it. We can't get into your Hummer like this. It'll ruin the upholstery."

He stopped and looked at her. "I've done it?" His grip tightened on her hand.

"Okay, okay. You didn't do it. Exactly."

They reached the Hummer. Trey opened the back passenger door, opened one of the drawers under the seats and retrieved a bath towel.

"Here." He handed it to her, pulled out a T-shirt and used it to dry his hair, and then he started unpacking.

She opened the front door and put the towel on the seat. By the time he found what he was looking for, her shoes and clothes were lying in a pile at her feet.

Trey tossed a pair of gym shorts and a T-shirt at her. "We need to get you home. There's lots to do before tomorrow. Ready?" He bundled her wet clothes and tossed them onto the rubber mat of the back floorboard.

She nodded. He closed the back door, waited for her to climb into the front and walked around the rear of the Hummer. Slowly, he eased up into the driver's seat.

"Are you still in a yes mood?" he asked and turned the key in the ignition.

Even if she hadn't been, she was too guilty to say it. "Um-hum."

"Then how about a week from tomorrow? Do you have plans?"

"What do you have in mind?" She grabbed a drink from the cooler.

"I thought I'd go up to the cabin for a day or two. Hoped you might like to go with me."

"What cabin?"

"My dad bought a cabin a couple of hours from here. He mostly used it for hunting. Even has a beautiful bearskin rug in front of the fireplace."

"I suppose he killed and skinned the bear himself," she teased as she looked through the dark-tinted window. In the distance clouds hung, waiting for a "go" from the weatherman. No breeze stirred the leaves of the trees outside or blew the clouds toward them. Everything was still.

"Actually, I did. My dad was a hunter. He taught me how to handle animals. I can shoot 'em, dress 'em, cook 'em. I can even tan their hides."

Chapter Sixty-One

TREY FONTAINE
En Route to Raven Bayou
Southeast Texas

Thursday Late Evening, 9 June 2005

TREY WISHED he could drive slower on the trip back to Raven Bayou, not wanting the day to end, not wanting to part company from Gemini Taylor, who'd proved, under the circumstances, to be a tough and strong-minded woman.

But he'd been through this before and knew she needed time and rest and the support of a good friend to get her through the next few days. He would be that friend.

At least he managed to get her mind off the killing for a short time. He'd been worried about her making this trip alone while under such stress. She needed a break. She needed someone to trust her. Trey was glad to have given her at least a little bit of peace. The coming weeks were going to be rough.

He didn't know why he told her about killing and skinning the bear. It wasn't really something he was proud of. Only his dad knew how he threw-up several times during the skinning process. The smell of dressing a bear made him sick. But more than anything, he wanted Gemini to be impressed with him, to admire him.

A stolen glance at her sitting in the passenger seat made him smile. She wore one of his T-shirts and a pair of gym shorts, the only thing he could find in his bag that tied at the waist.

A tiny smile curled her lips. Right now she faced one of the most dreaded events in a cop's life, and yet she could smile. He loved that about her. He loved her sense of humor, and though the water had been really muddy, he loved how she could take it as well as dish it out.

Realizing his mind was using the L-word, he tried to force his thoughts away from her. It didn't work. When they arrived at her house, he carried her wet clothes while she took her leather bag and opened the door. The cool of the A/C blew out against them.

"Just give me a minute and I'll change out of these."

"Not necessary. I can get them later." He hoped she would invite him in, but she didn't. Instead she took the wet clothes and dropped them on the tile floor of the entryway and moved into his arms.

"Thank you, Special Agent Trey Fontaine," she said with a smile. The kiss was warm and inviting, and when it ended he maintained his position an inch from her lips. For the first time, he noticed the yellow flecks in her eyes. She held him tightly against her, her eyes fixed on his mouth. She looked so vulnerable. Breakable.

It was late, the night sky still and moonless. "I guess I should go," he said reluctantly, hoping she'd insist he stay. She didn't. And he knew she'd made the right choice.

Chapter Sixty-Two

ENDRI CHERAMIE
Cheramie Residence
Raven Bayou, LA

Friday Morning, 10 June 2005

IT WAS TEN O'CLOCK in the morning when Endri heard a knock on the front door. She went to the locked screen to find Detective Coleman there. Blood drained from her face, leaving her cheeks cool. Her gaze swept the street. If someone was watching and told Jax...

"Good morning, Endri. I came to tell you something important."

"Who be that?" her mother called from the kitchen. "Who be that?"

"A friend," Endri said, and then turned to the detective. "You don't come here, no. Make Maman scared."

"I just wanted to tell you Jax Boudreaux was shot and killed last night."

Fear pumped through her. "I don't do it, no!"

"No, you didn't. There were lots of witnesses. He was shot by a cop. By my partner."

She saw a softness in his eyes. He didn't bring blame with him. He came to tell her she was safe. Her knees shook and her vision blurred with hot tears that fell over her lashes.

"Endri. Was he the one who hurt you?"

"Monsieur Boudreaux no like peoples talking bad 'bout his boy."

"I won't tell a soul. I promise."

But before she could answer, her mother was standing behind her. Endri kept her face turned carefully away, so her mother wouldn't see her tears.

"Why you standing here, rude like? Offer the genleman in," her mother said and pushed Endri out of the way. "Good you pass by, 'tective. Come on in. We got coffee."

"No, thank you, Ma'am. Just wanted to stop by and talk to Endri for a minute." His gaze shifted from mother to daughter.

"Good seeing you again, young lady. If you think of anything you can tell me, you have my number." He turned and left before her mother could say more.

"He a strange genleman," her mother said and returned to the kitchen.

Endri stood frozen. Afraid to move. If she moved, she might wake herself up from a dream. But if it was real, if Jax was really dead...Her knees shook, and she sat hard on the carpet. Finally, she and Maman were safe.

Chapter Sixty-Three

RUSS COLEMAN
En Route to Vance Residence
Raven Bayou, LA

Friday Morning, 10 June 2005

IT WAS THE FIRST piece of good news Russ could share with anyone. He hoped it brought relief to Endri. He was sure he saw it in her eyes, in the way her shoulders squared with the news. A big weight had been lifted.

Though it was early, he headed toward Darlene's, determined on keeping her safe. Strickland might cause a ruckus after Alexander's arrest and the death of his buddy Boudreaux. Who knew what Alexander might do? And it was possible the old man set up the whole thing. A vendetta because of the trial.

It was way too soon for Darlene to be out of the hospital. Her husband Frank thought so too. But Darlene, still bandaged and bruised, insisted on being home.

Russ hoped Trey's and Taylor's trip to Dallas would do some good. Until they figured out where that knife went—if there was a knife—his partner was in deep shit, and with Boudreaux stirring the pot, Russ just might get caught up in it.

With all the goings on in the department, it was ridiculous for his mind to drift toward Cora every few minutes, yet he wondered if she would be working tomorrow night when Taylor relieved him at Darlene's.

Chapter Sixty-Four

WILE E. WAYNE
Downtown
Raven Bayou, LA

Friday Morning, 10 June 2005

"WHY WOULD YOU WANT TO HURT HIM? I like him. So does Ginni and Taylor," Drew said with a pouty face.

"You haven't been listening too good. Did you see the way he looked at us? It was like he thought there was something wrong with us when we were at Grant's," I said.

"And you heard about the cabin, and the way he is with animals," Rocky pitched in, but quiet like.

"Well, it's just not fair," Drew protested. "He's the only guy who's nice to us. You said it was okay to kill bad men if that was the only way to stop 'em from doing wrong. But, Trey's not a bad man. Lots of people hunt. That don't make him bad."

"I didn't say we was gonna kill him. I said we need to think on what to do about him. What if he thinks we're crazy or something? What if he figures out about the bad men and what we did? You think he'd still be nice to us?" I just wanted Drew and the other girls to listen, but none of them would. Me and Rocky was the only boys and sometimes it was hard to get the girls to listen.

Trey was coming to the house later, and all I wanted was to talk to 'em about him before he showed up. But Ginni wouldn't talk about it at all. She don't like when we do stuff to people, even bad ones. And Drew was all ga-ga over the big FBI man and didn't want us to hurt him.

Rocky and me just looked at each other, and I knew he was thinking the same thing as me. If Trey shows up and starts being mean, we'll take care of him. We just won't ask the girls to help.

Chapter Sixty-Five

GEMINI TAYLOR
Downtown
Raven Bayou, LA

Friday Morning, 10 June 2005

GEM WOKE UP in her car, parked at Sonic. According to her watch, she was due for an appointment with the shrink, a doctor Quintina Griggs, Ph.D., in twenty-five minutes. Gem just wanted to sleep.

The attorney had been hopeful and kind, but she worried about the knife being missing. Trey did too. They were scheduled to meet at the department later this afternoon for the polygraph.

The psychologist's office was not far from the hospital and the lab Gem had gone to for her drug screen. She had to have another one today before taking the lie detector test to prove she was not using some exotic drug to help her outsmart the machine.

Arriving with time to spare, she stopped in the ladies' room off the hall before checking in with reception. The woman at the front desk was a no-nonsense professional with shoulder length chestnut hair and green eyes that tilted at the outside, like a Siamese cat.

"I have an appointment with Dr. Griggs at one," Gem said, expecting her to check the calendar on the desk.

"Yes. I'm Dr. Griggs. Are you ready?"

Gem was surprised at the lack of staff. She wondered if this was a regular occurrence or if someone had suddenly called in sick, but she didn't ask. Instead she nodded and followed the doctor into the office right past the reception desk.

The room was cozy, done in burgundy and hunter green with enough crème to keep it from being dreary. Instead of a desk, the doctor's swivel chair sat behind a small, elegantly carved table topped with a small lamp and phone and a picture frame turned so Gem couldn't see the subject of the photograph. Behind the table was a large window with a beautiful view of an old beech tree.

Dr. Griggs pulled a notepad and pen from the table and sat herself in a leather chair, offering Gem the one opposite. The doctor crossed her legs, her off-white linen pants draping softly at the top of her taupe pump. The office was nothing like she expected. Neither was Dr. Griggs.

Gem sat, placing her bag beside her in the chair, like a close friend and confidant.

"Well, Ms. Taylor, why are you here?" She looked directly into Gem's eyes and through them into her thoughts.

"Because I have to be if I want to keep my job."

"That's an honest answer. Would you like to talk about what happened? Why the department sent you here?"

Gem hesitated. The answer was a simple "no," but it wouldn't help her keep her job. "A man pulled a knife on me and threatened my life, so I shot him."

"And how do you feel about that?"

I feel like a murderer, like I've committed an unpardonable sin. "I did what I had to do to survive. The captain told me when he hired me that the most important thing was at the end of the day, all the officers get to go home. If I'd hesitated, I'd be the one in the morgue." Gem looked down and found the fingers of her left hand going white, the leather strap of her bag woven through them tightly.

Dr. Griggs wrote something on her notepad and brought her attention back to Gem. "Have you had any symptoms? Nightmares? Insomnia?"

Gem shook her head.

"Any other problems you'd like to talk about?"

"You mean, other than the fact that I'm on administrative leave pending an investigation to see if I should be fired or tried for murder? No. I don't have a care in the world."

The doctor leaned forward. "Ms. Taylor—may I call you Gemini?"

Gem nodded.

"Thank you. Gemini, our conversation is strictly confidential. My job here is simply to ascertain whether you're suffering any ill effects from the trauma you've been through. You took a life, and justified or not, that event will shape the rest of your life. If there's something I can do to help, I want to."

"Can you bring him back?" Her throat burned as she fought back tears.

"What if *you* could? If there were some way for you to relive that night and do it all over again, can you think of anything you could've done or said that would've made the night end differently?"

"No."

"So, you've given this a great deal of thought." Griggs leaned back in her seat and wrote something on the pad.

"What makes you say that?"

"You answered quickly so, either you don't care at all and never thought about it, or you've racked your brain trying to figure out if you really had to shoot him."

Gem took a deep breath, tried to maintain control. A single tear managed to get away from her and run down her cheek. Her fingers tingled from lack of circulation as she twisted the purse strap tighter. "He backed me in a corner. I couldn't get out, and he had a knife."

"What happened to the knife?"

The question startled her. Who told her about the missing knife?

"I don't know. When he lunged at me it was in his hand. I shot him." Gem closed her eyes, tried to envision the scene. Her weapon was pointed at his chest. He smiled before he came at her. He didn't expect her to pull the trigger. But she did. She must have, because Jax was dead.

Tears ran down her face as she remembered. There was a knife. Blood splattered all over her. She could feel it, wet and warm on her skin. She was disoriented, her knees weak. Her vision faded and she thought she'd fainted, but then she was there again, standing in the same position, the same body lying at her feet. But the knife was gone. She shivered.

"We both know nothing will bring him back," Griggs said. "No one can undo what's been done. The question is: what will you do now? Are you going to let it eat at you and destroy you? Your career? Your life? Or will you let me help you get through it?"

Gem looked the doctor straight in the eye. She looked sincere. "I really don't see how you can help, unless you know where the knife is." Her lips turned up in an effort to smile.

"Well, I don't know that, but I do know this—you weren't the only person in that room before the cops arrived. Someone must have picked up the knife. I don't know how much benefit I'll be at helping you save your career, but I believe I can assist you in getting your life back on an even keel. I'm willing to try. Are you?"

Gem didn't know how much longer they talked, but when she left Dr. Griggs office, she did feel better. She made an appointment for Monday morning. She even shook the doctor's hand before she left.

When she climbed in the Caddie, she leaned her head against the headrest, closed her eyes, and tried to think of where the hell that knife went. The doctor's words played through her head over and over like a tape—*you weren't the only person in that room before the cops arrived. Someone must have picked up the knife.*

The only other person in the room before the cops came was Trey.

Chapter Sixty-Six

TREY FONTAINE
Sheriff's Department
Raven Bayou, LA

Friday 13:00 hours, 10 June 2005

TREY PULLED OUT of the lot and headed to his mom's. He spent an hour listening to Ace through the tiny receiver behind his ear, mostly to get his mind off the sight of Jax on the metal table, his chest cut open while Barlow weighed his organs like a butcher in a meat department.

Ace had become close with another employee, and he listened as the woman whispered that her daughter had come here for a job and had disappeared.

"When did you last hear from her?" Ace had asked.

"It's been two months. She ran away, but then she called a couple of times to let me know she was okay."

"I'm really sorry to hear that, Sam. I'll keep my eyes and ears open," Ace said. After a breath, she whispered, "Did you hear that?"

"Yeah," he replied. "Get all the info you can on the woman and her daughter. As soon as you get back to me, I'll do some research. Other than that, all's well?"

"Oh, my achin' feet."

He knew someone had come too close for her to continue the conversation. She'd told him earlier she was to work Saturday and have Sunday and Monday off. Maybe she and this woman, Sam, could spend some time together.

In the meantime, he would return to the murder cases.

Russ had told Trey the only way to get answers about what happened the night of the Arnold Taylor murder was to ask someone who was there twenty years ago. There was no sense in telling Taylor what Russ had suggested, or what Trey planned.

He looked at his watch. *Too late today. Besides, I want to be at the polygraph. I'm staying with Taylor tomorrow, so I'll have to go Sunday. It's not like the witness is going anywhere. Not in this lifetime.*

Chapter Sixty-Seven

GEMINI TAYLOR
Sheriff's Department
Raven Bayou, LA

Friday 2:30 p.m., 10 June 2005

THE TABLE holding the dreaded machine sat to her left. Its wires hung toward the floor, and to her right was a file cabinet close enough for her to have opened the drawers if she wished.

"Detective Taylor." A bald guy shook her hand. "Jeffrey Cannes. You can call me Jeff. Nice to see you again." His voice was soft and reassuring. Gem had a polygraph twice before. Once for Dallas PD and once as a new hire here. It was required. Unfortunately, she didn't remember a thing about the one she'd had here. She didn't recognize this man. He looked like Ben Franklin. For all she knew he could *be* Ben Franklin.

An officer turned to Trey and Suzette DeCasse, her attorney. "I'm Lieutenant Coonce. There's a break room two doors down, if you two want to stay." They followed the man, leaving Gem with Ben.

"Have a seat so we can go over the questions."

She sat and took a deep breath. The room was cramped, and when he closed the door, she struggled with the coffin-like confinement.

"Now, I've been provided with a series of yes and no questions for you. I'm going to put some wires on you, which will measure your body's response to the questions..."

His voice was gravelly as he described the process. They reviewed the control questions, including the one Gem would answer falsely so he could get a reading of how her body reacted when she lied.

With practiced fingers, he wrapped the wire around her chest. He explained what each connection was for. It was hard for her to breathe with the wire tying her down.

He asked a few standard questions. Then control questions, making notes on the paper as it moved slowly through the machine. She averted her eyes, staring at the blank wall in front of her. She was afraid the sight of the needles bouncing would set her internal alarms off, and she'd end up having a heart attack.

She didn't usually use her Taylor face for anything except nasty crime scenes, and nastier criminals. But she needed all the help she could get. Sitting up straight, she allowed that part of her to take over, to distance her from the ugliness of what all this meant.

It didn't take long for him to start asking questions in earnest about the night of the shooting. She willed her body to behave and tried to think calming thoughts. It didn't work. She was scared shitless, afraid her career was being flushed down the toilet with each answer she gave.

His questions were the same ones she would, no doubt, be asked by the IA guys. Her answers would be the same. She didn't know where the damned knife was.

"I think I'm gonna puke," she said and started pulling wires from her body. The wastebasket was within reach. She got to it just in time. She hadn't eaten or drank much, but everything she did had stayed in her stomach until that minute.

Ben Franklin opened the door and called the lieutenant. Suzette rushed in, making the room even tighter than it already was.

The only shoes she could see were Suzette's. The woman squatted, her face close to Gem's. "Do we need to reschedule this?" she whispered.

Gem shook her head and sat the wastebasket on the floor, pulling a hankie from her pants pocket to wipe her lips. "I'll be fine. Just give me a minute and we can get this thing over with."

"Are you sure?" Trey asked from the doorway.

Gem nodded.

Suzette stepped out of the room and Gem heard her tell someone she'd be "ready to continue in a just a minute." She sounded so professional, so in control. Gem was glad to have someone on her side that was in control.

Gem heard footsteps and looked up. Coonce and old Ben Franklin had their heads together as they huddled a few steps down the hall.

Honey, you didn't do a thing wrong and all you have to do is tell the truth. Gem looked over her shoulder, sure to see Aunt Ginny there, but only the blank wall stared back at her.

Gem stood and looked down the hall. Trey and Suzette talked in a doorway not far from her. Their eyes were glued to her as though they feared she might escape. The thought had occurred to her.

She stepped out into the hall. "Could I get a drink?" she asked in the general direction of the kicking team, still huddled, arguing over their next play.

"Sure. Water? Soda?" Coonce asked.

"A diet co-cola would work."

"I'll see what I can do." He promptly entered the room where Trey lingered, reappearing a few seconds later with three cans.

"Regular co-cola, Diet Sprite, or Root Beer?"

Aunt Ginny used to give Gem clear sodas when she was sick. "Sprite, thank you." She popped the top and took a swig. It was cold and wet and managed to wash away the nasty taste in her mouth.

Just take a deep breath and get on with it. I'll be with you. It was Aunt Ginny's voice again, from right beside Gem. She looked at the huddle. "Hey, guys, let's do this," she said and walked back into the office. She took a drink, followed by a deep breath. By then, Ben Franklin was back.

He removed the wastebasket from the room and started with the wires again. This time Gem stayed calm, but it wasn't her. The calm came from inside. When he finished wiring her, he sat, tore the paper from the machine and turned it on again.

"Are you ready to proceed, Detective Taylor?" he asked.

Confidence washed over her. She sat taller in the chair, her posture improving. "Yes, sir. You may begin anytime you wish."

Chapter Sixty-Eight

TREY FONTAINE
Civic Building
Raven Bayou, LA

Friday Afternoon, 10 June 2005

THE HAIR on the back of Trey's neck stood up as he watched Gemini transform into a lady, her back straight, her face perfectly calm.

The examiner closed the door. The exam took less than thirty minutes, and when it was over, Gemini joined Trey in the break room while her attorney, Suzette DeCasse, spoke to the examiner and Lieutenant Coonce in the hallway.

Trey wasn't privy to those conversations. All he could do was watch the body language and facial expressions and make an educated guess at the words.

The lieutenant was a military type, his posture perfect, his face calm, his voice almost loud enough for Trey to hear, though he couldn't hear Ms. DeCasse at all. This man, Coonce, was in charge. He wasn't a particularly large man, but confidence oozed from him. Trey wouldn't want to face this man as an enemy.

After a short time, the lieutenant went into an office and Ms. DeCasse joined Trey.

"They didn't give me a lot of information, but from the look on the examiner's face, I think you did very well, Gemini," Ms. DeCasse said. "Call me if you need me. Otherwise, I'll be in touch as soon as I hear something."

"Thank you so much for your assistance, Suzette," Gemini offered her hand. The attorney gave it a cursory shake and left.

Gemini smiled at Trey and walked toward the pit, moving regally, like a belle of the Old South. Her pace was compact but smooth. Trey had to shorten his stride to stay beside her.

"How is Detective Coleman this morning?" she asked.

"When did he turn into Detective Coleman? Yesterday he was Russ."

"How is Russ this morning?"

Trey put a hand on her arm and stopped. She turned toward him.

"How is Gemini Taylor this morning?"

"Why, fine, of course. Why do you ask?"

"No headache?"

"No headache. Really." She started walking again.

"You're taking it very well. I'd be angry if they put me through that."

He slipped his hand into his pocket and thought about how badly he needed a Lortab.

"Nonsense. They're just doing their jobs."

They entered the pit and found only Bettencourt and the female vice detective, Justine Davidson.

"Where is everyone?" Gemini asked no one in particular.

"Russ went to call his sister. The rest are in a meeting," Bettencourt said.

Trey stretched and yawned.

Gemini froze, her face blanched. "I think I need to go home," she said shakily.

She must be thinking the meeting is about her. "Walk with me." Trey placed a hand on the small of her back and they headed back out to the hall. He stopped her, turned to face her, and took her hand. "Are you sure you're feeling all right?"

"Yes. I'm fine. I think I'll go home and change and then go see Darlene." She was sounding more like herself.

Then a tear fell.

"Hey. It's alright, Sweetie." Her body went rigid as steel as he hugged her. "Come on. Let's get you to your car. Unless you want me to drive you."

"No. Thank you. I'm fine."

He led her to her car and opened the driver's door. She slid into the seat.

"I'm going to Darlene's later. If I don't see you there, I'll come by your house and see how you're doing," he said.

"Thank you, Trey," she said with a tired voice, her fingers seeking his. He took her hand for a heartbeat, and then lifted it and closed the door. Her gaze fell to their hands, and her thumb rubbed gently over his fingers. She looked up, gave him a small smile, and cranked the car.

She waved as she pulled away. Trey slipped a hand in his pocket and pulled out the mint tin as he headed toward the conference room. A doctor friend, an old college roommate, managed to get him a single prescription of pain meds. Thirty wouldn't last him long.

He thought Taylor'd done well on the polygraph, and afterward she'd tried to keep a stiff upper lip. But she wasn't holding up as well as she wanted everyone to believe, as evidenced by the tears and her inability to look him in the eye.

He reached the conference room and tapped a knuckle on the door before opening it. Time to put his emotions on hold and do his job.

Chapter Sixty-Nine

GEMINI TAYLOR
Taylor Residence
Raven Bayou, LA

Friday Late Afternoon, 10 June 2005

GEM STILL SHOOK over what had happened during the polygraph. Not the fear of being tied up, or the puking when he asked about the knife, but the voice. Aunt Ginny had come alive inside her. *Did I really hear Aunt Ginny? Feel her presence?* She tried to think rationally of why such a thing would happen. And how. Aunt Ginny's wasn't the first voice Gem heard in her head. Were the others as real? How many had there been?

She could hear her and feel her. The way she talked and moved. It was as if Gem *was* Aunt Ginny. It scared the hell out of Gem. And if that hadn't been bad enough, she faded completely and came back to find herself downstairs in the hallway with Trey.

At home, she slipped into comfy clothes and sat for a few minutes, staring out the window. Her mind just couldn't pull things together. She looked at her watch. She'd sat there for more than an hour. She needed to change gears, needed to think of someone—or something—else before she drove herself crazy.

I'm hearing voices. How much crazier can I get?

Chapter Seventy

TREY FONTAINE
Downtown
Raven Bayou, LA

Friday Late Afternoon, 10 June 2005

TREY WALKED through Albertson's, wondering if this was such a good idea. If she knew of his plans for Sunday, would she want him in her house this evening with a surprise dinner? Best he didn't say anything. No sense making her angry.

He tossed everything into Streak and headed south, toward Aunt Darlene's house. Gemini was there, sitting with Russ on the porch. After visiting inside for a minute, he joined them.

"I don't want to wear Aunt Darlene out," he said as he sat.

"I just have to ask... *Aunt* Darlene?" Gemini said.

"Might as well be. Dad was Russ's partner. I've known this family my whole life. And Aunt Darlene has always been my favorite." Trey smiled at Russ.

"Thanks a lot," Russ said. "Taylor has just been telling me about the polygraph and her meeting with the department shrink."

"Sounds like a familiar subject."

She stood. "So, I'll come over Sunday evening and take a shift."

"That would be great," Russ said and reached out a hand.

She took it and gave it a gentle shake. A soft smile crossed her face. Trey knew what it was like to have a partner who trusted and believed in you. He slipped a thumb in his pocket and rubbed the tin.

"See you later?" she asked him.

"Sure. I'll be over in a few."

Gemini walked out to her car. Trey and Russ sat in silence until she disappeared.

"How'd it go?" Russ asked.

"I think she did okay. After she barfed."

Russ smiled. "Yeah. She told me. I've been thinking about that knife. Did you see anybody in the hallway before you went into the rest room?"

Trey tried to envision what he'd seen night-before-last when he left the table and crossed the dance floor of the Star-Lite club looking for Gemini. The crowd suddenly ran from the direction of the hallway, dozens of people pressing at him as they scattered. Any one of them could've been in the bathroom or the hall right after the shot, but by the time he arrived, the hall was empty, and only Gemini and the body occupied the ladies room.

"Not that I saw. People were running, pushing, screaming. But everyone was out of the way by the time I got through." He rubbed the back of his neck and stared at the floor, wishing he'd seen something. Anything. "You believe her, don't you?" he finally asked.

Russ looked him in the eye. "I think she believes she saw a knife. I'm just not so sure there *was* a knife."

"Did you discuss it with Wilkes?"

Russ nodded.

"And."

"He's never been too keen on Gemini, but he's willing to give her the benefit of the doubt. She was on the job in Dallas for almost fourteen years, and her work on the Grant cases have been..."

"What?"

"I started to say really good. Except for the incident at Michael Grant's scene."

Trey had forgotten that. Gemini had removed her glove and put her hand in Michael Grant's abdomen. Said she'd seen something. He wondered if she was reaching out to touch her dad. Maybe the sight of the body took her back in time.

"She was under a lot of stress, seeing a body in the same condition as her father's," Russ said rather defensively. "I didn't tell Wilkes about that."

"About which?"

"About what she did."

Trey wondered if the Taylor case haunted Russ enough to make him lose his objectivity. "Want me to stay here tonight?"

"Best you take it easy for a while. Between my partner and yours, you seem to have your hands full. I have a bad feeling. If I'm right about the Michael Grant and Arnold Taylor cases being related, you're going to be a busy guy real soon." Russ appeared to be in a relatively good mood, considering the circumstances. "So, you're going to see Gemini? At her place?"

Trey reflected a moment. "She's feeling really lonely right now. And I don't think she wants to burden her partner with her feelings. You seem to have your hands full too." He nodded toward the house.

"Just remember, she is my partner."

Trey flashed him a disingenuous smile and stood, anxious to get to Streak and take another pill. "You staying?"

"Yeah."

"I'll be back." As he drove toward Gemini's, he hoped he could get through the evening without doing anything he'd regret.

In his head he knew what he needed to do, but facing her sometimes made him do things he shouldn't. He only hoped she couldn't see the betrayal on his face.

It occurred to him that Gemini might be pleased with his idea. After all, he was trying to prove her daddy's killer was still on the loose, meaning her mother was innocent.

On the other hand, why risk upsetting someone who was already fragile? He told himself he was doing a good thing. A necessary thing. He was trying to help her. But deep inside, he wasn't buying his own lies.

Chapter Seventy-One

RUSS COLEMAN
Vance Residence
Raven Bayou, LA

Friday Early Evening, 10 June 2005

RUSS WENT back and forth between the department and Darlene's several times during the day. He was glad the workday was over and he could get back to the business of taking care of his family.

Grabbing his tea glass, he went back to the kitchen and checked the back yard through the sliding glass door. The girls sat at the table behind him. He turned his gaze to them.

Eight-year-old Chantelle was doing her homework. She looked just like her grandma Darlene at that age. And just like her mama Darla at that age.

Five-year-old Adoette had scattered her crayons all over the table and worked at coloring a picture, her tongue sticking out of one side of her mouth. Though she was the younger, she was almost as big as Chantelle.

Adoette took after her daddy. Big Deshaun lived up to his name, at six-foot-four and 260 pounds. When Darla joined the army, she never believed there would come a time that both she and her husband would be called up to go to war. Darla was lucky to have been born into a family who took care of their own

Russ pulled the cell phone from its charger and dialed Wilkes's number. "Was Terrand wearing a watch?" he asked when Wilkes answered.

"No. Why?"

Russ explained his feelings about Grant's watch.

"What about the Taylor case? Was Arnold Taylor wearing a watch?"

"Don't remember. I'll check in the morning."

"Keep in touch," Wilkes said.

Russ set his tea glass down and rubbed a palm over his short hair. Why would someone kill several men and steal nothing but their watches? As his mind sorted through the murders, a question nagged at him. Had Jax been wearing a watch? And more important, why did he even ask himself that question?

Chapter Seventy-Two

GEMINI TAYLOR
Taylor Residence
Raven Bayou, LA

Friday Evening, 10 June 2005

GEM WENT upstairs and changed into comfortable clothes. A firm believer that shoes and bras should be outlawed, the first thing she did was eliminate them. She chose an old, worn T-shirt and a pair of shorts made of the same fabric.

Downstairs, with a cold diet co-cola in one hand and her file on Daddy's case in the other, she sat in the overstuffed chair. She looked out the window at the shadowed yard on the northwest side of the house. Tucking her feet under her, she opened the file.

As her gaze fell on the copy of the report, her mind refused to think about the case. Since she'd returned to Raven Bayou, she kept hearing things and wondered if she was losing her mind. There was something else too. Since she'd been here, she'd had a lot of blackouts. And a lot of headaches. And she'd become a killer.

She closed the file and dropped it on the floor, leaned back in the big fluffy chair, and closed her eyes. The doorbell woke her. She stretched and got up. It wasn't dark outside yet, but the sun was already behind the trees in the distance. She must've slept for at least an hour.

When she opened the door, Trey stood there with sacks of groceries. He smiled and walked right past her to the kitchen. He set the bags on the counter.

She folded her arms across her chest and watched as he unloaded what he'd brought. Assorted cheeses, pasta, cans and bottles of sauces and tomatoes, olive oil, spices, herbs, salad fixings, and French bread.

She retrieved her diet co-cola and sat at the bar, watching him. He found his way around her kitchen easily. "Want a beer?"

She curled her nose at him. "I don't drink horse piss."

"Thought you might say that." He left and returned with the small ice chest he kept in the Hummer. "How about Zima?" He opened the chest and she looked inside. A six-pack of Miller Light in bottles and six Green Apple Zimas. She handed him the soda, grabbed a Zima, and popped the top. It was cold and sweet.

Trey put the soda in the fridge, opened a beer, and continued destroying her kitchen.

"Pots?"

She pointed to a lower cabinet and he pulled out two large pots. One he filled with water and set on the stove. While waiting for the water to boil, he filled the other pot with a jar of spaghetti sauce and a can of tomato paste. He turned the burner on low heat and grabbed the cutting board. It took him only a minute to chop the onion and toss it into a small skillet with a little olive oil before he started work on the salad.

"I'll be right back. I'm gonna go change." She stood to leave but he stopped her, coming around the bar to take her in his arms.

"Why? Aren't you comfortable?" He held her loosely.

"I'm not exactly dressed for company."

"I'm not exactly company. Besides, you look great."

"Are you crazy?"

"Let's not go there." He went back to the stove. "Didn't you put those clothes on because they're comfortable?"

"Yes."

"Then wear them. And have another drink."

"Are you trying to get me drunk and have your way with me?"

He laughed again and she returned to the barstool.

"Looks like you thought of almost everything." She took another sip.

"Almost?" He stopped and looked at her.

"What about dessert?"

His smile looked positively evil. "Got it covered." He went back to work.

"What is it?"

"You'll see."

"Where is it?"

He laughed. "Hey, beggars can't be choosers. Just relax. We'll get to it." His eyes met hers. "I promise."

They ate at the bar. Stuffed Cannelloni covered in marinara, garlic bread drizzled with herbed olive oil and stuck under the broiler until the edges began to brown, and tossed salad. The cold Zima was perfect for washing it down. She stuffed herself.

"How do you feel about baseball?" Trey swiped the sauce off his plate with his last bite of bread.

"Who's playing?"

"Washington Nationals."

She went to the living room, found the remote, and flipped through the channels till she found the game. Trey came in with their drinks. He looked around the room for a seat. Not a lot of options. Four dining room chairs around the big table, and one overstuffed chair facing the TV.

Placing their bottles on the side table, he tugged his boots off and kicked them out of the way. Then he picked her up and sat in her chair with her in his lap.

"They're a good team." He took a swig of his beer before handing Gem her drink. She shifted so she could see the screen. They sat, cuddled in her chair, watching the game, and drinking. She faded into a light sleep but was aware of him taking the bottle from her hand and holding her more firmly as she relaxed.

He carried her up the stairs, her arms around his neck and her head on his shoulder. "What about dessert?" she mumbled, so tranquil she was floating.

"I'll bring it up," he said and put her on the bed. She heard him go downstairs and outside. He came back in and locked the front door. Then he was in the kitchen. A few minutes later he came up with two plates and put them on the nightstand.

She reached over and tapped the touch-lamp to the first level of light, just enough to see the room. Whatever was on the plates looked killer good. "What's that?"

"Have you ever heard of chocolate decadence?" He handed her a plate with a fork. She took a bite and the bittersweet melted on her tongue. She thought she'd died and gone to heaven. Trey sat on the edge of the bed and watched. His dessert still sat on the nightstand.

"I wouldn't leave that there too long. It might disappear," she said with her mouth full of dark chocolate goo.

"If that's what it takes, have at it."

Half way through her dessert, she decided it didn't mix well with Green Apple Zimas. She put her plate beside Trey's and sighed contentedly.

He looked at his watch. "Guess I'd better get back to Russ and Darlene."

Gem didn't want him to leave. She wanted to go back to the fluffy chair and sleep in his lap. "I'll walk you out."

"No. I know my way out. Leave the dishes. I'll come back tomorrow and help out."

"Help out? You're the one who made the mess." She couldn't help teasing him. "So you'll pick me up in the morning? Are you sure you want to hang around the station while they interrogate me?"

"It's not an interrogation. Don't let them get away with it. It's a statement. You decide what you'll say before you go."

"Yeah, right."

"Yeah. Right. You have all night to think about it. You'll do fine. I'll be here at eight."

Her gaze swept the room as she avoided looking him in the eye.

"Gemini, you'll do fine. You're a strong woman. Just don't let them push you into saying anything except what you want to say. Get your statement in your head, say it, and get out of there."

She nodded, knowing it wouldn't be as easy as it sounded. They would pound her with questions, over and over.

"Good night." He kissed her forehead, grabbed the two plates, and disappeared down the stairs.

Chapter Seventy-Three

LIEUTENANT HORACE COONCE
Internal Affairs Office, Civic Building
Raven Bayou, LA

Saturday Morning, 11 June 2005

"So, WE HAVE THIS ONE BIG PROBLEM. The knife," Coonce said, sitting rigidly, eyes forward. This case was like falling into an outhouse with no good way for this to turn out. Put away a cop for shooting someone, and the department took a big hit. Let the killer of a Boudreaux go free, and his career was down the shitter.

His peripheral vision picked up the tension from Loe, who had kept silent since his arrival. Detective Taylor sat opposite Coonce, concentrating on the tabletop, her union rep to her left.

The camera caught every motion, every sound, or rather every second of silence. He waited, knowing how hard it was to face the enemy in front of witnesses. It wasn't like Taylor could scratch his eyes out or break down under pressure. Either response would show her weakness.

"Look, Taylor. I understand your position. And I want to believe you. But without the knife..." He let the words hang, letting her imagine the worst.

"Someone must have picked up the knife," she said calmly, her eyes giving him an even stare without fear or anxiety. Either she was innocent and believed in the system, or she was the coldest killer he'd seen since retiring from the Army.

Her hands were on the table, one hand picking at the nails of the other. A huge silver watch was pushed halfway up her forearm. Coonce placed his fingers on the insides of her wrists and stared into her eyes. This tactic usually rattled the interviewee. She didn't blink. "Do you know where the knife is?"

Her pulse raced under his fingertips.

"Do you know who picked it up?"

The trip hammer beat continued. She knew something.

"Have you ever used a knife on anyone?"

No change.

"Have you ever killed anyone other than Jamison Boudreaux?"

Her eyes changed, the pupils dilating as she took an easy breath. Her pulse slowed a bit, and her body relaxed just enough for him to notice. With a deeper breath, she met his gaze. Her expression could only be described as genteel. She was actually quite pretty.

"Did Coleman talk you into this?" Coonce had no love for the man. He could imagine Coleman's black blood and pure hatred driving him to rope Taylor into murdering a Boudreaux.

"What makes you think I need his approval so much that I'd kill for it?"

He sat back and watched her. Gemini Taylor turned into Sharon Stone in *Basic Instinct* when it came to Coleman. Coonce wondered why. He asked another dozen questions, which she answered easily and without hesitation.

"This is what we're going to do," he began. "You will put your formal statement in writing. Then you're free to go. I'm going to recommend you stay on paid admin leave for now. You will not leave the parish. You will not talk to the press, or to anyone else regarding any part of this statement or any case in which you have been involved as an officer or as a suspect. Or as a victim."

"I'm no victim of any case."

He flipped her personnel file open and thumbed through a few pages. Then he closed the file and locked eyes with her. Her mouth hung open, and her face blanched. He pushed a tablet and pen toward her, stood, and made eye contact with Loe. "I'm finished here for now. I'll need a copy of her statement, and the video."

Chapter Seventy-Four

RUSS COLEMAN
Vance Residence
Raven Bayou, LA

Saturday Afternoon, 11 June 2005

"UNCLE RUSS, can we go out and play?" Chantelle asked. Adoette stood right behind her sister, her arms wrapped around a doll.

Frank was nowhere in sight, and neither was Patsy. "I guess we could go out back for a while. Let me get some coffee." Adoette put her doll on the kitchen table. He poured himself a cup and went out the sliding door, his great nieces almost knocking him down as they pushed forward. "Hey...!"

But they were already playing tag, giggling, and gallivanting around like escaped prisoners. Russ walked around the yard, looked over the fences, and checked every bush and every back door of every house he could see. There were children in one yard, a tiny dog in another. Satisfied all was okay for now, he sat on the patio and watched the girls play.

It made him nervous for them to be out here, but he didn't want them to grow up scared of living. And he didn't want them driving Darlene out of bed with their squeals and laughter. They didn't need to know he had a .380 in an ankle holster and a patrol unit driving by every thirty minutes.

It didn't take the girls long to tire of their games. As Russ walked in the door behind them, he heard Darlene calling. He hurried to the bedroom and found Frank and Patsy hovering. "She wants you. I'll go see to the young'uns," Patsy said. Frank followed, leaving Russ and Darlene alone.

His sister looked better, stronger. She wore a scarf over her hair but all the bandages had been removed. He hated to see her face bruised, but her eyes were bright and that meant she was going to be all right. She patted the bed and he sat and took her hand. "When do I get to see Gemini?" she mumbled through her wired jaws.

"She'll be around soon. I think maybe tonight. How're you doing?"

"I'll be doing better soon."

The statement sounded like she was hiding something. Probably a lot. Maybe she wanted to tell Taylor more of what happened.

"How long have you known Gemini?"

"The truth is, I don't know her now," he replied.

"Well, I like her. She's got gumption."

"That's surely true." He smiled.

"Reckon that boy needed killing. That Boudreaux boy. Reckon she wouldn't hurt someone who didn't need it. She's pretty honest?"

"I guess. Why?"

"Now looky here, Big Brother. Some things are just for us women folk to know, so never you mind." Darlene smiled.

"Should I be worried?"

"I don't think so. I think everything's gonna be all right. You just take good care of that girl. I got a feeling about her."

Me too, he thought.

Chapter Seventy-Five

WILE E. WAYNE
Queen of Diamonds Casino
Raven Bayou, LA

Saturday Night, 11 June 2005

EVER BODY IN TOWN knows if you want to get something illegal, you go to the Queen.

Drew figured since Scott did dope, he probably spent a lot of time at the boat. Raven Bayou has got only two casinos, and just like other towns in Louisiana, they're on the water and shaped like boats even though they don't go nowhere.

We figured if we went back enough times, we'd catch him. It'd be easy to find Scott's car if it was in the parking lot. He drove an old green Ford Fiesta. That thing was ugly.

After parking the truck on the other side of the Breaden Street Bridge, we walked to the parking lot and looked around. It was our third trip when we finally saw the little car. Then we set ourselves down with our backs to the oleander bushes and watched.

"When do I get my knife?" Rocky asked.

"Soon," I said.

"Can I have my new knife now? Cain't I just hold it?"

Drew fetched the knife from outta her bag and gave it to Rocky. He ran his fingers over the shiny casing, unfolded it, and stared at the sharp blade and the gut hook.

"Put it away afore someone sees it," I whispered.

It was really late when Scott came out. His eyes looked funny and he walked kinda slow and careful like.

When he saw us he got all huffy. "Go away and leave me alone. Quit your harrassin' me."

"I'm not here to bother you," Drew said. "Just wanted you to know I think you're really cute."

He looked her up and down. She was wearing a skinny little top and a short skirt and I'm guessin' he liked what he seen, 'cause a couple minutes later...

"Look what I got," she said and held out a fat homemade cigarette. He smiled at her like she was Santa Clause and lit it. It smelled funny. It was mary wanna. I remembered that smell from when Taylor used to arrest people with that stuff.

Drew got us into his car with him. I still can't figure out why men always smile at her and let her have her way, but it works ever time. It's like they go in a trance and can't say no when she's around.

Anyhow, Drew told him to drive us over the bridge 'cause she left the truck there. I guess he didn't even wonder why, just did like she said. He drove like somebody's granny.

When he handed the cigarette back to Drew, she took a real deep puff and held her breath. It just took a couple minutes to get to the truck. Drew left it parked way off the road, kinda in between some trees, and she had him cross the bridge and park on the wrong side of the road, so the back of his car was pointed at the water. When he parked, they just set there, smoking and giggling until the cigarette was all gone.

There was an old piece of carpet in the bed of the truck. We put it there just for Alexander. Drew climbed up in the back in that short dress and that guy just followed her right on in and laid down.

He had a funny look on his face when he saw my knife, like he couldn't believe what was happening. I put my knees on his shoulders and held the blade against his Adam's apple. His eyes got real big.

"I saw what you did to Miss Darlene. What I wanna know is why. You just keen on hurting women?"

He stayed quiet, like he was afraid to talk. I sawed a little bit on his neck and let him feel his warm blood on his skin. I guess he thought he could wriggle away from me, but when he moved, I pressed harder on the knife and he settled right down.

"I'm waiting on a answer."

"I didn't mean to hurt her! I just wanted to scare her!"

His eyes rolled down toward his neck, like he was trying to see if the cut was bad.

"Why?" I pushed the blade a little harder to get his attention. He was shaking all over, and even with just the lights from the bridge to see by, I could tell he looked a little pale. He was sweating too.

"I...I just needed to scare her, that's all." He was trying to scoot away, but with my knees in his armpits, he didn't get far before the pain set in and he held still.

"Then why'd you hurt her?" I sawed a little more.

"I was messed up, man! I didn't mean to hurt her! I was just there to give her a message, but I was messed up! Please..."

"What message?"

He started to cry. What a sissy.

"Don't make me ask again." The blade went a little deeper, and he whined like a baby.

"I was supposed to slap her around a little is all."

"Who told you to?" I knotted up his shirt in my hand, like I was gonna hold him still while I cut his head off, and I leaned forward a little, putting more weight on the blade.

He sounded really scared so I backed off a little.

"Jax wanted to send that nigger detective a message to back off the Cheramie case. I was supposed to scare the shit out of his sister, and then get outta there. That's all I know. But I was messed up... and she was pretty...I couldn't help myself. I'm sorry. Man, I'm really, *really* sorry."

If this guy thought he was messed up before, I wondered what he'd think about himself when me and Rocky was through with him.

Chapter Seventy-Six

RUSS COLEMAN
Boudreaux Stables
Raven Bayou, LA

Sunday Before Dawn, 12 June 2005

RUSS JUMPED with the clash of thunder even though he was already awake. Cora jumped too, and then snuggled closer, her body pressed against him all the way to their toes. A gauzy curtain hung at the small window, a patch of black telling Russ even the sliver of a moon was hiding.

Palming his sleepy eyes, he sat up, the sheet barely covering his lap. A hand came around his waist and dipped down. He caught it before any damage was done.

Turning a little, he could see Cora's form stretched catty-cornered on the bed. "I have to go. Duty calls."

He bent and kissed her lightly and got up to dress, his eyes going back to the vision on the bed. In the feeble night light shining from the small bathroom, he took in her deep copper color, beautiful against the white sheets.

When he sat on the edge of the bed to slip on his shoes, the hand returned. He shifted his body again and gazed into her gray eyes. "I'm not as young as I used to be." He gave her another kiss, brushed her hair back with his hand. "Besides, I really do have to go." The smoothness of her cheek almost convinced him to stay, that and the sultry look she wore.

"If I gave you my number, you could call me. Would that be okay?" He wrote his cell number on the back of his card.

Cora took it and looked at it. "I don't have a phone. But you know where I work and where I live." She rolled over and closed her eyes.

The horse in the stall nickered, probably wanting breakfast, and Russ remembered there was only one inside. Cora told him the horse was injured.

He stepped out into muggy air. Yesterday the sun had been shining. The weatherman said there was a twenty percent chance of rain today. From the looks of the sky, he was pretty sure the odds had increased. A thin line of light from the east showed fast, angry clouds rolling in.

If he hurried, he could work in a shower and a cup of coffee before heading to Darlene's. She was healing. At least physically. But she was still unusually quiet. He wondered if the same could be said for Endri. The mind was such a tricky thing. A person could look fine on the outside and be shattered on the inside.

Taylor had been in strange moods of late, and it would, no doubt, get worse. She was a good cop, a good partner, and Boudreaux wanted her crucified. Russ couldn't say he was glad Taylor killed Jax Boudreaux. On the other hand, one less Boudreaux on the planet was a blessing for everybody.

Trey's behavior was unusual lately, at least for Trey. The boy needed to learn to use his instincts, to trust his gut.

And Russ himself had become involved with a woman twenty-five years younger than him, a woman who made him forget his priorities and do things completely unlike himself. He made a mental note to check the calendar for a full moon before sundown.

Then there was Endri. Russ's heart skipped a beat when he thought about the possibility that Endri could be carrying a Boudreaux child. What had made him think of that?

He'd been so worried about her state of mind and her physical health he never gave it a thought. Darlene had her tubes tied after her last baby, so she didn't have to worry about getting pregnant. But Endri...how could she not be at risk? His daughter and a Boudreaux?

Jax Boudreaux got what he deserved.

Russ got to Darlene's and found everybody asleep except the deputy.

"It's been quiet. I checked the perimeter five minutes ago. The back door is locked," the deputy said.

Russ thanked the young man and sent him off, and then decided to rest his eyes for a few minutes. He clicked the TV off and hadn't been settled long when the patter of small feet made him open his eyes. Chantelle and Adoette, stood in their pajamas, staring at him.

"Good morning," he said.

"We like cartoons," replied Adoette in her sweet whisper.

He recollected he was holding the remote against his chest. He handed it over.

"Thank you," came a chorus. They melted onto the floor, two feet from the screen and started the search.

Frank stumbled down the hall and into the kitchen. A few minutes later Russ followed the smell of coffee. As he poured a cup, sounds of the washer starting came from the laundry room. He checked the backyard. When he got back to the living room, the girls were fighting over the remote.

His cell beeped. He had a message waiting. He'd listen to it later, after a security check. He walked around the front yard, out to the sidewalk. The whole block was quiet, except for one car coming slowly down the street. It was Patsy, come to rescue him from the girls. Russ went back inside to refill his cup, forgetting all about the message on his cell.

Chapter Seventy-Seven

GEMINI TAYLOR
Vance Residence
Raven Bayou, LA

Sunday Early Morning, 12 June 2005

GEM PARKED at the curb. Halfway up the walk, she noticed a familiar face at the door.

"Good morning," Russ said.

"Good morning. How's Darlene?"

Before he could answer, Patsy came from the kitchen.

"Better today. Come on in. She'll be glad to see you. Even asked last night when you might come to see her."

Patsy went through the dining room to the sliding glass door and eased it open. "You girls stay in the yard and remember what Russ told you," she called before closing the door and motioning Gem to follow. "She's been looking forward to your visit."

Gem tagged along, down a narrow hallway to the master bedroom. It was homey, with lace doilies on the nightstands and dresser, a big overstuffed chair in pastel flowered fabric, and lamps everywhere. Miss Darlene sat propped against the headboard, her hair covered with a bright blue scarf. She looked neat and fresh. Her eyes were still swollen, the skin now green and yellow from fading bruises, but she smiled when she saw Gem.

A man Gem assumed to be her husband sat in a chair near the window, reading a book. When she visited earlier in the week, she never went in the house, and she suspected Frank Vance had not left his wife's side for more than a few minutes. He was quite handsome, in his fifties, with short gray hair, an oval face the color of creamy coffee, and a large frame.

"Gemini!" she said clear enough though her jaw was still wired. "Come and sit by me. Can you stay a while?"

"As long as you want." Gem sat on the edge of the bed and Miss Darlene reached for her, taking possession of Gem's hand, a lifeline. Gem had planned to go see Mama, but if Miss Darlene needed her here, she'd stay. She could always go see Mama on Monday, after her next torture session with the IA detectives.

"I better get back to the kitchen and keep an eye on those girls," Pasty said with a smile.

"Think I'll go and see if there's a ballgame on," her husband waddled out of the room, leaving the two of them alone.

"Heard anything about Alexander?" Miss Darlene asked. Her lips moved, but with her jaw still wired, her words slurred. "They let him out. You staying? Mostly strangers in my house."

"They're all good cops. You've been safe."

"Safer with you here."

"I think you give me too much credit," Gem said, feeling unfit for such confidence.

"I believed you. You meant what you said. You did, didn't you?"

"I'm not sure what you're talking about, but I don't say things I don't mean."

Miss Darlene leaned forward until they were only inches apart and lowered her voice. Her breath smelled of mouthwash. She must have been rinsing because she couldn't do much brushing with her jaw wired shut. "I remember exactly what you said—'I promise you, Miss Darlene, when we find the man who did this, I'll take care of him personal and you won't ever have to worry about him again.' You did mean it, didn't you?" She took a deep breath through her nose.

Gem froze. Something was not right. That didn't sound like something she'd say at all. Yet Miss Darlene's eyes begged her to confirm it. Gem's fear began to fill the room. Her grip tightened on the woman's hand. "Don't you worry. He'll be put away and you'll be safe."

Miss Darlene leaned closer to whisper in Gem's ear, "You said you'd take care of him! Said he wouldn't be around to hurt anyone!"

Gem tried to remember those words coming from her, but they just weren't there. Her eyes met the woman's. "Darlene, when—exactly—did I say that?"

"Oh, God…" Miss Darlene looked away, sheer terror on her face. She leaned back, releasing Gem's hand. "You don't remember. I should've known." Frigid anger—or fear—rolled off the woman. Her body stiffened as she sat up straight. She rubbed her jaws with both hands.

Gem scooted closer. "Miss Darlene, I don't intend to let anyone hurt you. I've checked with Russ every day to make sure somebody is with you, protecting you and your family."

Miss Darlene's face swung around to Gem, eyes penetrating. "You said you'd take care of him. And I trusted you."

Yes. It was anger.

"You can still trust me," Gem said.

Miss Darlene sat forward again, very close, her voice pressing, low. "You said you'd take care of him, Gemini. You promised. 'I'll take care of him personal and you won't ever have to worry about him again.' That's what you said. And there's only one way to do it!"

A chill ran down Gem's spine. She turned her body toward Miss Darlene, pulled one leg up on the bed, leaned forward, and whispered, "Miss Darlene, this is very important. I need you to tell me everything that happened from the second I arrived in your room that night, till the second I left." Gem took both of Miss Darlene's hands in her own and held them firmly. "Will you do that for me?"

Darlene nodded, her face serious. She grabbed a brown glass bottle from the bedside table, and used the eye-dropper lid to put some liquid in her mouth. Pain medication Gem guessed.

The woman didn't even wash the medicine down with water. She rubbed her jaw for a second, and then started speaking through her teeth. Her memory was quite good and Gem remembered just as Miss Darlene did, Gem's arrival, pulling up the chair, sitting for a long time and getting sleepy. She remembered Gem's words, and her own.

"And then I patted the bed and you held my hand and put your head down. Then sat up and said, 'I'm sure sorry that mean man hurt you, Miss Darlene. I sure am sorry,' and you looked like you were going to cry. You said, 'I promise you, Miss Darlene, when we find the man who did this, I'll take care of him personal and you won't ever have to worry about him again.' Then you laid your head back down and went to sleep. Then—"

"Then I woke up and apologized for falling asleep and you wrote two words on the note pad. 'Do it.' I wondered what made you change your mind."

Miss Darlene frowned. "You don't remember waking up...talking to me?"

What could Gem tell her? She surely wouldn't believe the truth. Gem didn't believe it. She must have been talking in her sleep. Gem closed her eyes, tried to remember, tried to picture what Miss Darlene told her. "I think I'm just so upset over the shooting. Ever since it happened I've been kind of fuzzy. I'm sorry, Miss Darlene."

"So, you'll do it?" she whispered, hope in her eyes.

Chapter Seventy-Eight

WILE E. WAYNE
Vance Residence
Raven Bayou, LA

Sunday Early Morning, 12 June 2005

I COULDN'T STAND how her eyes looked kinda lost, like she was depending on me.

"Miss Darlene, I made you a promise and I kept it. You won't never have to worry about Scott Alexander hurting you."

"Or anyone else?" she pleaded.

"Or anyone. Ever."

She hugged me then and her body kinda jerked like she was crying real hard. When she turned me loose and leaned back against the headboard, she was almost smiling, but there was tears on her cheeks. Sometimes ladies really don't make no sense to me.

"And I promise you I'll never tell anyone what you just told me, unless you ask me to."

"Thank you, Miss Darlene. You feeling better now?" I asked.

"Yes. Much." She pulled a tissue from a box on her night stand and wiped her eyes and blew her nose.

"Then I guess I better go."

She grabbed my hand and squeezed it. "Yes, I guess you better, before someone comes in. Will you come back and see me?"

"Sure, Ma'am."

We went to the living room and sat on the couch. A man was sitting there watching a ball game so we stayed quiet, me and Rocky watching the game while Drew thought about the knife.

I knew she wanted to talk about it, and we couldn't let anyone hear, so we went to the bathroom.

"I'm just not sure we did the right thing, leaving the knife there," Drew whispered.

"I didn't like it as much as I thought," Rocky said. "It's okay if we left it."

"But if they figure out Jax had the knife, they'll let Gemini keep working here and she might find out about that night. You know how she feels about her mama," Drew complained and did the girly, whiny thing. "If they make Gemini quit, we could go back to Dallas. But if they don't find the knife, they might put her in jail. And then what happens to us?"

"You know what happens to us. Besides, Jax was the one who hurt that girl Endri. People need to know. They won't know unless they find the knife," I said.

"They won't know even if they do find the knife. He didn't use the knife on the girl. He just threatened Gemini with it," Drew said.

"I know you wanna go back to Dallas, Drew, but it ain't up to us. Besides, we're doing good here. It ain't Gemini's fault if you're bored. They need to find the knife and prove Jax had it so Gemini can go back to work. Long as she's working, we know who the bad guys are and we can make things better."

"I guess," she said but stuck her lip out in a pout.

"So when Gemini gets the call, we need to make sure she goes, and then we need to make them find the knife." I said.

"Okay," Drew said. "Hey, maybe Trey'll be there."

"Yeah, maybe." Big as Trey was, it would take all of us to hold him down, if we could even then. We needed to come up with a plan, just in case he turned mean.

Chapter Seventy-Nine

GEMINI TAYLOR
Taylor Residence
Raven Bayou, LA

Sunday Mid-Morning, 12 June 2005

GEM'S STOMACH fluttered as she turned the key in the door. She should have known the day was going to suck. In the wee hours of the morning, she'd developed a massive headache, a queasy stomach, and the taste of something vile in her mouth.

Russ had taken one look at her when she came out of the bathroom at Miss Darlene's and told her to go home and get some rest. She didn't argue.

Not only did she have a migraine, but she was totally exhausted. And those stupid voices were in her head again. They weren't exactly voices, not like the Son of Sam heard. She was not crazy. They were thoughts, just in voices that weren't her own.

She adjusted the thermostat to sixty-eight and pressed the power button as she passed the TV. Sitting on edge of her chair, she sipped ice water and listened to the morning news.

The Stormwatch weather team said rain this morning. They were a little late with their prediction. Summer rains blew in and out randomly and were so common, she didn't know why they even bothered to mention them.

She still planned to go see Mama today, just as soon as she got her migraine under control. She'd already taken a pill on the way home but swallowed another, wishing she had heavy curtains to close against the light of day. Even though the sun's presence was subdued by heavy clouds, her eyes squinted to tiny slits, and she sat to keep from falling over.

Caffeine. Diet co-cola. That was what she needed. She headed for the kitchen, but the words of the anchorman stopped her. On the TV screen, a car was being winched out of the river. The phone rang, drowning out the details. Before answering, Gem muted the volume.

"Gemini Taylor?" The deep voice sounded familiar.

"Yes." Her attention was still focused on the TV screen.

"Deputy Long out in Verbois. Thought you'd like to know we found someone who says he saw an old pickup driving up Crowder Road the night Michael Grant was killed."

"That's all the description you got?" She had no idea why this man was calling her at home.

"He said it was a full-size truck with just the driver in the cab. It was sometime after oh-one-thirty, and his trailer sets back off the road a ways."

"Thanks, Deputy. Umm, how did you get my home number?"

"You gave it to me."

"I gave it to you? When?" She couldn't stop the panic in her own voice.

"Right before you left the Grant scene. Listen, I didn't mean to cause a problem. Maybe I misunderstood." He sounded sincere, and disappointed. Gem wondered if she'd know him if she saw him.

"No. No problem. I'm just not feeling well this morning. I appreciate the call. Can I get back to you on this?"

"Sure. Anytime."

Gem hung up, her eyes still taking in the chaos at what appeared to be an accident while she racked her brain for a memory of Deputy Long.

Chapter Eighty

RUSS COLEMAN
Vance Residence
Raven Bayou, LA

Sunday Late Morning, 12 June 2005

HE DIALED in the code to his home answering machine and listened. It was Wilkes. "You might want to meet me at the Breaden Street Bridge. ASAP. I'm sending one of my guys over to cover Darlene."

By the time Russ had his shoes on and finished his coffee, a deputy was knocking on the door. Russ checked his watch. Eleven-hundred hours. As he drove toward Breaden Street, he tried to puzzle out what bothered him about that night twenty years ago when he found Taylor in the closet, but Breaden Street Bridge was too close to give him time to figure it out.

He arrived as the clouds parted, showing patches of bright blue sky. The day decided not to give Russ more than he could bear.

Wilkes stood on the bridge, looking down.

"What's up?" Russ asked.

Wilkes motioned toward the water where a tow truck had pulled a car from the river.

"Whose is it?"

"Scott Alexander's."

Russ had conflicting emotions as he looked at the scene. He was relieved Darlene was out of danger, but he didn't believe Alexander acted on his own. Someone paid him, or forced him to hurt Darlene.

In his heart he took great pleasure knowing Alexander got his comeuppance. But he was also filled with sadness. Another life was gone, a life that might have been worth something if not for drugs, alcohol, and peer pressure. Or the influence of Jax Boudreaux.

Again, Russ would be barred from the investigation. The little Ford rolled up the bank, its front bumper connected to the tow truck winch. The ground was already soggy. Muddy river water poured out the windows, door frames and undercarriage, running down the bank and back into the river.

Wilkes spoke into his radio. "Anything?"

A minute later someone replied, "Not yet."

Russ checked his watch, impatient to call Trey.

When the car was clear of the water and sitting safely on ground, level enough to disconnect the winch, two deputies stuck their heads through the open windows and immediately backed out. One hurried toward the trees and Russ saw him bend and heave. The other looked up toward the bridge and gave the thumbs up sign with both hands.

Russ grabbed his cell and started making calls.

Chapter Eighty-One

GEMINI TAYLOR
Taylor Residence
Raven Bayou, LA

Sunday Late Morning, 12 June 2005

JUST AS SHE STARTED to release the mute on the TV, the phone rang again. Her blood pressure rose, her whole body thumping with the beat of her heart, cranking up the pain in her head.

"You see the news?" Russ asked.

His voice rattled her. For some reason, he was the last person she expected to hear from right now. Or maybe it was just wishful thinking.

Her eyes remained glued to the screen. "It's on now." A tow truck was parked close to the water's edge. Behind it hung an old rusted Ford Fiesta, the hatch pointed toward the river.

"Meet me here, but remember, you were just passing by."

"Where?"

"Breaden Street Bridge. The water wasn't deep enough to completely cover the car. Some walkers saw the front bumper sticking up and called the station."

She watched as deputies moved cameramen and on-scene reporters back. "I'll be there in fifteen minutes," she said, and then more to herself, "Why does that car look familiar?"

"You saw a picture of it at the station. It belongs to Scott Alexander." Now it clicked. She noticed how he didn't say she'd seen it at the Strickland house. Not on the phone. Not with him standing at the scene.

He hung up, and Gem sat with the phone to her ear, pictures of Alexander in a little car, that car, with a girl in the front and two boys in the back. Where the image came from, she hadn't a clue.

Angry dark clouds sat in the distance as Gem pulled away from the house. It would rain soon, so she left the top up on her car. The air was thick with moisture, but at least it was cooler than normal this morning—seventy-one degrees. The low pressure irritated her headache, but at least the voices had stopped.

Chapter Eighty-Two

TREY FONTAINE
Fontaine Residence
Raven Bayou, LA

Sunday Late Morning, 12 June 2005

TREY SAT on the back patio at the house, sipping coffee and thinking about the last few days. A thunderclap had woke him and made him roll out of bed, gun in hand. When he recognized the source of the boom, he slipped his gun back under his pillow and tried to go back to sleep, but thoughts tumbled around in his brain. He soon accepted there was no sense in lying there.

Dark clouds blanketed most of the sky. The air was warm and sticky. He sat in his jeans, barefoot and shirtless, the receiver picking up Ace's words as he sipped iced tea and gathered his thoughts. For the first time in the three weeks he'd been in town, he had a few minutes to do nothing.

Gemini killed Jax Wednesday night. Or rather, Thursday morning. Trey would rather it have been Monty. Muscles knotted in his chest at the thought of the oldest of the Boudreaux boys.

If Trey hadn't been trying to be cool, he would've told his dad about overhearing Monty talk about something "bad" going down at Smitty's. But Trey didn't want to be a snitch. It had cost him his dad. It had cost him everything.

The Boudreaux men were known for their womanizing and temper tantrums. If Jax was like his dad, he would've expected to get away with anything. Taylor said Jax threatened her with a knife. Trey believed her.

He sipped his tea and watched the automatic sprinklers come on. His mother's back yard was huge, with hummingbird feeders hanging from the patio roof. He couldn't imagine his mother filling a feeder with red liquid for the tiny creatures. After his dad was killed, Mom didn't feed much of anything. She refused to form attachments, or even maintain the ones she had.

The sound of the phone sent him hurrying through the sliding glass door. He grabbed it on the third ring.

"I need you ASAP, Bub." Russ sounded tired, but in control. He also sounded anxious.

"What's up?"

"Scott Alexander's car was found in the river this morning. He was inside."

Trey took a breath. "Where are you?"

Russ gave him the location and hung up.

Trey quickly showered and dressed in his standard uniform of black jeans, T-shirt, shoulder holster, and a jacket. He grabbed his wallet and keys, and he noticed the answering machine was blinking. Someone had called while he was in the shower. He pressed the play button and listened.

"Hey, Georgia, this is Jill. We're missing you at the conference. Tycoon Poole did the luncheon speech. You should've been there. It was hilarious. Anyhow, when you get home, give me a call."

His stomach did a little dance as he hurriedly put on his shoes. Mom's friend Jill was the exception to the rule of not getting attached.

Mom didn't make it to the conference? He walked out the door, digging the mint tin from his pocket and dry swallowing a Lortab.

Only one remained.

He called his mother's cell as he opened Streak's driver side door. "The subscriber is out of the area or unavailable at this time. Please try your call again later."

"What the...?"

He drove the few miles to the Breaden Street Bridge, his blood pressure skyrocketing. Georgia Fontaine was not the most open person in the world, but to be out of touch with her friend, and to miss a conference she paid for without so much as a word...It wasn't like her at all.

Trey didn't expect her to call him. She called him on his birthday every year, and that was about it. But she and Jill had been friends for ten years. They had worked together, and both were widows. They visited each other and talked on the phone when they were apart. Something was wrong if Jill didn't know where Mom was.

Maybe tomorrow he would drive to Baton Rouge and check things out. Maybe someone saw her. Maybe her little red T-bird was sitting at a motel or something.

By the time he arrived at the bridge, a crowd had gathered and he had to park a football field away from the scene. *Time to get your head back in the game*, he told himself.

Except Gemini Taylor was there. She wore dark slacks, and a crème colored blouse with short sleeves, her leather bag on one shoulder. She stood with one foot forward, the weight shifted to the other foot, hip outthrust. Her hair hung smoothly around her face. She looked not quite stern, but in control, her mouth showing none of the softness or vulnerability he knew to be behind the "cop" mask.

She set a fine example for him, made him want to stick out his chin and forget about injuries and losses and get on with the business of being an agent.

Maybe Russ was right. Gemini could change with the wind. She was so—

His thoughts were interrupted by the sight of the press and looky-loos peering over the yellow CRIME SCENE tape. He squared his shoulders and approached Gemini and Russ, positioning himself beside her, absorbing her strength.

He did not take her hand, or make any overt gesture to show his admiration or any of the other feelings he had fought so hard not to have. But he stood so close his little finger brushed the side of her hand, and for just a second, he caught a glimpse of a tiny smile.

Chapter Eighty-Three

RUSS COLEMAN
Breaden Street Bridge
Raven Bayou, LA

Sunday Late Morning, 12 June 2005

RUSS LEANED against a tree trunk fifty feet from the scene, hands in pockets, waiting; his mind far away in a poorly lit barn. Though his face was pointed in the right direction, he wasn't really staring at the open back of the vehicle. He eyed the clouds, and didn't envy the guys who would work this scene.

The crowd had been pushed back, and deputies worked the area where evidence tape stretched from tow truck to cruiser. "It's really him?" Taylor's voice came from nowhere.

Russ jumped, partly because of his guilt and the feeling that somehow she knew about Cora. "You should've joined the CIA. It gives me the willies when you creep up on me like that."

If he were a gambler, he'd bet a glint of humor hid behind Taylor's dark shades. Her hair hung loose, a good handle for someone planning to break her nose. She didn't usually wear it down. It was a rookie mistake. Then he remembered she was on administrative leave.

"Is it really him?" She kept her eyes on the car and the two techs combing the interior.

"Yes. It's him. Same as Grant. Why does he start skinning them but never finish? Not that I mind at all when it comes to this guy." He motioned toward the car with his head. "I had a mind to skin him myself."

Trey trotted toward them, making it official—the gang was all here. Taylor turned to the river as if something fascinating had suddenly grabbed her attention. Taking a quick look, Russ saw nothing but CSU working the riverbank.

"What are we waiting for?" Trey said like an eager teen being held at the door of a rock concert.

A minute ticked by in silence before Russ spoke. "I was waiting for you two. Shall we?"

Russ motioned for them to go ahead. Trey let Taylor lead the way. Wilkes would ignore Trey and Taylor as long as they didn't touch anything, but for Russ to be near the evidence might ruin any case that went to court, so he stopped at the end of the bridge, outside the CRIME SCENE tape, while his partner and godson scampered down the grassy hill.

Russ stood back, allowing others to do his job, feeling helpless.

Useless. He didn't know what he was doing here.

Someone did the world a favor when they killed Scott Alexander, sad as the truth was. "I was playing Jax"—that's what Alexander said when Wilkes questioned him about following Darlene—"I was playing Jax."

Jax.

Even if Jax hired Alexander, the threat didn't die with them. Behind these boys stood Jax's cowardly, rich, bastard of a father Alton Boudreaux. Russ was willing to bet on it.

Chapter Eighty-Four

TREY FONTAINE
Breaden Street Bridge
Raven Bayou, LA

Sunday Late Morning, 12 June 2005

THEY APPROACHED the back of the Fiesta, feet sinking several inches into the wet ground with every step. The grass stopped the mud from oozing into their shoes, but it didn't stop the water. By the time they stood by the bumper, their feet were soaked to the ankles.

Water still dripped from the doors and undercarriage of the vehicle. The body in the back was soaked too, its skin pale from being washed out, empty of blood. Scott Alexander lay on his back, entrails hanging down each side of his body like they'd been spewed out by puking through the slit in his belly.

Wilkes worked around them, clicking away with his camera while Trey and Gemini stood back and watched. Someone called for more underwater lights and an extra net. CSU techs in diving gear prepared to search the bottom of the river.

For the first time in his life, Trey was nervous about the turn of events. He, Russ, and Gemini had visited Nick Strickland's house Tuesday. Alexander was there.

Now Alexander was dead.

They hadn't done anything wrong. They weren't responsible for this death, but it still bothered Trey. Maybe it was because Alexander was so young. Seeing young people die reminded Trey how no one knew what would happen, or when. He could have easily died from the bullet he took or been paralyzed for life.

Trey looked again at the body lying in the back of the small car. He leaned over to get a good look at the victim's face and neck. Then he inspected the stab wounds and slit.

Alexander wasn't what Trey would call a good guy. What he did to Aunt Darlene was proof of that. But the only person Trey knew who thought Alexander deserved to die was Russ.

Russ didn't do this, Trey thought. *He couldn't do this, no matter how angry or hurt he was.* So who else could want Alexander dead? There was one other person who definitely had means, motive and opportunity. Jamison Alton Xavier Boudreaux.

He looked up at his godfather, standing up on the bridge, outside the CRIME SCENE tape.

"I need to talk to Russ for a minute," he said to Gemini. "I'll be right back."

She didn't even look his way. Her attention was so focused on the body he doubted she even heard him.

Chapter Eighty-Five

RUSS COLEMAN
Breaden Street Bridge
Raven Bayou, LA

Sunday Late Morning, 12 June 2005

RUSS FELT like a bystander, and not even a curious one. He'd called in the troops and now the best thing he could do was go back to Darlene's and have a beer.

Trey came up the hill and under the tape to stand beside him. "He's too young."

"Too young for what? He wasn't too damn young to rape and beat my sister. The bastard was plenty old enough." Russ's hands fisted.

"No, I mean too young to be a victim. He doesn't fit the pattern. The killer prefers middle-aged men." Trey looked out over the river. "We saw him alive and breathing Wednesday night, and now he's lying here dead by the same method used on Arnold Taylor, Terrand, and Michael Grant. Two of those cases are yours. I wonder if the killer was at the bar the other night. What if he's killing people you're investigating?"

That hadn't crossed Russ's mind. He couldn't believe it was someone in the department trying to get rid of him. No, this was not a grudge thing. This was an evil thing. "I'm not connected to the Terrand case. Besides, who hates me that mu—"

Boudreaux hates me that much.

Trey didn't react, but Russ was sure they were thinking the same thing.

"I have to say something. It's important," Trey said.

"Go on and say it," Russ said, sure of what was coming.

"Alton Boudreaux's son was killed by your partner. The man who attacked Aunt Darlene is dead. Listen to me. I need you to *hear* this: You need to have someone with you at all times. Don't go anywhere alone."

"Don't worry about me, Bub. I can take care of myself."

Trey turned toward Russ, leaning his elbow atop the bridge. "Russ, if Boudreaux gets as much as a flat tire, he's going to blame you. They're going to be all over you on this. Boudreaux will see to it. Now would be a really good time for you to take a few vacation days and stay at Aunt Darlene's."

Russ faced him. "I understand. Now you understand this: Alton Boudreaux is not gonna run me out of my department. Taylor acted out of self-defense, and we both know I didn't do this." He pointed toward the dripping car.

"I know," Trey argued. "But that won't stop Boudreaux from trying to blame you for both deaths. Besides, there's something else you could be doing, something important that would be a big favor to me."

"What?" Russ asked, his attention suddenly focused on his godson.

"Mom didn't make it to the conference." Trey gritted his teeth and pressed his lips together.

"You sure?" Russ understood Trey's worry. Georgia Fontaine would never pay for a conference, and then not show up. Even now, when she had a good income, she was practical and thrifty.

"There was a message on her phone this morning from her best friend wondering why she didn't show."

Russ considered this. Georgia was prompt, and kept her commitments. Something was wrong.

"I'll make a few calls when I get back to Darlene's." He jangled the keys in his pocket, stared at the ground as he tried to come up with something to calm Trey. Looking over the scene one more time, he saw Taylor staring at the dripping car, off in her own world.

"Think I'll leave the two of you to ponder the meaning of all this. I'm going to Darlene's. Let me know what you figure out."

"Russ," Trey called, taking a couple of steps to close the gap. He leaned in a little and whispered, "Please, if not for yourself, then for me, stay at Aunt Darlene's. If I know you and Aunt Darlene are safe and you're looking for Mom, I'll be able to concentrate on this mess. Maybe we can find some answers before Boudreaux knocks the shit into the fan."

He nodded, hugged Trey, and then went to his unit and crawled behind the wheel.

No matter how the jury decided, there was going to be hell. Russ gripped the steering wheel and envisioned his hands wringing Alton Boudreaux's throat.

Chapter Eighty-Six

GEMINI TAYLOR
Breaden Street Bridge
Raven Bayou, LA

Sunday Noon, 12 June 2005

SHE LOOKED UP the hill where Trey and Russ were talking. Russ had that Louisiana Hot Sauce look on his face. He knew he couldn't work this scene and it was apparent in the slump of his shoulders. He hugged Trey and walked to his unit. Trey came back down to the little car at the center of attention.

She and Trey stood watching as Wilkes walked around the car, talking into his recorder. Trey was so close she could smell him, but he hadn't said a word to her. It was impossible to keep her mind straight with him so near. His aftershave blew on the wind, surrounding her. She knew nothing of men's colognes or aftershave, but whatever it was, it smelled clean and tugged at her.

She wasn't the only one who thought so. Was that laughter she heard? It sounded like a teenage girl. She turned from watching Wilkes snap pictures to look over her shoulder at the crowd, trying to figure out where the laughter came from, but they were too far away.

The giggle was way too close to be coming from the crowd. It was coming from inside her head. A chill crawled up her spine making the hairs on her neck stand. Someone was watching her.

"Gemini?"

Trey's voice brought her back and she recognized the feeling that meant she'd started to fade away. Another second and she wouldn't have been there. She turned to him and saw concern.

"Yes," she said with deliberate conviction. "What?"

"You just looked a little strange."

"Thanks." She tried to smile.

"I can tell you want to jump right in there." He was so close she could've leaned back a few inches and touched him. Her head pounded and sweat covered her body.

"Excuse me," Wilkes said and moved between her and the rear bumper. She jumped like she'd been caught doing something wrong. Trey stepped back and slipped his hands into his pockets, projecting his intention to keep his hands to himself.

Tell Wilkes to look in the rip of the back seat. Gem looked behind her. There was only Trey. It wasn't his voice whispering in her ear. *The knife is there. Jax's knife.*

She swallowed hard and tried to smile, thankful her dark glasses covered her eyes. Without warning, her stomach contracted, but she was able to move a few steps away from the others before vomiting.

Instantly Trey stood beside her, one hand on her forehead and one on her ribs. The last thing she remembered was his soothing voice telling her everything was going to be all right while voices in her head argued over whether or not they should kill him.

Chapter Eighty-Seven

TREY FONTAINE
Breaden Street Bridge
Raven Bayou, LA

Sunday Early Afternoon, 12 June 2005

HE HELD GEMINI firmly until she stopped heaving. She straightened, her face pale and delicate looking.

"I think I'll take her to the doctor," he said to Wilkes, who stood back watching them, annoyance written on his face.

"Oh, for goodness sake! I don't need a doctor. It's just a migraine and it's gone now." Her voice sounded a little higher than normal after what her throat had just been through, but she did look better.

Trey was suddenly self-conscious about his hand on her ribs. He dropped it to his side and took a half step away.

"Where did Detective Coleman go?" she asked, looking around the scene.

Trey and Wilkes looked at each other in confusion, and then at her. "He went back to the station," Trey said.

"Well then, I guess I should do the same. If you'll excuse me." She stepped between them and turned her eyes to the body in full view through the open hatchback of the car. She shuddered and quickly averted her gaze, laying a hand softly against her chest. She hurried toward her Caddie.

Trey took all this in. There'd been no sign of a squeamish stomach at the Grant scene, or at the scene in the park, but the sight of this body really bothered her.

"I better drive her," he said to Wilkes. "She's seems to be a little off yet. Will the Caddie be okay there?" He nodded toward the vehicle parked just off the road.

Wilkes lowered his voice. "I'll have a couple of my guys take it to the station. You might need to take that girl to the doctor."

"Thanks," Trey said and jogged to catch up with her. He really didn't want to leave the scene. He'd rather keep an eye on the processing just in case someone here was friendly with Boudreaux. Strange things could happen to evidence when money entered the picture. Everyone had a price. He hoped no one here would sell Russ out. Several deputies were already in their units, ready to leave, but CSU would be there for a good part of the day, and Wilkes would stay with them. Trey trusted Wilkes, and someone had to take care of Gemini. She was really upset over this body and he wondered why.

Gemini was just reaching for the driver's door handle when he came up behind her. "Why don't you let me drive you? It's already been a rough day."

She turned to him with a frozen look in her eyes. Then her smile returned and she stepped away from the door. "How very kind of you, Trey." She passed her keys to him and walked around the rear of the car, headed for the passenger door.

"Why don't I take you in mine? The Caddie will be fine. I checked with Wilkes. He'll take care of it." He bent over and put the key in the ignition.

"Yes, that would be fine. I am feeling a little out of sorts. Thank you."

He opened the door of Streak for her, which earned him another curve of her beautiful lips, and helped her in, thinking all the while about the drastic change in her choice of words and mannerisms. There was no logical explanation for her behavior.

She sat carefully, and then swung her legs in and crossed them at the ankles. "Look at these sho—" The words stopped. She gazed at Trey before uncrossing her legs and tucking her muddy, sandaled feet as far out of sight as possible.

"Is something wrong?"

"Oh, it's nothing." She leaned away from the door so he could close it.

He climbed in the driver's door and scrutinized her. Something was terribly wrong, but she smiled, her cheeks now rosy and her eyes bright.

They rode to the station in silence. A slight wind stirred the leaves of the trees, and dark clouds roiled in the distance. Trey couldn't help notice the difference in Gemini's demeanor. Her perfect posture, hands folded demurely in her lap, feet hidden.

When he parked, she waited for him to open her door and thanked him graciously. He'd never seen puking have such an effect on a woman. She distanced herself from him, apparently embarrassed by his seeing her throw-up, and acted like she had to make up for it by being polite and reserved. It must've really bothered her.

He allowed her to lead the way. Her hips swayed gently, like she was gliding down the runway in heels. It was hard to think of Gemini as a model. Or a Southern lady. But he'd never seen her so genteel. Refined might be the appropriate word. And self-assured. Normally, Gemini Taylor was tough, capable, strong. But she changed too often to fit into any mold.

He couldn't figure her out, but that was all right. It wasn't necessary. Like it or not, he'd fallen for her, his mind on her much more than was healthy. So be it. Understanding her was much less important right now than just being with her any way he could.

They found Russ in the pit, sitting in his chair making notes on a yellow pad.

"Gemini wasn't feeling very well, so I brought her. Wilkes is having someone bring the Caddie."

Russ looked at his partner. "Are you okay?"

"I'm perfectly fine. Just give me a sec in the ladies' room and I'll be ready to go. I'd very much like to retrieve the Cadillac. I have some things to do before dark." She turned and walked away, leaving both men staring in bewilderment.

Chapter Eighty-Eight

GEMINI TAYLOR
Sheriff's Dept.
Raven Bayou, LA

Sunday Early Afternoon, 12 June 2005

SOMEHOW she had gotten herself from the Breaden Street Bridge to the women's locker room of the station without remembering how. She glanced in the mirror. The face staring back at her looked like a nightmare. Her eyeballs were bloodshot, her lips looked chapped, and her hair was loose and wild. She washed her hands, pulled a scrunchy from her leather bag and gathered her hair into it.

She stepped back, her shoes squishing and looked down to find her sandaled feet covered in mud. *Crap.* Slipping her shoes off, she rinsed and toweled them dry before washing her feet in the sink, one at a time, all the while wondering where the hell she'd been.

It was Sunday, and here she was at work. With muddy sandals and no clue. Her car keys weren't in her purse or pocket. Someone must have brought her here. After a final mirror check, she headed for the pit. Trey and Russ sat talking quietly.

"Feeling better?" Trey asked.

"Fine. What's up?" she said, pretending everything was normal.

"No way I can work the case. Wilkes will probably ask Trey to help, so I'm heading back to Darlene's," Russ said.

"Great. You have my cell number if you need me." She turned to Trey and lowered her voice a little. "And I assume if anything links the death to Jax or either of the Grants, you'll let me know?"

He smiled. "Glad to see you're feeling better. I'll walk you out."

Trey was silent as they headed to the parking lot. When she saw her Caddie parked so close to the building, she knew someone else had driven it here. She always parked in the back of the deputies' lot, straddling a space divider so no one could ding her doors. Having a gated lot for private vehicles was a real perk for employees in uniform.

"Got plans tonight?" he asked as they reached the car.

Gem looked at her watch. It was almost one-thirty. Almost one hour to the prison, no more than two inside, and one home. *I should be home doing laundry by evening until my shift at Miss Darlene's.* "Nothing special. What did you have in mind?"

"I make a mean chicken soup."

They settled on pizza and beer. He would bring it around seven. That left her plenty of time to get everything done. She cranked the car, and then suddenly, the little guy in her head started with the hammer again. *Tell Wilkes to look in the rip in Alexander's seat. The knife is there. Jax's knife.*

She stared into Trey's eyes, her belly, as well as her throat, burned. "There's something bothering me about Alexander's car."

"What?"

"The rip in the back of the seat," she said in a whisper, as if to herself. "Was that made by the knife the killer used?"

"What are you talking about?"

"Huh?" She blinked. "Oh, don't mind me. I'm just a little tired. Maybe it's just my brain working overtime. See you later." Gem spun out of the parking lot and down the old highway south of town.

Her mind swirled in confusion. Trey was so honest. Too much so to set her up. It wasn't possible that he took the knife. He believed in her. Defended her. Why would he take the knife? It didn't make sense.

The humid air stuck to her, leaving her face and naked arms moist. The top was still up on the Caddie, which turned it into a giant broiler and she was the daily special.

Her gas tank was full, but she stopped at the Gas N' More, the last station for the next twenty-five miles, for a bottle of water. The drive to the prison was a long one, and she'd skipped breakfast, but her stomach wasn't up to food. Pulling back out onto the highway, her mind returned to the knife.

Trey was Russ's godson. She trusted him. There had to be another explanation. As she cruised along toward yet another complication in her life, she tried to find it.

Thoughts of that *other* complication resurfaced as she drew closer to her destination. Mama. The last time Gem visited, her mother sent her away. Refused to talk to her. Mama had threatened to never talk to Gem or see her again if she didn't stop trying to find the truth about Daddy's death and gain Mama's freedom.

THE TOWERS and guards looked the same as Gem remembered from her last visit. The heavy clank of the metal doors locking made her light-headed.

She stood in line with several dozen other people, moving like cattle toward the feed. When her turn came, the woman behind the glass checked her I.D. and asked who she was visiting. Gem filled out the short form, took the key for the locker for her bag, locked it away and sat.

Ten minutes later her name was called. They stamped her hand with the date, and she was escorted through the locked door. After a cursory search, she was sent up the metal stairs.

When Gem arrived at the guard's table, her hand was checked under a blue-light wand. Then it was into the small visiting room for more waiting.

"Miss Taylor, the prisoner refused to see you." It was the officer on the other side of the glass. Gem's mind had been somewhere else, not paying attention to the empty room. The officer was a large woman, tall, muscular. She had a booming voice that didn't require the use of the phone to make Gem hear her.

She sat statue still, dumbfounded. How Mama could actually refuse her visit, just like that, not wanting help or even trying to help herself, was beyond Gem. She was so shocked she forgot her claustrophobia and sat in the empty room until the guard made her leave.

GEM SANK into her Caddie in the parking lot, not remembering how she'd gotten there. Trying to regain control, she wiped away tears and stared at the brick building looming over her, the sun a giant heat lamp too close to her skin. Humidity turned her crisp cotton shirt into a wilted rag. She looked to the northwest, toward Raven Bayou. Dark clouds blew across the sky in that direction.

Three guard towers were visible, and more stood on the far side of the building, toward the woods. It was at least five miles to the nearest house and ten to a wide spot in the road that some might call a town.

For a hundred yards all the way around the outside of the fence the grass was groomed with trees and underbrush cut back for a clear view. And a clear shot.

This prison was built in the fifties for hard-core criminals. Less than a decade later, the inmate population outgrew the facility and became a penitentiary for women lifers. As far as The System was concerned, Maine Taylor would spend the rest of her life behind those razor-wire topped electric fences. Entombed in a dark mass of bricks and mortar, her life was over. She was nothing but the walking dead. She believed it too.

It would've been easy enough for Gem to show her identification and have Mama delivered to an interrogation room. But it would've required her being chained and subjected to a strip search after the visit. Gem couldn't put her mama through that.

She closed her eyes and tried to remember the last words Mama had spoken to her. Then she understood the reason she couldn't hear Mama's voice was because of the other voices. The voices in her head had returned.

Her body suddenly became light as a feather. The seat and windshield and doors faded away into a beautiful blue. Calmly, she closed her eyes and gave in to the feeling of floating while familiar voices lulled her away.

SHE KNEW her eyes were open, but she couldn't see a thing. Her other senses worked just fine, but the information they transmitted to her brain threw her into sheer terror. Her body sat in her Caddie, but she wasn't alone. Though her car was big, she was being crushed like a sardine in a very small can.

Her self was squeezed in between the driver's door and another person. But that was not the half of it. There was someone behind her, and someone else sat on her lap. Although she felt their closeness, she couldn't feel their bodies. It was not like flesh pressed against her outer self. More like a constriction of her soul. The one on Gem's lap was weightless, but more powerful than she was.

She knew the smell of her car. The combination of the leather conditioner she used on the upholstery, and the gardenia body lotion she liked. Mixed together, they had a uniquely sweet, clean aroma. Yes, she was definitely in her car.

And then there were the voices. They all sounded familiar, like she had known them for years. They spoke like she wasn't there. She wanted to yell at them to shut up, but her mouth wouldn't cooperate. She couldn't even feel her lips. In the meantime all she could do was listen and think that she must be crazy.

"She likes Trey too much," said the voice of a young boy sitting to Gem's right, "We can't let her out."

"Well, we sure gotta keep an eye on Ginni. I thought for sure Trey and that detective knew something was wrong," the young woman on her lap said. The woman's voice was soft, with a seductive lilt. Gem immediately recognized it as the one who giggled at the crime scene. She must be young. A teenager.

"I can take care of Trey," sneered the boy by the passenger door, this one an older boy whose voice sometimes squeaked with the change so common at puberty. His words sounded threatening and Gem wondered if Trey might be in danger from him. Or maybe she was the one in danger.

"Well, we can't let Taylor out. She's too thin. Gemini can break through her any time she wants." The boy in the center of the front seat next to her said. He looked to be no more than five or six.

"We need to talk to Gemini. Once she knows the truth, she'll understand. She's not like Ginni. Gemini knows how bad some people can be. I've seen her be mad when somebody deserves to be punished and gets off," said the teenage girl in her lap.

"Maybe you're right. Let's try," The youngest boy beside her said.

Immediately someone flipped on a light and Gem could see. She turned to the right and looked the boy in the eye. He was young and skinny with green eyes and dark, straight hair. *What do I say to him? What do I call him?*

"I'm Wile. I take care of you." He almost smiled at her.

How did he do that? She must be losing her mind. This couldn't be happening. It was all just a bad dream.

"Oh, we're real," said the blond girl on her lap. "I'm Drew. I came when your bastard of a daddy tried to stop your mama from taking you away. I'm fifteen," she said proudly.

Drew turned to face Gem and Gem looked right into her blue eyes. She was pretty, with an oval face and full lips. Gem couldn't help but turn to the other boy by the passenger's door. He had huge brown eyes, chestnut hair, and his mouth was very small. He wouldn't look her in the eye. *And you?*

"I'm Rocky. You don't need to know much about me." His voice squeaked barely above a whisper.

How old are you?

"Twelve," Rocky said, still not looking at her.

"And I'm five," Wile told her.

She turned back to Wile. *Who's behind me?*

"Taylor and Ginni. Ginni came in Texas. Taylor came when you were in the academy and that mean trainer kept yellin' at you. We brought her to help you do your job."

Yes. She'd definitely lost her mind.

Why can't I talk? And how do you know what I'm thinking?

"We're not gonna let you out until we know we can trust you," Wile said, his face somber.

What do you mean, "let me out?"

They all looked at each other like it was a silly question.

"We all come to help you," Drew said. "We keep your memories so you don't have to. We protect you. If we were to let you out now, you might do something to get us in trouble." Drew looked to Wile. "Maybe we should let her talk while we're in the car. There's no one around to hear."

Wile thought that over while Gem wondered why Drew deferred to him. Then something changed. Gem could feel her body on the seat, her left arm lying atop the driver's door, elbow out the open window. Her chest rose and fell with the breathing she controlled. The humid air stuck to her skin. She closed her eyes and took a deep breath.

Thank God. It was just a nightmare.

"It wasn't a nightmare. We're still here. Don't be scared." Wile's voice said.

Her skin pebbled with goose bumps. This was worse than a nightmare. She wiped the sweat from her face with shaking hands and wondered if there was some way to escape them.

"Shut up! Everybody just shut up for a minute!" She almost screamed as her hands went to her temples, trying to hold everything together. She closed her eyes, hoping to clear her head.

A genteel voice came from behind her. "Gemini, don't be afraid. They're all good children. They mean well."

"Who is that?"

"I'm Ginni. The kids thought maybe I could help you understand who we are and that we love you. You're safe."

Gem covered her ears and squeezed her eyes shut. *God, please. Make it stop.* Her heart pounded so hard it hurt. There wasn't enough air to fill her lungs. Gem thought she might be having a heart attack.

When she opened her eyes, the brightness of the day made them throb. She squinted to shut out some of the light and looked around. Dozens of cars surrounded her as she sat in the parking lot of the prison.

Except for the call of a single gull in the air, blissful silence engulfed her. Finally, she was alone. After taking a deep breath, she put her hand on the keys dangling in the ignition.

Before she could start the car, her world tumbled. Dizziness overwhelmed her. Her eyes closed involuntarily and there in her car, surrounded by others who again controlled her body, Gem fainted.

Chapter Eighty-Nine

TREY FONTAINE
Breaden Street
Raven Bayou, LA

Sunday Afternoon, 12 June 2005

WHILE AT THE STATION, Trey learned nothing about his mom. Russ had called some other departments and some hospitals. It wasn't like her to disappear, and Trey was worried. He wondered if he would feel the same had there been no string of violent crime in the area.

He managed to get himself back to the scene on autopilot. Divers were still in the water. Wilkes was still documenting. The body was still in the car. Barlow and an assistant had arrived and most of the crowd had dispersed.

"Been inside the car yet?" he asked.

Wilkes shook his head.

The windows were down. Trey walked to the passenger side and stuck his head through the back window. Near the top was a small cut in the vinyl. His stomach lurched.

"Wilkes," he called and motioned the man to him.

"What?"

Trey pointed to the cut. "Make sure the techs open up that seat and look inside."

"For what?" Wilkes said, eyeing the slit.

"For evidence. I have to go somewhere, but I'll be back in town in a few hours. You got my cell number?"

"At the station."

Trey gave it to him again. "Anything comes up, give me a call?"

"Sure."

As he drove, Trey's mind raced through how to handle Maine Taylor.

Trey had seen mothers who would do anything for their children. If Russ was right about the sexual abuse, Maine may have killed her husband to protect Gemini. Or she might have hired someone else to do it. Trey didn't think either of those were the case. If he was right, the woman had confessed to a murder she didn't commit in order to protect the real killer.

Or Russ could be wrong about the incest, but was right about one thing. If Maine was not the killer, she knew who was. She was in the house and was found covered in blood. She confessed, not something she would've done for a stranger.

Chapter Ninety

WILE E. WAYNE
LOUISIANA CORRECTIONAL
INSTITUTE FOR WOMEN
ST. GABRIEL, LA

Sunday Afternoon, 12 June 2005

"WELL, at least while she's asleep we can plan stuff without her getting crazy," I told the others.

"So, what're we gonna do?" Rocky asked.

"I think it's time we got rid o' the man who started all this. And maybe the younger one too."

"And then what, Wile? You think she'll be alright if we get rid of 'em? I liked it better when we was in Dallas. Or maybe we can all move back to Aunt Ginny's. It was nice there," Drew said.

"Maybe. But first we're gonna make Gemini understand why we're here. You drive, Drew. We need to get back to town and figure out how to make sure that old man can't ever put his hands on another kid."

Drew turned the key.

"Wait! Duck!" I hollered.

All of us slunk down in the seat.

"What?" Drew asked.

"The Hummer," I said. "Trey is here. I told you he was dangerous." I peeked out the window. The big gray tank was pulling in the lot marked for law enforcement. Drew was all goo-goo eyes. She liked the truck almost as much as she liked that big ol' man. "Okay, let's get out of here."

"You got an idea, Wile? I mean about how to get to the old man?" Drew asked.

"I figure we need to get him alone first. So all we gotta do is have a woman call and say she's a widow and she has a five-year-old daughter."

"Yeah. That'd do it," Drew agreed and pulled out of the lot.

Chapter Ninety-One

TREY FONTAINE
LOUISIANA CORRECTIONAL
INSTITUTE FOR WOMEN
ST. GABRIEL, LA

Sunday Afternoon, 12 June 2005

HE FLASHED HIS BADGE at the gate, received a temporary placard and was directed to park in a state vehicle lot. Just as he turned the engine off, his cell rang.

"Chance found a knife," Russ said.

Alarms went off in Trey's head and the hair on his arms stood up. "Where?"

"In Alexander's car. The slit in the back of the rear seat. The techs took the seat apart and found a knife. A skinning knife. Avlee found a partial print on it. There wasn't enough for a positive, but it could be Jax's."

"Jax's knife? Or Jax's print?" Trey said.

"Both. The print was a six-point match. Looks like someone else handled the knife and smudged the print. Probably someone wearing gloves. The knife was bloody. Human blood, Alexander's type. They're still testing."

"So maybe Alexander went into the ladies' room and stole the knife," Trey said.

"I don't see how Taylor would've missed that, but it's possible."

"Yeah. She was pretty shook up. Thanks Russ."

"You want to come down and see what else we have?"

"Can't right now."

"Where are you?"

"The prison."

"Oh." There was a pause. "Good luck. Let me know what you learn."

"You got it. Any news on Mom?"

"Nothing. I'm still on it."

"Call me?"

"You know it."

Trey hung up, glad to know Russ was the one looking for his mom. He couldn't imagine any scenario that would make his mother change her plans and tell no one.

IT TOOK LESS than fifteen minutes to obtain clearance to interview the prisoner who was delivered to a small room where he waited.

"Good afternoon, Mrs. Taylor."

She was a small woman, her dark hair streaked with gray. She looked at him suspiciously as an officer led her to a chair and cuffed her hand to the steel loop connected to the metal table. The officer nodded to him and closed the door on her way out.

"Who are you?" Her voice was gravelly, like a smoker.

"I'm Trey Fontaine, a friend of your daughter's." He pulled out the other chair and sat opposite her. "I think she has a problem and I'm trying to help her."

A deer-in-the-headlights look pasted itself on her face. "You're a cop. You work with her?" she finally asked. Her hand went to the top button on her shirt. The wide, horizontal black stripes of the white shirt helped hide her rail thin body, but the short sleeves showed the skin and bones of her arms.

"I'm an agent with the FBI. Gemini's partner, Russell Coleman, is my godfather. He introduced us. She's too beautiful to ignore, so I asked her out. And the rest, as they say, is history."

"Did she send you?" She sounded hopeful as she peered toward the door where he had entered. "Is she waiting outside? I'm not going to see her." She sat silent a moment before asking, "What kind of problem?"

Trey shifted in his chair uncomfortably, and looked at his hands on the table like they belonged to someone else, clasped together, one thumb rubbing the other.

"Now that I'm here, I'm thinking maybe this isn't such a good idea." He still didn't look up.

"If my daughter is having some kind of problem, I have a right to know. What is it?" She no longer looked startled, or scared.

"Well, it's actually...kind of personal. We've been dating and..." *Come on, Maine. You can do it. Ask.* Trey willed her to respond.

"And what, Mr. Fontaine?"

He looked up to find her head tilted toward him.

"Well...she loves me, but I feel like she's keeping a big secret. One she can't tell me."

"Do—" Maine Taylor hesitated. "Do you love her?"

Trey looked at her, struggling to keep his mind in the game. "I do."

"Is she in love with you?"

"I believe so, Ma'am."

Her eyes shone with tears. "Is she still out there? Did she come with you today, Mr. Fontaine?"

"Please, call me Trey. No, she didn't come. She doesn't know I'm here."

"Gemi came. She was here not twenty-five minutes ago."

Trey wondered if Gemini saw him arrive. Too late now. "I thought maybe you could help me...could tell me why she seems so distant. If I just knew what she was holding back...I need to know about her past." He dropped his gaze to the table and waited. Again. Silence pounded through the room like a rapid heartbeat, only the tick of his watch echoing between them.

Finally, he raised his head. Maine Taylor stared back at him with pale blue eyes. Tears rolled down her cheeks.

"If you love her, don't give up on her. She's needed someone to love her for a long time. When she was little, I was so busy working to keep food in our mouths and a roof over our heads, I didn't have time to let her know how much I loved her. Didn't have time to do half the things I should of."

"What about her dad? Did he spend time with her? Surely she knew you both loved her."

Hatred filled her eyes. Her lips compressed to a hard line. "He was a bastard."

"I understand that you killed him because he was violent with you. But he must've loved Gemini. He didn't hurt her did he? How could anyone hurt Gemini? She's so lovely, so strong. How could any man not love her?"

Maine's gaze dropped, tears falling into her lap. She wiped her nose on the back of her hand. "If you love her, don't be dragging up the past," she whispered. "Did she send you here to get information out of me? Is this how she intends to help me? I told her and I'll tell you, I don't need any help. This is where I belong."

"She didn't send me. I told you, she doesn't know I'm here. But if there's something else in her past, something I don't know..."

Her eyes cut toward him and he thought she would scream. But in this small, sanitized room, far away from the rest of the inmates, there was only interminable silence. When she finally spoke it startled him.

"What was that, Ma'am? I'm sorry, I didn't hear you." But he had, and understood.

Her head snapped up, eyes throwing daggers. "I said that bastard couldn't love anyone. Arnold Taylor was a vicious beast. He beat her, tortured her. He'd been selling her, using her to keep his useless ass employed."

This wasn't what Trey had expected. He couldn't keep surprise from showing in his eyes. "You mean...he...?" After her confession, he struggled to keep it together.

There was no remaining distant. *Pull yourself together. Don't blow it.* He took a deep breath and looked again at Taylor's mother, yet another victim in this whole tragedy.

She sobbed, her eyes squeezed shut against his words.

"Gemini never said...I didn't...no wonder..." He twisted his class ring on one hand with the fingers of the other, averting his eyes, forcing his jaw muscles to relax. Trying to breathe the fury away.

"I knew he was an evil man, but I had no idea how evil until it was too late. Mr. Fontaine—Trey. Please, don't give up on her. I was blind and stupid and so wrapped up in my own problems I didn't see the truth. There's nothing I can ever do to make it up to her. But maybe if you stick with her, you can give her back some of what he took away."

"No wonder Gemini wouldn't share any of her past with me. She must think no one will believe her. And she probably thinks no one can be trusted." Sweat gathered under his arms. He trembled inside. His gaze went to the air vent that should have been throwing out cold air, but the A/C was silent. He hated to lie, but he had to gain her trust somehow. "Is there any more you can tell me? Anything about her history that might let me get closer to her?"

"You could talk to Ginny."

"Ginny?"

"My little sister, Virginia. I raised her. Raised half my sisters. I was the oldest girl, so by the time I was eight I was taking care of my younger siblings."

"You were the mom."

"Yes. By the time I was fifteen, I'd had enough of raising children. That's why I only had one. She was an accident. Swore I'd never have any, but when I learned I was pregnant, I couldn't..." She fisted the hand lying on the counter. "Virginia was the baby of the family. Ten years younger than me. When I was taken into custody, I had the police call Ginny. She took Gemi home with her."

"One more question, Mrs. Taylor. Gemini spends all her spare time trying to prove you're innocent. There have been some other murders in Raven Bayou Parish recently. They all have something in common with the way your husband was killed." He stared into her eyes, and then softened his tone just a little. "They were all stabbed in the heart, their abdomens slit open."

Maine's eyes conveyed shock. Sobs racked her body. Tears streamed, washing her cheeks, dripping off her chin, mucus running from her nose. Trey offered his handkerchief. She had to bend down so that her shackled hands could wipe her face.

"If you really love her, Mr. Fontaine, take her somewhere far away. Get her out of that parish, out of this state. Quit your job and move to Mexico or Canada. She's in danger here." She twisted the handkerchief into a rope and wound it through her fingers.

"In danger from whom? The killer? Did she see him that night?"

Surprise showed on her face. "Get her mind off me. Take her away."

"I believe her, Mrs. Taylor. I don't think you killed your husband." He leaned forward over the table. "Who're you covering for?"

She shook her head violently but didn't speak. Trey hoped he could out wait her. Hoped the wait was worth it. Minutes ticked by before she regained control. Finally, she sat up straight and stared into his eyes.

"If you really know my Gemi, if you really love her, you'll protect her.

Stop trying to find Arnold's killer. Just get her away. There's no way to change the past. Arnold is dead, as he should be, and I'm paying penance, as I should be. Take her away. Love her. The killings will stop. If you'll just love her, the killings will stop." Her words were spoken so softly he strained to make them out. He struggled to control his breathing, to stay calm. He took a deep breath and let it out slowly, wondering what he could say to make her tell him what he needed to know.

Before he could say another word, Maine yelled, "Guard! Get me out of here!"

Chapter Ninety-Two

TREY FONTAINE
En Route to Lufkin, Texas

Sunday Late Afternoon, 12 June 2005

TREY DROVE ninety miles an hour, but it would still take forty minutes to make it to Lufkin. He pulled out his cell. He could depend on Bobby Hopkins to find him some information without asking too many questions. Hopkins was his regular partner, the man who had his back when Trey was not on limited duty and baby sitting.

"Hopkins, I need a couple of favors," he said. "First, check on any crimes or accidents in the state involving a red, 1957 T-bird coupe. Call me immediately if you find anything. And—"

"Wait. You told me about that car before. That's your mom's car."

"Yeah. A long story. I'll tell you later. And pull whatever you have on dissociation. I need you to read to me."

"Will do, but wouldn't you rather talk to one of the pros?"

"No. Not yet."

"You talk to Red lately?" It was the nickname he'd given Tamlyn, his favorite analyst.

"No. She got something?"

"Found eighteen other missing persons reports involving young women who worked at casinos across the country. They're setting up a task force and we're gonna have some women go undercover."

"Great," was all Trey could think to say.

"You off on a wild goose chase of your own making?"

"I'm not sure it's a wild goose. You've heard the saying, 'if it quacks like a duck and walks like a duck, it's probably a duck?' Well, I think it's only pretending to be a duck." He pressed the END CALL button and dug through the console for his headset. Slipping it on, he waited for the phone to ring again.

It made no sense. Trey Fontaine prided himself on using empirical evidence. He didn't believe in hocus pocus, astrology, channeling, ghosts, and psychological crap. But he was in way over his head with this. What he was thinking was impossible, but going through the motions was necessary. He had to know for sure that Gemini was innocent.

The thermometer measured the outside temperature at ninety-eight degrees. The A/C was cranked up to frigid, but sweat poured down his sides.

Maine Taylor's words repeated over and over in his head—"if you'll just love her, the killings will stop."

Gemini's words echoed—"*when I was little I got my brain fractured.*"

The ringing of the cell broke into his thoughts.

"Okay, Trey," Hopkins said, "where you want me to start?"

THE DOOR of the condo swung open, and Trey came face to face with a smaller, older version of Gemini Taylor.

"Mrs. Phillips? Virginia Phillips?"

She nodded, a look of surprise on her face. Trey thought how very familiar she looked to him.

"I'm Trey Fontaine, a friend of Gemi's, I mean, Gemini Taylor's."

"Is Gemini here?" she asked, craning her neck around him.

"No, Ma'am. She doesn't know I'm here. I thought maybe we could talk."

One thing Trey knew about Southern women was that they were too hospitable. She would let him in without hesitation rather than risk insulting him.

Mrs. Phillips led him to the kitchen table and served iced tea before sitting herself. "Now, what is it you want to talk about?"

Trey swallowed hard and took a breath. He looked around the small house, his gaze sweeping over the spotless granite countertops, the kitchen cupboards with glass inset doors, and the small archway leading to a formal dining room. "You have a beautiful home," was all he could think to say.

"How very kind of you," she replied and the echo brought the hairs up on his neck like porcupine quills. Those were Gemini's words when he had offered to drive her to the station from the Alexander scene.

Call me Ginny. It's my nickname. His stomach turned as his mind continued to put things together.

"I'm not sure where to start," he said. Then he began by explaining his connection to her niece through Russ and the department. He ended with a simple statement, "I've been in love with Gemini since we were kids." Not a statement. A confession.

The woman's smile was one of pride. "Men fall in love with Gemini. It's just a fact but, for goodness sake! They don't usually come all the way to Lufkin to tell me!" Her hand flew softly to her chest and again realization hit Trey like a defensive center tackling the quarterback. She sipped her tea and set the glass back on the soft green placemat in front of her. Her gaze was focused on the table, her fingers wiping the fine, dark wood grain, removing imaginary specks of dust that might ruin the picture of perfection.

His next words were unplanned. "Yes, Ma'am. Well, I want to ask her to marry me—" Another confession, he realized and took a deep breath.

When he'd spoken to Maine Taylor, he was so intent on finding the truth he'd missed this.

"Marriage. That's a big step."

"Yes, Ma'am."

"Is that what you came here to talk about?"

Trey took a breath and looked the woman in the eyes. "I knew Gemini when she was a teenager. Just before her dad was killed. And then we didn't see each other for twenty years. I'd like to know what I missed."

"Did you ask her?"

"I'm afraid to. What was she like, those first few years after she left Raven Bayou? Where did she live? What did she do?"

"She lived right here. She was subdued and quiet for a while. She was afraid. Then sometimes I would hear her in her room, talking to herself, laughing, and I knew she was getting better."

"Those first weeks, when she was quiet, can you tell me about them? I really want to understand."

"Well then, I guess I should tell you everything I know. I think the worst of it was the dreams." She stopped and gazed at Trey's face, looking for reassurance. He gave her a small smile and a nod and she continued.

"Gemini suffers from terrible nightmares. Sometimes I would sit by her door and listen. She talked in her sleep, but her voice changed several times. It was like two or three different people were speaking. I rarely made out actual words, but the tones changed. It didn't make any sense to me. It still doesn't. I pray for her every day, mostly that she's found some kind of peace." She sipped her tea, and he noticed the tremor in her hands. "I feel like there's something in her past that she hasn't gotten over. Not just her dad's death and her mom being in prison. I visited my sister. But I think there are things in Gemini's past her mother doesn't know, things that make Gemini afraid to commit."

Trey saw a fleeting look of sadness cross her face. She laced her fingers together and sighed. "When Gemini came to me, she'd been through Hades. Maine and Gemini both refused to tell me exactly what happened that day, or why.

"When I got the call from the Sheriff's department, I couldn't believe it. I was just a couple hours away, so they allowed Gemini to stay at the station until I arrived." She stared off into another time and place. "We didn't even go back to the house for her clothes, just left Raven Bayou and never looked back." Her gaze came back to Trey for an instant. "That's why I was so surprised when she told me she was going back there to live.

"Anyhow, when she moved in with me, let's see...It's been twenty years, she was what you'd call a troubled teen. Her personality changed daily. One minute she was quiet and sullen, the next she pranced around the house like Paula Abdul, dancing those grinding dances that were so popular with the girls.

"One day she would be intensely interested in something, and the next day it was something else. Once it was martial arts paraphernalia. The next it was knives. She spent her allowance on them for a while.

"I never knew what it would be next. But we made it through. She finished high school here in town, and then started preparing herself for the physical part of the academy. Met a girl there from California. Krystal Randower. In a pre-academy class. They were inseparable. Then one day she came home with a beaming smile. She'd met Zach. He was so good for her."

"Zach?"

"Zachary Fulton. She was crazy about him. We had words more than once over him. Gemini had this wild idea that she and Zach would marry and live on love. Her grades dropped. She skipped classes. They drove me crazy." She shook her head, a little smile creeping onto her face.

"Then Gemini decided one time to spend the week-end with Krystal because Zach would be out of town..." Tears welled up in her eyes and she stood. "Excuse me." She walked away, by then the tears rolled down her cheeks.

Sweat gathered at the waistband of Trey's jeans. His breathing became fast and shallow. A minute later she returned with a box of tissues. She had wiped her face. She took a sip of tea.

Trey gulped some, though it did nothing to remove the cotton feel of his mouth. The A/C kicked on and cool air brushed Trey's neck.

"Zach was killed one Saturday night."

"Killed? You mean murdered?" Trey moved to the edge of his chair, forearms on knees, leaning forward.

Mrs. Philips nodded and wiped tears again. "He'd driven down to the Gulf and apparently planned to spend the night on the beach. They found him stuffed in the trunk of his car. He'd been stabbed. When I told her what happened, she was devastated."

She looked into his eyes for answers, but he only had questions.

"Did they find who did it?"

She shook her head. "After her dad...Well, it just seemed like Gemini couldn't get away from it." She averted her eyes to the window through which the back yard was visible. "I'm sure she must've felt that way, losing her boyfriend just like her dad. But that was years ago."

"So, Mrs. Philips—"

"Anyone in love with my Gemini can call me Ginny."

"So, Miss Ginny, do you think she's afraid to commit to me because she thinks I might die? Like her dad and her boyfriend?"

"I think she's tortured with the way both of them died. Zack's was a particularly brutal attack. The boy was stabbed in the chest three times and had a wound from his navel to his heart."

Chapter Ninety-Three

RUSS COLEMAN
Vance Residence
Raven Bayou, LA

Sunday Late Afternoon, 12 June 2005

HIS PHONE RANG but he thought about not answering it. He was in no mood to talk to anybody. On the other hand, he hadn't heard from Trey for several hours.

"Coleman," he said into the cell.

"It's me."

Russ waited for more but nothing came. He suspected Trey was in an area with poor reception or the call had been dropped. "Trey? Are you there?"

"I'm here."

Russ heard a heavy sigh on the other end. "What's wrong? Learn anything that would help us?"

"Maybe. After I left the prison, I went to visit Maine's sister, Virginia Phillips."

"That's the aunt who took Taylor to Lufkin."

"Yes. She had a lot to say. It's complicated. And I could be wrong. Russ, I need you to find out where Gemini is. I called her house. No answer. She's not picking up on her cell either. Find her and keep an eye on her, but listen. Don't approach her."

"She's my partner! What do you mean 'don't approach her?'" His hand moved over his hair and to his neck.

"Look, just be very careful. We don't really know what she is thinking. I'm on my way back from Lufkin now and I have more phone calls to make so I need to go. Please, just find her and as soon as you do, call me. I gotta go."

"How far out are you?"

"About thirty minutes, maybe less. I'm expecting a call from Quantico so I need to get off this line. I'll see you soon and, Russ...really...be careful."

"Trey!" The dial tone was all Russ heard. He hung up and rubbed a hand over his buzz cut again. Maybe there was a swamp-monster in Raven Bayou.

Chapter Ninety-Four

WILE E. WAYNE
Taylor Residence
Raven Bayou, LA

Sunday Late Afternoon, 12 June 2005

IT TOOK A LOT of talking to get Ginni to understand what we had to do. She didn't have no idea about the real Boudreaux, so it was hard for her. But after hearing us out, she finally decided to help us.

I listened as she made the call. I could only hear her end, but I knew the old man couldn't resist Ginni. It's just the way men are, especially around here.

"Is this Alton Boudreaux? The famous horse breeder?"

That would get him. He thought ever body knew him and his horses.

"When my husband died last year, his last request was that I contact you and see if I might purchase a stud from your stables. He was always going on about how wonderful your horses were. And of course, my daughter will be thrilled. She's only five, but she loves horses."

I was itchy to hear what he was saying.

"That would be wonderful, Mr. Boudreaux." She said it just right, kinda breathy, like Scarlett O'Hara. I hated that movie but Gemini watched it over and over, and most times I had to come out when the man carried Scarlett up the stairs. I don't think Gemini ever made it through that part.

"All right then, if you insist... Alton. Yes, I can come immediately. I'm in a sordid little hotel—" She listened with a smile on her face, like she thought he could see her.

"That sounds just wonderful. Thank you so much, Alton. Bye." She hung up the phone and turned to me. "He will personally show me several of his best breeding studs. At my convenience. Now would be fine. And he insists I stay at his house instead of a hotel."

That was fine with me too. Drew already had her bag packed. She'd been stealing Gemini's gun and cuffs for years. Ginni pulled a pretty dress out of the back of the closet and picked out some other stuff from the big steamer trunk upstairs on the other side of the bedroom wall. Me and Rocky left, and when we came back, she was all gussied up and ready to go.

The dress was brown, with white spots, and she had a big white hat that had a kind of ribbon around it that matched the dress. She had Gemini's sunglasses on and brown shoes with high heels. And she was carrying Drew's brown leather bag.

"I'll drive," she said and led us out the door. We piled into the Cadillac.

I just kept telling her ever thing was gonna be okay. She don't like it when she finds out me and Rocky have been out 'cause she always thinks we're up to something.

"Where do you think you'll get the money to buy such a fine animal?" she asked. Drew giggled and Rocky smiled.

"We don't really want a horse. We just want to talk to him alone, Ginni. He's always busy and his people are always around to butt in. Don't worry, ever thing'll be fine. I'm betting all of his people are gone home by now."

The good thing about Ginni is she's so lame. She always believes everything anybody says. Just like Aunt Ginny. The difference between 'em is Ginni knows us by sight and loves us. Aunt Ginny always calls us Gemini or Honey, like she can't tell us apart.

It was a perfect plan. I just hoped Boudreaux was gonna be his normal self. If I knew him, he was sending whoever might still be around somewhere so he could be alone with a rich lady widow with a five-year-old daughter who loved horses.

Chapter Ninety-Five

RUSS COLEMAN
En Route to Taylor Residence
Raven Bayou, LA

Sunday Early Evening, 12 June 2005

RUSS DROVE toward Taylor's house as he dialed the lab.

"CSU," Avlee answered.

"Have you seen Taylor today?"

There was a hesitation before Avlee said, "Wasn't she at the station this morning?"

"Yeah. Earlier. But I haven't heard from her for a while, and needed her help with something. If you see her, will you have her call me?"

"Sure."

He hung up and tried Taylor's cell again. Nothing. Two minutes later he pulled into her drive. The Caddie was gone and he saw no sign of life. He backed out and headed toward the donut shop. Maybe her cell was turned off, and she'd decided on donuts for an afternoon snack.

Taylor's car wasn't at the Southern Maid, nor the Rusty Badge. Russ parked in the lot and walked inside. The owner was working today.

"Looking for my partner, Gemini Taylor. Has she been in today?" Russ asked as the owner put an iced tea on the counter.

"Haven't seen her."

Russ nodded, his mind elsewhere. He took a large gulp of the tea, dropped a bill on the counter and thanked him.

"Listen, if Taylor comes in, have her call me?"

"Sure."

Russ was running out of ideas. As he slid behind the wheel of the Crown Vic, his cell rang. "Coleman." He cranked the engine.

"Where the hell have you been? I left a message on your phone at home, paged you, called your cell twice, but it was busy." It was Assistant DA Adam Walker.

The voice made Russ's blood run cold. There was only one reason for Walker to call him. He looked down at the pager on his belt. The LCD was blank, the battery dead.

"The jury foreman called me. They called the judge and court will convene tomorrow morning at eight-thirty. He wouldn't tell me the verdict, but from his tone..."

Whatever followed those words, Russ didn't hear. He struck the steering wheel with the heel of his hand as he sat in the unit, A/C blowing, the hand cradling the cell lying atop his thigh. Not guilty. Russ was sure of it. Boudreaux was free.

The bastard would get away with murder.

Russ tossed his cell into the passenger seat and left rubber on the pavement. He headed north on Lakeshore to Highway 31 and made a left on Old Latree Road, the shortest route to the Boudreaux Estate, not knowing what he'd do when he got there.

Between clouds, the fading sun glared through the windshield, burning through his slacks. Sweat gathered under the leather shoulder holster he wore over his shirt. He rubbed a sweaty palm down the hot fabric and tried to talk himself into a calm he didn't feel.

He planned to let Boudreaux know that the truth would come out, one way or the other. Russ would see to it.

It had been eighteen months since Boudreaux's arrest. Of course, Boudreaux never served a day in jail. He went free on his own recognizance within the hour while his victim, Julie Coleman, lay in a coma, spinal cord cut through, her body kept alive by machines.

What could Boudreaux do, have him arrested? All he was going to do was talk to the bastard. That was all. Russ kept telling himself this as he raced closer and closer to his wife's killer.

Chapter Ninety-Six

WILE E. WAYNE
Taylor Residence
Raven Bayou, LA

Sunday Evening, 12 June 2005

IT ONLY TOOK A FEW MINUTES TO GET THERE. We hid the car behind the trees by the old garage where our truck is hid, and we snuck down the hill toward the big Boudreaux Stables barn. When we were at the barn, we let Ginni go in front. She walked around the side of the barn and looked toward the house. The rain was gone and the dark clouds moved out of town so we could see the sun getting lower in the sky.

"You hoo! Mr. Boudreaux!" she called loud, and sure enough, Alton Boudreaux came waltzing out the front door of the mansion wearing an almost white suit that was all pressed and nice. He was tall and kinda wide, but his hair was the same as twenty years ago, except for the white stripes in it like a skunk's back. But it was shiny and greasy like it always was, with that flower smelling stuff.

"It's me! Ginni Phillips!" She waved and Boudreaux started walking toward the barn.

"What the...What are *you* doing here?" He looked around. "Where's your car?" He kept coming toward her, frowning now.

She smiled but didn't answer him. I reached into Drew's bag and took out Gemini's gun, the one she keeps at home. It's not like the one she carries at work. This one is big and holds six bullets. I got her cuffs out too. When Boudreaux got right up close to Ginni, I stepped in front of her and held the gun on him.

He saw the gun and kinda looked at me like I was crazy. He pulled his eyebrows together like black caterpillars creeping across his face. "What the hell is this all about?"

"Get inside. Walk nice and slow and keep quiet. I'll shoot you if I have to." I sure didn't want to though. It wouldn't be the same.

Boudreaux walked inside the barn, and I made him go to a big support post that holds up the hayloft.

"Put your back against that post." I handed him the cuffs. "Put 'em on one arm, and then put your hands back," I said.

"What do you think you're doing, young lady?" he said and I laughed. "You can't get away with this. You know who I am?"

"Yeah. We know who you are. And pretty soon you're gonna know who we are."

"Thank you, Ginni," I said.

"Now, Wile, promise you won't be too mean to this man," she said.

"I won't do nothing to him he don't deserve. I promise," I said and she left.

Big ole drops of sweat popped out of Boudreaux's forehead and he looked kinda confused. He tried to act all tough, but he knowed he was in deep ca-ca.

"I don't know who the hell you think you are, Detective Taylor, but I should've known. Killing my son wasn't enough for you? You intend to kill me now?"

"Gemini's with us, but she won't be killing you. She don't even want to see you."

"What the hell are talking about?" Boudreaux said, his face all red and wet. The white of his gray eyes had red squiggly lines, kinda like a road map has.

"Sit down," I told him. "We got some talking to do before you die."

Chapter Ninety-Seven

GEMINI TAYLOR
Boudreaux Barn
Raven Bayou, LA

Sunday Evening, 12 June 2005

THAT CROWDED ELEVATOR feeling was back. Her eyes must have been closed because she couldn't see anything. But she heard the voices loud and clear.

"We took care of her daddy. Now it's time to take care of you," Wile said.

"You really think you can get away with it? Really?"

Gem recognized that voice from her childhood, but she couldn't place it. Her eyes wouldn't open. Or maybe they were open but she was in a dark place. Someone breathed on her neck and she shuddered. She heard a noise, like metal clanking together.

"Maybe it's time she knew, time she remembered." It was the soft sweet voice of Aunt Ginny.

The windows of Gem's mind opened. She could see herself standing in the small group of people, watching Wile as he knelt beside Alton Boudreaux. Wile held a knife, its blade shiny even in the shadows of the barn. Right behind him lay her brown leather bag. She could tell someone had been rummaging through it.

Wile looked into her eyes, and then followed her gaze to the bag. "I just had to get my knife. It's all gonna be okay, Gemi."

Behind them the big door facing the mansion was closed. But the door toward the meadow was open, allowing air to circulate and light to slant in. Gem had been here before. Many times.

Her breath caught in her throat as she tried to speak. A second effort produced results. "What's he doing?" she asked the small group. Her heart pounded hard. "Why are we here?"

"It seems this less-than-a-gentleman has some alms to pay," said the petite version of herself. People always said Aunt Ginny and Gem looked alike. Now, finally, she could see it.

Her gaze returned to Boudreaux, sitting on the floor of his own barn, his hands secured behind a support post. Wile turned to look at Gem, his face serious, angry.

"Do you remember being here, Gemini? In this barn? With this man?" Wile asked.

"I...don't know..." Her throat burned with bile and her head began to spin.

"No. Gemini. You can't run anymore. You need to remember." Ginni's tone was urgent, yet her voice was full of compassion. Gem squeezed her eyes shut, like Dorothy in Oz, except she didn't have any red slippers. When she looked again the scene hadn't changed.

"Tell her, Wile," Ginni said.

"Yvette needs to tell her. Yvette knows what happened. She was the one who had to come."

"Wile, would you subject the child to that?" Ginni scolded, almost crying. "Would you make her come here?"

Wile stared Gem in the eye, his hand still on the knife. "Remember Gemini, when Alton here would mosey down to our house and bring you back to the barn? Remember how your daddy made you go?" His gaze swung back around to Boudreaux and he trailed the knife from the man's neck to this heart, and then down and down until the man's eyes grew into saucers and he held his breath.

"Remember, Gemini? He always said you was a pretty little thing, and you always came back with a candy bar and a sad face."

"No! It wasn't me!" Gem squeezed her eyes shut again.

"You're right, honey. It wasn't you. It was Yvette. Do you remember Yvette?" Ginni stroked Gem's back.

Behind her eyelids, images flashed. A little girl with blond ringlets and big blue eyes. The hay was harsh on Gem's skin. She had chubby cheeks and always wore a frilly dress or a sunsuit. His hands were too big and they hurt. She was always quiet and did as she was told. And he liked to put his thing...

Gem's eyes flew open and she gasped for breath. Pain struck her like a lightning bolt, from groin to stomach. She was so little. And a strong arm went around her waist, pulling her back. And it hurt.

"Oh, God!"

"You're okay, Gemini." Ginni's voice soothed. "We're here with you and you're safe. Nothing like that will ever happen to you again."

But Gem was too scared to be soothed. There was too much pain.

"It couldn't have been me. Reena went but I didn't." Gem looked at Ginni, and then Wile. *Reena went...Oh, God.*

Reena had volunteered in Gem's place. She knew what Boudreaux had planned for Gem and went in her stead. Gem shook with terror and cried with shame.

"Sometimes Reena went. Sometimes Yvette went. Yvette went for you. Do you remember, Gemini?" Wile said over his shoulder but still facing Boudreaux.

Boudreaux exploded. "You're crazy! What's going on here! You've gone nuts! Get these damned cuffs off me, you stupid bitch!" His eyes bore into Wile, but it didn't faze him. Wile pulled the knife slowly up Boudreaux's body until the point lay against the man's shirt, just over his heart.

Wile giggled, a big grin on his face. "Watch how hard he's breathing. Kinda like he's been running or something."

Gem concentrated on Boudreaux's chest. He stopped breathing altogether. Wile laughed at the man's fear.

Reena. Gem remembered the dream she had. The little copper-colored girl who was bigger and older than she. She remembered Reena walking hand-in-hand with Boudreaux toward this barn. And Daddy knocking Gem down, kicking her, because she saw. Gem couldn't breathe. Her chest was being crushed. "Who is Yvette?" she asked in a whisper.

"She came sometimes when Boudreaux came to the house," Drew said.

"I don't remember her," Gem said.

"I think she's had enough. We should let her rest," Ginni said. Gem hoped Ginni was talking about her because her knees began to shake and her head ached. And then she was gone.

Chapter Ninety-Eight

TREY FONTAINE
En Route to Raven Bayou, LA

Sunday Evening, 12 June 2005

STREAK BUZZED southeast on Highway 63 at eighty-five miles an hour, the portable red light flashing atop the driver's side, siren singing from the front grill. He had no idea where he'd go once he got to town. He only knew he had to get there, and fast. Hopefully, by the time he reached the city limits, Russ would call him and say he'd found Gemini and everything was fine.

Trey gripped the wheel with both hands. Not for fear of his own speed, but from the terror of knowing the truth. He didn't really have any proof, except for what his gut told him, and that was useless. Yet, this time he couldn't ignore it.

What bothered him most was that he hadn't figured it out sooner. This was his job. He was an FBI agent, after all.

His cell rang and he pressed the TALK button and listened through the tiny, fitted earpiece.

"Hopkins here."

"Anything on the T-bird?"

"Nothing. Sorry. But I have something else you asked for. Ready?"

He had to set aside the search for his mother right now. "Go," Trey said and turned on a small recorder he'd plugged into the phone. He listened to the details, his throat becoming dry at the words the agent on the other end of the line laid out. "Thanks. I owe you one."

"Ever think about just sharing what you have? I could be up there in a few hours."

"I may not have anything." *Just trying to put some pieces together for a friend.* "I'll let you know if I need help. If I have to bring anyone in on this, you'll be the first to know. What I really need help with is finding Mom. If I know you're working on that, it would help set my mind at ease."

"I'm on it, Trey. We'll find her."

Trey hung up and brought his attention back to the puzzle he was in the middle of. He didn't believe a word of what Hopkins had read to him. But if his only choices were that Gemini was guilty, or those words were true, he would choose the words. Because, if Gemini was guilty, Trey would have to arrest her, and he was pretty sure he couldn't do it.

He wiped his palms down his pant legs, leaving sweat stains on the dark fabric. *They never found Zach Fulton's killer.*

DNA was a relatively new science when the boy's body was found, more advanced by the time of the second murder. But no matches had been produced with the exception of a few hairs belonging to Gemini in Fulton's car. That would've been normal since they were dating. And Gemini had an alibi. Her friend, Krystal Randower, who now lived in California.

Hopkins had found a phone listing for her but there was no answer, only a machine. He hadn't left a message. Trey would try again later but doubted he could get anything out of her over the phone. If it came down to it, he could have an agent out there go to Krystal Randower's house.

Ten minutes later, he swung east onto a bumpy two-lane highway where trees and kudzu formed thirty-foot walls on each side of the pot-holed pavement. The big vehicle filled the eastbound lane as well as a portion of the westbound, which was fine since Trey's was the only vehicle on the highway.

The music of the radio stopped for a news report, and he turned the volume up:

"The jury has made a decision on the trial of millionaire horse breeder Alton Boudreaux of Raven Bayou. On trial for vehicular manslaughter, Mr. Boudreaux's verdict will be read tomorrow morning when court convenes."

Son of a bitch! The jury had been deliberating for nine days. It wasn't a good sign. The evidence in the case was straightforward, so nine days of deliberation meant they couldn't agree on something. Trey pressed the speed dial number for Russ. It rang but there was no answer.

Boudreaux had already ruined enough lives. Trey's dad was dead. Julie was dead, and Russ would never be the same. Boudreaux might be behind the Cheramie case, and probably Aunt Darlene's rape and beating. And he was pushing to ruin Gemini's career.

Russ hated Boudreaux. If he heard about the jury coming in, he'd go after the miserable bastard. Trey looked at his watch. The best bet was to go straight to Boudreaux's. There was a good chance he'd find Russ. Hopefully, he'd beat him there.

Where the hell could Russ be that he can't answer his phone? Maybe he had already found Boudreaux. Or maybe Gemini. Trey's heart hammered in his chest. Or maybe she found him.

Chapter Ninety-Nine

RUSS COLEMAN
Boudreaux Barn
Raven Bayou, LA

Sunday Evening, 12 June 2005

BOUDREAUX WAS ARRESTED a week after the hit-and-run.

A month passed before doctors convinced Russ that the wife he knew and loved was gone. She lay in the sterile bed surrounded by ugly industrial green walls, wrapped in a cheap cotton hospital gown. NASA didn't have as many machines as they had hooked up to her. Russ could still remember the feel of the cold pen in his hands as he signed the papers and let them to pull the plug.

The big white house with its black shutters loomed at the end of the drive. The noise of the tires on the oyster shells, followed by his footsteps should have declared him, but when Russ climbed the stairs, crossed the wide veranda, and knocked on the front door, there was no answer. The windows were closed, as was the storm door. The big security door was open, but the inside of the room too dark to see much. Even people who used central air only used glass storm doors during the day. The Southern way was to have a solid glass door instead of a screen, and to keep the front door of the house open and welcoming to visitors. Except Russ didn't think Boudreaux would be so welcoming when it came to him.

The sun set just above the treetops, heat rising, making far off things shimmer in the distance. Russ knocked again, his anger building. Boudreaux's Lincoln sat in the drive so he had to be home. He scanned the property. No other cars in sight. No people either. If Boudreaux was inside, he could see Russ. That thought wasn't comforting.

He approached the barn and heard voices. Angry voices. Pressing himself against the wall, weapon drawn, he listened but couldn't make out what was being said.

There was the office and another room, Cora's room, at the end of the barn nearest the house, a curtain blocking the view. Moving slowly and carefully, he stepped over to the office window and peeked in. Empty.

Chapter One-Hundred

TREY FONTAINE
Boudreaux Property
Raven Bayou, LA

Sunday Evening, 12 June 2005

TREY PARKED on Old Cypress Road fifty yards from the spot where Gemini had kissed him twenty years earlier. He eased the door open, stepped out and pulled his shoulder holster and weapon out from under the jacket that lay on the seat. After slipping his arms into his holster, the nine millimeter lying against his ribs, he pulled on the net vest, its bold, yellow FBI emblem glowing on the back. He popped another Lortab in his mouth. It was the last one.

He moved silently, sure of what he would find, but not sure where he would find it. In his head a litany of thoughts and prayers resonated. *Let me find Boudreaux before Russ does. Let me be wrong about Gemini. Don't make me have to hurt her. Let me get there in time.*

Approaching the old house where Gemini once lived, he cautiously peeked in the side windows. Nothing. A quick glance around the corner gave him a view of the barn that had been converted to a garage years ago. One door stood ajar, giving him a glimpse of a bumper, bringing back a memory of the bright, reflective flash he and Gemini had passed here earlier in the week.

He took a deliberate deep breath. The distance from the house to the garage was only a matter of feet, thirty at most. There wasn't a soul in sight. He stepped lightly to the garage.

No sound came from within. He moved through the door and took a good look at the truck. A 1960 Ford step-side. Dark blue. It was dirty, the seat covered with a colorful beach towel. No other details were visible in the dimness. *It must be the same truck Mr. Taylor used to drive.*

Finding the old truck was not a good sign. He hoped Gemini's absence meant he was wrong. *Where in hell could she be?*

Trey took a few steps, and then stopped. There in the shade of an old weeping willow sat the Caddie, completely hidden from view by the garage and the tree. No one could've seen it from any other angle. He looked to his left, toward the Boudreaux mansion.

Chapter One-Hundred-One

RUSS COLEMAN
Boudreaux Barn
Raven Bayou, LA

Sunday Early Evening, 12 June 2005

RUSS MOVED QUIETLY around the building and saw a door at the other end. One window faced the hill. He peeked in and saw an empty tack room. Bending, he passed under the window and stopped at the edge of the big barn door. The voices came to him clearer, but it was still hard to understand the words.

He took a quick peek around the corner, and then withdrew. In that brief span of time, he saw Boudreaux sitting against a post at the end of the barn toward the house with a woman squatting beside him, her back to Russ. She looked like Taylor. He eased through the barn door and into the tack room, and then peeked around the doorframe. His heart pounded, lungs struggling for air. Wiping sweat from his forehead, he stood inches inside the room, listening. A young boy's voice, full of hatred, floated to him. Then a woman's voice, but not Taylor's. He wondered if he'd been wrong about her identity. Then came another female voice. They talked about killing Boudreaux and going to Lufkin.

Russ stopped breathing when the voices quieted. In their place he heard footsteps inside the barn, coming his way.

Chapter One-Hundred-Two

TREY FONTAINE
Boudreaux Property
Raven Bayou, LA

Sunday Evening, 12 June 2005

TREY STARED at the Boudreaux stables, the barn door standing open at the end facing him. He hid in the shade of the old willow as a woman inside pulled the rolling door, bringing it to within a couple of feet of being closed. Even from that distance he knew it was Gemini.

Moving a few feet along the backside of the garage gave him a view of the driveway at the mansion. His heart stopped at the sight of a tan Crown Vic parked there.

His worst nightmare slapped him in the face. He hurried back toward the Hummer and called Russ. No answer.

He hopped up into the seat of the big SUV, started the engine, and threw the Hummer in gear. The gate to the Boudreaux stables was only a quarter mile down the road. There was no cover between the road and the stables, just white rail fences around pastures filled with horses.

Driving around the corner to the front of the mansion, he parked outside the gate near a half dozen crepe myrtles in full bloom, their limbs heavy laden and hanging almost to the ground, providing cover for the SUV.

The drive was lined with magnolia trees, big ones with low hanging branches. He moved from one to the next, eyes darting in all directions. Finally, he reached the barn and leaned against it, panting. Wiping sweat from his eyes, he headed to the back, to the door left ajar. It was just like someone expected him.

Chapter One-Hundred-Three

RUSS COLEMAN
Boudreaux Barn
Raven Bayou, LA

Sunday Evening, 12 June 2005

RUSS FROZE behind the tack room door, watching through the crack as Taylor walked back toward Boudreaux. So it was her. He wondered where the others were, the boy and the other woman. Before he had a chance to sneak a look, or even speculate, a shadow near the outside door caught his eye.

Trey was just outside the barn, gun drawn. "Gemini, I'm coming in!"

Russ was not in Trey's line of vision. He didn't move.

Trey turned his body sideways and eased through the door, weapon pointed at the sky. His head turned left, and then right. Russ remained still and out of sight behind the tack room door.

Sound echoed from the other end of the barn.

"How're you doing, Gemini?" Trey called.

"Go away, mister FBI man," a young boy's voice answered. "We don't need no help."

Trey's body began to shake so badly he couldn't aim his pistol. Russ worried that he might lose it.

"You don't want to do this," Trey said. "Come here to me."

The boy's voice answered. "Nobody's going no where."

Trey took a couple of steps and lowered the weapon to his side. Russ listened, hypnotized. "Are you the one who killed Gemini's daddy?" Trey asked.

Stepping from behind the door, Russ squatted and leaned his head far enough past the frame to see into the barn. There were only three people—Trey, Boudreaux, and Taylor.

Russ's heart raced when his eyes met Taylor's. She smiled, but it was the smile of a child. He stood and stepped out slowly, knowing Trey was still unaware of his presence. His right hand gripped the pistol, but he didn't move or raise the weapon. Instead he remained still, listening.

"Remember when we was waiting for Aunt Ginny to come get us and you sat down and talked to us?" she asked Russ in a soft teenage voice.

Trey's head snapped around. There was fear in Trey's face, but Russ kept his attention on Taylor and nodded again as he raised a palm toward Trey, motioning him to calm down.

"And you told us stuff about we could remain silent and we could talk to an attorney if we wanted?"

Russ nodded again.

"And you said sometimes a mom loves her kids so much she'll do anything to protect 'em? And how sometimes it's best if we forgive people for stuff they did?" the girl continued.

Again, Russ nodded, his eyes glued to hers.

"And you said sometimes there's bad men and they hafta be stopped?" This was a different voice, a little boy, probably under ten years old.

A prickle of fear ran down the back of Russ's neck.

"Well, this is one of 'em that hafta be stopped. We decided we ain't gonna forgive him."

Chapter One-Hundred-Four

GEMINI TAYLOR
Boudreaux Barn
Raven Bayou, LA

Sunday Evening, 12 June 2005

GEM FLOATED on clouds, buoyed by a warm current of air. It was peaceful here, quiet. A small whimper dragged her out of her slumber.

Noises hovered around her. She tried to ignore them, but it was impossible. The combination of sounds didn't fit together, the grunting sound came from a pig at a trough, and then the softer mew from some kind of small animal in distress. When they didn't stop, Gem opened her eyes.

She stood in the Boudreaux barn. The firmly packed floor was cool on her bare feet. Her head pounded, sharp pain hitting both temples. Then she saw them in the office. A little girl with blond curls with her sunsuit lying on the wood floor.

Boudreaux sat in his big office chair, the leather one that rocked. The girl squirmed on his lap, her back to him. She couldn't have been more than three years old. His hands gripped her tiny waist as he bounced her up and down rhythmically on top of him. The girl's eyes were squeezed shut. Tears streamed down her cheeks as her tiny fingers clawed at the hands holding her.

Gem bent and retched, bile splattering on the floor. The grunts and whimpers continued. No matter how hard she tried, she couldn't block them out.

"That's Yvette," Ginni said, stroking Gem's back.

She pulled herself up but refused to look into the office.

"She came when you were very young, to take your place, to protect you," Ginni said.

"No! Don't say that. I'd never allow that!"

"Gemini, what Boudreaux did wasn't your fault. Just as what your daddy did wasn't. We all came to help you."

"What?" She looked first at Ginni, and then turned to see Wile still on the floor by Boudreaux. Her gaze whipped back around to the office, but it was empty. Then it dawned on her that the Boudreaux she'd seen with the little girl was much younger than the one sitting in front of her.

Her gaze passed over Rocky and Drew, and then returned to Ginni.

"Maybe you should let each one say why they're here." Ginni spoke softly.

Gem pressed her hands against her ears and closed her eyes. "No! Stop! Just leave me alone!"

"Maybe she's not ready yet," Drew said. "What good will it do for her to know anyhow? What makes you think she can take it now? It won't change her mind 'bout what we gotta do. Let's just do it and get outta here. Go back to Lufkin."

Gem dropped her hands and stared at Drew. Out of nowhere numbers filled her mind. Five. Twelve. Fifteen. The ages of Wile, Rocky and Drew. The numbers of the combination lock on Gem's locker. She knew. She must've known. Somewhere deep inside, she'd known all along.

Wile turned to face her. "Whadaya think, Gemini? You strong enough to finally know the truth? 'Cause when you do, you'll wanna be the one holding the knife. It took Drew to get to your daddy, and it took me and Rocky to put a stop to what he done to you. He was an evil man. Remember him, how he treated you? You remember the time he beat you with the hose 'cause you tripped on it while he was washing the truck? You think you were the last little girl this...hunchback critter...hurt?" Wile nodded toward Boudreaux.

Gem's head throbbed. She had to get away from these people. They were talking crazy. Doing crazy things. "Just let me go. I don't want to be here anymore. Ple-e-ease," she cried. "I won't tell anyone. I'll go away. You'll never see me again."

Drew and Ginni pressed against her, one on each side. They would never let her go. Gem had to figure out a way to get free. She sobbed.

"We know what you're thinking, but Gemini, you can't get free of us," Ginni said. "Any more than you can get free of yourself. The things you can't remember, those are the things we came to help you with."

Gem looked up and saw Rocky standing before her, his eyes as sad as ever. "Remember Twitch?" he asked, tears forming.

Twitch was the most beautiful black and white rabbit she'd ever seen. How could she forget him?

"Remember what Daddy did?" Rocky whispered.

Gem squeezed her eyes shut, not wanting to see. But the visions came from within. Daddy coming home with a rifle in the crook of his arm. His hunting bag empty. He pulled Twitch out of his cage and then...Gem couldn't remember, didn't want to remember what happened then.

"I had to skin Twitch for you. But I couldn't finish it." A tear slid down Rocky's cheek.

"No!"

"If she saw the stuff in the bag, would it help?" Drew offered. Her gaze went to the brown leather bag Gem used as a purse before joining the PD in Dallas. It sat open beside Wile, the contents within view. She stepped over to the bag and looked in. Nothing unusual. Her hands had been inside that bag thousands of times. She knew the contents.

Wile reached in with his free hand, dug to the bottom, and withdrew what looked like a chamois. He tossed it to the ground and it clinked like fine metal chunks. Gem stepped back, not wanting to see what was inside.

Wile unfolded the edges of the piece of leather and Gem's mind tumbled. Watches. A half-dozen men's watches, Daddy's among them. And a fancy glittery one.

"That's my boy's watch!" Boudreaux proclaimed. "You murdering bitch! You stole my son's watch!"

While Gem's gaze was glued to the pile of watches, Wile withdrew something else and tossed it onto the heap.

Another knife. A skinning knife.

Gem heard feet shuffle and looked up to see Trey shifting to get a better view of the pile of evidence. His face turned sweaty and pale like he was in shock. She didn't want to see it or believe it either. But proof of her guilt lay there for anyone to see. It was impossible to say she was innocent.

Her knees gave way. Drew and Ginni eased her to the floor and sat on each side of her as if they were all attached at the hips. Gem could feel them in her mind, could feel their compassion and anger and determination.

They were real. And they were really in her body. In her mind, not beside her or in front of her as she thought. The only way she could get free was to overpower them. Could she put on her Taylor face? Would that make her stronger? She tried.

Taylor stepped in front of her. Gem could see her. She stood, melded herself with Taylor. Then she looked at Boudreaux and hatred welled in her. Not just her own, but the hate of the little blond girl, Drew, Wile and Rocky.

Gem had been a cop for too many years to allow this to happen. Boudreaux would pay, but within the rules. "Wile, give me the knife."

His head turned, but the knife's gleaming blade moved not an inch.

"Give it to me!" Gem demanded.

"I told you Gem could walk right through Taylor," Drew said.

Wile looked almost sad, but resolved. "We gotta do this, Gemi, and you can't stop us."

Chapter One-Hundred-Five

TREY FONTAINE
Boudreaux Barn
Raven Bayou, LA

Sunday Evening, 12 June 2005

MOVIES AND BOOKS, and even the few psych classes Trey'd been required to take didn't do justice to what he witnessed. He'd seen Taylor's body go through changes. Her posture, the way her eyes looked, her voice, her gestures.

He'd seen a half dozen people who all looked similar to Gemini, but were different. Seeing with his own eyes made him question his own sanity rather than hers. And yet, it was true. There was more than one person in the body of Gemini Taylor. And at least one of them was a killer.

His mind went to the mint tin in his pocket. The empty one. The pain was unbearable and he had nothing to ease it. Then a light bulb flicked on and he recognized this sensation was not really physical. His chest tightened with pain caused by the ripping open of his heart. Lortabs would not fix that.

His eyes cut to Boudreaux, sitting there looking arrogant half the time, and scared the other half. The barrel of Trey's pistol shifted focus from Taylor to Boudreaux. He kept a tight grip on the gun but was shaking again. That son of a bitch was responsible for all the misery in Trey's life.

Bringing his other hand up to steady his aim, Trey pointed the barrel at Boudreaux's head.

"No one would like to see Boudreaux dead more than me. But not this way." It was Russ's voice, a little behind Trey.

Gemini's head turned toward them, though Trey wasn't sure which personality was staring through her wild eyes.

"See? Our way is better," said the boy's voice, holding the knife to Boudreaux's chest. The big man was sweating. His white suit was dusty, wilted, and wrinkled. His oiled hair was mussed and his eyes were the size of saucers.

"No, Wile." Gemini's voice came from the same mouth. She turned to Trey. "Please don't shoot him."

Hearing her voice directed at him shattered his defenses. He wanted to drop the gun and run to her. Hold her. Tell her it would be okay. Hair stirred on the back of his neck, a familiar feeling he couldn't describe. How could he not have known? He'd spent days with her, had fallen in love with her all over again. He lowered his weapon again.

"I know how you feel," Russ said. There was a tremor in his voice. "Believe me. I'd like to kill Boudreaux too. But we're the good guys. Remember?"

Trey wasn't feeling like a good guy right now. He wanted to kill the bastard and be done with it. "This is justice. Boudreaux deserves to die. For what he did to Gemini. For what he did to Julie, to you..." He paused, the gun shaking. "For what he did to me."

Trey heard Russ take two steps forward and saw his godfather in his peripheral vision.

"What are you talking about?" Russ whispered.

"Monty."

Boudreaux, who had been looking at Gemini with a mixture of fear and contempt, snapped his head in their direction. "What about Monty? You know what happened to him?"

"What happened to *him*? Who gives a fuck what happened to him? His involvement in Smitty's dope deal got my dad killed." Trey leveled the gun toward Boudreaux again. A lump formed in his throat as he remembered overhearing the conversation between Monty and another man. A conversation that could have saved Trey's dad. But Trey never told. And his dad died for Trey's need to not be seen as a snitch.

"You don't know what the hell you're talking about." Disgust covered Boudreaux's face. "Monty was never involved with Smitty. Monty was his mama's boy. Too damn perfect to dirty his hands with the likes of Smitty."

Trey's finger tightened on the trigger.

"He's right," Russ whispered.

"The hell he is. I overheard Monty talking to someone about Smitty. Told the guy not to go to Smitty's that night because something was going down. We all know what went down. My dad was killed." Trey's blood boiled. Sweat trickled down his back. The muscles in his arms and back were tensed to the point of spasm. The gun shook.

"It's okay, Trey," Russ said. "It wasn't your fault. Everybody tries to fit in. You were a kid, just trying to be one of the guys. You didn't know it was going to happen."

Before Trey's eyes, Gemini's countenance changed and became young, wild eyed, and he knew she was gone. He swallowed hard, hating how others could see into him so easily. Tears burned the back of his throat. He eased the shaking barrel toward the body that housed Gemini.

"Trey, Monty was the witness." Russ's voice was soft. "Didn't you ever wonder why he suddenly disappeared and was never heard from again?"

"The boy ran. That's why. The little prick snitched and then ran," Boudreaux spat.

Trey refocused and changed targets. He squinted his eyes and tilted his head, sighting the weapon between Boudreaux's eyes.

Russ took a step closer to Trey and whispered, "He's in witness protection."

Trey's head whipped around to meet Russ's gaze.

"Monty heard about the delivery and came to me. If you want to blame someone for your dad's death, blame me. I'm the one who called him as my back-up."

Trey barely withheld a sob. He took a deep breath and steadied his hand. After hating Monty for twenty years, it was hard to accept what Russ told him.

"Hey, Bub. How about you lower the weapon? I got this one," Russ said. But Trey didn't respond.

"C'mon," Russ said as he slowly reached out and touched Trey's arm. He pressed gently and Trey's arms collapsed, the pistol gripped loosely in his right hand, pointing to the ground.

Chapter One-Hundred-Six

GEMINI TAYLOR
Boudreaux Barn
Raven Bayou, LA

Sunday Evening, 12 June 2005

GEM HEARD Trey's voice, heard Wile answer him. How could she get free? How could she take control? She needed to take the knife from Wile. And then what?

If she didn't stop Wile, Russ would shoot. *What will happen to me if Wile dies? Am I wearing my body, or is he? Is Wile just a part of my imagination, or am I the imaginary one?*

Tears welled as she watched the scene before her. Wile turned to her, his eyes shimmered too. Was it a coincidence? Or did she have some power over him? Gem took a step toward Wile and Boudreaux. Her gaze went from the knife in Wile's hand to the one on the floor, the one that had been in her bag with the watches.

"It's Rocky's," Wile whispered.

Gem turned, looking for the other boy. He stood beside Drew, his gaze on the pile of items from Gem's bag. Then she remembered. Daddy made Rocky skin Twitch, the rabbit. Two boys. Two knives. Wile stabbed his victims in the heart. Rocky opened their bellies and started to skin them, the same way Daddy had made him open up Twitch.

"Trey?" she said.

"I'm here, Taylor," he replied with a crack in his voice, but his eyes stayed on Wile and the hostage. Either he didn't see Gem, or...Was it Wile that Trey saw? Was Gem just a part of Wile's mind? She was so confused. Was she real? She swallowed hard and squeezed her eyes shut for a minute. After a deep breath, she looked around again, and understood. Gem was real. She was sure of it. And she had a decision to make. A vital one.

If she let Wile kill Boudreaux, they would all die. There was no explaining how she knew, but it was a fact. Russ would shoot. And it might be a blessing because the only other option would be to take them into custody. Lock them up. Maybe forever.

Gem didn't know if she and Wile could overtake Russ. Didn't know if they were strong enough together to get the gun from him. If they did, could they get away? Would Wile even trust Gem to help him?

"No, Gemini," Wile said. "What if something bad happened?"

She looked behind her. Drew, Ginni, and Rocky were gone.

"I gotta do this, Gemi," Wile repeated, his eyes on Boudreaux. "For you and Yvette."

"Stop this crazy bitch before she kills me!" Boudreaux yelled, his gaze never leaving Wile's face.

Bitch. He's calling Wile a bitch. Gem looked down at her body. It looked real, looked like her, Gemini. Wile looked like a boy. But Boudreaux called him a bitch.

"Russ, don't shoot him," she urged. How could she make him understand? "Wile, don't do this. Let's just go. We can go back to Lufkin and live with Aunt Ginny."

"Yeah, we can," Drew said from behind Gem and she turned, half expecting to see nothing, thinking Drew's voice was in her head again. But Drew was there, just a foot away.

"Just put the knife down and let's go," Gem repeated.

"That's a good idea," Russ agreed.

"He ain't gonna let us go, Gemi. And besides, this is why we come here." Wile shifted his weight and put a hand on Boudreaux's shoulder to brace himself.

Gem sent her mind out on an expedition, fingers, feeling the way toward Wile. What she reached was as hard and cold as a brick wall. Wile recognized her attempt and refused to let her in. His eyes flashed and she saw fear and pain. He pressed the knife enough to make Gem back off.

"Don't make me shoot you!" Russ's voice strained as he redirected the barrel of his gun on Wile.

"Gemini, you don't want to do this." It was Trey. She took a quick look at him. His shaking hands were empty. He must have holstered his weapon. His eyes shimmered with tears, shoulders slumped in defeat. "Remember the rule. The cops all get to go home at night. You're a cop, Taylor. Put the knife down and let's go home."

Her heart pounded into her throat, choking her. She fisted her hands and took deep breaths.

Wile shifted the knife, pressing the point through the shirt and into skin yet again.

Boudreaux sucked in a breath and held it, his chin drawn into his neck, his eyes trying to see the tip of the blade without moving his face.

"Don't do this!" Trey said.

Gem looked at him again. His face was pale and grim.

"She won't. Neither will he. Will you Wile?"

That voice was a new one and came from a woman walking through the door standing ajar at the end of the barn.

"Cora, get back!" Russ shouted.

"Cora?" Gem said. It sounded so familiar. She took a good look at the woman, and then she saw it. "Reena?"

She had freckles across her nose, just like when she was a little girl. She was shorter than Gem, and curvy. "Yes, baby girl. It's me. Been a long time." She stepped closer to them. "Wile, this is not your job."

"You know Wile?" Gem said unbelievably.

"As well as I know you, girl. He took your daddy's beatings for a long time. He came when you were five." Her voice was soft and gentle. Having Reena nearby gave Gem a little confidence.

Gem's mind suddenly pressed up against Wile's. The wall was gone. Pictures flashed in her mind, distant pictures. *Daddy with a belt. Daddy with a stick. Daddy with a hose. Daddy hitting, kicking, yelling. Daddy slapping my face, dropping me into the trunk. Slamming the lid.* "Stop it!" she yelled, ready to fight back, ready to kill.

Boudreaux pressed his back and his head against the post, sat up as straight as he could. He looked at Cora. "I'll give you anything you want if you just get her away from me."

Wile looked at Gem, and then at Reena. "You see, Gemi?" He shifted his gaze to Reena. "I gotta do it, Reena. It's for you too."

He shielded his mind again, cold steel shutting her out.

"It's okay, Wile," Reena said. "I'm a big girl now. I can take care of myself. Gemini's a big girl too. She's a cop. Boudreaux won't ever hurt her again." Reena moved closer still, her eyes riveted to Wile. "Don't you think it's time you let someone else take care of Boudreaux?"

"You know how he is. Only one way to take care of him." Wile pushed on the knife, drawing blood.

Boudreaux inhaled deeply, squinted his eyes. His face covered in sweat and drained of color.

Russ moved closer, only a few feet from Wile and Boudreaux, gun pointed at Wile's...her head.

"Wile, look at me," Reena said.

He did, his hand white-knuckling the knife.

"You had to grow up too fast, been through too much. Put the knife down and come," she opened her arms. He didn't move.

Gem had to do something. She stepped over to Wile, squatted behind him. He didn't so much as flinch, his eyes glued to Reena. Gem gripped his hand in hers and whispered to him. "Let me have the knife, Wile."

Knowing a physical struggle could end in Boudreaux's death, Gem held Wile's hand steady. The only way to do this was with her mind.

She looked at Trey and Russ one more time. She was sealing her own fate. This could end in one of two ways—with her dead or locked up—neither a good option. But she was the responsible one here, the one who had to pay the piper.

"I'm taking the knife, Wile. I'm stronger than you. This is my body and my mind."

His hand gripped the handle, his mind set against her.

"Stop, Gemi. We gotta do this! You know how he likes to hurt people. It don't matter none to him if it's girls or boys, or even grown-ups. When he's gone we'll be safe."

"We're safe now, Wile. You said you were doing this for me and Yvette and Reena. But we're all okay. Look at Reena. Look at me, Wile." He remained still, his back to her.

"What about Yvette? What'll she think if we let him go?"

Gem didn't have an answer for him. Her hand still encircled his, gripping steadily. Her legs burned from squatting, though she'd been there for only a minute or two. It was the tension of Wile's legs that caused her pain.

Pictures flashed again. Memories of her, walking hand-in-hand with Boudreaux. Fear welled inside as she saw the things Boudreaux had done to her, to Yvette. The riding crop he liked to penetrate her with. Giant tears ran. But she couldn't wipe them away, couldn't do anything but concentrate on taking the knife.

She pressed at the edges of Wile's mind. Tried to gain entrance and thereby control. His mind blocked her. Solid steel stood between her thoughts and his. But Gem probed and searched until she again found a way in.

Another vision flashed in her mind—Jax dead on the floor. She'd killed him. Her gut clenched. Hot liquid came up in her throat. Tears started again. *I can't do it again. I won't.*

Gem wrapped her hand more tightly around the knife, feeling it instead of Wile's hand. She gently bent her elbow until the knife was near her chest. Boudreaux exhaled and slumped, and from the corner of her eye, Gem saw Russ lower his gun.

It would've been easy enough to turn the blade into her chest and press. The thought of being put in a cage made it seem a good choice.

"That's my girl," Reena said and squatted beside her. "You always were a strong one."

It was then that Gem realized that Wile had disappeared. His sadness was inside her.

"Thank you, Wile," she whispered as Reena took the knife from her hand.

Chapter One-Hundred-Seven

RUSS COLEMAN
Boudreaux Barn
Raven Bayou, LA

Sunday Evening, 12 June 2005

SADNESS OVERTOOK HIM as he watched Gem crumble. Her tears poured down a face with no emotion. Her body shook violently. Dead eyes stared into nothingness, her pasty face covered with sweat.

Russ glanced at his godson and fought back his desire to shoot Boudreaux himself. Trey's feelings for Taylor were plain. They were also of no use.

He'd been all wrong about Arnold Taylor's death. Arnold Taylor tortured the little girl, gave her into the grip of Alton Boudreaux until her mind could take no more. Finally, Taylor's alter egos put a stop to it.

That was why, twenty years ago when Russ found Taylor in the closet, she was near catatonic. She'd seen the body. She'd witnessed the murder. She'd seen Wile kill her daddy. A part of herself was the killer.

His gaze fell on Trey, tense and still shaking. Russ knew his godson was not ready for the emotional torment he was going through now.

Chapter One-Hundred-Eight

TREY FONTAINE
Boudreaux Barn
Raven Bayou, LA

Sunday Evening, 12 June 2005

TREY HADN'T REALIZED how taut he was until Cora took the knife from Taylor. At that moment he wanted nothing more than to reach into his pocket and pull out the pills that gave him power over pain. But there were no more pills. And all the drugs in the world wouldn't stop the torture of his heart breaking.

He sensed rather than saw Russ beside him, so totally focused on the scene in front of him, everything else was blocked from his vision as well as his mind. Taylor stood and Cora held her as she cried.

"Get these damn cuffs off me!" Boudreaux yelled. "And get that crazy bitch out of here!"

Cora walked Taylor away from the men, but neither Russ nor Trey moved, both satisfied to let the bastard fume. Trey figured with any luck, the man would have a heart attack.

He turned when he heard the cuffs Russ held in his hand. They looked at each other. His lips trembled and tears stung his eyes. He swallowed hard and took the cuffs from Russ.

"Gemini?" Trey said and waited. Cora's hard gaze cut him to the bone. When Taylor turned and saw him holding the cuffs, he read the terror in her eyes, the vacillation. Was Wile still inside her, arguing, urging her to do something, anything?

Tears poured down her cheeks as she stepped toward him, and then, finally, she raised her arms. "Guess our pizza and beer is off. Not even any chicken soup? I would like to have met your mother."

When he clicked the cuffs into place, he thought she would faint. Her face blanched even more. Then she began to sob uncontrollably.

Trey wrapped his arms around her, his throat burning, swallowing back tears. His soul shook as he held her close. He remembered her words—*when I was little I got my brain fractured*. It had been a strange way of putting things, but now he knew how very true those words were.

Chapter One-Hundred-Nine

RUSS COLEMAN
Boudreaux Barn
Raven Bayou, LA

Sunday Evening, 12 June 2005

RUSS WATCHED as Trey rolled the door open and Taylor shuffled toward the Crown Vic. Fresh air blew into the stifling barn. Outside, the sky was a soft, clear blue. The sun had fallen behind the trees and a light breeze blew.

Cora stood, her gaze following the couple, knife still gripped in one hand. Russ noticed the hand was steady.

"Damn it! Get these things off me!" Boudreaux yelled again. Cora and Russ both turned toward him. Russ suddenly realized how pathetic the man was. Boudreaux's expensive shirt sported a slit stained with blood and the armpits of his jacket soaked through with sweat. His face was pale, his eyes suspiciously moist as he stared up at Russ.

Russ dug around in his pockets, making a big production of looking for something. "I guess I lost my cuff key," he said, his attention on Boudreaux's face.

"You bastard! Quit fucking around!"

"Sorry, Mr. Boudreaux. Guess you'll have to wait until a uniformed officer gets here. He can take your statement." Russ turned back to Cora. "Thanks for your help," he said weakly to her.

He heard Boudreaux fumbling behind him, grunting with the effort and continuing the tirade of cussing.

Russ stepped close to Cora and lowered his voice. "If you ever decide to do something about him, about what he did, let me know." Reaching out, he gave her forearm a gentle squeeze.

She shook her head. "Who, in this community, would take my word against the great gentleman Alton Boudreaux? No, thank you."

He looked over his shoulder, and then back at her. "Guess I'd better get out there and help with Taylor. I'll call for a deputy. Let's take that knife and put it on the desk in the office. I'll explain about your prints on it." She looked at the hunting knife in her hand, the tip covered in blood, and then turned toward the office. The other knife, the skinning knife, lay among the watches. Cora smiled and nodded to Russ as they walked away from Boudreaux.

Chapter One-Hundred-Ten

CORA LYON
Boudreaux Barn
Raven Bayou, LA

Sunday Evening, 12 June 2005

CORA STOOD in the door of the office and watched as Russ walked away, leaving Boudreaux cuffed and sitting with his back against the post. Trey and Taylor were nowhere to be seen. Cora assumed they were walking out to the big silver-gray Hummer she'd noticed out front.

One of the conditions of her sleeping in the barn was that she would make herself scarce should a buyer arrive, so when she saw the big SUV near the road, she'd kept going and drove in the back way on Old Cypress Road.

Now, looking out the front of the barn, she watched Russ slip behind the wheel of his Crown Vic and pick up the mic. With his attention elsewhere, she sauntered back toward Boudreaux.

"That nigger bastard son of a bitch'll pay for this!" Boudreaux spat.

Cora turned to face him, and he looked up at her. Even when at someone's mercy Alton Boudreaux's gray eyes cast nothing but superiority. "Don't sit there and pretend you don't know me, not after what just happened here," she almost whispered, her jaw set.

"I don't know what you're talking about," he declared, raising his chin haughtily.

Squatting near him, she spoke gently. "Well, let's see if I can clear it up for you." She picked up the skinning knife from the pile of watches and brought it up near his throat. "I would think you'd recognize the gray eyes. They're just like yours."

Realization set in when he stared into her eyes. "What is it you want?" He pressed his head back against the post. "Name it," his tone lowered.

"Your head on a platter would be nice." She smiled.

"Coleman might be a son of a bitchin' nigger, but he won't let you kill me."

"Coleman's not here. And I have a few minutes before a deputy arrives. So, let's start with some confessions. How about that? Let's start with owning up to me...Daddy."

His jaw muscles jumped. "You don't know what the hell you're talking about."

"Sure I do. You've always said that the world was fooled with your charm. Your mama thought you could do no wrong.

"So, when you molested my mother and got her pregnant, your dear sweet mama Frances thought my mama'd been fooling around with some boy. So your mama sent her away until after I was born. She was only twelve. And you started on me when I was four...Daddy."

"Stop calling me that!" His eyes met hers. "What is this shit? What the hell do you want? Is it money? Fine. How much?"

"Now that Jax is dead, I guess I get it all." She trailed the knife down his throat to his chest.

"How about you just stop this bullshit." His gaze flashed quickly toward the door. "Name your price, take your money, and get out."

"Throwing me out again... Daddy?"

The "Daddy" threw him into another tirade. "Stop acting all righteous. You liked what I did to you, and so did your mama and that little whore out there who just tried to kill me."

His eyes narrowed and his voice dropped even lower. "The both of you were always parading around in those little cotton things with strings to hold 'em up. Half the time they hung off. And the two of you squatting and bending like you were pretending to sit on a cock or take one in the butt. Don't tell me you didn't like it. You asked for it!...You begged for it!"

Cora stood and looked out the door. She saw Russ wave from his car before returning his attention to the papers he'd pulled from the dark recesses of the front seat. She'd tucked the hand holding the knife behind her thigh enough so he couldn't see it.

"I protected Gemini when she was little. There was no way I'd let her kill you right in front of a cop and an FBI agent." She looked down at the man at her feet. "But that don't mean you deserve to live."

THREE MINUTES LATER, Cora lit a cigarette as she slipped into the old pickup that had once belonged to Arnold Taylor and drove slowly down Old Cypress Road. Headed west out of town, she looked in the rearview mirror, a smile curling the corners of her lips.

One thing she was sure of—Alton Boudreaux would never hurt another child—not with three holes in his chest and a knife hidden under the pile of intestines in his lap.

Chapter One-Hundred-Eleven

WILE E. WAYNE
Pineville Mental Institution
Pineville, LA

Thursday, 15 July 2005

"DREW, CAN YOU GET THE GEEK TO GET US DOWNSTAIRS?" Drew was always good at that stuff.

"Don't you think you three have gotten us into enough trouble? Leave Warren alone," Ginni said.

"We ain't to blame," I said.

I didn't know Ginni was listening. The counselors are always telling Gemini that we can all be friends and work together...but I figure doctor people are out to kill us off.

It's been kinda hard for me and Drew and Rocky to have playtime without ever body watching. But I figure if we wait till all the grown-ups are asleep, and Drew can get that funny looking computer guy to take her out to smoke, we can get away.

Anyhow, that's the way I look at it. Gemini is cool and all. And I like Ginni and the others. But I don't like being in here. They don't even let us go out and fish or nothing.

But, while we're here, there are some kinda mean men in here that like to push the girls around. We been planning how to take care of 'em. One at a time.

Chapter One-Hundred-Twelve

GEMINI TAYLOR
Pineville Mental Institution
Pineville, LA

Thursday, 15 July 2005

"HOW YOU DOING, BABY GIRL," Maine Taylor said to her daughter.

Gem looked around the day room, the windows were high, but they let the sunshine in. The pale yellow walls contained cheap metal tables surrounded by folding chairs. "I'm okay, Mama."

When she looked at her mother, Gem smiled. Finally, she had managed to see her mom out of prison.

"I brought you something," Mama said and pulled a chocolate bar from her purse. She laid it on the table, but Gem didn't reach for it. "I talked to your doctor. She says you're strong and she expects you'll get better pretty quick. I like her."

"I do too," Gem said, thinking of Quintina Griggs. If there was anyone in the world she could trust, it was Quintina.

"I'm sorry, Gemi," her mama said. "I'm sorry I didn't do better by you. I'm sorry I didn't listen. I'm sorry about all of it."

"Mama, you don't need to be sorry. Quintina says when you know better, you do better. When you figured it all out, you went to prison for me. I'm the one who is sorry. You spent all those years in prison. For me."

"And if I could be here instead of you, I'd do that too. That's what mamas do." She gently patted Gem's hand, her tears threatened to fall over her lashes.

"No, Mama. I did wrong. I need to be here. I need to be with Quintina."

"Is there anything you need, Gemi? Anything I can bring you?"

"No Mama. I have everything I need."

"Well, then, I guess I'd better go. I have to be at work in a few hours. But I'll be back Saturday. Okay?" She stood and so did Gem. They hugged, and both shed a few tears before Mama waved bye and left the room.

Gem sat back down. She picked up the candy bar and looked at the dark brown label.

"Open it," said Wile's voice.

"Yeah, I want some," Drew said.

"I think we should save this until after dinner," Gem told them. She slipped it into the big pocket of her blouse, her fingers rubbing against the envelope hidden there. She pulled it out, ran her fingers over the writing. It had come in the mail a week after she got here.

A letter from Trey. She held it against her chest and closed her eyes. A smile came from deep inside. Opening her eyes, she looked at the envelope again before slipping it back in her pocket.

Maybe someday, she'd open it.

Epilogue

TREY FONTAINE
Fontaine Residence
Raven Bayou County

Tuesday, 20 July 2005

TREY SAT at his mother's desk in the office of her home. Though the transmitter and receiver were on, he heard none of Ace's words. His body had stopped shaking from lack of drugs. Now he just suffered from insomnia.

He had to admit to himself that the pain in his butt had eased. It wasn't nearly as bad as he'd thought it was, as he'd wanted it to be.

Gemini was in a secure asylum, awaiting further testing before receiving orders from the judge. Everyone knew how it would go. She was too ill to stand trial.

Cora hadn't been found. The truck she drove away in was discovered just a few miles out of town. Every agency in the state was looking for her.

Russ took a long vacation and was spending time with Darlene, but every day he got updates on the cases from Wilkes, and between him and Bettencourt, Russ continued to stay on top of the search for Trey's mom.

Bobby Hopkins sat in a crème colored leather chair, filling it from one armrest to the other. His black hair was cut short, his face clean-shaven, and his left ankle was atop his right knee, the foot keeping a fast rhythm as it bounced up and down. Hopkins wasn't good at sitting still.

"Stop that," he said. "You're thinking too hard. You keep frowning like that, your face is gonna freeze in that position." Hopkins was like that. He could look at Trey and know what was going on.

"Want a soda?" Trey asked.

"I want you to get your mind back in the game. If you need some time off, I can take over with Ace." His black eyes flashed with humor.

"Screw you." Trey stood and headed for the kitchen.

"C'mon, Trey. Sitting here going over everything in your head won't change the facts. Taylor needed help. You're no shrink. And it's about time Russ retired. We'll find your mom. But right now, we have to be ready to back Ace up. This is a big operation."

Trey came back with two icy sodas and passed one to his partner. "I know." He took a deep breath. "I just...I need to know where Mom is."

"She doesn't fit the profile, partner. Besides, she's not the victim type. Maybe she ran away with a traveling salesman. Maybe she hit her head and has amnesia. We have a whole team on her case. They'll find her."

Hopkins took a swig of the soda. "After the last month, you should know how useless you'd be on a case as personal as this. Just take a breath. Then get your head back in the game."

"Yeah. Get my head back in the game." Trey tossed his head back and drank half the soda before stopping. He started to tell Hopkins to go to hell, but the ringing of a phone stopped him. Hopkins pulled the cell from his pocket.

"Hopkins." He listened, throwing in a "yeah" here and there. His eyes narrowed as he looked at Trey. "Got it. Thanks." He closed the phone and swallowed hard. And Trey knew.

"They found her?"

Hopkins averted his gaze to the floor.

"Say something!" Trey almost shouted.

Hopkins nodded his head. "Her T-bird was pulled out of a lake this morning."

"She wasn't in it?"

His partner hesitated and Trey saw his eyes squint a little at his reluctance to say any more.

"Tell me, Hopkins."

"They found...a foot. In the floorboard."

Pain struck Trey again. His chest ached with fire. His head pounded. He rubbed the place where the mint tin used to be.

In one swift motion he stood and stepped to the whiskey decanter on the mini-bar. He poured a short glass half-full and lifted it to his lips. His hand shook and a burning knot lay in his stomach. He choked back what would have been tears, refusing to go there. With a vicious overhand throw, the glass and its contents went flying. It crashed against the wall, whiskey splattering the antique wallpaper.

Swallowing hard, Trey Fontaine straightened his back, and turned to his partner.

"Let's go."

Read on for a preview of

Ultimate Game
A Trey Fontaine Mystery

THE MUD OOZING around her broken body should have been a comfort. At least she wasn't lying on concrete. Pain stabbed her ribs with every breath and the salty taste of blood covered her tongue. Ace shivered, struggling to breathe through the metallic smell that filled her nose.

Stillness permeated the air as the car pulled away. Then the egrets settled, the flapping of their wings, and their calls announcing safety. But she couldn't see their white feathers against the black of night. Couldn't see anything.

"I'm coming, Ace! I'm almost there!" A voice, tinny and weak, echoed through the receiver behind her ear. It sounded like Trey. Or was it God?

Ace wanted to respond, but couldn't control her mouth. Her face burned as cool air brushed across it. Trey wouldn't make it in time. She lay here dying at the edge of the muddy Raven Bayou, wishing she was in New Orleans, sipping a cold one with other agents, instead of lying in this forgotten swamp a hundred miles northwest of The Big Easy.

Thirty-five is too young to die. I haven't been married. Never had a baby. Oh, God! I'll never see Mom again.

Her final thought before agony brought on a different kind of blackness was that no one would ever stop JoDell Papillion. The arrogant, selfish bastard would continue to trade American girls for Columbian drugs. He'd ruined too many lives, and when Ace was dead, he would have eliminated the only person who knew enough to put him away.

TREY SWUNG the big SUV off of Gypsum onto Bayou Road and drove down the center line, shining the spotlight from side to side in a desperate attempt to find Ace. His voice cracked as he incessantly talked into the receiver. "Hold on, Ace. I'm on my way. Almost there! Hold on." The bleeding knot on his head throbbed, and his vision blurred a time or two, but he drove on toward the signal. "Be all right, Ace. Please be okay," he whispered.

When he turned onto the dirt road that separated forest from swamp, the signal got stronger, and he knew where he'd find her. In the bayou.

"Tracker One. I'm on the dirt road off Bayou. The signal is stronger here," he said into the radio.

"Copy Tracker One," the dispatcher said and began sending units in that direction, her voice broken by static, and by officers responding from everywhere.

It was pitch black outside. He slowed. A pair of wild eyes darted into the trees. A deer, maybe. He didn't know how long he laid unconscious back there in that parking lot. Was he too late? The signal got stronger until finally he knew she was within fifty feet of the Hummer.

"Tracker One. She's here. Send a bus."

He stopped, left the lights on, and pulled out the battery-operated spot light. "Ace," he yelled. No answer. He started the search, his heart racing at the thought of what he'd find. He called over and over, but Ace didn't respond. Then his light reflected on a bit of white. Ace wore a white blouse at the casino.

Running to her, Trey shined the light over her body. The blouse lay unbuttoned, exposing her chest, a big boot print dead center on her skin. His heart jumped into his throat at the sight of her face. Her nose was crooked, and so was her jaw, which may have just been dislocated. Both eyes were black and swollen shut. Her face had half a dozen deep cuts. He checked her carotid for a pulse. Barely there. He thought he heard her speak, and when the beam of his flashlight fell on her mouth, he saw foamy blood trickling down her cheek, to the ground.

"Get that bus here now!" he shouted into the radio. Ace lay on her side, her blonde hair covered with mud and blood. He sat back on his heels, his gaze glued to the gruesome sight before him.

Ace had been so beautiful.

The only noise was the thump of his heart. Even the cicadas stopped playing their song. The fastest thing would be to take her to the hospital himself. He could lift her easily enough. She was tall, but lean, and Trey was plenty strong enough. But she was so...broken. He couldn't risk more damage. Then he heard the faint sound of a siren. *Finally*. The medics were close.

Trey knew what it was like to be on the other end of an eleven-eleven call. Officer down. Every law enforcement officer, whether city, parish, state or federal, listening within the range of his radio would swarm the site immediately.

"Copy Tracker One. Site code four?"

"Affirm. Code four. Hurry." He ran two fingers up the furrow between his brows. This couldn't happen again. Ace had to live. This couldn't be the second partner he got killed.

About the Author

A graduate of the University of California and former officer for a large sheriff's department, **RYDER ISLINGTON** is now retired and doing what she loves: reading, writing, and gardening. She lives in Louisiana with her family, including a very large English Chocolate Lab, a very small Chinese pug, and a houseful of demanding cats.

She can be contacted at RyderIslington@yahoo.com or visit her blog at http://ryderislington.wordpress.com

Other Titles at LL-Publications

www.ll-publications.com

The Dead Detective Agency – Peg Herring

This is the first book of a clever new detective series by Peg Herring. Tori VanCamp wakes in a strange room with a vivid recollection of being murdered. The memory is startlingly clear, but she functions normally. Determined to find out what's happened and why, Tori enlists the help of an odd man named Seamus. Together they embark on an investigation that is like nothing she has ever experienced. Death is all around her, and soon, two people she cares about are prime candidates for murder.

Murder at McMurdo – A. J. Walker

Mark Collins came to McMurdo Antarctic Research Station to study ice cores, cut down on drinking, and patch up his marriage. He's failed. His equipment arrives broken, and he's having an affair with a coworker who drinks as much as he does. When they witness a murder and the wrong man gets blamed, they must solve the crime for themselves or reveal their affair to prove his innocence

Cure for an Ailing Alien/Retribution – Darrell Bain

Two short stories from multi-award winning author Darrell Bain.

In "Cure for an Ailing Alien," nurse Joanne Levy is called upon to treat her strangest patient yet - an alien, harbored in secret by a government agency. Just how does a human treat a sick being from another planet? The results are not what you expect!

"Retribution" sees Jim's family shocked by the visit of a tiny alien. Armed with his gun, Jim sets out to protect his family, but his best intentions turn out to have horrendous consequences.

Devil Don't Want Her – Zetta Brown

A humorous short story where Faith Darling, a young, spiritually righteous woman, must face the fact that you cannot escape from your family and the truth.

When Faith's notorious great-grandmother Miss Sunny Vincent dies, Faith, as the only surviving relative, must arrange the funeral. However, Miss Sunny Vincent's remains are hard to dispose of because God won't have her ... and the Devil don't want her.

LL-Publications
"...taking the reader down a different path."
www.ll-publications.com